I0610466

# An Unexpected Homecoming

Sharon Hughson

©2020, Sharon Hughson

All rights reserved. Except as permitted under the U.S. Copyright Act of 1976, no part of this publication may be reproduced, distributed or transmitted in any form or by any means, or stored in a database of retrieval system without the prior written permission of the publisher: INKSPIRED.

**Cover Designer:** Covers by Kay

This is a work of fiction. Names, characters, organization, places, events, and incidents are either products of the author's imagination or are used fictitiously. Any resemblance to actual persons, living or dead, or actual events is purely coincidental.

*Freedom is never free.*
*Thank you to all those who have served to protect*
*the freedoms enjoyed in the United States.*

# Book One

# One

J azlyn Rolle snuck into the hallway at oh-dark-thirty. She tiptoed on stocking feet toward the light her mother left burning in the kitchen. A few more feet and she'd be home free.

The crackling of a newspaper broke the silence, and every muscle tensed.

"Why are you sneaking around like a teenager?" Her father's voice dripped disapproval.

Her spine stiffened, snapping her into the military attention stance as if he was her commanding officer.

She forced herself to relax and lifted the running shoes she carried. "Didn't want to wake anyone up."

*More like trying to get out of the house before he was awake.*

He grunted. "Are you sending your application to UT? It's not too late to finish your degree."

She turned the water faucet on full pressure, hoping the splashing in the sink would convince him she hadn't heard. Because what could she say?

*I don't know what to do with my life now?*

After chugging two glasses of water, Jaz sat in the nook and slipped into her running shoes. She jerked a wave in her father's direction and hustled toward the door.

Outside, the powerful smell of her mother's petunias greeted her. She breathed deeply and crammed one ear bud in, cranking her running playlist.

Her feet set an easy pace and headed away from Sweet Grove. Only three days back in her hometown and her spirit craved its independence.

*Any chance you can help me get a job?* Making demands of God when she hadn't exactly been paying attention to him the last few years wasn't fair.

What was?

She inhaled and exhaled, focusing on the sound of the air entering and exiting her throat and lungs. Her sneakers pounded a hypnotic tempo against the asphalt. The familiar rhythm carried her into the runner's zone she craved.

When her feet slid on loose gravel, her mind slammed back to reality.

The rising sun stretched her shadow to the curve in the packed dirt road. She breathed in a hint of dust along with the tickle of farm fresh manure. Sage shrouded a barbed-wire fence on her left. Pungent juniper bit into her nose, smelling like a litter box that needed changing.

Sweat tickled above her brow, and she backhanded it away. She checked the fitness tracker on her left wrist. Nearly seven and she'd gone more than three miles. If she turned around, she would get home before her father left. She'd rather swallow a cockroach.

Long grass lining the road's shoulder rustled. A jack-rabbit leaped into the road. Jaz stumbled as it dodged her. Her heart jackhammered and her steps faltered.

An instant later, a brown and white dog burst from the scrub a yard behind her. Its pink tongue lolled to the side, but nothing slowed its pursuit.

Jaz shortened her stride. Typical Sweet Grove. The traffic included wildlife rather than automobiles.

The dog scrambled down the berm on the opposite side of the road. Before disappearing, it stumbled tail over nose with a yelp of agony that shivered up her sweat-coated spine.

Jaz slowed, already past the dog's crashing point. She couldn't even run in the middle of nowhere without something interfering. She paused her music and glanced toward the ditch. Nothing.

Her finger hovered over the play button when she heard a whimper. She sighed, scraping more sweat from her brow. Only a jerk could ignore an injured dog.

Jaz plodded to the edge of the road. The furry pile lay near the white rail fence. An obstacle course of gopher holes had tripped up the poor animal.

Jaz squatted a few feet from the dog. "Good boy," she crooned without thinking.

Another whine pulled her intestines like taffy. She extended her fingers toward his nose, slow and steady, and he barely snuffled them before letting out another pitiful cry.

"Gopher hole get you?" She spoke quietly, scanning his body for signs of injury.

The dog rolled his eyes at her. The brown pools begged for help. Jaz edged closer, hands grazing gently over the long hair. When she smoothed across his hind leg, a yip startled her. The lolling tongue flapped toward the injured area and coated her hand with spittle.

Jaz huffed out air. So much for a quiet morning run.

She knelt in the grass, wincing when her knee found a sharp rock. She cooed and slid her arms under the dog. If anything was broken, moving him might make it worse, but the dog didn't make a sound.

As she rocked back, rolling the pup against her chest, a warm tongue swathed her chin. Ugh. Dog kisses. But then again she was a walking salt block.

With a grunt, she stood and staggered to the top of the ditch, glancing in both directions. Further along the road she noticed an iron gateway. The steer head emblem in the center had nearly rusted loose, and the double-bar T brand beneath it shook like a leaf in a windstorm.

*May as well ask at that house.* Her brain sifted old memories for the owner of the brand while her feet carried her beneath the arch and down a rutted driveway.

A fence, paint flaking, lined one side while a collection of fruit and nut trees speckled the grass on the other. It didn't look much like a working ranch to her. Who had she gone to school with that lived out here?

She was still trying to work it out when a horse snorted off to her left. Her steps slowed. After all, she was trespassing and that could be a shoot-first-ask-later offense in small town Texas.

Jaz stopped and squinted toward the rising sun. A saddled horse on the far side of the corral swiveled its head in her direction. The cowboy kneeling at the horse's feet stood. Broad shoulders tapered into a trim waist and long legs kept her gaze dropping all the way to the heels of dusty cowboy boots.

She opened her mouth to call out at the same moment

he twisted toward her, but the word petered on her lips.

"Hey." The stranger jogged toward her, bent arms flexing firm biceps. Jaz stumbled away from the fence. With his face in shadow, she couldn't decide if he was angry or concerned.

Her experience with men advised her to back away and keep her guard up.

"Poppet?" His rough voice matched his ruggedness.

The dog rolled its eyes toward the cowboy and whined.

A moment later, the tall stranger vaulted over the fence and landed a foot away from them. Jaz stumbled back another step, nearly turning her ankle in a rut.

"What happened?"

He stepped closer, and Jaz could finally make out his features. Heavy eyebrows peeked from beneath the hat's brim. His face had high cheekbones and a shapely jaw covered in yesterday's whiskers. Her heart leapt to attention.

Jaz cleared her parched throat. "She was chasing a rabbit and caught her foot in a gopher hole."

"Silly girl." His work-roughened hands smoothed over the dog's head, and she licked his dusty fingers.

The scent of hay, fresh-cut grass, and salt accompanied him into her space bubble. Jaz stared into his face, trying to place him. He didn't look much older than she was, so they probably went to school together. In Sweet Grove, everyone knew everyone.

It was one of the things she'd been glad to escape from ten years ago when she left for college.

"Let me take her." He stepped closer, hesitating for a fraction of an instant before jostling his arms beneath hers. Firm muscles scraped along her damp arms. A platoon of shivers marched across her skin and down her spine.

Then he stepped back, and her empty arms dropped to her sides. She tugged at the hem of her shorts, aware they'd ridden up during the dog rescue.

The cowboy trod toward the buildings. Shadows danced in the breezeway between a flaking red barn and a workshop. Jaz trailed after him, trying not to notice the swagger of those muscular shoulders or the way his Wrangler's hugged his backside.

"Do you think...Poppet needs a vet?"

He stopped beside a rusty truck. "Would you open this?"

Jaz's pulse raced as she jogged past him. When she tugged it open, the door squawked like an angry goose.

The cowboy brushed against her shoulder and squished her into the door. Acrobatics in her stomach sent Jaz sidling back until the creaky door groaned to a stop.

The stranger slid the dog onto the ratty cloth bench seat. He whispered unintelligible sounds while his hands smoothed along the dog's spine, chest, and legs. When he touched the back leg, Poppet yipped and rolled her baleful gaze toward him.

"Doesn't feel broken."

Jaz craned to see around him. He twisted, and his chin nearly collided with her forehead.

Awareness zinged through her shoulders. She jerked her gaze to his, caught in the hypnosis of Gulf blue eyes.

He tapped the brim of his hat upward and pink flooded his tanned cheeks. Her lips twitched. Too much time around army guys who strutted and tutted, acting like women should bow to them, increased her appreciation of his shyness.

"Excuse me." His voice seemed gruffer.

"Jazlyn Rolle." With her back pressed to the door, she barely had room to hold her hand out to him.

He stared at it. His Adam's apple bobbed in his throat and he slid away from her. He rubbed his hands down the seams of his jeans before clearing his throat. "Thanks for bringing Poppet home. I should see to her."

Without another glance, he sidled around the truck and slammed into the workshop.

Jaz blinked. What just happened? She didn't even know his name.

She shook her head and gave Poppet's fluffy ears a gentle rub. Her tail flopped against the seat.

Jaz stared toward the closed door, but when the cowboy didn't return, it was obvious he wanted her to leave.

Turning back to the road, her gaze roved toward the house. A compact car was parked near the porch, shaded by the branches of a nut tree.

Jaz plugged her ear bud back in. Who knew what had

driven the handsome cowboy away. She refused to feel bad about rescuing the dog.

A warm flush heated her chest. Good deeds like this had motivated her to follow in her brother's footsteps.

A breeze whirled the dust along the driveway. She trotted around the minefield of potholes.

What sort of career could she pursue that would allow her to experience warm fuzzies daily? The cadence of her footfalls and breaths lulled her into the ideal state of mind for mulling the question.

Easing into the zone chased away the nagging feeling she should know that cowboy, too.

⁂

Bailey Travers smoothed his hand down Poppet's back leg. While he probed and the dog panted, he tried to ignore the tremors ricocheting through every cell in his body.

Jazlyn Rolle. Why did she have to run across his dog's path? God surely hated him. At least she hadn't seemed to recognize him. One small favor.

"Everything will be okay, girl." A cramp in his empty stomach didn't believe the lie.

He cared too much for the brown-and-white mutt. Once Bailey cared for a person, place, or animal, he was guaranteed to lose it. He'd lost his parents to drugs and prison and his foster mother to a botched surgery. His foster father hovered near the edge with terminal cancer, so why shouldn't Bailey expect to lose the dog, too?

Not that the dog held the same importance as Dad. But she was important. He'd rescued her five years ago, shortly after MaryAnn graduated to Heaven, and the dog had been a bundle of cuddles when Tess left for college.

Bailey decided the dog probably didn't need a vet. An elbow nudged his lower back. He glanced over his shoulder to see his sister standing with hands on her hips.

"Poppet will be fine." His gruff voice made her scowl.

"Who was that?"

Bailey ignored the question by rearranging the gauze in the first aid kit.

"Why didn't you offer her a ride?"

Bailey's stomach bucked into his heart and zapped his

pulse into overdrive. He'd had the same reaction to those muscular chocolate milk legs exposed to the creeping sunlight. When he'd lifted Poppet, he'd brushed against firm muscle and smooth, damp skin. His heart and stomach crashed together while warm tingles dive-bombed his body.

He hadn't meant to be rude, but his throat constricted. He didn't want her remembering how her brother had to rescue him. Drew rescued everyone.

Seven years ago, Drew Rolle had been killed on active duty. What was Bailey supposed to say to the sister Drew could no longer protect? Not that those sculpted arms and legs left any doubt about her ability to take care of herself.

"She took off before I thought of it."

A finger dug between two ribs. "You have the social skills of a hermit. How do you expect to host tourists if that's the best you've got for a pretty lady?"

"You're going to be the hostess." The guest ranch was her game plan.

"In the house, sure, but you'll be leading the ranching stuff."

"Maybe there's a class I can take." He ruffled the dog's ears. She grunted and laid her head on the seat.

"What class would that be? Personality acquirement for the socially inept?"

"That hurts." Bailey mimed pulling a stake out of his chest and flicking it over the truck. He dug through the first aid kit.

Behind him, Tess huffed and grumbled. "She was pretty."

He wasn't going to argue that fact. His fingers were wondering how to get a replay of the skin-to-skin contact. "She's Drew Rolle's sister."

Silence greeted his offhand comment. Why had he told Tess that? Since returning from college, his sister had a penchant for meddling in his personal life.

"Am I supposed to know who you're talking about?"

His mind spun through all the things his sister missed in the five years she'd been gone. She'd been little more than a teenager in grief when she'd left for school.

"Probably not. He was a year ahead of me." He closed the kit. "Big football and track star that headed off to the military when he could have played college ball."

Poppet whimpered as he rubbed his hands gently over one forepaw.

"You were a book geek, so how were you friends with him?"

"Didn't say we were friends." More like Bailey was the invisible man. But that suited him fine—then and now. "I knew him. He was a great big brother."

"You should have asked him to tutor you." Tess giggled as she nudged him with her shoulder.

What would she think if he admitted the truth? That he'd copied Drew's method of brothering?

"He was KIA in Afghanistan seven years ago."

Tess gasped.

Bailey frowned over his shoulder at her. Her bright blue eyes filled with tears and her hand covered her mouth. Thank the Lord she had been too young to remember the hell that hardened his heart.

"I'm heading to the pharmacy for those new meds the nurse prescribed. You need anything?"

Bailey shook his head and rolled the dog against his chest. He'd take her in the house, see if she could hobble around. If nothing else he could leave her bed in Fritz's room.

The stereo blared when Tess started her little Kia. After he hip-checked the truck door, Bailey nodded to his sister, who was singing along with the radio as she backed around to head for the road.

He'd missed his sister's zest for life while she was away. *Please, God, don't let Dad's death destroy that.*

Praying as if God would answer? They hadn't been on speaking terms since his mother's death.

Inside, he set Poppet on the floor. She whimpered and wobbled to her feet but managed to hobble to her dish and give him a gloomy look since there wasn't any food.

Normal behavior.

He grabbed a cup of coffee and a muffin Tess baked yesterday, another thing he appreciated about his sister. He could cook a passable meal, but baking seemed like too much effort.

He elbowed his dad's bedroom door open. The gray head turned toward him, haloed by the lamp on the bedside table. The hospital bed raised Fritz into sitting position, and his hefty Bible lay open across his lap.

Some things never changed.

"Morning." Fritz's voice was rough but louder than it had been the previous night.

Bailey sat in the armchair at the side of the bed. The worn cushions embraced him. Tess's muffin melted on his tongue, and something like peace draped itself over his shoulders.

"How's the ranch?"

"The cows busted out of the east pasture, and Poppet stepped in a gopher hole."

Fritz's gray eyes blinked, and his hand petted the open Bible. "Your sister is talking nonstop about Travers Guest Ranch." His lips twitched into a smile, brightening the pasty pallor of his skin.

"It's going to take time to get this place fixed up, but Herman Wells has promised to help me."

Bailey watched his dad's face for signs of the melancholy that marked the years between his wife's death and now.

"I thought you planned to head back to the city, son."

Bailey polished off the muffin and sipped his coffee. In the light of Tess's excitement, his plans didn't matter. Once Dad was gone, she was all he had in the world.

"You need to follow your heart." His dad stroked the gold band on his ring finger.

Follow his heart? What did that even mean? Since the day he'd been dumped like yesterday's lunch, he had worked hard to be useful. If people relied on him, maybe they would keep him around. But nothing he did ever kept them from leaving.

"This family is my heart, Dad." He ignored the memory of sage green eyes and the magnetic pull they had on him.

"Not family like Delores. She would steal the ranch."

Bailey stiffened. Why was his dad bringing up his sister? Could the woman come and take the ranch?

"She's gone." His dad's voice faded, and his eyes closed.

Did that mean the woman was dead? The muffin congealed to an ache in his gut.

A withered hand rose off the sheets. "You are my son. Tess is my daughter. I've taken care of things." His father's voice cracked on the last word.

A pang tugged at Bailey's chest. If his dad said it was taken care of, he should trust him. Maybe there was a will somewhere.

He opened his mouth to ask about it, but Fritz's eyes were closed. His wrinkled fingers clenched the Bible's bulk. After a long blink, he rolled his head toward Bailey.

"I want you to have my Bible." He lifted the book, but it plopped back on his lap.

Bailey nearly choked on his next breath. This strong man he'd idolized for two decades couldn't lift a book. Another pang of loss spiked through his chest.

Bailey settled his palm on the book's cover. "You keep it for now."

His father licked his lips. "Everything you need is in here, son." His voice was a mere rasp. "Everything."

Bailey nodded. Fritz and MaryAnn had lived out the Bible and taught their children its principles. But it didn't save them from death.

With the thickness in his throat and the prickling burn behind his eyeballs, he didn't trust himself to speak. Pain, like someone yanking his intestines out, wrenched through him. He wasn't strong, but he could pretend.

The old man's eyes drifted shut, fluttering lids struggling against the effects of his pain medication.

Bailey reached toward the Bible. "Want me to read to you?"

"Later." He swallowed, and his next words were a mere whisper. "Get to work."

As Bailey stood, Poppet hobbled into the room. When he glanced her way, the dog whined. It almost made him smile.

He scratched her head, staring at the man he'd called father.

The impending goodbye echoed through his heart.

## Two

The blue truck loomed large in the driveway. Great. Her father hadn't left for work.

Jaz ducked around the side of the ranch-style home located north of Sweet Grove, about ten minutes closer to the hospital in Rosewood where her dad had worked forever. She tiptoed across the garage, hoping to sneak through the laundry room and into her bedroom.

One conversation with her father a day had to be enough torture. *Right, God?*

After kicking her dusty sneakers off in the laundry room, she cracked open the door to the hallway. With muffled footfalls, she slunk down the hall to the room her mother hadn't changed since Jaz left for college.

Her hand rested on the doorknob to her room when she heard her dad say, "You're the most beautiful woman in the world."

The husky tone of his voice made her throat close. He would never say those words to her. She doubted any man would.

"I'm the luckiest woman." Whatever else her mother said was concealed by the bark of her miniature boxer.

Jaz skipped into her room, closing the door before the energetic pooch could out her completely.

If only she could slam the door on the memories.

But the tone of her father's voice reminded her of *him*—Captain Cutthroat. After what he'd done, she refused to think of him in other terms.

In the same raspy tone of voice, he'd told her, "You make softball look sexy." But he hadn't meant it.

The courtroom voice he used a year later proved that.

"You wouldn't fit in the Virginia lifestyle."

Jaz twisted the nozzle on the shower as hot as it would go. The water pounded her face, cooling as it sluiced down her athletic body. No, she wasn't a slender, beauty queen like her mother, but she wasn't an ugly cow either.

And she could fit it in anywhere. Couldn't she?

As an older memory pushed its way to the surface, Jaz scrubbed her face, hair, and body. This time it was her father's square face and hazel eyes glaring at her. She could almost feel his fingers on her bicep. To banish the thoughts, she began a mental checklist for the day. Would getting a job help her find a sense of direction? Without the driving purpose of the past six years, she needed something.

A few minutes later, dressed in jeans and a flowing blouse, Jaz poured a cup of coffee and popped it into the microwave. Her mother called from her office across the family room.

Jaz shuffled into the room. Several ledgers lay open across the desk. Pencils stuck up from a ceramic fireman's boot. Geraldine Rolle glanced over the top of emerald green reading glasses, and her face creased with a smile.

A hard place in Jaz's chest melted. A mother's love could do that.

"I'll be at the library perfecting my resume and submitting online applications."

Her mother shook her head. "What has this world come to? Will someone hire you without ever meeting you, too?"

"I'm sure they'll set up at least a phone interview."

The microwave beeped.

"Dinner's at six."

The knot returned to Jaz's stomach. She couldn't eat at the same table as her father. But the look of hope on her mother's face kept her from saying anything.

"I'll let you know."

Jaz returned to the kitchen and peeled a hard-boiled egg and an orange. She stuffed the food into her messenger bag and stalked out of the house.

Her car coughed and heaved but eventually started. The thing needed to be replaced, but it was her biggest tangible connection to Drew. Dad had been too busy with a work convention—surprise—so Drew had driven down from Fort Benning to look at cars with her. They'd had a great time, and when she'd pleaded for the shiny red Subaru, he'd negotiated the best price he could.

Eight years ago. And it hadn't been on the new car lot when they'd found it. She'd racked up more than 100,000 miles on the car, and it deserved to be put out of its misery.

But she couldn't do it.

The brick Sweet Grove Library shared a parking lot with the police station. Across Third Street from the elementary school, it was a one-stop book haven for the education community, too. Jaz planned to spend her time on the public computers searching for jobs and accessing her Google Docs and email.

By the time her stomach gnawed her backbone, Jaz had updated a professional resume and applied at several Austin law firms and county courthouses. One military promise rang true. Her education, experience, and training as a paralegal with the Judge Advocate General's Office translated into a lucrative civilian career.

When she stepped outside, sunshine reminded her that Texas springtime wasn't meant for denim. Her blouse glued itself to her back before she reached First Street.

"Jazlyn!"

Her eyebrows shot up as she turned. A lanky woman with a pony-tail bouncing across her shoulders beelined for her. Behind her, the white steeple of First Street Church was visible.

Elise Nelsen had been a couple years behind Jaz in high school, but they had been in the softball program together. Now she was the youth pastor at First Street Church and the coach of the high school softball team.

Jaz smiled and waved, slowing to allow her to catch up.

"I saw you at church yesterday. Glad to have you back in town."

Jaz appreciated that Elise made no mention of Jaz's slight to her parents by attending a different church than they did. Getting back on speaking terms with God had a better chance of happening if her dad's angry aura wasn't stifling the prospect.

"Where you headed?" Elise's easy grin slid in place.

"To grab something at the market." She paused at the curb to check for traffic. There wasn't any.

"Kristina's on shift at Mabel's."

"Finding a job is more important than Mabel's pie."

"Blasphemy!" Elise laughed, and they crossed the street together.

The youth pastor followed her into the market, and she waved to the cashier.

Jaz had barely picked up a basket near the door before Elise said, "I need help with the softball team."

A carnival ride started in Jaz's stomach. For many years, softball had been everything to her.

Elise gabbed about the poor budget while Jaz picked up a couple apples, a small jar of chunky peanut butter, and two liter-sized bottles of cold water. As soon as she set her purchases on the counter, Elise grabbed her hands.

"Our batting stinks to high heaven. Will you help us?"

Jaz glanced between the hands clutching hers and the serious brown eyes. "I might only be here a couple of weeks."

"Any time you could spare would help. And you'd get to swing the bat every day."

Her fingers itched at the thought, and a tingle beneath her shoulder blades gushed an emotional waterfall into her stomach. It was the most emotion she'd felt since the day she faced off with the man who supposedly loved her. Jaz powered off that thought.

"I've never coached."

While the cashier rang up her purchases, Elise explained the routine. "Your name dominates the records board," she added. "You're like a celebrity to the girls."

Celebrity status for hitting a softball? Was that all she had to show for her life?

"You don't have to attend games or make any long-term commitments. It's not a paying position."

By this time, they were back outside. A breeze ruffled the plastic bag in her hand. Jaz cracked open a bottle of water, chugging half of it.

Every inch of Elise pleaded. "My assistant coach knows pitching, and I can't focus on hitting and defensive fielding at the same time. But if you were there..."

What else did Jaz have going on? It wasn't like she was in a hurry to head home when the library closed. Hadn't she been looking for an excuse not to join in family meals?

"Deets."

Elise threw her arms around Jaz, crushing the bag of apples against her stomach. "Four to six at the high school softball field." She grinned. "You remember where it is, right?"

"Unless they moved it."

"Nothing moves in Sweet Grove."

Exactly why Jazlyn needed to find a job, load up the Drew memorabilia her mom promised to give her, and put Sweet Grove in her rear-view mirror.

༄༅༆༄

The caterwauling in his stomach wouldn't be ignored. Bailey chalked it up to having nothing but a muffin to eat that morning. He steered the Chevy into the lot behind Mabel's. Maybe he could ease his worries and fill his belly at the same time.

Bailey tossed his hat on the seat and snagged a water bottle. His gut protested his forgotten lunch all the way to the back door.

He pushed through the employee entrance and ducked into the kitchen.

Jeffrey Berkley manned a grill with one hand and whipped something in a bowl with the other. The relaxed set of his shoulders announced to the world that he'd found his sweet spot.

"One special." A waitress snapped a slip onto the old-fashioned order turnstile. Her gaze swung to Bailey. "You got company."

Jeffrey sidestepped along the counter, flipping something on the grill. He glanced backward and white teeth flashed in his dark face. "B.T. Sneaking in again?"

"I got a question, and you're the smartest guy I know."

Jeffrey laughed. "You don't get out much."

While Jeffrey slapped together a special and finished his other order, Bailey leaned against the dish station. "I'm hungry too."

Jeffrey barked out, "Order up."

Before Bailey could say anything, his friend flipped a second corned beef sandwich onto a plate. With an expert twist of his wrist, he whipped a basket from the deep fryer, flipped fries into a metal pan, and sprinkled a seasoning blend over them. After filling the other half of the plate with the fries, Jeffrey slapped it onto the cutting block near Bailey's hip. His mouth watered.

"Eat up."

Bailey washed his hands at the sink, grimacing as the water scalded through his callouses. He gobbled half the sandwich and was munching fries when he remembered his other purpose. He swigged the rest of his water, swishing it around his mouth before swallowing.

He glanced toward Jeffrey, who was pouring yellow batter into a pan. "What do you know about inheritance laws?"

"Law?" Jeffrey shook the pan and tapped it on the counter. "Not much."

As Bailey reached for the other half of the sandwich, his front pocket vibrated. He dug out the phone and read a message from his sister.

*Plans for the guest rooms?*

Bailey grimaced. They wouldn't need the plans he'd labored over if an actual blood relation showed up and claimed the ranch. He tapped out a reply.

After his friend tucked the pan into the oven, he gave Bailey his full attention. "Doesn't your dad have a will?"

"Not that I've been able to find."

Jeffrey's hand clamped onto Bailey's shoulder. "Glad Tess made it home to have some time with him."

Bailey agreed. "Thing is, he mumbled something about his sister." Bailey recoiled at the thought of a sister betraying her brother. "She stole his parent's ranch, and I'm afraid she might show up and do the same thing here."

Jeffrey frowned. "I don't know how to help you."

While Jeffrey typed a message on his phone, Bailey scarfed the rest of the meal. He was still munching on fries when Jeffrey tucked his phone away.

"Elise knows someone. She says you could stop by the library now and ask about it." Jeffrey reached for the plate. "Finished?"

Bailey nodded, wiping his hands down the back of his jeans. A glance at the phone as he tucked it back in his pocket showed he still had thirty minutes until he needed to be at the high school. And the library was on the way.

"What do I owe you?" His hand rested against his wallet.

Jeffrey waved his hand. "Lunch rush is over and the special would have went to waste."

"Thanks, man." They bumped fists and Bailey headed out.

Clouds scudded across the blue sky, shading him from the sun's rays. He breathed deeply of the cooler air before hopping back in his not-so-cool truck and driving the few blocks down First and onto Birch.

Cool air stole his breath as he pushed into the library. At her post behind the counter, Sally Scott looked up, and her sour expression transformed.

Hat in hand, he scanned the library. Where was this guy who knew about the law?

A row of computers sat along the back wall, and Bailey made a wide circuit around the circulation counter, raising his hand in greeting when Sally stepped his way. He wove through the section of nonfiction books and spotted a woman hunched over a computer. The only other people in the place were some mothers and young children in the back.

As he approached the lone woman, she stretched like a cat and stood up. Even covered by long pants, he'd recognize those legs anywhere. Jazlyn Rolle was the legal expert?

Bailey stopped a foot away and cleared his throat.

She whirled toward him, pale green eyes widening. "You're the guy with legal questions?"

Her befuddlement matched his so well, his frown eased. He raised an eyebrow. "You're the legal expert Elise knows?"

Her laugh rolled over him. She slapped her hand over her mouth and gazed beyond him.

He extended his hand to her, wishing for a moment he'd given it a proper wash after lunch. "I'm Bailey Travers." *Please don't recognize the name.* When her face showed no recognition, tension bled from his shoulders. "Thanks for agreeing to help me."

"Of course." Her hand gripped his in a hearty shake.

Bailey tried to prolong the contact, enjoying the tingling sensations, but when she tugged, he let go. He took a deep breath and steeled himself. He should have said something when she'd delivered Poppet to him.

"Is your dog okay?" She asked like she'd read his mind.

He nodded, searching for something else to say.

"I'm glad." She paused for a moment. "What sort of legal questions do you have?"

Her intelligent green eyes made his heart flutter. He gazed at a point beyond her right shoulder to center his thoughts. "My dad is going to pass soon, and I don't think he has a will. Since he never adopted us, I'm afraid we'll lose the ranch."

*And we can't lose the ranch. It's all Tess has.*

Jaz slid into the chair she'd been using and opened a new search window on her computer. Her fingers flew over the keys. Bailey edged closer until the scent of oranges overwhelmed him. The food in his stomach felt like a weight.

"You were fostered by the Traverses, right?" She glanced at him.

He bobbed his head.

"Mrs. Travers has already passed?"

He nodded again. "Five years ago."

Jaz stopped typing and looked up at him. "I'm sorry. I can't imagine losing my mom."

Bailey's gaze met hers. Something dark flickered behind her sympathetic expression, and she turned back to the screen as if to hide it.

"Even if you weren't legally adopted, there's a thing called equitable adoption that should allow you to inherit from your dad." Jaz pointed to a paragraph on the screen.

Bailey leaned closer until the heat of her warmed his side. He swallowed to wet his mouth before he could squeak out a question. "What's that?"

She swiveled in his direction. Their faces were inches apart, and the full impact of her struck him like a punch to the gut. He couldn't breathe.

She scooted her chair back a foot and took a deep breath. Did that mean she was affected by him, too? His gaze drifted to the rise of her chest beneath the feminine shirt she wore. His ears burst into flame, and he snapped his gaze back to her face.

A small smile tugged on her lips. "Also called adoption by estoppel. It exists if the relationship began during the child's minority, continued throughout the parent's lifetime, and clear evidence shows the foster parent would have adopted except for legal barriers." She counted the conditions off on her lithe fingers.

Bailey straightened. Although the subject of legal adoption came up several times, the Traverses had never followed through. Would a judge think that meant they didn't want to adopt Tess and him?

The fries in his stomach turned to stone.

"Were there legal barriers to adoption?" Jaz glanced at him again, finger still pointing to the text on-screen. "The other two requirements are met."

Sweat beaded beneath his hair, and he scratched at it. Jaz's gaze followed the motion, so he tucked his hand in his pocket instead.

"Some. My biological father protested giving up his parental rights." Bailey shuddered as a memory of the man's harsh voice replayed in his mind. "He was in and out of jail but always made contact before the 20-month period expired."

MaryAnn had been frustrated when the man's letters came, but she was too honest to toss them in the trash. It wasn't like they meant anything to Bailey, but Tess seemed to cherish them.

"You never lived with him again?"

Bailey's heart jolted at the idea. He didn't have as many gruesome memories of his father as he did of his drug-using mother, but life before he'd come to Sweet Grove was better left in the past.

"By the time he'd went back to prison for more than two years, I was already 18. MaryAnn had documents drawn up to adopt Tess, but those were never filed either."

"Because…" Jaz worried her bottom lip.

The sight made flutters start in his chest. He couldn't take his eyes off the white teeth nibbling the berry-colored skin.

He dragged his attention from her mouth and studied the computer without seeing it. "I was surprised to learn she hadn't finished the process." MaryAnn had been irritated by the delays and gung-ho about making the adoption official.

"Maybe you can find some documentation. Do you know for sure there's no will?"

Bailey shook his head. His gaze shifted to the clock in the lower corner of the computer screen. "I'll check Dad's office." He stepped back. "I've got to get to work."

Jaz ducked her strong chin. "Let me know if you have more questions." She stood in a single graceful motion. "I'm sorry about your dad."

"I'm sorry about Drew."

She blanched at the name. Her lips opened and closed. His mind grappled for something else to say, but the tasks waiting at the school called him.

"Thanks for checking on this." He reached to tip his hat at her and realized it was in his other hand.

"No problem."

His cheeks burned as he twisted toward the entrance and strode away. At the door, he glanced back, but she had already returned to the computer.

He hated the idea that Tess might lose the ranch, and his roiling gut confirmed that. But knowing he needed to continue talking to Jaz about the situation sanded the sharp edges from his anxiety.

# Three

Later that day, Jaz slipped into shorts and a t-shirt in the library's restroom. Something about changing into softball clothes in the locker room at Sweet Grove High felt a little too much like reliving the glory days.

Like everything good in her life, they were long gone. And she had no clue what her future looked like.

As ready as she'd ever be, she dropped her other clothes into the back seat of her car, snagged the bag of gear and the cleats she'd tied together, and jogged down the sidewalk, swerving into the athletic field parking lot. The ricochet of tennis balls thrummed along with the thump of her footsteps. One cleat drummed a beat against her shoulder blade while the other sat snuggly in her armpit.

She pushed through the turnstile and slowed to a walk. The pulsing in her neck had nothing to do with the short run. Back in the day, her mentoring style had always been impatience married with demonstration. Would these girls respond to that?

When she capped the rise at the end of the football field and began the descent into the groomed softball field, Elise hailed her. The tickling scent of fresh cut grass melded with the stir of dust and chalk in the air, and the familiarity of it dispelled her inhibitions. Softball's stalwart friendship had pulled her through the grief of losing Drew and the anxiety of fitting in with the JAG crew.

Jaz leaned her bat against the dugout fence and swung the shoes off her shoulder. Teenage girls in shorts and red t-shirts sporting the shorthorns mascot scanned her from the infield where they tossed balls back and forth.

"What's the plan?" Jaz sat on the metal bleachers behind the backstop. She'd already replaced one sneaker with a cleat when Elise joined her, arms crossed over her chest and shoulders leaning against the chain link barrier.

"Lynn's going to be late, so how about you run the pitchers and catchers through batting practice first? I'll head to third base and nag the fielders about their performance."

Jaz nodded.

"Once Lynn takes her crew, you can work the outfielders and the three designated hitters." A glint in those green eyes made Jaz narrow her own.

"What aren't you telling me about the infielders?"

Elise's grin ignited. "I'll let you figure that out on your own."

"Delightful." Jaz double-knotted her shoes and hoped the muttered word didn't give away her trepidation.

After pulling on her batting gloves and stretching, Jaz grabbed her bat. Elise gathered the players to the pitcher's mound where she explained the drill. Furtive glances from the girls became bolder, more speculative.

"We're about to turn a corner in the batter's box."

A few girls snorted. One said, "If quicksand doesn't swallow us first."

Several girls laughed at the remark, but many shook their heads and glared at the speaker.

"I'd like to introduce you to Jazlyn Rolle." Elise gestured as if she was Vanna White and Jaz was a lighted letter awaiting a turn.

Jaz nodded, bringing the bat to her shoulder and scuffing dirt over home plate.

"Not THE Jazlyn Rolle?" A stocky girl with a long blonde ponytail gaped at Elise.

"Most career home runs with 283. Fifty-nine home runs in a season, and three home runs in a single game. Yep, that's the one." Elise beamed as if the records were hers.

A grumble swelled among the girls.

Elise held up her hand. "She's volunteering her time to help us improve our hitting consistency, so I expect you to treat her with more respect than you give me."

She stared around the circle of girls. "Pitchers and catchers, you're up first. Starters, take your positions on the field." Elise nodded to the dugout, indicating the other six girls should wait there. "Bix, you pitch a few to Coach Rolle."

Jaz stiffened at the title. She stepped away from the batter's box while one of the girls grabbed a mitt and crouched behind the plate.

"Better protect that pretty face, Dan." This came from the blonde girl who grabbed a ball and mitt and scanned Jaz through slitted eyes.

Bix jogged toward the mound while the catcher pulled her helmet into place and another girl secured her chest protection.

Jaz watched the pair warm up. The catcher signaled and the pitcher windmilled the ball over the plate. Leather snapping against leather proved they worked well together.

"Batter up," Elise called, winking at Jaz.

Jaz swung the bat once more and stepped into the box. She toed a groove with her right foot and sank weight onto her back leg. She squinted at the pitcher and choked up on the bat.

Bix glared at her, adjusting slightly to a left-handed batter. Her first pitch dropped at the last moment, and Jaz adapted her swing. Her shoulder muscles sang as the bat's vibrations jarred through her and the spinning ball soared over the shortstop's head.

The next pitch looked like it was way outside but curved violently into the zone. Jaz connected again, the neon ball striking a little too close to her hands for depth, but it slammed the ground to the right of the mound and bounced over the first baseman's head.

Bix narrowed her eyes and moved through her windup. A fastball sailed into the zone.

Jaz twisted, one with the bat. Energy sparked through her, and the wood connected with a solid crack. She watched the ball soar over the outfielders and the fence, straight toward a man mowing the field.

The girls gaped at her. The pitcher's mitt hung at her side.

Jaz turned to the line of girls wearing batting helmets. The one in the warm up circle snapped her mouth shut. Jaz waved her in, stepping behind the plate so she could see the oncoming ball and watch the batter's stance and swing.

"Let's start with a fast ball or two." Jaz raised her chin toward the pitcher. "Then let Dan call the pitches, like in a game."

Bix blew a bubble and offered a curt nod. No one liked to see her fastball pounded over the fence.

"How about a couple swings?" Jaz turned her attention to the batter.

Girl after girl stepped up to the plate. Jaz watched their first few swings and then stepped in with advice to strengthen their individual style. Some needed help in hand placement, while others didn't have a strong base because their feet were too close together or their weight was distributed awkwardly.

The other coach arrived, and a different pitcher and catcher took over while a new rotation of batters came through the line.

Eventually Elise called a halt and had the girls circle up. Rather than joining the huddle, Jaz collected the bats and balls and stuffed them into the equipment bag.

She'd changed into her street shoes by the time the girls grabbed the equipment and headed toward the locker room, most looking glum and many red-faced.

Elise stopped in front of her, hands on hips. "And I thought I was a taskmaster."

Jaz glanced up. Elise wasn't smiling, and Jaz's eyes widened. "What do you mean?"

Elise nodded and pursed her lips. "Some of the girls were practically in tears. You need to go easy on them."

Jaz blinked. She hadn't paid any attention to the girls' emotions. She'd talked them through batting the same way she'd coached herself for decades. Compared to her father, she was kindness personified.

*Is that a comparison you want?*

"I told you I'm not a coach."

Elise sighed. "Your style might work for college girls, but most of this group plays for the fun of it or to stay in shape for another sport. None of them expect to get scholarships."

Dust scratched her throat. Jaz swallowed, giving a curt nod. The lift of her spirits crashed into the pit of her stomach.

Even softball couldn't offer the sort of homecoming she wanted.

⁂

At lunchtime on Thursday, Bailey drove down Birch Street toward his afternoon job, lunch on the seat beside him. He craned his neck and his foot eased off the gas as he approached the library.

A lovely dark-skinned woman pushed her way out of the doors at that moment. His foot smashed the brake pedal, and his chest careened forward, jamming into the steering wheel.

Jaz slid into her car before he could park the truck. Now what?

Over the sound of his engine, he heard her car whine but the motor didn't turn over. His heart leapt in his chest. Car problems he understood.

Before he talked himself out of walking up to a virtual stranger, he shut off the pickup and shoved open the cab door. He would help anyone whose car was giving them problems. This had nothing to do with sage green eyes, teasing lips, and legs that had no right to be so distracting. Nothing at all.

His heartbeat drummed a cadence for his footsteps, and his fingers ground into his palms.

He stopped beside her car and cleared his throat. Her head was crumpled against arms crossed over the steering wheel. His heart nose-dived into his stomach.

*Please don't let her be crying.* Tears from someone he cared about demolished him.

"Car trouble?" The husky sound of his voice had him coughing.

She startled, and wide green eyes met his. "It won't start." She shrugged.

"Try it again."

She heaved a breath, and his gaze wandered to her fitted tank top. He jerked his attention away, listening as the key clicked.

"Alternator is my guess. Should be an easy fix."

Relief smoothed the wrinkles in her forehead. "I guess I'm walking."

She opened the door, and he sidled backward. A single graceful movement later and she stood beside him. The sight of her athletic form covered in fitted crop pants and a shirt that flowed with every motion revved his pulse into overdrive.

She tilted her head back slightly to meet his gaze and caught him scanning her womanly curves. At least she couldn't know he'd begun to salivate like a starving dog at mealtime.

He licked his lips. "I think I can fix your car."

"I was going to grab a bite and then head back in." She nodded toward the library. "To finish up some job applications."

His gaze lingered on her lips after she'd finished speaking. Their red plumpness reminded him of ripe strawberries.

He blinked away the thought. Maybe he should have eaten the lunch Tess packed him before he stopped here. His hunger was affecting every thought.

"I have a lunch in my truck." Which sounded rude and like he didn't want to spend time with her. *False.*

"Are you offering to share?" Her grin sent a whirlpool spiraling through his gut.

"Uh." He gulped air. "I can give you a ride." Her smile acted like a vise on his lungs.

"Maybe to the market?" Her eyes flicked over his face. "Unless you've got other plans."

"No plans." He'd learned the hard way that family responsibilities came before any plans he might make.

"Want to walk?"

"I've got to be at the school in less than an hour."

She pursed her lips together, and he forgot what he'd said. What did they taste like? It had been years since he'd kissed anyone.

"Bailey?"

He shook off the stray thoughts. "I can drop you at the market. Then I can head for work when we're done."

She nodded and leaned back into the car. He whirled away, stomping toward his truck to keep from leering at her again. Sweat itched where his hat pressed his hair against his head.

The truck door groaned open, and Bailey hopped into the driver's seat, leaning across to open the passenger door from the inside. Jaz rounded his truck, hips swaying.

The sight of her stopped his heart. Lord, he'd been so infatuated with her in high school. Apparently, he still was.

She was only in town until she landed another job. He remembered her determination on the softball field. If she applied the same drive to her career, she'd have offers rolling in before a week passed.

Jaz appeared beyond the opening, and he turned his attention to starting the truck. As soon as she snapped her seatbelt in place, he backed out and drove the two blocks to the market.

"I'll wait." His throat felt tight.

"Thanks."

She jumped out of the truck. He tried to stare straight ahead, but his traitorous eyes followed her. The thrumming of his pulse nearly deafened him.

His hands flexed on the steering wheel. His knuckles whitened, which reminded him of her hands on the bat at so many softball games. Once Drew had joined the Army, Bailey had become the cheering section at Jaz's games.

He'd been there the evening she'd scored three home runs. Everyone had leapt to their feet, cheering as the three runs scored with her third homer. His pulse had hammered like a construction crew that night, too.

When he'd congratulated her after the game, her light eyes had fixed on him, and his heart had stopped. Then she'd smiled, squeezed his hand and said, "Thanks for being Drew's stand-in."

Because that's how she'd seen him—the weak kid her heroic brother had to rescue from bullies, and the guy who watched her games because of a promise to her brother. But who could watch her inspire a team of competitive girls to the state championship and not fall for her?

A squeal of hinges snapped him out of his reverie. Jaz climbed in, a plastic bag over one wrist. "There's a picnic table in the church yard. How about eating there?"

Bailey nodded and started the engine. It wasn't even a block up First to the church. Two cars were parked at the far end of the building closer to the office entrance. Of course, Pastor Bernie would be there.

Hopefully God wouldn't strike Bailey down for using a table in the yard when he hadn't darkened the door in months.

Once they were seated, Jaz pulled out a bag of carrots and some sort of dip. He opened the insulated lunch bag Tess had packed for him and grabbed one of the sandwiches. The roast beef from Sunday's pot roast exploded with flavor on his tongue.

"Why Sweet Grove?"

Bailey swallowed the bite. "Family. Why not Sweet Grove?"

"It doesn't feel like home without Drew."

He choked down another bite of his sandwich, sensing the grief behind the words. "He was a true hero. I wasn't surprised to hear he died in the line of duty."

Jaz drank some tea from a bottle. She tilted her head in a way that drew his attention to the nape of her neck. Such a smooth expanse of hot cocoa. "Is that the rumor?"

"Your parents didn't really say much about it. Nothing was in the papers. But I know Drew."

She licked her lips and he almost missed her next words. "I'm trying to place you."

Bailey chomped down on the sandwich so he wouldn't say something stupid. Something like, "I'm glad you can't. I'm not memorable." Because being forgettable was better than being remembered as the weakling he was.

He polished off one sandwich and opened the second at the same time she popped the lid on a salad covered in grilled chicken.

"Do you play darts? Elise said there's some sort of dart tournament next week."

Bailey stopped chewing. His gaze swept toward her. She concentrated on stabbing lettuce with a plastic fork.

"Not since college."

"Where'd you go to college?" She shoveled in a bite of salad and glanced up at him. The fork halted as their gazes collided.

Bailey's mouth dried up. Those beautiful pale eyes in that dark face could render him senseless like a blow to the head. When she glanced back at her food, he forced himself to look at his sandwich and finish chewing the bite in his mouth. After he chased it with a swig of water, he cleared his throat.

"Colorado. An architectural design school."

"Why Colorado?"

He pushed away the horror show called his early childhood that tried to awaken in his mind. College and working with a drafting firm had been good experiences. It wasn't Colorado's fault his grandmother didn't want him.

*They're too much trouble.* The words from the courtroom resounded in his brain.

Jaz touched his knuckles. He stared at the point of contact, noticing for the first time that he'd pulverized the half sandwich still wrapped in plastic. Warmth oozed along his arm.

"I didn't mean to bring back painful memories." Her lips quivered into a small smile, distracting him from the past.

He sucked a deep breath, staring at where their hands connected. "College was great, but my childhood wasn't. Until Fritz and MaryAnn." He tilted his chin and found her studying him. "I don't know what will happen when Fritz passes."

Her hand wrapped around his. "I hope you find a will."

Bailey loosened his death grip on the sandwich and turned his palm into hers. Her gaze unlocked something in his chest. She really saw him. He stroked his thumb over hers and his stomach bucked.

After sharing a look that flayed his armored heart, Bailey licked his lips and leaned slightly toward her.

Jaz flinched away and started forking her salad again. "Were you good at darts?"

Bailey froze, realizing he'd been close to kissing her. It was crazy to even consider that. He took a deep breath, and the tangy scent of oranges overlapped the freshness of flowers and grass. "I was better at pool."

Jaz asked him what billiard games he liked, and his spine relaxed. They ate lunch, conversing like two normal people without hang-ups and ghosts.

*God, I don't know what I did to deserve a break like this.*

A breeze swept over him, and he heard his mother whisper, *It's called grace, and God gives it freely.*

A bird swooped toward Jaz's bowl of lettuce. She ducked and tossed a leaf on the other edge of the table. Her laugh when a second bird joined in pecking at the greenery sent a shudder of warmth spinning into his gut.

Maybe there would be life after Dad died.

# Four

After practice that night, Jaz jogged back to the library. Bailey waited beside his truck. Sweat glued the shirt to her back, and it jerked as she raised a hand to him. As promised, he'd borrowed a trailer from a friend. Together they rolled her car's front wheels in place and he secured them.

Jaz stared at the Subaru, a sort of anxious grief balling in her stomach. Tears burned behind her eyes.

She whirled and paced toward the passenger door of Bailey's truck. Crying over a broken car? So what if it was her last connection to Drew. She should be more worried about having transportation for an interview in Austin next week.

Bailey pushed his ever-present hat higher on his head. "Ready?"

She gulped away the emotion and nodded. Their doors squeaked in chorus as they climbed into the truck.

"Thanks for giving me a ride and fixing the car."

"Just being neighborly."

She relaxed into the cloth-covered seat and glanced at him. This cowboy had a heart of gold.

The face of her most recent heartbreaker swam into her mind. She'd assumed every man in uniform would share her brother's integrity. Boy, had she been proven wrong.

"There's a scrimmage tomorrow." She would be in the dugout giving the girls last-minute hitting tips and encouraging them. Maybe she'd coach first base a few innings. An old desire longed for a cheering squad. *For coaching?*

"I'll have the field mowed and chalked."

She pressed down the welling disappointment. "Elise was nagging about the dart tournament again."

Bailey stopped at the intersection of Fourth Avenue

and Orchard Way. He glanced toward her. When his brilliant eyes fixed on hers, her staccato heartbeat sent blood rushing toward her cheeks. How he could be thirty and single shocked her senseless.

Gals in Sweet Grove were blind or slow. Maybe both.

"Tess mentioned it, too."

"There'll be food."

His warm chuckle rolled over her. An army of goose-bumps marched up her arms. "It's for members of the Twenty and Single small group."

Jaz arched an eyebrow. "What? You're too old?"

After he turned onto Orchard, he shot her a smoldering look. Her heart plunged into the seat beneath her, taking her empty stomach with it. If only that look meant something.

She shook the thought away. After the brutal decapitation of her last relationship, she wasn't looking for romance. Especially not in Sweet Grove.

"I'm not a member of the class." Bailey's masculine voice hammered its own tune along her backbone.

"Tess is. They're encouraged to bring guests." She slapped her thigh. "At least that's how Elise convinced me to go."

She touched his arm. The muscles bunched beneath her fingers, and flutters exploded inside her chest. "Turn here."

He followed her directions, the movement of his arms dislodging her touch. Sadly. She wouldn't mind another excuse to hold onto him.

Heat flushed her face. Time to think about something else.

He braked at the end of the short drive in front of the single-story house. He slammed the truck in park and hopped out, racing around the front of the truck before she could fathom his hurry.

The door beside her opened. Bailey stood there, chin ducked and hat shading half of his face. "Texas, where gentlemen live and breathe." His lips twitched.

She slid to the ground, her sneakers landing inches from his grass-covered boots. She tilted her head up, nearly choking at the intensity of his gaze.

"Thanks for the ride." Her voice squeaked worse than the hinges on the door. She cleared her throat. "The car—"

"I should be able to get the part tomorrow and replace it on Saturday."

Her shoulders relaxed. "So it'll be working by Monday?"

He nodded. His lips parted, as if he was going to say something. No sound came out.

She stared at his full mouth, and her toes tingled to press her upward. One small peck as a thank you would be appropriate.

Bailey ducked his head and strode to the truck rail, where he reached in the bed and grabbed her two bags. She blinked, having forgotten about them.

A breeze whispered across her burning face. When she took the bags, their hands brushed. Awareness chilled her, sending goosebumps marching up her arm.

"Thanks."

"Don't mention it." He tipped the brim of his hat.

Before she could fully debate it, Jaz pecked him on the lips.

Hot hands pressed into her lower back, and he returned the kiss with sizzle and swiftness. She gasped, and her heartbeat deafened her. Before she could enjoy the extended contact, he pulled back.

His eyes were darker than a stormy sky. "See you later."

She gulped, nodding because her voice was MIA.

Replays of the kiss dogged her through dinner and monopolized her dreams.

※※※

Early Saturday morning, Poppet whined at Bailey. Once Bailey dragged himself upright, the dog trotted toward his father's room. Fritz's face was slack, colorless but at peace.

Tears choked Bailey. His fingers brushed the Bible beside his father's hip. The Bible he insisted held all the answers Bailey needed.

What use was the Bible? It hadn't kept his parents alive.

His father's voice echoed in his mind, *The cost of life is death*. While God might heal some people and extend the lives of others, it was only a stopgap measure. Death won in the end.

Bailey stroked the Bible and dropped it on his dresser before heading to the kitchen. He brewed a cup of tea and car-

SHARON HUGHSON

ried it into Tess's room.

Her blonde hair peeked over the sheets. He'd never understood how she could burrow so far beneath the covers, especially when it wasn't the slightest bit cold.

He set the tea on her nightstand. The mattress sank as he sat at her back. Her silky hair smoothed beneath his touch. He wiggled her shoulder. She groaned.

"Tess, it's Dad."

She twisted toward him, eyes wide. Whatever she saw on his face brought a rainstorm of tears. She flung herself against his chest, arms squeezing around his neck. He patted her back and cupped her head. Before he could think, the crooning lullabies he used with the rescue animals poured from his lips.

Her shoulders shook, and her need made his own tears evaporate. He could be strong. A lifetime of practice wouldn't fail him now.

When the outburst finished, she leaned back, fluffing a pillow to cushion her. She wiped her face and took the proffered tea. Bailey snagged a box of tissues from her dresser, exchanged it for the teacup.

"What now?"

"He's already planned everything with the funeral home."

Tess sighed. "We're orphans again."

The woefulness of her tone opened a pit beneath his stomach. They'd always been orphans. Even when the Traverses took them in and gave them a name, they hadn't legally adopted them.

"We have each other."

Her lips twisted. After she sipped the tea, she stared past him toward the door. "What do we do?"

"There's a list, Tess." His heart and stomach tangled. "I'll take care of it."

A few quiet minutes later, she nudged him with her legs. "I want to see him."

Bailey nodded, squeezed her calf, and left the room. There were cows to look after.

But first, he called the funeral home.

By late that afternoon, his hair stood on end. He'd checked off everything on the list, going through the safe and the folders in his dad's desk. There weren't any legal documents.

The one thing he had found scalded his hand as he picked it up again. The curling script on the outside looked so innocuous.

His fingers trembled as he pulled the single sheet of paper out of the envelope.

*Uncle Fritz,*

*So you're dying. I suppose that means I'll be inheriting that ranch. I have no desire to live in the middle of nowhere Texas, but I suppose the land will sell for a tidy sum.*

*Why not invite me up to see my inheritance before you pass?*

*Or maybe I'll say my farewells to your lifeless body.*

*Your Niece,*

*Honey Campbell*

The words etched themselves into his eyeballs. He closed his eyes, rubbing at the burning sensation.

Campbell. Dad's sister's name had been Campbell. The one he'd mentioned on Monday. When their parents passed, his sister had edged him out of the inheritance. Bailey never heard how it had happened, but he remembered one thing.

"She's a gold-digging, heartless woman. And her daughter's just like her," Fritz would say.

The heartless gold-digger assumed she would inherit the ranch.

Tess pushed open the office door. Bailey flipped the letter facedown and stood.

She fell against his chest. They'd spent the day's tears, but the feel of her against his chest reassured him. He wasn't alone.

"Let's go for a ride." Her voice was muffled against him.

It was a perfect idea. There'd be no answers about Honey Campbell's claim on a weekend.

"Okay. Let me straighten a few things."

She peeked around him at the various piles on the large cherry desk. "Find anything?"

"Not yet."

Her brow and lips pinched with worry. He smoothed a hand over her blonde ponytail, tugging the end.

"I will."

She smiled.

Once she left, he returned to the desk, and stuffed the letter in the envelope and folded it. After straightening the piles, leaving the copy of the life insurance policy he'd located in the safe on top, he headed to the room he'd been using.

The ugly letter got buried beneath his socks. He'd deal with it later.

It was nothing to worry Tess about.

But the knot in his stomach refused to loosen.

※※※

Monday morning couldn't come soon enough. Bailey rushed through chores and listened to Tess's litany of cleaning tasks. When she mentioned their mother's craft and sewing room, he straightened.

"Keep an eye out for any legal documents."

Tess gaped at him. "Why would Mom have those?"

"I didn't find anything about the adoption in dad's study. Maybe she had those papers."

Tess's face fell. "The adoption never happened, Lee."

He covered her hand with his. "But there could be papers. Which would be helpful if there are inheritance questions."

"Why would there be inheritance questions?"

Bailey gulped. Her eyes had widened, and he read the panic there. Exactly what he'd been trying to avoid.

He forced what he hoped appeared as a nonchalant shrug. "Jaz mentioned something about the adoption."

"Jaz." A mischievous smile stretched across Tess's face. "You like her."

Bailey stood and took his coffee cup to the sink. "She's only passing through, Tess."

But that didn't stop him from thinking about her. Would she be at the library if she didn't have a car? Maybe he should stop by her house.

His mind flitted back to the brief kiss on Thursday night. She'd been saying thank you and he'd turned it into something else.

If he was lucky, she wouldn't remember it. Like she hadn't remembered who he was.

Less than an hour later, he breezed into the library. No one was at the circulation desk. He strode toward the bank of computers. His steps echoed in the patron-free library.

Before he reached her, Jaz turned in his direction. Her lips curled into a smile. His heart played leap frog with his stomach. Before her beauty distracted him, he dug in his back pocket, fingering the envelope.

She stood up. "I heard about your dad."

Her arms suddenly wrapped around his waist. His hands went to her lower back automatically. The scent of summer and spices filled his senses.

Just as quickly, she stepped back. "I'm sorry."

"He's in a better place." He cringed at the platitude. How many times had he heard it after his mother passed? And it never made him feel better.

Her chin dropped. "I can tell you're a man with a mission."

Bailey's heart crashed into his fluttery stomach. He wasn't here to hug Jaz or imagine kissing her again. Not when they could lose the ranch and derail Tess's dreams.

He extended his hand to her. The crinkled envelope looked like he'd been sitting on it for days. "I didn't find a will, but I found this."

Jaz read the short note. "A niece? We'll need to do some research."

It was nearly time for him to be at work.

He slapped the hat on his thigh and she whipped toward him. "I've got to head out."

She glanced between the letter and his face. "Can you meet later? No, that won't work." She picked up her smart phone. "How about tomorrow afternoon?"

"Sure."

She held the offensive letter toward him, but he shook his head. If he took it home, Tess might find it, and she had enough worries to occupy her mind.

"Keep it."

"I can check out this..." She glanced at the note. "Honey Campbell, too."

"Thanks again."

As he wove his way out of the library, he realized the knot that had twisted his innards since he found the letter had loosened. Had talking to Jaz about the problem really changed anything?

He looked forward to spending more time with her, but it was dangerous. Not just because she might remember him, but because his heart felt too much around her.

And she would be leaving while he had to stay.

# Five

The next day, Jaz took her morning run and then wheeled her old bicycle out of the garage. She didn't blame Bailey for not getting the car fixed. After all, his dad died the day he planned to work on it, and since then he'd been worrying about the inheritance issues.

Back in the library, Jaz took up her regular post at a computer. She clicked through to her email inbox and could hardly believe her eyes.

Jaz tilted the computer monitor and reread the message from one of her UT softball teammates.

*OMG. You're back in Austin? Can you still swing a bat? I might have something for you with the Longhorns.*

Her heart skipped wildly. Practicing with the high school team reminded her that softball could be her home. With a bat in her hand, she felt right and welcome.

A job with the UT softball program? It was more than she had ever imagined for herself.

Nothing was certain, though. The pay could be horrible. Or it could be a volunteer position, and that wouldn't pay the rent.

After asking her friend for details, Jaz concentrated on the job search. She finished up her third application to law firms in Austin. Sally's voice pitched in the unmistakable way of flirting women everywhere. Jaz hit the submit button before standing to stretch and turning to face the front of the library.

A lanky cowboy strolled in her direction. The crown of his head retained the impression of the hat he held in one hand. Light brown hair curled around the back of his ears. Deep-water blue eyes stared at her.

Jaz ignored her acrobatic heart and gestured toward the chair next to where she'd been working all morning. Bailey ducked his chin toward her seat.

Her eyebrows winged upward. "How could I forget I was in Texas, land of the last gentleman?"

Pink tinted Bailey's tanned cheeks. Was he remembering how he'd mentioned being a gentleman Thursday before she kissed him?

After she sat, he stood over her. "I've been meaning to tell you. Drew inspired me to act right as much as my dad."

Sudden stinging in her nose made Jaz blink.

Bailey sat in the chair she'd pointed out, and set his cowboy hat on one of his knees. "Drew was an amazing brother. I tried to be just like him for Tess."

Jaz's mind spun, trying to place this man. He would have been several years ahead of her in school, but certainly someone with eyes like his, never mind the broad shoulders, couldn't have been overlooked. Even if she hadn't been all that interested in boys back then.

Or now.

"Little sis has done well. She got her hospitality degree and wants to convert the ranch into some sort of resort." Pride glowed from his eyes, and his chin rose when he talked about his sister. Jaz recalled Drew looking the same way at her.

A twist in her chest made her rub the spot over her heart. Bailey's gaze followed her gesture, and his face reddened.

She fought to hide a grin. He tugged on one ear and stared toward his boots. That's when it hit her.

"I remember now."

His head snapped up. Dread washed across his handsome features.

"You trained a dog. Some guys were giving you a hard time."

*A crowd of teenagers circling the thin guy with a pimply face. The yellow lab cowered behind his skinny legs. His fists were clenched, and blood trickled from his nose.*

*Drew shoved the largest guy in the mob back a step. "Go through me to touch him again."*

*A murmur of curses shuddered through the group, but when the big guy backed off, the rest of them followed. Jaz glowed with pride over her brother's actions.*

"Drew was driving us to the dentist. I'd walked over

from the middle school." Her mind returned slowly from that distant time. "He was a junior, I think."

Bailey swallowed hard, scanning the room like he needed an emergency exit. She put her hand on his knee, and he froze.

"I can see why you would consider Drew heroic. He rescued me dozens of times."

Bailey's gaze flickered to hers. Her heart sped during the short stare-down. When he shifted his focus to her hand —still on his knee—lava rushed into Jaz's face. She pulled her hand away.

"Not the best first impression, huh?"

Jaz furrowed her brows. Was he serious? "What makes you say that?"

"I couldn't protect myself from those guys."

Jaz shifted closer and gripped his forearm. The muscle twitched beneath her fingers. "Seriously? Those guys were jerks. Drew hated bullies."

A flush crept up Bailey's neck and tinted his ears pink. "I usually succeeded in my plan to be invisible. But I was proud of my class project." He shook his head.

She squeezed his arm. She should let go, but something in his posture wouldn't let her do it. No one should think they had to be invisible.

"Drew stood up for me a million times, and it wasn't because I couldn't protect myself. He couldn't stand to see me..." A clog in her throat stopped her words. Jaz blinked, but the moisture popped into her eyes anyway. If anyone was weak, it had to be her.

Rough fingers closed over hers, sandwiching her hand in soothing warmth. Compassion stretched from Bailey's gaze to hers. Her embarrassment fled, steamrolled by attraction.

He saw her like Drew did, and he understood how important Drew had been.

"Mostly it was my dad." Where had those words come from?

Bailey rubbed circles on the back of her hand. A current of electric awareness bolted straight to her chest.

"There was this piano recital. I had this fluffy dress on." She scowled at the memory. "I did alright on my piece, but afterward I chased Drew around the parking lot, fell into a pothole. I ripped the stupid dress, and my dad was furious."

*"Why can't you ever act like a lady?" He'd jerked her arm so hard it brought tears to her eyes.*

"Drew was your hero."

Bailey's husky words pulled her away from the worst moment of her childhood. She blinked at him, reorienting into the present.

"I'm sorry you had to lose him."

Jaz stacked her other hand on his and gripped like she was hanging from a cliff. Something she'd never experienced wove a thread through their locked gazes.

Her lips trembled into a smile. "Our hero. And I want to be just like him."

Bailey licked his lips. Jaz's attention shifted to his mouth. That brief kiss the other night had been sweet. Would he be tentative if she kissed him again? Or would he free the desire she saw in those haunted eyes?

She blinked and drew back. Their hands slid apart, but her temperature skyrocketed into the realm of hot-August-afternoon.

"You're helping me." Bailey's voice sounded strained.

Had he been affected by their touch? Jaz peeked at him, but his wide-eyed look was as wild as it had been from the moment she'd remembered him.

That wasn't why he was here. "What did you find out about a will?" She needed to get back on track.

He shook his head. "Dad swore he'd taken care of things, but I can't find a will."

She pursed her lips. "A safe? A family attorney?"

Broad shoulders shrugged. "Safe was a bust. There was nothing in the files about an attorney."

"What about the adoption issue?"

He shook his head. "I haven't found anything about that either."

If they could prove his biological father stopped the adoption, the court might rule in favor of estoppel. "Let me do some more digging for statutes and cases supporting equitable adoption."

"If we can't prove they planned to adopt us?"

Jaz shook her head. "You lived with him for decades. Both you and your sister took his name. Texas courts are favorable to equitable adoption."

"And Honey Campbell?" His lips curled as he said the name, like he'd bitten a moldy grape.

"Resident of Colorado. Current driver's license but doesn't own any property."

"Except the ranch."

Jaz grabbed his fingers. "No. You and Tess are his children, and that claim supersedes anything Honey Campbell might have."

"But she's related by blood."

Jaz nodded, the knot in her stomach tightening. "Twice divorced. Never takes the husband's name, but she does take as much money as possible." Women like that disgusted Jaz. She had firsthand experience being used, and she'd never do it to someone else. Especially not through something as special and binding as marriage.

He lurched to his feet, fumbling with his hat. "I've got to get to work."

Jaz stood. "I'll see if I can find some cases of equitable adoption. A will would solve everything."

Bailey's jaw clenched. "I've got Tess looking as she's going through Mom's things." He started to turn, then locked gazes with her again. "I'll get your car fixed tonight, too."

"No rush. My mom's letting me borrow hers for the interview I have tomorrow."

"You have an interview?" His eyes widened and darkened.

"For the Travis County District Attorney." It wasn't her first choice, but it would get her out from under her father's roof.

"In Austin. Of course." His Adam's apple bobbed. "I will get the car fixed."

"I know."

"It's the least I can do to repay you—"

"Friends help each other. Or maybe I'm just being neighborly." She tried to grin as she threw his words back at him.

They shared a long look. His gorgeous eyes were a stormy sea of emotion. She curled her fingers into fists because they ached to reach out and wipe that expression away.

He nodded again and about-faced. His broad shoulders

swaggered as he walked away. She scanned him from head to toe in a way neither neighborly nor indicative of friendship.

With a shake of her head, she returned to the computer. The attraction served no purpose. Bailey was fighting to keep his ranch, and she was pushing to escape Sweet Grove at the earliest possible moment.

They walked diverging paths, and that truth soured her stomach.

# Six

Jazlyn's days fell into a pattern: mornings at the library and afternoons on the softball field. One day she waded through an interview for a job she didn't want, tense as she wove through Austin traffic in her mother's car.

On Friday morning, after her mom headed to Ernie's to do some bookkeeping, Jaz pilfered through the box of Drew's items, fighting tears when she touched his face in a photo of four soldiers in BDU's. His squad. She could barely look at the medal he'd won, an insignificant memorandum of a life he'd spent for others. She shoved everything to the back of her closet.

Finally, it was time to don the Shorthorns jersey. She tossed a change of clothes into her backpack. Certain Elise would give her a ride home and feeling too dependent on her parents, Jaz hopped on her bike.

At the school, a crowd of parents filled the bleachers, and Jaz was proud of the way the girls played. They won by a run.

Afterward, Jaz and Elise changed in the locker room. Once the girls left, it echoed with a forsaken air. She'd spent four years changing into and out of uniforms and PE clothes in this place.

*And now you're back at twenty-eight.*

The thought depressed her.

Elise drove beside her as Jaz pedaled the few blocks to the church.

"Afraid I'm going to bolt?"

Elise shook her head. "Sticking close so someone else

doesn't claim you."

Jaz laughed and jumped the curb while Elise stopped to check for cross traffic on First Street. By the time Elise parked, Jaz had the bike rolled into the rack beside the steps.

Inside, they followed the sound of raised voices to the fellowship area which doubled as an auditorium for youth church. A dozen people milled around while two guys argued over placement of a dartboard.

Jaz scanned the room, counting four dartboards. Kristina smiled at the sight of them and scurried over. Several people raised their hands or called out greetings to Elise.

"Did you win?" Kristina stopped in front of Elise.

Elise nodded and hugged Jaz's arm. "Thanks to brilliant batting instruction."

Kristina giggled and Jaz shook her head. "I can tell by my recent pay raise how much you mean that."

The three of them laughed and melded into the crowd. A man closer to thirty-five led the small group. He offered up a few game options. Did they want to do Cricket or 301? The three electronic boards would keep the score automatically and either game could be selected from their menu, but the fourth board would require teams to self-monitor and keep score.

"We don't have enough for even teams," Elise said.

Kristina and another girl volunteered to sit out or be scorekeeper, if needed.

Pencils filled the silence as everyone wrote their game choice on a slip of paper.

A cheery voice called, "We're not late, are we?"

Jaz finished by crossing her T and glanced up at the new arrival. Her heart jackhammered at the sight of Bailey standing behind the perky blonde woman. She chattered with the leader, who handed them slips of paper and explained what was happening.

Bailey stood ramrod straight, and his jaw jerked as if he was gritting his teeth. Jaz willed him to look her way. When he did, she was unprepared for the softening of his lips and smoldering in his eyes.

Her breath caught in her throat. Elise glanced at her and then toward the door. A huge grin split her face. Kristina glanced between Jaz and Elise, eyes wide.

"Do we get to choose our partners?" Elise called out.

"Sure." The leader was collecting folded slips of paper.

"With shoulders like that, Bailey's a good choice." Elise raised her eyebrows, challenge implied.

Jaz shrugged. "Said he hasn't played since college, so it's your funeral."

"Well, then, I'll leave him for you."

"Wait. I thought you wanted to be my partner." Jaz narrowed her eyes.

"Kristina's my best friend." Elise slid her arm around Kristina's elbow and tugged her toward the leader.

"Great," Kristina grumbled.

Bailey, hat in hand, seemed glued in place. Two guys flirted outrageously with his sister. Jaz started toward them.

"Maybe I should be Bailey's partner." Tess sounded sad, but Jaz could see she didn't want to hurt anyone's feelings.

Fighting the yawning pit swallowing her stomach, Jaz turned to the two men. "I need a partner." Jaz stuck her hand out. "Jaz Rolle."

The shorter guy, whose black hair curled up on the ends, grasped her hand. His name got lost behind Tess's exclamation.

"Oh! Well, Jaz is Bailey's partner. So, which of you wants to lose first?" Tess poked each of the male shoulders, casting a sly glance at her brother.

Jaz blinked. She'd been out-maneuvered twice in two minutes. Her experience in the dating game was showing like torn underwear. "I didn't know if you'd show," she said.

Bailey set his hat on the nearest table and smoothed his hand through his light brown hair. It was damp, as if recently washed, and the usual ring wasn't present.

A dance inside her chest made Jaz reach for a chair to steady herself.

"Looks like you get the handicap." One corner of his full mouth curled up.

Jaz gripped the back of the chair to keep from falling over. His grin had enough sex appeal to stop traffic. Spots dotted her vision. "How do you know I'm not the handicap?" Her voice sounded light, not breathless. Thank goodness.

"I've watched you swing a bat and throw a softball." His gaze flitted to her mouth. "And you wouldn't sign up for any sport you weren't good at."

"Sport? Are darts a sport?"

The leader whistled and waved them over. Bailey matched her steps like they were on parade grounds. Jaz tried to listen as the rules for Cricket were explained amidst groans from several people. Good thing she knew the game because with the heat of Bailey's arm pressing against hers, she couldn't concentrate on anything else.

Thankfully, they moved apart during the actual game. Which they won. He hit the bullseye to increase their score, and she closed out the numbers.

The high five they exchanged shot tingles through her fingers, up her arms, and into her heart. She really shouldn't be so attracted to him.

After the leader muttered a short prayer of thanks, Jaz grabbed a plate of snacks and a pop and headed toward the doors. The cool evening air relieved the tension building between her ears.

She wandered over to the table where she'd had lunch with Bailey.

Bailey who needed her help. Bailey who admired and respected Drew. Bailey whose grin did all sorts of crazy things to her intestines.

Bailey who she could not care about because he belonged to Sweet Grove.

The doors swished open. Peals of laughter and light spilled into the yard. Jaz turned.

The man she was trying to evict from her thoughts strolled toward her.

⁂

As soon as Jaz walked his way, Bailey's spine relaxed. He wanted to hug Tess for forcing them together.

During the game, he and Jaz ribbed each other until they found their rhythm. After that, the other team, which included the group's leader, had no chance. Jaz could hit a double with one of every two darts she threw, and even he was sick of hearing the dartboard's female voice say, "Triple. 60!"

Of course, he could hit the center of the board with regularity, too, so it wasn't all Jaz who gave them the win. A flush of pleasure he hardly remembered warmed him by the time the game finished and the leader asked a blessing on the snacks.

He checked in with Tess, whose two admirers were being held at bay by a group of ladies. When he grabbed a plate, Jaz was gone.

The warmth receded. His stomach bucked a little.

Elise elbowed him in the kidney. "She's outside." She glared at the doors leading to the yard.

Bailey wanted to play dumb, but it wasn't worth the effort. Between Tess and Elise, he and Jaz were being thrown together. Why fight it?

Balancing his plate on the pop can, he opened the door and gulped the cool air. After a few blinks, his eyes adjusted. Jaz sat at the table they'd shared the week before, a bemused smile on her generous lips.

Bailey's heart sling-shotted toward her, as if it could make his feet move faster. After setting down his plate, he took a drink of pop to buy time for his brain to manufacture words. The carbonation burned a path down his throat.

"We make a pretty good team." His knee bumped the table as he tried to fold himself onto the bench.

Jaz snatched up her drink. Heat flashed up the back of his neck, and he fought the urge to rub the spot with his hand. He reached for his hat only to realize he'd left it inside.

"We're unstoppable." Jaz grinned and tipped the can to her lips.

Bailey stared at the aluminum with envy. When her eyelids flickered, he snapped his traitorous gaze to his plate. He fumbled a chip into the pile of salsa beside it. The crunch of it between his teeth deafened him.

"How many bulls eyes was that? Six?" She fingered a square of cheese onto a cracker. "And you haven't played since college?" She snorted.

The sound should have been unattractive, but Bailey's pulse skittered like a spooked horse. Everything she did made him crazy.

Bailey jerked his chin down and stared at his plate. He needed to get a grip.

"Did you play a lot in college?" she asked.

Bailey swallowed another chip. "Most of the guys preferred pool, so the dart boards were available."

"Pool. I played plenty of that on the base, too."

Of course she did. How could he forget that she'd spent six years in the Army? And what had he done with his life?

He shook the critical voice away. Bailey took care of his family. That's what was important to him. He would never let Tess feel the abandonment he'd experienced when they became wards of the state.

"A dart master and a pool shark." He grinned to chase away his dark thoughts.

She laughed. The sound rolled over him like cool water on a hot day. He memorized the lines of her square jaw and broad cheekbones.

She popped half of a cracker with cheese into her mouth. Her movements mesmerized him.

She froze, her eyes locking with his. "What? Do I have something on my face?" She swiped at her chin.

Bailey swallowed, and it felt like razor blades. If he didn't stop staring, she was going to run away screaming.

He forced himself to look at the pop can beside his plate. "Just a whole lot of too-pretty." The words came out in a strangled whisper.

She laughed again. "Who knew you had a line like that in you?"

He blinked at her. "Line? I don't have any lines."

Her smile fell away, and her eyes flickered between his, looking for something. He would never joke about the way a girl looked.

"Wow." The word was an exhale. She shook her head, but disbelief clouded her features. After chewing a few more crackers, she asked, "So how much did the part for Old Red cost?"

He kept his attention on his food. "A hundred bucks."

"I'll get the cash to you tomorrow."

He looked up. "Carrier pigeon?" And smirked.

"Ha ha." But her gorgeous lips twitched into a smile.

Maybe he could make a joke.

An hour later, he loaded her bike into the back of his truck while Tess slid into the passenger seat of Elise's car. Their matchmaking was so obvious it made him want to roll his eyes.

But why? He was eager to spend more time with Jaz. It would never lead anywhere, but he'd crushed on this gorgeous woman for too long not to enjoy the time with her.

On the drive to her house, they teased each other about their defeat in the second round of darts. The group had played 301, a game where you subtracted your score from 301 and had to land exactly at zero to win.

"Hey, I can hit the bullseye. I never claimed I could hit any number." Bailey's grin stretched across his face.

"Which was proven true multiple times tonight." Jaz poked his arm.

Tingles spiraled from the point of contact. He pulled into the drive beside a much newer Chevy truck.

She reached for the handle at the same time he threw the truck in park. He tugged on her elbow. "Gentleman, remember?"

Her white teeth flashed in the shadowy cab. He jumped out of the truck.

"Who can't hit a two on the dart board."

Her laughter wafted after him, sweeter to his ears than any bird song. He was still smiling when she slid out of her seat and bumped into him. His arms encircled her. The scent of corn chips and salt rushed him.

Light from the porch cast a triangle of illumination across her face. Her smiling mouth trembled as her pale-eyed glance swept from his chin to his eyes.

Her breath stuttered, sending warmth across his neck. Nothing could deter the automatic lowering of his face toward hers. When she tilted her chin to meet him, his heart twirled in glee.

Those luscious lips didn't taste like strawberries, but they were sweet. Their softness pressed into him, and something between a sigh and moan fled up his throat. Her fingers swept into the hair at the nape of his neck, and he deepened the kiss.

There could never be enough of her. Her taste, her smell, and her presence filled something he hadn't realized was empty.

She drew back, far enough they could look at each other. His eyelids fluttered, and his lips prayed for another taste of her.

"I'm not staying." The whisper sent heat to his face and chills down his spine. "The only reason I'm here is because of a breakup."

She stepped back. His hands brushed the sides of her hips, longing to hold her closer.

"A guy I was with for more than a year burned me good. Traded our relationship for a promotion." Her mouth twisted into a sneer but her eyes screamed her pain.

Abandonment and betrayal. He knew their bitter flavor.

He squeezed her waist. "I'm not that guy."

After a lengthy pause, filled only by the humming cicadas, she said, "Tonight was fun."

In her eyes he read the plea for understanding. And his mind accepted it. He ducked his head, nearly jamming the brim of his hat into her forehead.

Her smile returned in a slow spread that made his knees weak. He clenched his hands to keep from pulling her to him. He lifted her bike out of the truck, giving his hands something else to focus on.

Her fingers brushed his when she grabbed the handlebars. "Thanks for the ride."

"Don't forget." He handed her the backpack he'd tossed into the bed, careful to release it before their fingers touched.

He watched her hips sway as she walked to the house. The gears on the bike clicked as she rolled it toward the garage and leaned it against a wall.

Spotlighted on the porch, she turned back. "See you tomorrow."

Then she was gone. The pained cry of the hinges when he shut the passenger door echoed something deep in his soul.

Tomorrow couldn't come soon enough.

Then again, it would be one day closer to saying goodbye to Jaz. And his chance for love.

# Seven

J az rolled the bike to a stop beside her car. Sunlight glittered off the windshield. A low woof sounded from the direction of the farmhouse. Dust swirled at her feet and flooded her nostrils with the aroma of animal sweat and dung, and a sweet, grassy scent that reminded her of Bailey.

Her pulse throbbed in her neck. After that sweet kiss, her dreams had featured the handsome cowboy.

He belonged to Sweet Grove. She was only here to pay for the alternator.

The screen door creaked and slammed. Jaz pushed her bike toward the porch.

Bailey's sister wiped her hands on the front of a pink-flowered apron. Her face beamed and light sparked in her sky-blue eyes, several shades paler than her brother's and not nearly so captivating.

Jaz shoved away thoughts of those soulful eyes and leaned her bike against the trunk of a fruit tree. "Morning. Bailey around?"

Tess waved toward the barn. "Doing chores. He'll be up for breakfast in a few minutes. Care to join us?"

A groan from Jaz's stomach pleaded one answer while her better sense told her to drop the money and run.

"Biscuits and gravy, home fries, sausage patties and lots of coffee."

Jaz grinned. "You had me at gravy."

Tess stepped back, nearly tripping on the brown and white dog Jaz rescued from the ditch. "Poppet, move." More laughter than scolding filled the woman's voice.

Jaz followed her into the house and stopped at the sink on the screened porch. Poppet drooled on her bare calves. She crouched down and ruffled the dog's ears. "Looks like you're doing better."

Tess popped her head through the doorway. "Her limp disappeared after a couple days. She's been mopey since Dad passed."

A weight slammed into Jaz's chest. Their father had died. She was supposed to be helping them keep the ranch. With a final pat to the dog's head, Jaz pushed to her feet and scrubbed her hands in the sink.

She was still drying her hands on a paper towel as she entered the kitchen. Peach walls whispered of sunrises while a yeasty aroma blended with the greasy scent of fried meat. Her stomach rumbled.

"I haven't had home-cooked gravy." She paused to consider and count back. "Since Christmas three years ago. My grandmother's giblet gravy is a staple for holidays."

"No gravy in the mess hall?"

Jaz grimaced. "The thin, lumpy, flavorless goop they drowned the potatoes in was *not* gravy."

Tess's tinkling laugh filled the space between them. Jaz dropped her used paper towel in the trash and picked up the plates stacked on one counter. Her glance drifted through the window to the ramshackle outbuilding as she set the dishes on a table in a nook. If they wanted to make this place ready for guests, they needed an injection of cash.

*Which will be a moot point if that niece inherits the ranch.*

Jaz asked about Tess's business plans while relocating silverware, napkins, butter, two kinds of jelly, honey in a crock, and two trivets from counter to table. Tess elaborated her plan to find investors to help with the necessary upgrades.

"Are you going to cook and clean? What's Bailey's role?"

Tess stirred gravy in a cast iron skillet. Her shoulders heaved. "I wish he'd head back to the city."

*What?* Jaz's heart tripped over itself.

The screen door slammed and boots clumped across the wooden floors. Jaz turned in time to see Bailey duck through the door and hang his hat on a peg. When he saw her, he froze.

"Jaz is joining us for breakfast." Tess peeked in the oven. "Wash up. Biscuits are ready."

"Yes 'm." He headed back to the sink where Jaz had

washed. Rings of sweat circled beneath his arms, and his t-shirt clung to a muscled back. Her pulse tangoed and her stomach dropped. Did the man have to be so gorgeous?

She tore her eyes away in time to catch Tess grinning at her. The kitchen's temperature spiked, and Jaz fanned her stomach with her t-shirt.

Tess filled a basket with golden buttermilk biscuits, and Jaz transferred it to the table. Bailey strode across to snatch a piece of sausage from the plate Tess had in her hand. She swatted at him with a spatula, and he made an exaggerated dodge.

Something curled low in Jaz's gut. It had been too long since she danced those brother-sister moves. A hole in her chest chimed Drew's name. She ducked her head and shuffled to the far side of the table.

Bailey carried the skillet to the table and set it on the central trivet. "Coffee?"

His blue gaze singed her. A seizure behind her breastbone delayed her response.

"Sure."

In short order, the three of them were seated. Tess bowed her head and Bailey followed suit. Jaz dropped her gaze to the table as the sexy masculine voice said, "For what we're about to receive, Lord, we thank You."

Tess said "Amen" along with him, and hands reached for the food. Jaz snatched a biscuit just as Bailey seized the basket. The handle of the spoon in the pan of potatoes was untouched, so she scooped a serving onto her plate. Tess passed her the plate of meat at the same time Bailey forked the largest patty from it.

"Manners!" This time it sounded like scolding. "Mom would snatch that right back."

Bailey shrugged, cutting a corner off his prize and popping it into his mouth.

Jaz sampled some of everything. She was savoring her second bite of gravy-smothered biscuit when she felt his eyes on her. She glanced up and licked the fork clean. Heaven.

Bailey's eyes darkened.

"The gravy's not quite right," Tess said.

"It's wonderful." Jaz prepped her fork with another bite.

"It's missing something, isn't it, Lee?" Tess stared at her brother while licking some gravy from her fork.

Bailey swallowed a mouthful. His plate was half-empty. He sipped coffee and glanced at Tess. "Maybe. Still haven't found a recipe?"

"She probably didn't write it down. I'll have to experiment."

Jaz swallowed another bite. "My grandmother adds a dash or two of Worcestershire Sauce to her country gravy."

Tess snapped her fingers. "I'll try that."

Breakfast passed in a flurry of delicious tastes and smells and light conversation. Tess tried to shoo them from the kitchen, but Bailey insisted on cleaning up. Jaz volunteered to help, and Tess, wearing a sly smile, scurried out of the kitchen.

They worked in tandem, Jaz clearing and Bailey washing dishes. As she dried things, he directed her to the correct cupboards. Camaraderie blanketed the room.

She patted her stomach and groaned. Bailey glanced her way, his devastating grin sneaking onto his kissable lips. Heat melted her fullness to something else.

Once she hung the damp dishtowel over the back of a chair, Jaz reached into the armband that held her phone. She cut off Bailey's retreat toward the door and held the folded bills out to him.

He grunted and ignored her hand. Jaz stepped onto one of his booted feet and slapped the center of his chest with the money.

Balance fled and she wobbled. His hands cradled her hips, steadying her. She tilted her face toward his, sucking air at the expression on his tanned face.

"I'm fixing it as a friend." His voice was gravel.

Chills rippled up her spine. "Did you buy a part?"

He pursed his lips and nodded. That mouth.

"I'm reimbursing you." She smacked his chest again. "I might let you do the repair as a favor." She arched an eyebrow at him, daring him to argue.

His gaze flitted to her lips. An exhale fanned her features. She leaned toward him, tugged by a gravity that defied all reason.

"For parts." His hand folded over hers, trapping it

against his chest.

His head lowered, and his lips crushed hers. She whimpered and opened to him, drawing him into a deeper kiss. Her legs turned to jelly. When he ended the contact, she crashed against his chest.

Harsh breaths ruffled hair at her ears. "I'm not getting anything done."

Jaz grinned, shoring up her strength to ease away from the magnetic heat of his chest. "I wouldn't call that nothing."

A snort from behind them made Jaz whirl. Tess stood in the hallway, one thin hand over her mouth and nose.

"Nice." Bailey snatched his hat from the peg and strode out the door.

Jaz stared after him and shrugged off the pull to follow. "Thanks for breakfast."

Tess smiled. "Thanks for making my brother smile."

What did a person say to that?

Jaz had reached her bike before she heard Tess, now on the porch, call her name.

"Don't let him scare you off."

Jaz laughed, backing her bike toward the rutted driveway. "I don't scare easily."

After every crushing loss she'd faced, maybe she should.

# Eight

Honey Campbell knocked on the door at half past noon on Sunday. "I'm here to see my ranch."

The shrill voice acted like acid on Bailey's nerves. He heard her from the study, and his stomach plummeted through the floor while some part of him hardened against more pending loss.

He reached the doorway by the time Tess, eyebrows pressed together in confusion, led a stranger into the room.

The woman's heels clattered on the plank floors. Too much makeup highlighted her rusty brown eyes. She flipped her straight, white-blonde hair over her shoulder in a haughty gesture. Curves bulged beneath the fabric of her too-tight dress.

"Do you know this woman?" Tess's voice trembled.

Bailey draped an arm over his sister's shoulders. The stranger stepped closer, a feral smile moving her hot pink lips. Nails in the same shade, long and pointed, adorned the hand she extended toward them.

"I'm Honey Campbell, Fritz's niece. The owner of this ranch."

Bailey glared at her hand. "Dad said you have no right to this property."

One thin brow arched up. "And there's a will to that effect?"

Bailey gulped. This nightmare was becoming all too real.

"I see." She gazed around the room, clacking over to a bookshelf and fingering the Lennox crystal decanter and glasses. Fritz had given the set to Mary Ann as an anniversary gift. Sharing a drink had been their special way to unwind together on the overstuffed love seat that sat beside the window.

"I heard Fritz passed." She whirled toward them. "Rude of you to make me learn about my uncle's death through gossip."

"We don't know you." Tess pressed quivering hands to her lips.

"You're not welcome here." Bailey stiffened. "I'll show you out."

"You'll show me my ranch, foster brat. Then I'll stay at that quaint B & B until the funeral. Which is when?"

"Thursday afternoon." Tess's voice was smaller now.

Bailey squeezed her against his side. His roiling stomach gushed acid into his throat. He would not let this woman take over. Dad promised the ranch would be theirs.

"I'll show you around." Bailey gestured toward the door.

Once the woman's clicking footsteps retreated down the hall, he pressed his phone into Tess's hand. "Text Jaz. Tell her it's an emergency and will she please come."

Even though her eyes were wide, Tess's lips twitched into a smile. "I knew you liked her."

Bailey closed his eyes. His heart sped at the thought of Jaz, but it wasn't like that. "She's helping me with something. That's all."

"You want her help in an emergency, that's something."

"Tess."

His sister took the phone, which he unlocked with a four-digit code.

"My birthday? Still?" Tess's laugh sounded tinny.

Bailey strode out of the room to find the intruder looking in the drawers of the master bedroom. He gritted his teeth to rein in the fury that pushed into his throat. "I'd appreciate it if you wouldn't snoop."

Honey sniffed and gave him a prim look. "It's not snooping when it's mine."

"That's for the courts to decide."

Her garish lips parted into a sneer. "My uncle never adopted you or your little sister. The courts will rule for a blood relative."

A knife raked through his chest. He clenched his hands to keep from clutching it. "There's adoption by estoppel." He stabbed the intruder with a glower.

She froze, eyes narrowing. Without a word she swept past him and clattered down the hallway.

Every moment in the kitchen felt like an hour. Her heavy perfume draped like a veil in the air, choking him as he followed her upstairs.

"How many bedrooms in this place?"

"Seven." He'd been sleeping in what had been the parlor since Tess took the bedroom beside the master. She'd declared the five bedrooms upstairs were perfect for guest rooms once they added bathrooms.

"You will clean this clutter out before you leave." She'd stopped beside an antique dresser with elegant scroll work. "But not this. I'll mark the things I want left here."

Bailey's stomach bucked. He gripped the doorknob until it branded his palm. He gritted his teeth and glanced out the window, wishing for escape.

An age later, Honey clambered down the porch steps, gripping his arm with her claw-like nails. His gut churned.

She stopped on the threshold to his dad's workshop. The sign he and Tess had been working on lay across two sawhorses. The rustic wooden planks were burnt around the edges. "Travers Guest Ranch" it read, and the double-bar T brand was burned into the boards beneath the name.

"What's this? A little business venture?" She turned a hard gaze on him. "You don't seem the type."

He stiffened. "Tess has a degree in hospitality, and she's worked several different resorts."

An eyebrow arched. She stepped closer to the sign, her spiky heel catching in the cracks between planks in the floor. She stumbled and righted herself on the sign.

"This is rustic. Fits the place." She tapped a nail against her lower lip.

Sweat prickled his scalp. Her expression made his skin crawl.

"Maybe you won't have to move out. If we go ahead with this guest ranch, you two could be the on-sight managers."

The guest ranch was Tess's plan, and they weren't sharing it with this interloper. But before he settled on a comeback, she tiptoed across the floor and out toward the barn.

As the barn door squawked open, the barn dogs lunged forward. Both backed away at the sight of the stranger. Or maybe they were terrified of the shoes. If she stepped on a paw, it would make being crucified look painless.

The golden lab slouched backward, his ruff rising. The shepherd gave the stranger a wide berth and came to slobber on Bailey's boots.

"The tax records indicate there's 85 acres here. How much livestock?" Her nose wrinkled as she peeked into the nearest stall.

Tax records? How long had she been gathering information?

She stumbled along the passage toward the feed and tack rooms. The pitch of her voice grated as she asked other questions, but Bailey was done. He didn't want to pretend he was okay with her assumption of ownership.

He crossed his arms and leaned against the doorway. The dogs circled like vultures, but he hadn't grabbed any treats. He stared toward the road, searching for a telltale rumble of dust. But only the puffs stirred by the wind churned as far as he could see.

"I have questions."

He straightened his hat and stared into her face. "I just lost my dad. This isn't the best time for giving tours of the ranch."

Her lips curled. "It's about to be time for you to move off my property. If you don't want to work with me—"

He held up a hand. "Can we put this off for a day or two? Until after the funeral?"

The thin brows rose. "Time won't change the facts."

Time to search for the will or an attorney who knew about one was all he had on his side. He squeezed his arms more tightly across his chest to keep from shaking sense into the woman.

"Thank you for giving us a few days to process our loss."

She huffed. Her ankle twisted on the rough ground as she tried to stomp her way to the white Jeep parked behind Tess's car.

He glanced up in time to see his sister duck out of the upstairs window. The Jeep revved and bounced down the drive.

Time to convince his sister they had nothing to worry about.

*Please, God, don't let it be a lie.*

❧❧❧

When Bailey brought her car by on Sunday afternoon, Jaz heard all about Honey Campbell. Things weren't looking up, and her heart plummeted into her stomach at missing the call for help.

"You have more right to it than her." Electricity tingled across her fingertips as Jaz gripped his forearm. "Possession is nine-tenths of the law."

Cliché, but true.

Monday, she drove her repaired car to Austin for an interview with Boldt and Associates. The partners were brothers who liked employing veterans. After a smooth interview, they offered her the job and piled her up with documents outlining their tuition reimbursement programs and a host of other benefits.

As she pulled out of the parking structure, she cursed herself for not accepting the job. Two weeks until they needed her to start, and she had no reason to wait until Friday to give them an answer.

Broad shoulders, blue eyes, and a grin that gave her a heart attack vaulted into her mind. The salty taste of Saturday's kiss still stung her tongue.

She wasn't a teenager who could be befuddled by physical attraction, and she wasn't ready for it to be more than that. Surely losing her military career taught her to be cautious before loving a man.

*It's too soon to love Bailey Travers*. The Drew connection was confusing her.

Her heart pretzeled into her backbone. Her brother had been gone so long, and she'd been lost without him. Now Bailey filled that space.

Their kisses burned into her mind. That soul-scorching lip-lock in the kitchen? It felt nothing like kissing her brother.

Her cell phone vibrated in the cup holder where she always tossed it. She slowed and glanced toward the lit screen. Deena, co-captain of the Longhorns back in the day, had been emailing her about helping the softball team.

Jaz signaled and turned into the next parking lot. The phone finished its fourth ring at the same moment she answered it.

"Hey girl."

"Jaz! Didn't you say you were in Austin for a job interview today?"

"Done."

"Why don't you join me at softball practice?"

A long-silent cheering squad raised a racket inside her chest. Drew and softball were her two loves.

"Sounds fun." She licked her lips. "Why?"

"I might have some good news." Deena paused. "But it all hinges on how you swing the bat."

Jaz laughed. "Didn't I tell you I've been hitting with the team from my high school alma mater?"

"Hitting a high school pitcher is one thing."

Her lips hurt from the stretch of her smile. "Be there soon."

"Practice is at three."

Jaz ended the call, and then dialed her mother's phone to let her know she wouldn't be home until late.

"How was the interview?" Her mom's interest was clear.

"Great. I'm heading to UT to reconnect with some people." Jaz debated telling her about the offer but wanted to get to the college.

With help from the map app on her phone, she determined her best course to the university.

As she pulled into traffic, she sensed she'd found the right path. One that led to her future purpose.

⁂

Hours later, sweat and dust mingled on her skin. Jaz slipped into her car, glancing at her phone. A notification on her lock screen stopped her.

*Found the papers.*

Her heart floated higher, choking off her air. She closed her eyes, willing the feeling to pass.

Today proved she belonged in Austin. Bailey was fighting hard to keep his family ranch in Sweet Grove. As much as she connected with him, she wasn't ready to make concessions for another man.

After she drove through a burger place she'd frequented often during college, Jaz turned her car toward Sweet Grove. She made short work of the chicken strips and fries and slurped the iced tea until the ice rattled at her.

On the highway, she maneuvered to the slow lane and pulled up her recent call list. She pushed the icon to redial Bailey.

"Hey." A single word spoken in his smooth baritone increased her heart rate. The man was like an instant cardio workout. But not good for her heart in other ways.

"What'd you find?"

"Are you home?"

They spoke at the same time. Her phone coughed up static.

"I'm driving. You're on speaker."

"Oh." Tires spinning on pavement filled the silence. "I thought your interview was early."

She couldn't dampen her excitement as she told him about her afternoon hitting softballs and talking to the coaching staff. "They're looking for someone to help with practices. It wouldn't pay much, but the hours wouldn't interfere with the paralegal job."

After a pause, he asked, "So the interview went well?"

"They offered me the job."

Silence answered. It went on long enough for her fingers to start twitching on the wheel.

"When do you start?" Was she imagining the cooling in his tone of voice?

"I haven't accepted it."

"Why not?"

That was the real question. The pay, benefits, and hours fit her ideal future, and she couldn't wait to get out of her parents' home. Why not jump at this position?

The greasy food congealed in her gut, and a cramp seized her. She didn't want to consider the reasons too closely.

"I like thinking things through."

His sigh sent a knife through her chest. "But you will."

After a few swallows, once she was certain her voice would be even, she said, "What did you find?"

"The adoption papers."

His voice flooded the interior of the car as he explained how Tess had been cleaning one of the rooms upstairs. Apparently their foster mom had stacks of fabric and crates of yarn. Buried on a cabinet filled with patterns was the envelope from the attorney's office.

"Did you call?"

"By the time I got home, the office was closed."

But they could call tomorrow. Her breathing shallowed. If they found a will, he wouldn't need her anymore. Pain stabbed the small of her back.

He needed her. That's why she was attracted to him. She'd been a throwaway to her father and the captain. But Bailey needed her, and he had given her purpose.

The lawyers at the new firm would need her and so would the coaches at UT. The new purpose she'd been seeking waved at her from Austin.

Her heart and stomach wrung together like rags stuck beneath the agitator.

"I'll call in the morning." His words pulled her back.

She needed to make her own calls. The time to move on had come.

"Keep me posted." The clip of her words made her cringe. It wasn't his fault she couldn't stay.

"Later." Melancholy laced the single word, and then he was gone.

Heaviness pressed into her nose and blurred her eyes. She blinked, pulling to the shoulder to end the call and start some music that would take her mind off those deep blue eyes and tender kisses.

*God, take away these emotions.*

The tears dried, but the specter of Bailey remained.

# Nine

On Thursday afternoon, a crowd milled inside the entrance to the funeral home. Flowers scented the air with sweet, heavy syrup that coated a person's throat. Jaz tried not to wrinkle her nose as she squeezed between Jack and Maisie Bryant.

A woman whose makeup caked into fine lines around her eyes and mouth blocked the path to the guest book. Bleached hair sprayed stiff to mimic Heather Locklear's style never moved with her many gestures. Her shrill voice grated against Jaz's eardrums.

Fritz Travers' niece held court like some sort of princess. Sweet Grove had lost one of its own, and the inheritance-stealer soaked up the town's condolences like they belonged to her.

The woman had probably never even met the uncle she claimed to mourn.

Jaz circled the back of the clot of well-wishers and hurried through the chapel doors. People milled around the few rows of walnut pews. Murmuring voices blended with the instrumental hymns piped through unobtrusive speakers. She glanced toward the curtained family room where Pastor Bernie and his wife stood with Bailey and Tess.

A black jacket stretched across Bailey's broad shoulders. His fingers fumbled at the knotted tie around his neck. The pale blue shirt beneath it matched the sweater Tess wore over a navy sundress.

Jaz gripped the back of the nearest pew to steady herself. The man looked good in grass-stained Wranglers, but in a suit, he could stop traffic. Or her heart.

Tess glanced up and smiled. It was a wobbly expression. She waved Jaz over, and Jaz couldn't deny the girl anything when her face looked ready to crumple.

A moment later, Bailey's gaze snagged hers, and she almost tripped over her feet. Breath stalled in her chest where her heart palpitated at top speed. The tension in his jaw relaxed.

She slid between Tess and Tabitha Olson. Jaz squeezed Tess's hand while greeting the pastor and his wife.

"Are you hiding in here?"

Tess shrugged.

Bailey's eyes narrowed. "Avoiding Honey Campbell. Yep."

Bernie Olson squeezed Bailey's shoulder. "No matter what she says, the town supports you two. Fritz's kids."

Bailey nodded, and Tess leaned into Tabitha's embrace. While the women hugged, Bailey slid behind his sister and wove his fingers through Jaz's.

Warmth from his skin melted the iciness that had formed at the sight of Honey. Jaz peeked at him. Anxiety lurked in his expressive eyes. Her fingers tightened, and she pressed into his side. The thrilling tingles at the contact shouldn't be allowed at a funeral.

Once the Olsons left, Tess whirled toward Bailey. Her chilled fingers gripped Jaz's elbow, and she grabbed her brother in the same manner. "Tell me she's lying through her teeth." The whispered hiss crawled along Jaz's spine like a lazy snake.

Bailey clenched her hand. Jaz hugged Tess with her free arm. She whispered in her ear, "Don't worry. I'll handle that money-grubbing pretender."

Tears clung to Tess's lashes, but she nodded as the women broke apart.

"Sit with us?"

Jaz straightened. "I'm not family."

"We want you to sit with us. Don't we, Lee?" Tess's knuckles appeared white against her brother's dark jacket.

Bailey's Adam's apple bobbed.

"It would send the wrong message." Jaz tugged her hand free from his. "I'll see you after."

The background music ended, signaling the start of the service. Honey Campbell hustled through the door from the foyer into the family alcove, and Jaz slashed the woman with visual daggers before squeezing beside Elise on the back pew.

Her friend leaned and whispered in her ear, "Did I see you holding Bailey's hand?" Elise waggled her eyebrows.

Jaz rolled her eyes. "You're so juvenile. I was comforting him."

"The way his eyes followed you when you walked away." Her eyes widened. "Thought it might set you on fire."

Pastor Bernie started speaking. Jaz sighed, grateful not to have to address Elise's teasing.

The funeral director pulled the privacy curtain in the family room. She could make out three silhouettes in a row. Her fingers fisted at the thought of that woman.

Did Honey truly have the strongest claim? Jaz couldn't let those claws grasp the ranch Tess planned her future around. Surely a judge would agree that the continued relationship between Fritz, Bailey, and Tess merited estoppel.

What sort of proof should she be trying to amass to help them in court? Her stomach dropped.

*Please, God, don't let this be a lengthy court battle.*

She stole a glance at the ceiling as the congregation stood. Jaz bolted up a beat later, earning a frown from Elise.

If she couldn't figure out this mess, everything Fritz Travers worked for would go to the daughter of a woman who robbed him of his own inheritance.

Jaz gritted her teeth. Not on her watch.

During the closing prayer, a nudge in her spirit twisted her heart. She'd been so frantic searching for a job and trying to help Bailey she'd forgotten her plan to pursue the Jesus she'd first met in Sweet Grove.

*If you still care about me, help me find a way to save Bailey's ranch.*

As far as she could tell, her prayer hit the ceiling. Pastor Bernie said his amen. People filed past the open casket at the front of the room, and Jaz slipped out the back door while Elise talked to a woman in front of them.

Jaz scribbled her name in the guest book and slid into a spot in the reception line. Town folks spoke to Bailey and Tess on their way out the door. Honey Campbell stood on the opposite side of Bailey, dabbing at her perfect makeup and gushing over everyone who passed.

Jaz narrowed her eyes. What sort of person snatched everything away from so-called family members? They'd already lost so much.

The line deposited her in front of Tess. Jaz hugged her, noticing the jab of shoulder blades against her palms.

"I'm so glad you're helping us." She squeezed Jaz's shoulders. "And I'm glad Bailey found someone."

Jaz ignored the surge of guilt. Her heart wasn't ready to fall for a man, no matter how handsome and generous he might be. Besides, she was leaving in a week.

Then the man who'd invaded her dreams and tried to steal her heart stood before her. He stretched his hand out, but she pushed it aside and threw her arms around his neck. His warm breath fanned the sensitive spot beneath her ear, and her heart revved its engine.

"We'll figure this out." She put as much confidence into her words as she could.

Warm hands squeezed her waist. A line of people stared at them, she was sure, but Jaz didn't want to let go. Some unexplainable force she had never felt pulled her into him like gravity kept her feet on the ground.

"Thank you." His husky whisper sent thrills through every cell of her body.

He released her, and she stepped away, the tug toward him unchecked. She fought it and sidled in front of Honey Campbell. The warmth fled, and she narrowed her eyes.

In response, the woman's rusty eyes slitted. Her fingernails scraped across Jaz's palm as they shook hands.

"I don't know what you're hoping to accomplish, but you won't get the ranch." Jaz kept her voice low.

Honey ducked toward her. "Oh sugar, the ranch is mine. Whoever you think you are, you can't stop me."

Her heart dropped into her stomach.

"The law's on my side." Jaz snatched her hand away.

"The law never keeps me from what I want." Honey sneered and turned to grace the next person in line with a syrupy smile. Jaz gagged.

"I understand your land adjoins mine." The southern accent was so false it grated on Jaz's eardrums. "I'll be selling, if you want to put in an early bid."

Jaz whirled. The woman clung to Herman Wells's hand. Behind him, Norma Wells stepped out of hugging Bailey to extricate her husband from the vulture's claws.

"Fritz's son and daughter will inherit the ranch." Herman Wells's gruff voice carried well.

"They were never adopted." The smug look on Honey's face needed to be swatted off. "So the ranch comes to me. I have documents."

Norma glared at the woman's hand like it was a viper. "We're not interested in purchasing the land."

Jaz held the door for the older couple, willing Bailey to look up at her. His attention was on the people in front of him.

She stepped into the warming afternoon. The stew inside her sloshed and burned.

She had to stop Honey Campbell. But how?

# Ten

Honey Campbell relentlessly dogged them to the cemetery and then to the church. Bailey couldn't stand her grating voice, and when he caught her cornering Tess, he was done.

Tess stared straight ahead on the drive to the ranch. His firm grip guided her into the house. After changing into normal clothes, he knocked on her bedroom door. She didn't answer.

In the entryway, Poppet whined. The dog stared at the closet's ajar door. Bailey's heart plummeted. Their first night in this house, Tess huddled in that closet, but she wasn't five years old anymore, and the idea of her feeling that scared and insecure ripped away the veneer he'd been wearing all day.

He nudged the dog with his boot and swung the door wide. The ball of flesh curled in the corner killed any residue of hope inside him.

"Tess."

She didn't look up.

He knelt in front of her, smoothing her hair. The soothing sounds he used with injured animals flowed from his lips. Her sniffles escalated. In his arms, she shook with sobs.

Bailey hauled her against his chest and carried her to her bedroom. His throat ached and eyes burned while he held her on his lap until the tears stopped.

"We're not losing our home." There was no strength in her words, which almost sounded like a question.

"We'll hire a lawyer." *With what money?*

He had to find a way to hand his sister her dream. She wasn't the throwaway child. The adoption documents—un-

76

signed but emphatic—on her dresser proved as much.

"I should pack things. Just in case."

Bailey bristled. His arms tightened around her thin frame. "Only pack what you want to donate." The growl in his tone made Poppet, who'd followed them into the room, stare at him.

When Tess pushed away, Bailey let her go. In his own room, he stared at nothing until his gaze landed on Dad's Bible, forgotten on the dresser. The leather was soft against his palm, and an inky fragrance drifted upward when he opened to a bookmark.

A highlighted verse in the corner of the page drew his attention. "When a man's ways please the Lord, he maketh even his enemies to be at peace with him."

Guilt stabbed him. This was his fault.

Since his mother passed, Bailey had banished God from everything. What use did he have for a deity who wouldn't protect those He loved? For a while he'd almost been convinced that he wasn't cursed, but once MaryAnn was gone and his dad slipped into melancholy, the old fears returned to plague him.

So he'd stopped going to church. And his father hadn't nagged him like his mother would have.

He closed the book and tucked it under his arm. As he headed for the door, he called, "I'm going out."

Footsteps scuffled out of the master bedroom. Tess cocked her hip against the doorframe, one of Dad's flannel shirts hugged against her chest. "Don't be gone long. That... woman will be back."

Bailey's stomach knotted. Through gritted teeth he said, "Text me if she shows. I'll lock up."

Tess shook her head. "Dad never locked anything."

Bailey's arms itched to hug his sister, but she shuffled through the doorway before he could.

After securing everything that had a lock, Bailey gunned the truck's engine and headed for Mill Creek Pond. He took a left turn before he reached the park's main entrance. The dusty path wound through the trees and dead-ended in a wide spot on the opposite side of the pool.

Decades ago, Drew Rolle had brought him here. A huge willow shaded a portion of the pond, and the two of them had climbed up, legs dangling as a late spring thunderstorm dumped a gallon of water on their heads.

Since then, Bailey had returned on only a few occasions: after his mother's funeral, and now after his father's. Would he live to see this place in the wake of his sister's death, too?

He shook off the macabre thoughts. As he squatted beside the pond, he stared into the murky depths willing them to provide the solace he'd found at other times.

Instead, Honey Campbell's threats swirled through his mind. The woman might be related by blood to his father, but she'd never been part of their family. What about Dad's promise?

"No will. No adoption." He grunted and tossed a stick into the water.

It floated on an invisible current for a moment and then sunk. Like his dreams and plans. Unless he found a way to fight that greedy woman, Tess's dreams would drown, too.

He surged to his feet and paced along the curving shore. A line of thick underbrush blocked access in one direction, hindering people from circling from the park to this side of the pond. His boots crushed twigs as he stomped from one edge of the clearing to the other where a line of shrubs marked the boundary of a homestead.

With every step, he cursed his horrible luck. Eventually, the sound of a car rattled him from his dark musings.

An old red Subaru parked beside his truck. Shadows made it impossible for him to see the driver, but his mind recalled the straight black skirt and royal blue blouse she'd worn at the funeral. He licked his lips and shoved his hands into his back pockets.

Maybe that would keep them from grabbing her and holding on until this nightmare passed.

His life was a nightmare.

Jaz stepped out of the car. She'd changed into brown walking shorts and a lighter brown shirt with filmy cap sleeves.

The sight of her punched the air from his lungs. He pressed his fingers deeper into his pockets until they curled against the seams.

"I didn't know anyone else came here." Her voice was breathless as if she'd sprinted to meet him, but she'd hardly taken two steps away from her car.

"Drew brought me here." Bailey forced his gaze to her face.

"Me too." A small smile curled one corner of her luscious lips.

Maybe looking at her face wasn't the best idea. He stared at the ground in front of her.

"I'm sorry about that woman." Jaz walked closer until a scent of ginger and oranges breezed toward him.

His pulse throbbed in his neck. He curled his fingers tighter and angled toward the pond.

"We'll call that lawyer tomorrow. And fight her." He'd worry about the cost of such a thing later.

"You have a strong case for equitable adoption. Maybe the attorneys will convince Miss Campbell to settle out of court."

Bailey doubted anything weaker than a stampeding herd of wild horses would divert Honey Campbell's attention from the ranch. Her mother stolen Fritz's inheritance, and it looked like she was proving the truth of that adage about the apple and the tree.

"It doesn't make sense." Jaz stood beside him, and the heat of her bare arm taunting.

From the corner of his eye, he saw her face him. Those green eyes stared past him, and a furrow marred her smooth forehead. His stomach bucked into his heart, which skittered like a rabbit on the run.

"You asked your dad about this situation. He said it was handled." She crossed her arms. "That means there has to be a will or something."

"There's no will." Bailey sounded like death.

"Think, Jaz," she muttered and paced away.

His gaze followed. She continued talking to herself and shaking her head. When her arms flailed upward, he smiled.

She turned back, and her eyes widened. That undefinable cord locked their gazes together. Her lips were slightly parted, and Bailey licked his. On the edge of losing everything, and still his body screamed for her.

"There has to be something. Maybe he gave you an envelope. Months ago?"

Bailey shook his head. "Nothing."

"He left you something. Mentioned something was important but it didn't mean anything to you at the time."

Bailey sighed. "There's nothing."

Except his Bible.

A jolt shot through him. *The Bible.*

Bailey strode past Jaz and yanked open the truck door. The worn black book lay innocently between the seatbelt locks.

*Everything you need is in here, son.* His father's words whispered to him. Why had Bailey assumed his father was referring to spiritual things?

*Son.* The echo of that word reverberated in his heart as he gripped the book and pulled it to his chest. No matter what Honey Campbell said, Bailey had been Fritz's son. And there was no way he would let his family's ranch become carrion in her clutches.

He set the book on the seat and fanned the pages. Jaz squeezed in beside him, warm breath tickling his forearms.

"Is that your dad's Bible?" Excitement pitched her voice higher.

He nodded, glancing at various bookmarks, a small pink envelope, and a strip from a string tie. Curling the cover in the opposite direction, he thumbed the thin pages, making them tumble more slowly.

*Please, God, let me be right about this.*

Toward the end of his flipping, a folded paper slid forward. He opened the Bible and stared at the yellow page from one of the legal pads his father favored. A verse near Bailey's right thumb was circled in dark ink.

"But my God shall supply all your need according to his riches in glory by Christ Jesus."

Bailey covered the sudden fluttering in his chest. His other hand lifted the paper. Jaz bumped his arm, and he glanced toward her.

She reached for the paper. "Want me to read it?"

Bailey pulled the paper out of her reach. "You'd think your ranch was at stake."

"It would be easier for me to handle that than to think of you…and Tess losing everything."

She glanced up at him, color riding high on her cheekbones. He believed her. It made no sense, but she cared about this issue as much as he did.

Bailey unfolded the paper. His heart stalled and his gut twitched. What if this was another dead end?

*I can't take it. Please.*

His father's scrawling cursive filled the page. In places the ink thinned, as if the pen he used was running dry, but all the words were legible. Bailey scanned them. His lips twitched, and the hundred-pound weight that had settled over his heart when he found Tess huddled in the closet lifted.

He handed the paper to Jaz. "What's your opinion? You're the legal expert."

Rather than snatching the paper, Jaz pushed his hand lower, keeping hers on his while she scanned the page. She whistled.

Bailey stared at her dark fingers against his work-tanned hands. They weren't so very different.

She whirled toward him and threw her arms around his neck. Warm lips pressed against the pulse point, and his heart lunged toward her.

"This is a will. Your father left everything to you and your sister."

Paper forgotten, Bailey wrapped his arms around Jaz. A smile lit her face, and she tapped his hat, pushing it up.

"You shouldn't even need a lawyer—"

He couldn't stop his lips from cutting off her excited spiel. Breaths mingled as he savored the sweetness of her soft mouth. She sighed, sagging against him.

His arms tightened. He nuzzled his way to her ear. "Thank you."

He started to pull back, but her strong, hot hands pressed against the back of his neck, fingers twining in his hair. Their mouths joined. His heart frolicked in his chest, and when she opened to him, his tongue dove in. She tasted of sunflower seeds and fresh vegetables.

A minute later, he gasped and broke the contact. He pressed his forehead to hers, knocking his hat even higher. He closed his eyes and imprinted the scent and feel of her in his mind. It was already engraved on his heart.

"Tess!" He stepped back, slamming into the open truck door behind him. How could he forget his sister? And what if the greedy niece showed up?

Jaz looked dazed, smoothing her lips together to close her gaping mouth.

"Honey threatened to kick us out today."

"Not happening." She traced a finger along his jaw.

A shudder of pleasure trilled along his nerves. He reached out to touch her face in the same spot.

She blinked and twisted toward the interior of the truck. Her fingers pinched the edge of the yellow paper—the will—and she sidled out of the narrow trap his body and the truck formed.

82

A chill robbed some of his euphoria.

"I'll show this to the sheriff. He'll have a legal reason to chase her off."

Bailey closed the door, granting access to her car. He leaned against the truck, wondering at the void in his chest.

"See you out there." She ducked into her car and tucked the paper in her folded visor.

The engine rumbled to life, and she backed along the rutted trail.

When the dust concealed her, Bailey drew a deep breath. The hole in his chest ached.

He might have secured the ranch, but Jaz had driven away with his heart.

# Eleven

J az checked the rear-view mirror again. When the vehicles bounced onto the dirt road, the police cruiser had fallen further behind. A glance at her speedometer showed her at the speed limit.

Her toes itched to floor the accelerator. Although her watch told her only forty minutes had passed since she'd left Bailey beside Mill Pond, her tumbling gut urged her to hurry.

"This sheet of paper changes everything," Sheriff Grant said when she'd barged into his coffee break at Mabel's. By now, everyone in town knew the latest development.

The game-changing page lay innocently on her passenger seat. Bailey's dad had come through for them. In his own handwriting, he bequeathed the ranch and the personal property on it to his children.

*I know of a blood relative who will make a claim, but Honey Campbell (or whatever her married name might be) has no business on my property.*

Jaz could feel the malice through the rough cross on that final T, and having met the woman in question, she understood it, too.

Finally the archway marking the ranch drive came in sight. She slowed and turned onto the rutted road. A white Jeep blocked the stairs to the porch.

Jaz stopped her car behind Bailey's truck under the breezeway connecting the barn and shed. The thrill of competition rolled through her stomach as she snatched up the precious will and scrambled out of the car.

Bailey and Honey faced off to the side of the paddock. Tess rushed outside, sending the screen door banging against the house.

Bailey's crossed arms emphasized his firm biceps. Jaz blinked and focused on Honey, still parading in the too-tight navy-blue dress and stilt-like heels from the funeral. Her arms flailed like branches in a windstorm, but Bailey's face was stone.

"Jazlyn." Tess latched onto her arm. "Is that it?"

Jaz handed her the paper they'd been turning their world upside down to locate. As the pale blue eyes stared at the page, tears welled and spilled. Tess caught them with her fingers before they could mar the paper.

"Let's get rid of her." Jaz stepped forward, and Tess matched her pace.

The police cruiser turned into the driveway.

Jaz marched up to Honey and planted herself between the woman and Bailey. "Time for you to leave."

Tess waved the yellow page.

"I'm not leaving." Honey's garish mouth hardened.

Jaz stiffened and edged closer, the toes of her sandals touching the points on the uncomfortable-looking pumps. "This will clearly bequeaths this property—land and personal effects—to Bailey and Tess."

"They're nobodies. I'm Fritz's niece."

Tess cleared her throat. "Honey Campbell, right?"

The woman bobbed her head.

"Dad mentioned you in the will, too."

The lined eyebrows screwed up, and the hot pink lips formed an O. "Let me see."

Jaz intercepted Tess's hand as she tried to make the exchange. Sheriff Grant strolled up to the group.

"Miz Campbell, you seem to be a smart lady. Let's not have any trouble." The sheriff tipped his hat at Tess.

Honey stepped back and fluttered her eyelashes at the lawman. "I'm mentioned in the will, and she—" Honey made an angry gesture toward Jaz. "—Won't let me see it."

Jaz handed the document to the sheriff. "This is the

original, sir. I couldn't let her take it and possibly try to destroy it."

A sneer twisted the woman's pink mouth. Jaz had been around her share of people who attempted to destroy evidence, and Honey fit the type.

"She won't try anything in my presence." The sheriff glared with sternness. "Besides, there's a photocopy at my office."

Honey snatched the paper from the sheriff. Her heavily mascaraed eyes scanned down the page. Jaz knew when she read the portion of the will addressed to her because her teeth ground together.

"Well, I never." She dropped the paper like it was contaminated.

Jaz snagged it from the air.

Honey turned a false smile on Tess. "You still need investors for your little guest ranch." The syrupy drawl was back. "I'd be happy to partner with you."

Tess huffed and crossed her arms.

Bailey edged up beside Jaz. "Thank you." He added his own drawl, allowing an extra-long pause before saying, "But no thank you."

Honey's vicious fingernails dug into the side of her legs. Sheriff Grant gestured toward their vehicles.

"After you, ma'am."

Honey glared at each of them in turn, her eyes narrowing dangerously at Jaz. "This is no way to treat family."

Jaz blinked and innocently widened her eyes. "Since you say they aren't your family, what did you expect?"

Honey huffed. The sheriff placed a large hand on her shoulder. Together, they marched toward the house.

Moments later, Honey's engine revved and the Jeep bounced like popping corn down the drive. The sheriff followed at a more sedate pace, raising his hand to them.

Tess squealed and spun around. She brushed past Jaz and hurled herself against Bailey's chest. He caught her.

A sense of isolation pinged against Jaz as her lips trembled into a smile at the joyful sight. Tess and Bailey deserved a little happiness.

Tess whirled and hugged Jaz, knocking her back a step. A waft of vanilla embraced Jaz, who gripped Tess's sides to keep from crashing to the ground. She patted Tess between the shoulders. Behind her, Bailey's sexy half-grin parted his kissable lips, and a shudder rumbled through her.

"I'm going to call the investors." Tess narrowed her eyes at Bailey, flashing a sibling communique his way. When she turned back, her smile widened. "We can never thank you enough." Another glare at Bailey. "Although Bailey is about to give it his best shot."

The girl dislodged the will from Jaz's grip and trotted toward the house.

Bailey shuffled from foot to foot. "So, thank you." He stared over her shoulder as the words tumbled out.

Jaz crossed her arms. "That is not your best shot."

He closed his eyes. Praying? When his eyelids opened, those gem-like orbs riveted to her face. "There are no words." He glanced to her mouth.

Jaz stepped toward him, and he closed the remaining distance. He gently braced her shoulders instead of sweeping her into his arms. Jaz furrowed her brow and gave him a questioning stare.

Troubled waters stirred behind his eyes. The man thought too much.

Jaz slid her hands behind his neck, pushed onto her tiptoes, and pulled his face down. His mouth responded to hers. Shivers pelted her stomach. She inched closer until their chests molded together.

She lost herself in the taste of him—honey and sweet grass. Their lips melded, and her face flushed. The kiss rendered her senseless.

With a groan, he stepped back. Her hands slid across the top of his shoulders and down his muscular arms, stopping on his forearms. His rancher hands burned into the skin at her waist. Jaz blinked the stars out of her vision, and his serious expression pummeled her.

"I like the way you show your appreciation."

His fingers tightened for a moment before relaxing again. His breath feathered across her cheekbone. "I know you're not staying."

The words scorched away the haze of pleasure inspired by his kiss. That's the conversation he wanted to have?

"Deena isn't expecting me until next Saturday." His jaw clenched, and she laced her fingers through his. "Austin's not that far away."

Bailey tugged her toward the paddock fence, leaning on the freshly painted white rails. The brilliance made the peeling barn seem even shabbier.

"There's so much work around here. Tess wants to open this summer, and I don't know how..." He stared at the dappled gray horse tugging grass from under the bottom rail at the far side of the corral.

"What was she saying about investors?" Jaz leaned her hip against his, needing to touch him.

"She's lined up some silent partners. Owners of the resort she worked at. But what she needs is people to move walls, mend fences, and repair these buildings." He motioned with his free hand.

Unease limped into her gut. Was this a letdown speech?

"And the horses we have aren't right for green riders." He shoved his hat higher on his head and shifted an inch away from Jaz.

Her hand tensed in his. *I'm so stupid.*

"It's a relief that you won't have to fight for the ranch, then." Her eyes darted in his direction.

He shrugged. "Tess's dream isn't ruined."

"What about your dreams, Bailey?"

His thumb flicked across the back of her hand, sending

a lightning-strike of awareness up her arm. She ground her teeth.

"I'm her brother. She needs me to run the ranching part of things." He glanced toward Jaz and away.

"Brothers can have their own dreams." The words nudged the secret "Drew closet" of her heart. He joined the Army and put himself on the line for others. Was Bailey the kind who never left home?

"Maybe someday." His tone said he didn't believe it.

She squeezed his hand, tugged him closer. Their gazes collided, knocking her windless. But his eyes whispered the truth.

Something hot bubbled from a chasm that had long been empty.

"Tell me what you really want, Bailey." Her fierce whisper broke on his name. She gritted her back teeth and ordered her emotions to cease fire.

His face lowered to hers. The gentle brush of his lips exploded in tingles along hers. His grip tightened, and she returned the squeeze. His mouth lifted a centimeter, and hot breath caressed her face and neck. She stilled her fluttering eyelids.

He kissed her again, a firm, decisive motion that didn't linger. "I want you to be free." His gruff voice awakened the beast in her chest.

"What do *you* want? Not for Tess or for me. For you." She glared at him, but his gaze strayed toward the ground.

She pulled her hand free and used both hands to force his chin up. His eyes were a barren sea. Her pounding heart fled into her stomach, and she nearly gasped at the physical pain seeing his raw grief caused.

"To do my duty."

Jaz understood about that. She'd joined the military to fulfill a sense of duty to her brother. She came home because her mother expected it. But dreams and duty couldn't coexist. She wanted acceptance and an opportunity to help people.

She blinked and bit back a barrage of words. It wasn't her place to berate him. Who was she to determine what would make him happy? Not the woman who completed a man. A lifetime of experiences proved that.

Jaz kissed his chin, close enough to his lips that she felt them tremble. "You know where to find me." She held her breath. *Please, God, aren't I worth loving?*

When he blinked and dipped his head, shading his eyes from her sight, she heard the loudspeaker announcement.

Goodbye. It was always goodbye.

# Twelve

The Subaru kicked up dust, and a tether on his heart tugged Bailey toward the woman inside. When the car turned the bend on Armstrong Road, the thread of longing snapped against him with physical force. He gulped and massaged the aching spot on his chest.

Shamgar snorted, spooked by the sudden movement. The horse tossed his head and danced away from the fence. Bailey's frame folded against the rail. The barn dogs circled his legs, whining.

The screen door slammed. A few moments later, Poppet scratched at his ankle. Bailey's arms were too heavy to reach for the dog.

Another grunt sounded behind him before Tess punched his shoulder. "What are you doing?"

Bailey glowered at her but without heat. Emptiness swelled to fill the hole Jaz left behind, an abyss deeper than when MaryAnn died. He hadn't experienced anything so devastating for twenty years. Nothing could hurt as much as hearing his grandmother pass him off to the state because he was too much trouble. Until now.

Shamgar trotted to the far side of the paddock.

"I'm standing here with my sister."

"Don't be a jerk." Tess faced him, arms hugging her waist. "You shouldn't have let her leave."

The words were like a slam to his heart.

"She has a job. In Austin."

"Did you even ask her to stay?"

Poppet whimpered at his feet. Wide brown eyes stared

up at him. Bailey crouched to tousle the dog's ears. She leaned into his knees, eyes closing in pleasure.

"Why would she stay here?"

Tess huffed. "Because she's falling for you. Because you two make a great couple."

Pressure built in his chest. A couple? He wished. But it was safer for her to avoid his whirlpool of doom.

"Sweet Grove is just a stopping point for her. She doesn't want to live here."

Tess tossed her hands in the air. "So go to Austin."

Bailey patted Poppet's head and stood. "I can't leave you, Tess. You're the only family I have left."

His sister glared at him, her light blue eyes glinting with icy resolve. This was something new, something she'd learned in the years away from him. What happened to the easygoing girl who wanted to please everyone?

"I love you, Lee, but you're being an idiot."

Heat flushed his neck. "Standing by my family is idiotic? I don't think so." He shoved his hands into his front pockets. "Not when you're all I've got."

Her hand gripped his forearm, cool somehow in the gathering heat of the day. "And you'll still have me if you're in Austin. Right? We didn't stop being family while you were in college." She squeezed. "Or I was."

The ranch was his responsibility. She had a solid business plan, but it would take a ton of work before she could make a profit.

"You don't need my help to get ready for guests?" He blinked. "Didn't you say I'd be the one in charge of the dude ranch aspect?"

She shrugged. "I can work it out. Mr. Wells and his son have been helpful."

"For a fee."

She pinched his arm. "Stop changing the subject. I'm a big girl. I can handle a guest ranch."

"The bills won't pay themselves while you're fixing

things up."

Her glare could have frozen a steaming pot of coffee. "This isn't about me. It's about you." She swallowed, and her voice dropped to a whisper. "I want you to be happy."

Bailey hugged her to his chest. Happy? What did that even feel like? His entire life had been about making himself useful so he wouldn't be sent away. There had been moments when the weight of responsibility hadn't pressed so hard he could barely draw a breath, but not on the ranch. Not since his mother died.

Tess stepped out of his arms. She shook his shoulders. Or tried. Her petite frame wasn't moving him. "Does Jazlyn Rolle make you happy?"

Life sparked in his chest. His stomach bounced into his heart. She made him feel alive in too many ways to count.

Tess grinned. "The way your eyes lit up tells me all I need to know." She grabbed his arm and tugged him toward the house.

"Tess," he chided, but followed anyway because he didn't want to hurt her.

"You're going to get in your truck and drive over to her house. You're going to ask her to stay."

His heart plunged into free fall. "She won't."

Tess stopped and shoved his shoulder. "You're blind. I see the way she looks at you."

His pulse pounded. He hadn't imagined those heated gazes? It seemed like wishful thinking to hope someone as smart and beautiful as Jaz would see anything worthwhile in him. He gulped.

Tess jerked open the door of his truck. "Go already."

The pounding increased inside his skull. He couldn't do this. For too many reasons to calculate, but two rose to the surface.

"She's better off without me." He shrugged off his sister's grip. "And her dream isn't in Sweet Grove. I'm not asking her to give it up."

He'd walked away from his design job so Tess could attend college. It was what he did for the people he loved.

The people he loved? Pale green eyes and a squared-off chin flashed before his eyes. His heart skidded against his flipping stomach. Fine. Maybe he did think he was half in love with her, but that was all the more reason to let her go.

Tess circled him and yanked his arm again. This time she marched them toward the house.

"I can walk."

"But not in the right direction. Or fast enough to keep Jaz from getting away."

Bailey stopped, and Tess's hand slipped off his arm. "What are you talking about now?"

Tess twirled and slammed her hands on her hips. "Get upstairs and pack a bag. Then go to her house and ask her if you can go with her."

His jaw dropped. "You're addle pated."

She narrowed her eyes. "I'm the only one who's seeing sense here."

"We haven't even dated, and you want me to move to Austin with her?"

Tess shook her head. "Not like that." She stomped up the steps.

Bailey followed, Poppet at his heels. His sister had lost her mind if she thought Bailey could move two hours away with a girl he'd only been hanging out with for a couple weeks. And yet, his lips buzzed at the memory of the searing lip-lock they'd shared at Mill Pond and the ones by the paddock.

He thrust the visions away and caught the screen door before it slammed in his face. Tess marched straight down the hall to the study. Bailey and Poppet trailed her.

She whirled on him, hip resting against the side of the big oak desk. "You weren't planning to stay here when Dad passed. Tell me the truth."

Bailey's throat dried. What did his plans matter? He shook his head because his tongue stuck to the roof of his mouth.

She snatched the drawings for the farmhouse renovations and additions to the barn from the desk. "You love drawing plans, using your education to design things. When you showed me this—" Her voice cut off and moisture sprung to the corner of her eyes.

He stepped forward, arms outstretched. She backed away, holding the plans like a shield.

"The only time I've seen this spark is when you're working with the animals, drawing these changes, and when you're with Jaz." She lowered the plans. "Bailey, I want you to be happy."

The words strained past the lump in his throat, "I'm not leaving you."

She straightened to her full five feet three inches. "I don't want you here."

Bailey blinked. "You need my help."

"I don't." She crossed her arms over her chest, and the paper crackled.

A weight sunk through his stomach. Something curled around his lower back.

"Tessa." His warning came out hoarse.

"I mean it, Bailey." She gestured with her hands. "I can handle the ranch. I've been lining up private investors, and I think I've figured out a way to get it off the ground by the end of summer."

"And who will take care of the stock?"

"There's that therapy ranch out toward Harrison."

Bailey shook his head. How could she even suggest this? Didn't she know he wanted to support her? "Tess, I want to help you."

"Fine. Then go after your dream." She stuck her chin out.

"How does that help you?" He tilted his head and crossed his arms in a pose mimicking hers.

"Get a great paying job in Austin and feel free to send

money." She glared at him. "Am I right that you could earn as much in a week of architectural design as you make in a month mowing fields and working maintenance for the school district?"

He opened his mouth to argue, then shut it. She was right. He'd been earning a goodly sum five years ago at the custom home design partnership in Houston. They'd probably be happy to give him a recommendation after they tried to talk him into returning.

A hiccup jerked inside his chest. The back of his tongue tasted like hope.

"Let's get this guest ranch operating first." He lowered his voice to the pitch he used with spooked horses.

She grunted. "Don't try that whispering magic on me." She set the plans on the desk and grabbed his arms. "Let me do this, Lee. Please."

The pleading in her eyes undid him. She knew he couldn't say no to that look. He tried to manufacture ire at her manipulation, but his soul held its breath. "She's not going to want me following her to Austin."

Tess pouted. "But you can do it anyway." She slipped her hand in his. "Go talk to her."

Bailey kissed his sister's sunshine-scented hair.

As he worked through the next day, he tried to plan a convincing argument, something that wouldn't sound desperate or stalker-like. In the end, he tossed shoes and clothes into an old duffel he used to carry laundry home in during college and prayed.

*Let her want me.*

# Thirteen

Saturday afternoon, Jaz hugged her mother tighter, breathing in the scent of lilies, memorizing it. She'd only be two hours away, much closer than she'd been for the past six years. Why the ever-widening chasm in her chest then?

"Next weekend I'll help you apartment shop." Her mother smoothed a hand over her hair and kissed her cheek.

They broke apart, and her mom climbed into the idling car. Her father waved, his expression the same grim set he'd had since she told him she'd be leaving. He wanted to know how much money she'd earn and when she planned to finish her degrees.

*Thanks for all the support, Dad.* But she hadn't expected anything more.

A flash of Drew's smile echoed across her memory. He gave her two thumbs up, as he had whenever her dad walked away frowning his disapproval.

She jiggled another box into the back of the car. She still had to load the linens her mother had set aside for her and the clothes hanging in the closet. Maybe she'd be in Austin sooner than she'd told Deena.

In her bedroom, she scanned the walls and shelves. Bare. Not as colorless as the barracks when she'd left the Army, but a similar ache throbbed in her chest. Why? This room hadn't been home for a decade. The past weeks were a hotel stay, a pit stop in her post-Army life.

Jaz tilted the box on top of the sheets. Light from the window played across the bronze facets. Her brother's too-short life condensed into a single medal, appropriate since it represented his valor and his goal to rescue others.

Like he'd done for her as long as she could remember.

She snapped the lid closed and tucked the medal into her messenger bag. She scanned the room, grabbed another bag, and hustled to her car.

Outside, a rusty white pickup blocked the end of the drive. Jaz froze. Crossed arms emphasized the mass of his biceps as Bailey leaned against the truck. He used one hand to tilt his hat up, a salute she'd come to recognize as his form of greeting.

With the hat pushed back, she could see those devastating eyes. His gaze was as dark as the shadows lengthening across the eventful day.

"Heading to Austin?" The low gravel of his question raced up her back—a chilling pleasure.

Jaz dipped her chin and dropped the bags she carried in the passenger seat of her car. Her heart danced against her breastbone, but her mind went mute. What was left to say? She'd helped him save his ranch and tied him to Sweet Grove.

She stole a glance at him as she ducked back through the open garage. Her lips tingled, anticipating a goodbye kiss.

In her room, she slung the handle of one of the remaining bags over her shoulder and hefted the one holding sheets and towels. She swiveled and barreled into firm pecs and steely abs. She grunted.

"Is this the last of it?"

She stared at his lips, tempted to push onto her toes and revel in the concussion of emotion and pleasure of his kiss. Instead, she gulped and focused on his calloused fingers wrapped over hers on the handle of the bag. She released it automatically, and when he held his other hand out, she passed the second one off, too.

"Back seat?"

She licked her lips, trying to swallow around the hive buzzing in her throat. Bailey's gaze dropped to her mouth. Her heart revved like an engine in overdrive. She sidled away from him. "Yeah. I just have to grab what's hanging in the closet."

His gaze flicked back to hers. Then he was gone and the room chilled. How could one cowboy be so hot?

*You're walking away from that?*

She shrugged, hating how her stomach plummeted. Her life was a litany of walking away from one dream after the other. She squeezed her eyes shut.

*Lord, help me find what I'm searching for.*

Her eyes snapped open. She piled the clothes onto the bed and closed the closet doors.

He was back. His large hands could easily span all the hangers, but he only lifted half of them. Even the hem of her longest dress didn't skim the floor. He edged away from the door, waiting for her to precede him.

Always the gentleman.

Jaz draped the rest of the clothes over her arms. She scurried around him like a rat avoiding a well-baited trap.

After she lay the clothes over the packed back seat, she scooted away. When he leaned into the car, his toned backside looked as fine as ever.

She gulped. He wasn't a player, and he'd already told her goodbye. Bailey respected and understood her, but he belonged to Sweet Grove. Jaz needed to spread her wings.

She fidgeted with the handle on the door. He closed the back door and hatchback of her car. He stopped inches in front of her.

"Thanks." Her voice wobbled. She clenched her fingers into a ball.

"I don't want you to go." The words were quiet and carried a world of doubt and longing.

Jaz choked on her next breath. Bailey slid closer and cupped her cheek. Her eyelids veiled her sight, and the sensation of his rough skin stroking her smooth cheek traveled through every nerve ending. She tried to capture the experience and store it for later.

"I can't stay, Bailey." She stared into his steady gaze, pouring every reason for leaving into a silent communique. "Not even for you."

The corner of his mouth twitched. Her heart stumbled, longing to see that grin again.

"But you're tempted to stay?" He lowered his face toward hers. "By me?"

Firm lips swept across hers. Sensations crashed in a flash flood through every atom of her being. Her arms groped his waist as his fingers swept beneath her ear and into the hair at the nape of her neck. She opened her mouth to taste all of him, and suddenly she was kissing air.

She blinked up at him, trying to catch the breath he stole. After a few swallows, she found it. "It's not just the job. Or my dad." Her voice shook, so she stopped talking.

He shoved his hat higher, and his gaze brushed across her features, a caress she felt as much as the one at her neck and hip.

"You're not running from memories of Drew, are you?"

She pressed her lips in a line. "I came to collect them. They're going with me." She thought of the photo album and the medal.

"Take me with you, too."

She pinched her brows together and tried to step away from him. He dropped both hands to her hips and held her in place, so close his heat melted the resolve she'd donned as body armor.

"But, Tess. And the ranch."

"Tess told me to go after you."

Of course she did. Jaz shook her head. "What would you do in Austin? Where would you stay?"

His fingers drew a circle on one of her hips, igniting a firestorm in her gut. She covered his hand with hers. The full-fledged grin appeared then, turning her insides to a circus of monkeys.

"I have a degree. I could get a job."

"But I know how much the ranch means to you."

"It's a home for Tess."

Swelling in her chest made her breath catch. She couldn't risk this again. Could she?

"What about your home, Bailey? Isn't the ranch all you have?"

Bailey studied her face, a slow perusal. The distracting swirl of his fingers started on her opposite hip.

"Is the ranch all I have?" He leaned closer. His breath fanned her cheek when he whispered, "I thought I'd found something with you."

Her heart sprang toward him, pounding against her breastbone. She inched closer without meaning to do it. The cotton of his shirt slid beneath her palm as she raised her hand to cover his heart.

She'd lost everything, but what if all of that was so she could find love? Doubt rattled like buckshot inside her brain.

"I know it's only been a couple of weeks." His throat bobbed. "But I crushed on you so hard in high school. And when I saw you with Poppet, it all came rushing back."

His fingers tightened on her waist. In those summer night eyes, hope called to her.

What if God was answering her prayer?

"I don't—"

Her fingers covered his mouth, pushing until he stopped talking. Their gazes melded.

"You've got my number, cowboy. No need to uproot yourself today." Her stomach plunged, already missing him.

He stared into her eyes until he drilled her soul. "You'll be my girl?"

Her lips twitched. Had she ever been anyone's girl? She rose onto her toes, kissing away the half frown.

"Will you be my guy?"

His mouth claiming hers told her everything she needed to know.

✧✧✧✧

### One Month Later

Afternoon sunlight pounded against her skull. Jaz swatted the behind of the last girl and followed her out of the heat and into the locker room.

So much for the championship bid. The Longhorns had been ranked in the top five before this week, but it ended at regionals today.

As her eyes started to adjust to the dimness of the hallway between the dugout and the locker room, Deena pulled her aside. "Someone's asking for you." She thumbed toward the exit into the stands.

"Not that I'm sad to miss the tongue-lashing—"

Deena held up her palm. "Your part-time gig isn't worth that."

Jaz thanked her friend, snagged a bottle of water from the ice chest near the door, and downed half of it as she climbed the stairs. Her mom planned to attend the game this weekend. Jaz loved seeing her but was a little tired of shopping for her barren apartment.

A sigh escaped as she hit the bar and stepped into the shadowed hallways beneath the stands. A cowboy leaned against the far wall.

Jaz halted, rubbing her eyes. Her lungs forgot to breathe.

"Good game, coach."

She was an assistant to the assistant who was on medical leave, not anyone's coach.

Jaz stepped out of the doorway. The clang of the closing door echoed in the enclosed space. "Hey."

Even though they texted each other every night, her heart was jigging around her stomach.

"I wanted to surprise you."

He stepped closer. Her eyes devoured his half-smile, the fit of his shirt across broad shoulders, and the loose way he ambled toward her.

"I'm a mess." Old insecurities reared into her throat, stalling her words.

Bailey's hands framed her chin. "You're beautiful. Mind-boggling." His calloused fingertips stroked her cheek and he gulped. "Sexy."

Before Jaz could argue, his lips covered hers, caressing, confirming. She melted into him, stunned at the flood of energy shooting through her. His hands slid to her shoulders.

A trail of kisses crossed her sweaty cheek. Hot breath chilled her neck.

"I missed you."

The truth of it soothed across a too-often-broken heart. A tear in her soul stitched together.

She rested her palms on his waist. "So, cowboy, what brings you to Austin?"

One corner of his mouth curled up and then the other. Her chest ached at the sight of that grin and the light sparking blue fire in his eyes.

"Besides my gorgeous girlfriend?"

She blinked at him. He dangled a set of keys before lacing his fingers in hers and dragging her forward.

"I need to change."

His eyes scanned her. "You're perfect."

She stumbled behind him, wincing when they stepped into the sunlight. He'd taken her to the service entrance of the parking lot. She recognized the beater truck parked in a tow away zone.

"Haven't been here long?"

Bailey's grin widened. "I saw the last two innings."

"You're lucky you didn't get towed."

Bailey led her to the truck. The bed was packed with boxes, and the crew cab was stuffed with jeans and shirts.

Jaz gaped at the sight. He waggled the keys again. Her gaze riveted on those sexy lips.

"I start my job on Monday." He angled the bill of his hat

up further so she wouldn't miss his wink. "These keys open my studio apartment."

Her jaw slackened even more. No matter how often he speculated about moving away from the ranch, it had seemed like some distant future event.

"What about Tess?"

"She's a big girl." His lips curled into a frown. "She's got a vested partner now. And she kicked me out last month."

His exaggerated drawl sent a flush of shivering tingles up her arms. She loved the sound of his voice. Technology was great, but it didn't replace moments like this when his hand warmed her hip and his eyes proclaimed a million truths she struggled to believe.

As Bailey pulled her closer, her stomach shivered. In his unblinking gaze she saw a future, and his circle-drawing thumbs reassured her it wasn't all a dream.

She bit her lower lip, sucking it in her mouth. "You never said anything. What's the big—"

His lips covered hers with hot urgency. A few pulsing heartbeats later, he slowed and sweetened the kiss and drew back. He whispered on her lips, "I'm here to win your trust and love."

"I trust you." The breathy voice sounded foreign to her. "I don't want you to regret—"

He pressed his lips to hers, waking every nerve from head to toe. When he edged back, her insides churned and her knees buckled. He flashed a flirty grin and plopped his hat onto her head. "Want to see my place?"

She sighed and arched one brow. "My stuff is in the locker room. My car..."

The squawk of the passenger door opening cut her off. Pressure from his hand guided her into the blast of hot air escaping the truck.

"We can pick it up later."

Jaz slid onto the seat, gripping his hand before he could step back. "Are you sure about this?"

The glint in his eyes said he understood that she was asking about more than the move from Sweet Grove. Her stomach twisted.

His luscious lips slid into the grin she adored. "I've been sure about this since you nearly knocked my head off with a softball."

*Lord, it's too perfect to be real.*

Bailey interlaced their fingers. There was no mistaking the adoration sparkling in his steady gaze.

Love threw a fastball but doubt struck out.

# Book Two

## Fourteen

A sweet bubble gum scent swirled around Jazlyn Rolle during what had become her favorite part of her position at Boldt & Associates. In front of her, the girl smiled, ignorant of the wheelchair beneath her caused by a manufacturer who didn't care about the faceless statistics harmed by their products. When the girl's small hand squeezed around Jaz's, it pulled strings in her heart. Suddenly, Jaz was transported twenty years in the past where she was the little sister sharing cotton candy with her brother.

Jaz blinked the old memory away and firmed her smiling mouth before pumping the girl's pale hand in her bronze one and sliding away from the wheelchair.

"Can we play catch next time?" Hope shone in the girl's pale blue eyes.

Jaz glanced to the woman whose hands gripped the handles on the back of the chair. Red shadowed the mother's eyes, and her thin brown hair hung limply to her shoulders. In contrast, the girl's hair was in two tight braids, evidence of Jaz's care while the mother met with Mr. Boldt.

After the woman nodded, Jaz said, "I always have a glove and ball in my desk." Because softball had been Jaz's saving grace at that girl's age, long before she'd played on scholarship at the University of Texas.

"Thank you, Miz Jaz," the mother said in accent-thickened gratitude.

Jaz gripped the woman's hand for a moment and opened the door. Heavy air rushed to fill the coolness, and a gust swirled yellowed leaves across the sidewalk. Jaz waved until the wheelchair was out of sight on the far side of the van in the nearest handicapped parking spot.

When it became clear most parents in the large lawsuit proceedings couldn't afford babysitting during conference appointments, Jaz came up with a compromise. She entertained the children while parents attended the lawyer-client meetings. Now she was forced back to the job she'd been hired to do.

Jaz rolled her shoulders and returned to her desk. Most of the research on the negligence case against the pharmaceutical company had been completed weeks ago, but there was always another case. Always some other big company taking advantage of the little guy. Those cases called to the part of her that wanted to protect others from bullies, as her brother had always done for her. Until being the hero cost his life.

Jaz scooted up to her desk and woke her computer screen. Thoughts of Drew and life callings faded as she copied pertinent case numbers into her research file and highlighted the court summations, working with three separate applications open until words swam on the screen. Just another day in the life of a paralegal.

She leaned away from the monitor and closed her eyes. A stinging burn ebbed as darkness soothed the eye strain. She'd almost prefer fumbling through the dusty tomes in the library on the second floor. At least she had to get up and locate the next resource. Chained to her desk, she didn't know if her eyes or her rear ached more.

She squirmed, and her chair rolled an inch to one side and squeaked like a mouse beneath an elephant's foot.

The case she was working on was important. It would secure funding for several nonprofit groups, but that didn't make the research any less tedious.

Maybe she should apply to law school again. At least then she would be working on briefs and motions rather than this constant search for precedents and statutes. If she got her law degree, someone else would find that information for her.

An old longing for her father's approval ached in the vicinity of her heart. He wanted her to become a lawyer, but her short list of accomplishments had taught her whatever she did would never be enough to please him. Because she wasn't a beautiful lady like her mother, and no one could escape the shadow of a brother who sacrificed everything for duty.

The pang sharpened. Most days, her work satisfied her sense of purpose and she didn't feel her brother's loss. Other days, the monotony fueled doubts into rocket ships bent on destroying any sense of significance she might have found since leaving the Army.

Her smart phone vibrated on her desk. Jaz snapped her eyes open and flipped the device face up, glancing at nearby desks.

Dad. No photo flashed above the single word because Jaz didn't have one. That simple truth spoke volumes about her relationship with him. He demanded, and she conformed. She couldn't recall a time he'd ever listened to more than a dozen words she said.

The ache in her chest became a whirlpool in her stomach. He would never call her. Unless something bad happened, and her mother couldn't make the call.

Her fingers trembled, and she nearly dropped the phone which chose that moment to vibrate again. She swiped the answer button, swallowing the terror clawing at her voice box.

"Hello?"

"Jazlyn, this is your father." The medium baritone voice echoed in her ear. Was he on speaker?

"Hey. I'm at work."

"I wouldn't call...It's your mother." The words jumbled together.

The bottom dropped out of Jaz's world. She wilted against the chair and numbness had her fumbling the phone again.

"What about her?" *Please, God, don't let her be dead.* She couldn't lose another person she loved.

"There was an accident Saturday."

It was Monday. Why had he waited two days to tell Jaz

the news? A familiar pang slashed at her sense of duty. When the weekly call hadn't come last night, Jaz should have called Mom.

"How bad?"

"The car's a loss." Like Jaz cared about a collection of metal and wires. "They took her to St. Joseph's, thought it was a fractured pelvis."

He said it like breaking the bone that divided the body into upper and lower halves was a small thing. Only her father would be so blasé.

"Is she still there?"

After a pause, her father choked out, "No. They had to transport her to Travis County General."

That was Austin's foremost trauma hospital. A bubble burst inside her chest. Spots danced along the edges of her vision.

"She had emergency surgery this morning to stop internal bleeding."

Moisture blurred across the ever-narrowing view in front of Jaz. Her mother had to be okay.

"Prognosis?" She snapped the word out.

Her father's voice cut off. Sounds of shuffling at his end of the phone scratched her ear.

"She's in traction for at least six weeks, but they found the bleed and stopped it. Both of her legs are also broken." His voice faltered.

Jaz knew this hurt him more than it wounded her. Her father idolized and adored her mother. It was the gleam of that relationship that made his dismissal of Jaz all the more obvious and painful. She didn't measure up. Her athletic interests and tomboyish antics were nothing like her mother's beauty queen face and figure.

"I'll come to the hospital."

"She's still in recovery. It might be hours."

*You shouldn't be alone.* That's what she knew she should say. But her being there would practically be the same as him being alone. They wouldn't talk or hug. No, they'd circle each other like territorial porcupines.

"I'll be there soon." Jaz asked where she could meet him and, after he gave directions, she ended the call.

She expelled a long breath. The room spun. Jaz leaned elbows on the desk and propped her forehead on her palms.

*Lord, I thought my life was looking up.*

After forfeiting her military career to fraternize with an officer who then dumped her, Jaz had lost all sense of purpose. She'd wanted to follow in Drew's footsteps, carry on the heroics he lived daily. She'd found a great job in Austin, only a couple hours from her parents, and had even spent some time working with the softball team at UT where she'd played on full scholarship for three years.

Until Drew died.

Once her heartbeat returned to normal and she could breathe again, Jaz opened the ongoing text thread with Bailey. At least he would understand. *Ca! me.*

If they needed to talk during work hours, the standard method was a simple text. Once the other person had time, they would call back or respond to a text request.

Jaz had informed her boss of the situation and closed the projects she was working on before her cell phone rang. A picture of Bailey lit up the screen. He wore his sexy grin and tapped the brim of his cowboy hat with two fingers. The sight twisted her chest with a different sort of pain.

Why did someone so gorgeous and hardworking admire her? She couldn't comprehend it, but she knew he would stand by her like no one else. Only Drew had ever been so stalwart.

And today she needed him.

# Fifteen

Bailey Travers clutched the yellow legal pad. Its familiarity clung to him, a single link to the father he'd buried five months ago.

*I'm in the city, Dad. Chasing my dreams like you wanted.*

The pale sage eyes and white smile of his girlfriend flashed across his mind. If she hadn't come back to Sweet Grove, he would still be riding a tractor and living out of his truck. Jaz and the designing job had spurred him away from the only home he'd ever known. But she was worth it. Someday, they would have a new home together.

He stepped through a large room divided into cubicles and lined on three sides by offices, a conference room, and a break area. At his design table, he set the paper aside. His phone had vibrated twice while he was meeting with his boss to discuss changes to a custom remodel on an upscale home in West Lake Hills. Who pulled out walls and replaced rooms in a house barely ten years old?

Bailey couldn't imagine the audacity of it. He pulled his smart phone from his hip pocket and tapped the screen. A text from Jaz blared, *Ca! me.*

His heart jigged behind his ribs, a familiar sensation around Jaz. It still amazed him that a woman from strong roots thought a former foster kid was worth dating. He understood why she'd helped him hold onto the ranch his sister converted to a resort after their father died. She was like her older brother that way. Drew had rescued Bailey from bullies in high school and offered friendship. Still, when Jaz followed up her rescue by asking to date him? Bailey jumped at that and returned to the drafting career he'd left behind when MaryAnn

Travers passed away.

The twinge of loneliness at the thought of his little sister Tess and his recently deceased father Fritz hardly registered. Somehow, Bailey had walked away from his father's funeral with more to live for rather than less. In a world where he loved and lost, the turnaround constituted a modern miracle.

Bailey snagged his hat from its hook and strolled out of his cube. A few other designers greeted him as he wove through the maze of cubicles to exit into the parking lot behind the building. He shoved open the fire door and sunshine blinded him. The wave of hot air suffocated, and it took him a moment to catch his breath.

After plopping his hat on his head and strolling into shade cast by the neighboring building, he pressed the button. Tinny ringing sounded in his ear.

"Thanks." Jaz's voice made spring bloom in his stomach. Something in her tone had Bailey standing straighter.

"You okay?"

During a pause, he shuffled his feet. *Lord, whatever it is, let me be able to help her.*

"My mom was in a car accident."

His heart exploded, pounding, flipping, and trying to escape from his chest. Not her mother. They were so close.

"This weekend, but Dad didn't bother to call until there

was some sort of internal bleeding scare." Her bitterness bit into him.

"You need to go to her."

"She's at Travis County General. Still in post-op recovery."

He swallowed a lump swelling from somewhere deeper than his stomach. Hospitals meant death. "I'll meet you there."

Her sigh told him he'd said the right thing. She didn't get along well with her father, who always ragged on her about becoming a lawyer.

"Are you sure your boss will let you come? My mom isn't exactly your family."

*Not yet.* But Bailey planned to change that relationship by marrying Jaz as soon as the stubborn woman overcame her doubts about his feelings. Today was another time he could prove his commitment to her.

"I'll work something out." Bailey's deadlines weren't so pressing they couldn't be met if he stayed late a few nights.

Jaz shared information about the waiting room, promising to text him if they should meet elsewhere. Steadiness returned to her voice. Did that have anything to do with him?

Once the call ended, he paced back into the building, whisking his hat off as he strode to his boss's office. An assistant typed madly on a computer keyboard in the outer office. Behind her, the door to his boss's domain stood open.

"Back so soon" The woman's blonde hair draped over one shoulder and across her ample chest. She winked, and heat crept up Bailey's neck.

Everyone at the firm knew he'd moved to Austin to be close to his girlfriend, but that didn't stop most of the women from flirting with him.

Bailey shifted from foot to foot and nodded toward the other door. His fingers pinched the band on his cowboy hat. "Go on in." Her hazel eyes flickered down him as she returned her attention to typing.

Bailey strode into the office, blinking at the flood of light from the window behind his boss. It overlooked a small green space that separated this building from the much taller one beside it.

"More questions?" His boss stood. Iron gray hair dotted his temples, and the dress shirt tucked loosely into dark slacks concealed the middle-aged bulge. He motioned Bailey toward the two chairs in the far corner of the room, a space the man preferred to conduct meetings and interviews.

Bailey nodded in response to the question and stopped beside one of the chairs. "I'd like to take off early. Jaz's mother was in an accident and just got out of surgery at Travis County General."

The shorter man halted. "Of course. Do you need to go now? I would like the proposal for Inder Realty by day's end."

Bailey knew his boss was meeting with the broker the next afternoon. It wouldn't take him long to finish the additions they'd discussed. "I'll get that to you before I leave."

"Will you need a few days off?" His boss had the steeliest gray eyes Bailey had ever seen, but at the moment they softened.

"I don't know."

"Call me once you do."

"Will do. Thank you." Bailey ducked his chin and left the room.

It took less than thirty minutes to clean up the plans his boss requested and email him the link to the file. That put him in Austin traffic at the same time as most of the school buses. At a stop light, he texted to let Jaz know he was on his way.

*Please let her mother be al right.*

He'd prayed the same for his own mother and MaryAnn passed anyway. Lately it seemed like God might be paying more attention to Bailey's prayers, but who knew how long that might last?

After too many slams on the brakes and several rounds of the hospital parking garage, Bailey finally emerged from the elevator onto the appropriate floor. Around a corner and down a long hallway, Bailey found Jaz pacing one end of a mid-sized waiting area. On the opposite side her father, arms crossed over his chest, stared out the only window in the room.

When Jaz spotted Bailey, her green eyes lit up and some of the tension eased out of her jawline. She flew into his arms, and the familiar scent of oranges and ginger tickled his nose. Catching her father's stern gaze, he fought the urge to bury his face in her hair.

"Thanks for coming." Her words were for his ears only.

"Sorry it took so long."

Her father edged a step closer. His face appeared pasty, and his hazel eyes were wide and bloodshot. The puff of hair he usually kept gelled into a deep side part stood on end in a few areas and flattened against his skull in others.

Bailey shook Ronald Rolle's hand. "How is she?"

Ron's cool hand clasped his firmly and, after a single squeeze and pump, he withdrew it. "Still waiting to hear."

A woman popped her head into the room. "Mr. Rolle? The doctor can meet with you now."

Ron stiffened and walked toward the doorway. Jaz, her spine arrow straight, followed without waiting for an invitation. Her fingers gripped his as she tugged Bailey along behind her.

Further along the hallway, the woman gestured to an open doorway and assured them the doctor would join them momentarily.

Ron's gaze flitted to Bailey and Jaz's joined hands, and Bailey fought to keep from flinching or drawing away. He'd only been around Jaz's dad one time, and the air of disapproval weighed heavily. Her mom had chattered and flitted about, an ideal hostess who still couldn't warm the room in the presence of Ron's aloofness.

A man in scrubs and a white coat with a mask and stethoscope dangling from his neck hurried into the room, shutting the door behind him. The snick of the latch sounded ominous.

Jaz stepped closer so their hips touched, and her fingers tightened on his.

"Mr. Rolle, Geraldine is stable. We stitched a couple contusions and insured the spleen was intact. The hardware placement in her hip seems fine, but we'll want to run a full treatment of antibiotics." The doctor gestured toward the grouping of furniture. "Why don't we have a seat while I discuss the prognosis?"

Before she sat, Jaz said, "She's out of danger, right?"

When the doctor confirmed this, Jaz's tension drained further, but she still leaned into Bailey. He draped his arm around her shoulders and drew spirals on her upper arm.

"The triple traction remains for at least a week, and she'll stay here where we can keep her fluids steady, screen for blood clots, and monitor any infections. After that, I might recommend a rehabilitation center for up to a month."

Ron clenched his hands between his knees. "What about home care?"

"Because of her fractured femur and fibula, she won't be able to walk for at least six weeks. I'll want her up in a wheelchair as soon as possible, and physical therapy will keep her legs from atrophying, but she'll need a full-time caregiver."

Jaz wilted further into Bailey. Ron straightened but held the doctor's gaze. "How soon can she come home?"

"Unless you want a hospital bed rigged with the pulleys that keep the bones aligned in your living room, two weeks minimum."

Ron's shoulders slumped. Jaz twitched toward him but pulled short of touching him.

"I can help take care of her." Jaz drummed her fingers on her thigh. "Does that mean she can come home sooner? The house is a single level with only one step up to the stoop." She straightened away from him. "Mom would prefer to be at home."

The doctor glanced between Jaz and her father, studied Jaz

for a second longer, then pursed his lips together. "We'll discuss it. She's being transferred to a room now, and I'm sure you want to see her."

They stood. The doctor shook hands with Ron and nodded to Jaz. "I'll have the nurse provide the recovery timeline and instructions, so you can talk it over with Geraldine. I'll check her progress tomorrow afternoon."

A moment later, another man in scrubs directed them to follow him. The sterile, antiseptic atmosphere choked Bailey, but he pushed away the dark memories of MaryAnn's supposedly routine surgery that ended up claiming her life.

*Please, Lord. Don't let that happen to Jaz's mother.*

# Sixteen

straight jacket couldn't have been more confining. Or so it seemed as Jazlyn clambered from the double bed she'd slept in as a teenager. Sweet Grove wasn't home without Drew and was even less welcoming since Bailey lived in Austin rather than up the road at Travers Guest Ranch.

Once the doctors released Geraldine Rolle from Travis County General, her father lined up a hospital bed, wheelchair, walker, and everything from a bedpan to a home health nurse. Ignoring her father's dubious looks, Jaz relocated and became her mother's primary caregiver while her father continued his job at St. Joseph's five days each week.

"Jaz," her mother called from the family room.

As she turned toward the sound, Jaz glimpsed Drew smiling from his Special Forces graduation portrait. Her heart clenched. She ducked out of her mother's home office—now Jaz's workspace for the foreseeable future. Thankfully Boldt & Associates had a remote system, allowing Jaz to continue her work online.

At the foot of the hospital bed, weights dangled from two separate pulleys. Jaz's thoughts spiraled into the realm of science fiction horror flicks. The doctor couldn't visit soon enough with his portable x-ray machine to determine if the pelvic bones would stay in position without traction. Cleaning the sites of the bolts and screws in her mom's knee and thigh was her least favorite task. Yes, she preferred emptying the bed pan.

Jaz stopped beside her mother's raised head. A drama series streamed on the television behind her. Her mother's fingers could have been icicles, and Jaz forced away a shiver as she clutched her mother's hand in hers.

Her mother's lips trembled in her pale face. The skin that was always two shades lighter than Jaz's looked nearly yellow.

"A drink." She lifted the glorified sippy cup, its flexible straw flopping like a wagging tail.

"You want a snack, too?" Her mother's appetite had dwindled to nothing, and the physical therapist had stressed that she needed to eat high-energy foods, especially before and after therapy sessions.

Jaz glanced at the clock on the stove. Another three hours until the therapist showed up to torment her mother again. The bending and lifting made the pulleys creak and the weights clank, and the sounds grated on Jaz. At least physical therapy only happened twice per week. Once the traction was gone, the torture sessions would increase to five days out of seven.

The ice maker ground out some crushed ice. Jaz filled the cup with water and snagged a protein bar from a nearby box. She returned the cup to her mother. After Mom took a drink, Jaz tore the package and handed the bar over.

Geraldine stared at the bar, finally taking it after Jaz nearly stuck it in her mouth.

"How's work going?" Her mother nibbled a corner off the bar.

"All right. Researching negligence claims against pharmaceutical companies. It's a little disheartening that there are so many to sift through." Jaz fidgeted with the edge of the sheets.

"Did you go for a run this morning?" The shadows under Mom's eyes made a rock drop in Jaz's midsection. Her mother shouldn't be worrying about her.

Jaz nodded. "I miss Bailey."

"I thought he called last night." Brown eyes studied her,

reminiscent of her brother's searching gaze.

The first month she dated Bailey, they'd carried on their budding relationship long distance, but since May they'd spent time together every day. Going back to the phone calls and video chats left an aching loneliness behind her ribs.

*You could be in traction.* Things could always be worse but being trapped in the same house with her father was pretty high on Jaz's list of things to avoid.

After her mother had eaten a few bites, Jaz squeezed her thin shoulder. On her trip back to the desk, Jaz tried to ignore the shrine of pictures, medals, and certificates adorning the office wall. A shelf supported several trophies from Drew's high school football career. Three all-league trophies and two all-state trophies proved he was destined to be a running back, in exchange for a college education at least.

But after the Twin Towers attacks, Drew changed. News of oppressive regimes in too many corners of the world escalated, and after high school graduation, Drew enlisted in the Army instead of accepting either of the full scholarships he'd been offered.

That was the only time she'd ever heard her father rail at her brother using the disapproval reserved for her. She'd been floored, but Drew had shaken it off like a just-bathed dog sheds water.

She forced her focus back to the computer. By the time her backside felt numb, she'd filled out three of the five research requests due that week.

When the doorbell chimed, Jaz stretched. "Do you need anything?" she asked her mom on her way past. The protein bar was only half-eaten, but her mother shook her head, eyes fixed on the television.

Jaz swung the door open, and Tabitha Olson stood on the stoop.

"I'm here to spell you." The woman smiled.

Since Jaz returned from the military, she'd attended First Street Church where Tabitha's husband pastored. Her parents attended a Baptist church in Rosewood, and this offer seemed out-of-place.

Tabitha squeezed Jaz's hand. "Elise mentioned you're feeling cooped up. I know she takes an afternoon walk with Kristina. Maybe you could join them. Get some fresh air."

"Mom can't be by herself." *And my father expects me to stay with her.*

Tabitha gestured to herself. "That's why I'm here."

"I couldn't impose on you that way. There are bedpans—"

The pastor's wife held up her hand. "I'm offering. And I'm no stranger to nursing."

Jaz and the woman stared at each other for a few more beats. The pounding in her chest escalated, straining toward the taste of freedom beyond the door.

Jaz nodded and stepped back, sweeping her hand toward the doorway to her right. "She's set up in there."

Tabitha strode past, a cross-body bag bouncing against her hip with each step. Her mother's voice pitched in greeting, and after settling Tabitha with a cup of tea, Jaz dodged into her room for walking shoes.

A few minutes later, Jaz backed her car out of the driveway and headed toward Sweet Grove. Elise replied immediately to her text and told Jaz to meet them at Cider Creek Park. Obviously, this had been a staged intervention, but Jaz couldn't muster any irritation. She needed to escape the oppression of being a caregiver. How did anyone do it full-time?

She parked the car and vaulted from the seat. Her arms reached toward the sky, and she wished to hug the humid air and swirl through the parking lot on giddy feet. Instead, she smiled upward.

*Thanks, Lord. I really needed this.*

Elise and Kristina sauntered along a nearby pathway. Elise waved, and her ponytail gyrated wildly. Both women were younger than Jaz but had gone out of their way to befriend her when she'd attended First Street Church in the spring.

Jaz fell into step with the other women. She inhaled the

sunshine. Golden leaves crunched beneath her sneakers. "This is perfect."

Kristina talked about an argument between the sheriff and a couple regulars at Mabel's. Elise griped about separating a pair of over-eager high schoolers who were making out during youth service. The stories grounded Jaz in the world of normal.

"How's Bailey?" Elise smirked and elbowed Jaz.

"Great. We talk every night. He worries about Tess."

Kristina nodded. "Jeffrey says he's always been an overprotective brother."

"Not overprotective," Jaz argued at the same time Elise said, "That's not a bad thing."

The three women burst into laughter. Tension oozed from Jaz's shoulders, and her palm covered the ache in her side from the hysterics. Fresh air and friendship were good for her mental health.

Elise discussed possible changes to her job at First Street Church, and the wrinkles between her eyebrows indicated more worry than she admitted with her words. Jeffrey had plans lined up to slowly evolve the diner's menu, and Kristina's voice infused with excitement.

"You're blessed that your employer is letting you work from Sweet Grove." Elise glanced toward Jaz.

A trio of birds swooped toward something in the path ahead. Their twitters distracted Jaz, but her walking partners said nothing.

She sighed. "It's boring. I miss Austin."

"Sure it's not Bailey you miss?" Kristina grinned.

Jaz shook her head. "Sure, I miss him, but as far as work goes, I miss talking to the clients. Most days I spent time with kids while their parents discuss pending lawsuits."

"Kids?" Elise arched her brows. "Must not be teenagers. You were pretty hard-nosed with the softball team."

When Elise first asked Jaz to help coach the high school team, Jaz's strict, no-nonsense style hadn't been popular. After a few weeks, it mellowed into something more encouraging and, more importantly, the girls had improved their batting averages.

"Maybe it's your biological clock." Kristina frowned, still staring straight ahead.

*Maybe* her *biological clock is ticking, but I'm not even engaged.* Did she want to be? Her heart thrummed.

"This could be the Lord's way of directing you to something better." Elise's eyes slitted.

"Not in Sweet Grove." Jaz shook her head. "Not as a caregiver." She chuckled to take the sting out of the admissions.

"Let's pray about it."

Elise jerked both of her friends to a stop and said a quick prayer, not even bowing her head or closing her eyes. It was like Jesus stood on the path with them, and shivers prickled along Jaz's arms.

As they returned to the parking lot twenty minutes later, Jaz hugged each woman in turn, thanking them.

"Let's do this a couple days a week." Elise stated it like a done deal.

"Is there someone I can hire to stay with Mom?" Jaz had turned toward her car, but the stiff silence halted her.

"Tabitha enjoys getting out and visiting."

"I can't ask her to take care of Mom."

Kristina apologized and ducked into her car. After she pulled out, waving at them, Elise glared at Jaz. "Then I will. She's not doing it just for you, you know."

Jaz shrugged off Elise's offer, saying she'd text Elise the next time she was available. Mom didn't need the strain of entertaining someone, and Jaz knew her father would see Jaz's break as shirking her responsibilities.

Jaz called a greeting as she entered the house. In the great room, the television was off, the bed was nearly in a full sitting position, and her mother's fingers wrapped around a tea cup. Two glossy magazines were open between the women, who barely paused their conversation when Jaz walked past them into the office.

In fact, Tabitha was still there when Ron Rolle banged through the garage door and called out, "I'm home."

Jaz saved her work and typed an email to her boss. She typed carefully to delay the inevitable, and by the time she emerged from the office, Tabitha was gone. Her father sat on the hospital bed holding her mother's hand.

"I like that sparkle in your eyes." Her father's voice rumbled and tickled. The special tone he used with his wife was so different from what he turned on Jaz that it almost sounded foreign to her ears.

"Tabitha asked if she could stop by a couple times each week." Her mother's eyes lifted and met Jaz's.

The silent message sent mixed emotions flooding through Jaz. Apparently, Elise had been right.

"As long as you don't overdo it." Ron squeezed her hand.

"I need to do more. Just wait until the therapist comes." And like that was an announcement, the doorbell chimed. Jaz scooted around her parents. She felt her father's gaze boring into her back as she hurried to the door.

Once she'd admitted the lithe woman carrying an athletic bag filled with exercise bands and assorted medieval devices, Jaz ducked into her bedroom. She flopped on her bed, her heart racing and stomach tightening as she pressed Bailey's name on the screen of her phone.

Three rings later, he answered.

"Hey, cowboy."

"Well, hello, beautiful. How's your day?" He drawled the words. The lazy Texas accent spiraled through her, awakening a flight of birds in her chest.

"Better."

The timbre of his voice soothed her, and the trapped feelings melted away. How could she go another month without seeing him every day?

# Seventeen

Digital technology didn't remove the quaver of relief that flowed through Jaz's single word. His heart galloped across his chest.

Bailey slumped into the ratty camping chair that accounted for one-fourth of the furniture in his loft and stared at the photo of Jaz he'd clipped to the icebox. The fire in those green eyes and the smirk playing with her berry-delicious lips would be absent.

"How's your mom?" Bailey had lost two mothers—one to jail and drugs, and then MaryAnn's botched surgery. His heart buckled at the thought of Jaz losing hers.

"Bored out of her mind. Hating the dependency."

Bailey hadn't spent much time around Jaz's parents, but Geraldine Rolle seemed loving and nurturing, and Jaz adored her enough to imprison herself within range of her father's air of disapproval.

It was her father Bailey didn't understand. Why should the man be disappointed in his daughter? Jaz was an amazing athlete, a strong woman in mind and body, and someone who made softball a dance of desire. Maybe Bailey was the only one affected by her determination. He hoped he was the only one tasting the sweetness of her lips.

"And you're stir-crazy." Should he address the elephant in the room? No. He'd wait for her to bring up her dad. Bailey could relate to daddy issues even if his own biological father had been in prison for twenty years.

"I'm running every morning, but by mid-afternoon it feels like the room is shrinking." Her sigh dropped a coal in his stomach.

"Why not take another run in the evenings?"

"You realize this is Texas, right?"

He imagined her arching those expressive brows at him. His pulse leapt against his neck. "You could visit Tess."

"She's busy with guests. I've been hanging with Elise some. She convinced Tabitha Olson to spell me this afternoon."

The preacher's wife had been reaching out to Tess since before Bailey moved to Austin. If he'd stayed in Sweet Grove, he could hold Jaz's hand right now and lose himself in the deep waters of her incredible eyes.

But then again, if they'd had only a long-distance relationship over the past four months, she might have found someone else. Foreboding thrummed in his roiling gut.

*You don't have to earn love.* MaryAnn Travers had told him that often enough for the sentiment to still echo in his mind. Some days he even believed it was the truth, but today, not so much.

"Maybe I'll come up this weekend." Bailey held his breath.

"I was thinking about coming back to Austin, picking up a few things and checking in at the office."

He pushed the smart phone away from his face and exhaled. She hadn't decided to leave him behind. His heart ballooned against his ribcage.

"Friday night, late dinner?" His voice sounded like a growl.

"How about I text when I get there? I'm thinking a DVD and popcorn at my place."

They'd spent plenty of Friday nights curled together on the futon in front of her wide screen television. It was his all-time favorite date activity, snuggling and kissing. Heat flushed through him.

"The next three days are going to drag."

"You're such a flatterer." Her voice grew husky, and his heart surged for release from his chest. "Sweet dreams, cowboy."

That night, her voice echoed through his dreams, making

them a little more like the Mexican dinner special than an ice cream sundae.

☙❧☙❧

WHEN THE TEXT CAME AROUND NINE ON FRIDAY NIGHT, Bailey told himself he wasn't pacing. In his apartment, four strides took him from bed to door. Anything less than ten steps couldn't be considered pacing.

His palm slipped across the back of his phone as he flipped it to read the text announcing she'd finally reached her apartment. He shoved the device into his hip pocket, picked up the bag containing kettle corn and Jaz's favorite bottled drink, and jetted out the door. The steps groaned as he trotted down them.

Interminable minutes later, Jaz flung opened the door at her place, flashing her beautiful smile. Bailey pulled her against him, and she sagged into his chest. His palm swept over the soft cotton shirt covering her back. She staggered into the apartment, and he closed the door before cupping her face between his hands.

"I missed you." Her breath caressed his cheek.

Bailey rested his forehead on hers and breathed in the scent of oranges and musky perspiration. His chest pulsed, squeezing his heart and lungs. He couldn't decide if he would faint from lack of oxygen or have a heart attack first.

She pushed upward and brushed her lips over his. Bailey held his eager response in check, letting his mouth soften and mold to hers. His girl tasted as good as she smelled.

Too soon, Jaz stepped back. The smile on her freshly-kissed lips put fire in her green eyes. Bailey couldn't catch his breath for another moment.

"How's your mom?"

"Getting better. The traction should be removed next week."

"Must be tough to be tied to a bed." His neck heated at the alluring picture the words tried to paint in his mind.

Jaz linked her fingers through his and pulled him toward her futon. The bottles clanked together in his bag, cooling his thoughts.

"What'd you bring me?"

Another soft smile chased away the tired lines around her eyes and mouth. Bailey offered her the drinks and kettle corn. She squealed like it was Christmas morning and gave him another quick kiss.

Soon they snuggled together while the movie played. He didn't care that his skin burned where they touched, pasting his shirt to his sweaty torso. The fact his back was flushed and damp where it rested against the cushion didn't faze him.

With his girl in his arms, all was right with the world.

# Eighteen

Saturday surrealism carried Jaz along while she sorted clothes and straightened up the apartment. How did the place get dirty when no one had been there for a couple weeks? Still, the fragrance of her citrus candle welcomed her home.

Mid-morning, she and Bailey jogged a half-mile to the UT campus. When she'd moved to Austin, Jaz wanted an apartment close to campus since she'd been helping with the softball team. Now, being there stirred something in her that couldn't be defined as healthy. The nagging sense of unfulfilled purpose that had dogged her from discharge to Sweet Grove a few months before reached dark tentacles toward the peace she thought she'd found.

At least running dulled those sensations. After several miles around the track and the campus paths, they stopped at a bench. Jaz rested her heel on the wooden slats and began stretching the major muscles in her legs. Bailey, hands on hips, paced in a circle. She'd become accustomed to seeing him in shorts and t-shirts, but she preferred the Wranglers, button up shirts, and cowboy boots. Her slowing heart rate spiked at the mere thought.

A pair of guys wearing jeans and hoodies ambled past. One of them backtracked, stopping a few feet away. Jaz glanced up into golden eyes and a face nearly a brown as hers.

"Ming?"

"I didn't expect to see you here, Jazzer." The smile made his thin features attractive.

Jaz dropped her foot and rounded the bench. They shook

hands, Ming holding on after she'd let go. They'd been in the pre-law program together, and she hadn't seen him since joining the military seven years ago.

"Are you a student at UT?" His gaze raked down her, lingering on her exposed calves.

She shook her head. Why did guys do that? Look at a girl like something to be devoured? "I live nearby, and this is an easy place for a run."

Ming glanced toward Bailey, who stretched his quad muscle nearby, glaring at the guys like he'd noticed their devouring perusal, too. Jaz tried to communicate that he should join her without saying anything.

"What brings you here?" Jaz shifted her weight away from Ming. "Didn't you graduate years ago?"

Ming nodded and shuffled closer. "Right on track. Somehow I made it without my genius-grade study buddy."

Jaz sidled backward and grabbed the bench with one hand. She stretched her quad, hoping to cover her retreat with normal actions. She glanced toward Bailey, and he dropped his foot and side-stepped closer, but every muscle in his body tensed like a mountain cat read to pounce.

"I'm on staff, teaching a few of the pre-law classes." Ming straightened to his full height which barely matched hers. "Planning to get a graduate degree in contract mediation, and I attend classes free if I'm employed here."

She nodded, not really interested. Was he bragging about his accomplishments? She thought she'd accepted her role as a paralegal, happy to help people without the stress of being responsible for winning court cases.

Bailey stopped within arm's reach. Jaz dropped her foot and slid her hand into his. "Bailey, this is Ming. We were in the same pre-law cohort back in the day. Ming, this is my boyfriend."

Ming's eyebrows rose. He scanned Bailey before extending his hand. By the way Ming grimaced during their shake, Jaz guessed Bailey was showing his cowboy strength.

"What do you do?" Ming rubbed his hand on his hip.

"Architectural design." Bailey's voice rumbled, and shivers dove into Jaz's stomach. That deep voice.

"You're an architect, then? With a firm? Or independent?"

"A firm." Bailey gritted his teeth.

"Nice to see you again," Jaz said, "but we've got to run." She laughed at her pun, but it sounded false in her ears.

Her former classmate shook his head. "Did you ever finish law school? I was shocked when you dropped out." His lips pursed into something that made Jaz think he'd bitten a green persimmon.

"I'm working with Boldt & Associates." Her abdomen ached like she'd sprinted on a full stomach. Why not give her job title? Or admit she had no college degree?

"A small firm. Two brothers, right?"

Jaz's fingers tightened in Bailey's. "Right. Great place to work, but we're late." She twisted toward the path they'd finished running. "See you later."

Bailey didn't resist, and soon they left Ming and his friend behind. Bailey slowed from their near jogging pace.

"Ex-boyfriend?"

Something in his tone made Jaz stiffen. She glanced at his profile, but his face could have been granite. "No. Nothing more than study partners and friends."

Bailey sighed. "You didn't tell him you're not a lawyer. Do you wish you were?"

A riot started in her stomach and made the ache in her side grow. Did she? And since when was she ashamed of her job?

"Haven't really thought about going back to school. Lots of other things on my mind lately."

Bailey's thumb rubbed the back of her hand. Tingles raced like a shock treatment through her, revving her pulse again.

"He thought you were too good for me." His tone was resigned.

Jaz stopped, pulling Bailey to a halt a half-step later. Doubt troubled the deep water of his eyes, and the ache moved higher in her chest.

"He doesn't even know you."

"But he knows you."

They stared into each other's faces for several pounding heartbeats. Was he jealous? Or was this about Bailey's low self-esteem?

"He knew me seven years ago. I'm not the same person." Losing Drew and her military career had certainly changed her. Whatever Ming thought, becoming a lawyer didn't mean anything. Some of the worst people she knew held that job.

He dropped her hand, and his jaw tensed. "You don't have to be a lawyer to impress me."

Jaz leaned into him and pecked his cheek. "One of the many reasons I'm with you and not someone like that." She gestured vaguely toward where they'd met the other men.

When she took his hand, he didn't resist. They walked toward the nearby Chipotle hand-in-hand, but a silent question lingered between them.

⁂

SUNDAY CAME TOO SOON FOR JAZ WHO WASN'T IN A HURRY to return to Sweet Grove. The storefront where Young and Alive Fellowship met was no one's typical church, but peace rushed through Jaz's veins upon pushing through the glass doors. Upbeat contemporary music filtered through a speaker overhead, and the air-conditioned air held a hint of warmth.

As Bailey followed her inside, a couple stepped from a room along the makeshift hallway toward another set of doors into the assembly hall. The man smiled, his gray flecked hair making him look older than thirty-five. The woman's face lit up, and she grabbed Jaz into a hug. Her pregnant stomach pressed against Jaz, and the child kicked its protest.

"Whoa! He's active today." Jaz refrained from touching the swollen belly. She wouldn't want people presuming that way on her.

Melanie's hand dropped to her stomach. Her slanted eye-lids creased further until the joy-filled brown orbs nearly disappeared. "He missed you."

"Nice to see you, Bailey." Melanie's husband shook Bailey's hand.

When Bailey pulled away, Jaz's lower back chilled. She'd attended this church years ago, but it was a transitional group with hardly any of the same members. More than half the congregation was between twenty and thirty, though, and the atmosphere was open and inclusive. Exactly the home her wayward spirit needed.

As they pressed forward, more people greeted them. Jaz enjoyed the small group studies but had chosen to sleep later today, knowing she'd need those extra hours. Since her mother's accident, her sleeping patterns had been off, plaguing Jaz with aching muscles and relentless wakefulness in Sweet Grove.

One of the guys who played basketball with Bailey waved them into a row of chairs. They'd barely sat down when his girlfriend raced over. Her face glowed like she'd swallowed a thousand watts of illumination.

"We're getting married." She stretched the final word out and shoved her left hand at Jaz's face.

A sparkling diamond solitaire glinted. While Jaz's heart dove into the floor, she forced her lips into a smile. These two had started dating after Bailey moved to Austin. Maybe it was her own limited experience with the steadfastness of men that made her wonder how they already knew they wanted to spend forever together.

"Congratulations." Jaz stood and hugged the younger woman.

*Lord, let this be the right choice for them.*

The negative feelings floated away. God could handle their future. Jaz's smile relaxed into something genuine.

In a few moments, the praise band began playing and the worship leader led in prayer. Jaz sang the repetitive words.

Melodies flowed around and through her. When they sat for the sermon, she leaned towards Bailey, and his arm rested along the back of her padded seat.

*Lord, I needed this. Help Mom get better. Thank You for being with her.*

Her father's stern visage intruded on the prayer, and Jaz's eyelids fluttered. The pastor still spoke in his excited tenor, and a different slide projected on the wall behind him.

*The trial of your faith works patience,* she read.

She sighed. Hadn't her father been trying her patience for a lifetime? She'd hoped being an adult would change things somehow, that maybe he'd stop foisting his expectations on her. Or at least stop being disappointed in her decisions.

*Lord, You'll show me if You want me to go back to college, right?*

The delicate web of peace wrapped around her searching heart again.

She was only in Sweet Grove for a few more weeks. She could endure whatever her father doled out.

Bailey squeezed her shoulder. She glanced at him and released the last of her worries. One of his eyebrows twitched upward, asking if she was okay.

Her lips relaxed into a smile. His heart-tugging grin answered.

Yes—she was home.

᪥᪥᪥

BY THE NEXT TUESDAY, THE CONSTANT CITY NOISE AND Austin traffic ground through Bailey's even temper. The city strangled him. He was there to pursue Jaz and his design career. Without the girl, the career and its associated paycheck lost appeal.

During his evening call with Jaz, Bailey paced like a caged animal. His studio apartment located above a second-hand clothing store, while cheap and only a few blocks from his office, wasn't much larger than a zoo exhibit. He'd snagged it months ago because there was no commute and Jaz's place was five minutes away.

Except when she was a hundred miles south.

Bailey scrolled to his recent calls and selected his sister's mobile number. He'd talked to her on Sunday, but the constant whoosh of automobiles passing outside his single paned windows wasn't filling the void.

She answered on the third ring.

"Everything okay?" Her sweet concern melted him.

Bailey slumped into the folding chair and leaned his elbows on the square card table. He imagined the scarred walnut table in the ranch dining room and couldn't remember why he'd thought moving away was a good plan.

"I miss you."

"Huh. You miss Jaz, you mean."

Bailey rubbed his forehead over his knuckles. "I miss you. And the ranch." He swallowed a lump rising in his throat. "And yeah, Jaz. We just talked on the phone."

They'd tried video calls, but Bailey didn't have wireless Internet at his apartment, and his older phone couldn't keep up with the streaming. Maybe tomorrow he'd stay late at the office and use their Wi-Fi.

"You've got it bad." Her laugh tinkled across the miles.

The hardness in his chest eased. He wasn't going to argue the obvious. "Need some help around the ranch? I'm thinking about asking for a week."

"You haven't worked there long enough to take time off."

He hated that she was right but despised the yawning emptiness of days— or nights — without Jaz even more. And he missed the barnyard smell and the feel of a horse moving beneath him. Morning came alive when he watched the sun rise from horseback. Nothing freed coiling tension like galloping across a pasture.

"So how is the ranch?"

Tess's pause told him what he hadn't wanted to ask outright. On Sunday, she'd raved about the two families who'd spent the weekend and how wonderful it was to bake Mom's cinnamon rolls for them.

"I'm running some web specials, but tourist season is about over. I'll come up with some holiday packages and hope to rent a few rooms during the winter school breaks."

When he'd left in the spring, her major private investor had been on site helping with repairs and organizing the business side of the guest ranch. The guy had a major crush on Tess, but sometime during her sold-out summer, the guy took off again.

His money was still backing things, but Bailey knew running the day-to-day ranching activities was beyond Tess's capabilities. She'd outsourced to a few neighbors, but all that did was cut into her profit margin.

"Did you get that last guest bath in?"

The seven-bedroom house made a great guest lodge. Tess had taken over the master suite downstairs and converted the room he'd used when his father was ill back into a parlor. The investor had funded and overseen the addition of bathrooms to four of the rooms upstairs, dividing a smaller bedroom into two nice-sized bathrooms and adding smaller ones to two of the larger bedrooms.

The final room—used by MaryAnn for crafting and sewing—still needed to be renovated. He'd drawn the plans and helped get the permits and county approval, but he'd been busy making sure the barn and corrals were safe and accessible for their city guests.

"I wanted to wait until the other rooms weren't booked." The sadness lacing her tone told the true story.

Boxing up projects that had been the heart of evenings with their mother was too difficult. He could understand. He'd helped her clear out his dad's things before moving to Austin, and every item held bittersweet memories.

"I could help with the demo and remodel."

"I can handle it, Lee. It's my ranch."

Her possessiveness of the ranch had grown exponentially

after they'd secured ownership of the property. His stomach clenched as he thought of those grim days when there had been no will and an over-zealous blood relative circled like a buzzard. Of course, if it hadn't been for that trouble, he probably wouldn't have spent time with Jaz.

*Every trial is a blessing, if you look at it "om the right angle.* More wisdom from his mother.

"I didn't say you couldn't handle things. I want to help." He was her big brother. She could pretend she didn't need him, but in this case, he knew the truth.

"A weekend is plenty of time." She sighed, and he heard a yip from her end of the call.

His lips curled into a smile. Poppet was probably begging for dinner leftovers or anything else she thought was edible.

"There's an empty room for me this weekend?"

After a lengthy pause, she said, "I have four empty rooms. Unless someone drops in or books last minute."

"I can stay in the barn."

In June, her investor had cleaned out the largest storage room and fixed it up, saying it would be perfect for a future ranch manager. Once the dude ranch could support someone to oversee the stock, ranching demonstrations, and horseback rides.

"See you Friday night, then?" She sounded less irritated about the prospect.

"Wild horses couldn't keep me away, little sis." He drawled out the words, imagining them sitting with the Traverses watching John Wayne movies. *True Grit* was one of Tess's favorites.

She giggled. "You're so NOT the Duke of anything. Love you."

Before he could respond in kind, the call disconnected.

No matter what she said, Tess still needed him. That assurance lightened the discontent nibbling at his master plan.

As he plugged his phone into the charger, Bailey grinned

and imagined surprising his girl. Her face blooming with shock and joy became a central part of his dreams.

# *Nineteen*

**T**hursday, the orthopedic specialist visited the house. As he started unscrewing bolts from Mom, Jaz evacuated, excusing herself to find boxes for the unnecessary weights.

For the first time since she'd been home, Jaz sat across the table from her mother at dinner. After warning her mother to take things slow, her father helped Geraldine with her first real shower. Jaz tried not to grit her teeth at her father's needless words. No one wanted the traction back.

Recovery sped forward. Except when her mother asked to return to her own bed, the doctor told her to wait at least another week.

"It's easier to get in and out of the hospital bed. I expect the pain will spike now that you're moving around." The surgeon gazed over the top of wire-rimmed glasses, reminding Jaz of her high school chemistry teacher.

By the time Friday afternoon arrived, Jaz's lower back throbbed from shifting her mother from bed to wheelchair to restroom to wheelchair to recliner and back again. Once Tabitha arrived for her afternoon visit and assured Jaz she could assist Geraldine into and out of the chair, Jaz ducked into the garage.

The afternoon was warm and breezy, and she decided to bike into town and visit with Elise. The ache in her back eased as she rolled the bike into the driveway. After topping off the air in the tires and greasing up the gears on the back wheel, Jaz pushed the bike toward the road.

An older coupe slowed and eased past. Tinted windows made it impossible to see inside, although a shadow made it seem like only a driver occupied the vehicle. Hair at the base of her neck snapped to attention. Was the person watching her?

The car barely cleared the driveway before shifting into reverse. The passenger window rolled down. A broad-shouldered man with short, wild dreadlocks leaned toward the opening. His dark features blended with the shadowy interior.

"Is this the Rolle place?" White teeth flashed.

Jazlyn rested the bike against her stomach and crossed her arms over her chest. The flimsy mountain bike wasn't much of a barrier, but it eased the tension the stranger's question raised. "Who wants to know?"

The engine noise changed, and the car rolled slightly. The man leaned closer and studied her with somber brown eyes. "Jazlyn, right? Zoom said you were feisty." Now he smiled, but the emotion in his eyes didn't match his easy tone or expression.

A war entangled her pounding heart and churning stomach. Jaz took a steadying breath. Zoom was the nickname Drew's unit gave him. "How do you know Drew?"

"Afghanistan. I'm one of the guys he saved." The intense gaze dropped to the passenger seat.

"You know how he died?" Excitement leaked into her tone. How macabre was that?

The Army declared that her brother had died in a "training accident," but everyone knew that meant he'd been on a covert op. He was a Special Forces munitions expert. Eight years later, the files still hadn't been declassified. While she served in a JAG office, Jaz had tried to discover the truth behind his death but she had no access to paper records at the Pentagon and her security clearance wasn't high enough to view the computer database.

If this stranger knew the truth, it might be worth wading through the pain of reliving the loss. They would have answers, and that would grant them a modicum of closure.

"I was on the mission."

Jaz studied the stiff features. He was a handsome guy, and even the world-worn expression couldn't hide the fact that he was closer to her age than her brother's. Blood pounded against her skull. She sidled back, listening to the clicking of her bike's gears.

"Why are you here?"

"Drew asked me to come."

Jaz snorted. "Nearly eight years have passed since Drew asked anyone anything."

Full lips pressed into a white line. "I was recovering. Or not."

He'd been injured. Why hadn't she realized that?

"I'm sure my parents will be thrilled to hear your message, but my father's at work and my mother has company."

He shrugged and leaned closer. "The message is for you."

The bottom dropped out of her churning stomach. Jaz gaped at him, eyes blinking while her mind spun.

"I—okay." Her fingers dug into the handlebars on the bike.

"Were you going somewhere?"

She nodded. "I don't know your name."

"Billy." He stuck his hand out the window. "William Jefferson. The guys called me Prez."

She blinked, wondering if the letters she'd saved and carried from college to base after base in a plastic shoe box mentioned this guy. She hadn't read them in more than a year.

A spike twisted in her chest, and she covered the spot with one hand. The bike seat slapped against her hip bone, but she hardly noticed.

He withdrew his outstretched arm back into the vehicle. "Is there somewhere we could talk? Somewhere public since you don't even know me."

Jaz swallowed and tried to make her voice work. After a long pause, she said, "Let me put my bike away. There's a place in town."

Her leaden feet made the return to the garage burdensome. Still her mind whirled, and the thoughts dizzied her until brown spots danced on the edges of her vision.

Drew had left a message for her with a guy from his platoon. Someone who had been injured, too, but who Drew trusted to deliver his final thoughts to his little sister. Was it a letter? Or would the guy be reciting something? How did she know this guy was for real?

*Lord, I need help here.*

Assurance whisked away the anxiety in her gut. Why would someone pretend to have a message from a dead guy? And if he'd intended harm, wouldn't he have come while Jaz was in a more vulnerable spot? He'd been recovering, he said. Maybe his injuries had been severe enough to require years of surgery and rehab.

A ribbon of certainty wove its way around her pounding heart and clenching stomach. God's answer to her plea for help?

Jaz sent a text to her mother and Elise, letting them know she'd be at the high school with a friend of Drew's.

The scent of gasoline and grease swirled up her nose as she took calming breaths. She'd been waiting for years to learn about Drew's final mission. And if he had a message for her, she wanted—no, needed—to hear it.

By the time Jaz returned to the idling car, the passenger door stood open. Billy leaned against his own seat, staring out the side window away from her. When she slammed the door, he jolted like he'd been hit with a bullet.

His foot slipped onto the gas, revving the engine. His eyes, wide and wild like a spooked animal's, stared at her.

"Sorry." Jaz forced the word from her suddenly tight throat. She directed him toward town, keeping the conversation light by relaying tidbits about Drew's high school years.

"No one could believe he passed up a full-ride to play football." Billy gulped and glanced her way. "Not the football part, but who chooses Uncle Sam over that?"

"Drew. It was his mission to rescue everyone."

Billy nodded. "Once we got to know him, we all understood."

They pulled into the lot beside the high school stadium. Jaz ducked inside the chain link fence and strolled out to the track. Billy fell in beside her, his loosely tied high tops flopping with every step. He walked with a slight limp, favoring his left leg and holding his back stiffly, arms hardly swinging as they paced side-by-side in the outer two lanes.

"Can you tell me what happened? How Drew died?" Jaz studied the man's profile. "I know it's classified, and I don't care about locations or even the mission."

Billy stared straight ahead. His Adam's apple bobbed, and Jaz decided staring at him probably didn't help.

"I was the newbie on the squad. Hadn't been there for six weeks. It was my first incursion." He paused. "Last, too."

Jaz squeezed his forearm. The contact shocked her, and she pulled away before he could read anything other than comfort into the gesture. It unsettled her to feel so at ease with this stranger. *It's the Drew connection.*

"Zoom set the charges while I watched the perimeter with most of the team." He looked at her. "Zoom is—"

"Drew. He told me his nickname." A ball of tears choked her. After she gulped them away, she said, "Thought it was an ironic twist since he had the quickest 40- and 100-yard dash times in the state."

Billy dropped his chin. His shoes clopped. A bird called from a nearby tree, and another answered from the stands. "Everything seemed quiet. Then they passed a doorway that was in the shadows. It burst open, and Hell broke loose."

Jaz stumbled and wondered if she'd tripped over her stomach which had plunged with those last three words. Drew went through Hell on his way to Heaven. Moisture burned her wide, blinking eyes.

"Doc was nearest to me, and when Zoom and Panther fell

to the automatic fire, he pulled me with him, wanting to get them out of harm's way and treat them."

Jaz tried to picture a dark, dusty street with gunfire punctuating what should be a peaceful scene.

"Anyway, Panther wasn't hurt as bad as Zoom, so Doc pulled him back to the perimeter while I laid down cover fire."

*Thunk. Thump.* The slap of his soles on the track added an eerie soundtrack to the tale.

"I'd rolled Zoom behind a rattletrap car. His breath was wheezing." Billy paused, and when he continued, his tone was thick. "He asked how far to the building he'd wired. Said he was going to blow it and I needed to get out of range."

Jaz could see her brother, gasping for breath and deciding to sacrifice himself for all of them. Did he think the explosion would kill the insurgents? Or did he figure it would be the perfect cover for his team to withdraw and fight another day?

"No man left behind, I said. He looked at me—deep, the way he did that made your soul feel naked—and told me to get out of there." Billy slashed at his face and turned his head away. "Then he pulled something out of his hip pocket and made me promise to deliver it once I got stateside."

Jaz scolded her rising emotions. She'd mourned her brother already, and this confirmation of his heroism should make her feel proud, not weepy.

"I shoved the folded envelope into my pocket. He told me he'd count to three once I started running." *Thump. Thwack.* "There was a lull of a couple seconds, and I barely heard him tell me to go. I fired toward the enemy and bolted back to the perimeter." He shook his head. "The explosion knocked me down and made my ears ring for a week."

"Is that how you were injured?"

A grim smile curled his wide lips. "We were ambushed at the evac site. Doc and I were running with Panther's stretcher when machine gun fire cut our legs out from under us."

Silence stretched. Jaz focused on the sound of her breathing, shallow like she'd been running. She inhaled deeply and waited to exhale.

"Only two of our guys made it out without serious injuries. Our objective was destroyed, but so was our team." "Intense." What could she say to such a story?

"It was a month before I was coherent enough to talk to anyone. Doc asked about the envelope. I guess they'd found it while they were putting tourniquets on my legs."

Another yawn of silence. A whisper of wind cooled Jaz's flushed face.

Drew had sent her a message. After they'd completed half a lap, Jaz said, "So you got sent home?"

"I lost one leg, and the other knee was blown apart. That was a long recovery, but the nightmares…"

Jaz squeezed his arm again. "I'm sorry you had to go through that."

Billy stopped walking and glanced at her fingers resting on a muscled forearm, a shade more pecan pie than her smoky quartz hand.

She dropped it to her side. He dug in the front pocket of his shorts and withdrew a wallet.

Her heart palpitated, and she tried to catch her breath. He flipped open the bi-fold and pulled a dirty, wrinkled envelope out of the bill pocket.

"I tried to locate you a few times about three years after, but you'd left the university, and I hung up when I called the Sweet Grove number. Then that was disconnected."

She nodded, feeling like a bobble-head doll. "They use mobiles now."

"After I met Reesa, she told me the way to get closure was to keep my promise. I started searching for you again. I didn't expect to find you today. I figured I'd have to beg your parents for your address."

Their gazes locked. "You could have mailed this." The envelope felt smooth beneath her fingers. An electric current tingled its way from the palm of her hand into her heart. Jaz yearned to hug the paper, sniff it for lingering traces of her hero.

Billy shook his head. "Nah. I needed to deliver the message in person."

They stared at the envelope. Jaz swallowed. An unreasonable dizziness made her wobble. His hand on her upper arm steadied her.

"I'd like to know what it says." He shrugged. "But Reesa said you'd want to read it in private."

His dark eyes begged her to deny it. She couldn't. The flimsy envelope held the final link to her idol. She wanted to savor the words. Alone.

"Reesa's one smart gal."

He barked out a laugh. "Maybe not since she's going to marry me."

Jaz blinked her burning eyes. "Congratulations," she said in a barely audible whisper.

They strode toward the fence and his car. Jaz's feet itched to run, but she stayed beside Billy, slowing her pace as they started down the slope toward the gate.

"Did you want to meet my mom? She'd love to hear the story."

Billy walked on. Just before they reached the exit, he stopped. "I delivered the message. I'm done."

The hollow behind his eyes reminded her of her own reflection for a couple years after Drew's death. Jaz stepped into him and wrapped her arms around his shoulders, hugging him like it was her final moment with Drew. His hands grazed her back, barely touching, but she couldn't move away for several heartbeats.

She stepped back, blinking away the tears. "I can never thank you enough."

He nodded. The ride back to her parents' house stretched on endlessly. The letter burned against her palm.

Drew's message from beyond the grave whispered to her soul.

# Twenty

On his way to the ranch— earlier than Tess would expect—Bailey detoured down Main Street. Not that he missed mowing the athletic fields and fixing every loose bolt at the schools, but there were good memories, too. Like the day Jaz hit a record number of home runs, and the day she hit one right in his lap.

He grinned and cranked his window all the way down. He shoved his hat higher, tapped his fingers along with the contemporary Christian song playing through his scratchy old speakers, and drank in the smell of country. Tension bled from his shoulders and back, and a sense of homecoming welled as he drove past First Street Church and other familiar buildings.

He tapped the brakes at the parking lot beside the stadium. The steering wheel fought the turn as his wheels bounced over the speed bump. A souped-up Honda Civic parked near the gate took up a couple spaces.

Bailey kept his foot off the gas, and his truck idled its way closer to the car. The chrome wheels and wide tires reminded him of some of the racers he'd studied as a teenager. Not that he'd ever have the sort of money to doctor a car that way. It wouldn't have been practical on a ranch anyway.

But he didn't live on a ranch anymore. He stopped beside the car, squinting to see beyond the tinted windows.

His peripheral vision caught movement inside the fence. His gaze swept upward, and his eyes bulged.

Long legs sporting fitted yoga capris covered by a long, fitted t-shirt filled his vision. He'd know those legs from any angle. His heart leapt, and he reached for the gear shift. A smoke-skinned stranger stood beside Jaz, his hands buried in the pockets of baggy jeans.

As Bailey's fingers latched onto the shifter, Jaz threw herself against the stranger's chest. Her arms gripped his shoulders, and Bailey's stomach bucked into his heart. His breath left in a whoosh.

Who was this guy? Why was Jaz throwing herself at him?

As the man's hands came up—did his wrists graze her hips? — Bailey's control flew out the window. He stomped on the gas, made a U-turn, and sped out of the lot. When he bounced over the speed bump, his chest slammed the steering wheel. The rattling of the truck's bed couldn't drown the thrum of blood rushing through his head and pounding in his ears.

The truck's back end skidded around the next curve. Bailey plowed mindlessly through town, turned on Orchard Way, and finally bumped onto dirt-packed Armstrong Road. His foot relaxed on the gas and the jouncing lessened.

Jazlyn with her arms around another man's neck branded itself into his mind's eye. The distance was too much for her. Or maybe her old military boyfriend came back. Whatever the case, she'd replaced Bailey. He knew it would happen.

At the ranch, he pulled next to the barn and shut off the ignition. Closing his eyes brought the scene alive. Would he ever unsee it? His heart throbbed out its usual rhythm. Amazing that a broken heart still worked.

When his breathing slowed enough to hear the snuffling dogs rather than his pumping blood, Bailey shoved open the door. The squealing hinges sent the dogs ducking out of the way. They were back before he could slam the door, backsides wagging and tongues flapping at his hands.

Bailey crouched beside them. He ruffled the Aussie's ears while the other shepherd sniffed his chin. After giving the dogs a thorough petting, Bailey stood and glanced around. The buildings were freshly painted. Afternoon sunlight glistened off the white paddock fence.

Shamgar whinnied, and another horse answered from the back of the barn.

*Home.* Among these animals who were also cast off and unwanted, he belonged. He understood them, and they accepted him. No one wanted the animals, either, so Bailey rescued them. Their brokenness soothed his ragged soul while his hands fed their bodies and his steadiness calmed them.

Why had he thought loving Jaz would work out? Whenever he loved someone, they left.

He let himself into the paddock. Shamgar trotted over and snuffed at Bailey's pockets.

A few months ago, Bailey had stood at this very fence. He'd told Jaz goodbye because his heart knew they couldn't have a future. Maybe he didn't know it was because her old boyfriend would come back, or she'd realize he wasn't worth loving, but he sensed it.

His palm slid down Shamgar's mottled gray neck and cooing whispers eased from his lips.

Bailey had let Tess convince him he could find love. He'd believed that Jaz was different, that she saw beyond his foster-child-throwaway exterior. And he'd chased her, all the way to Austin.

Shamgar tossed his mane and bumped his forehead into Bailey's chest.

"Miss me, boy?" The words croaked out of an aching throat.

Bailey scratched the dark spot covered by the gray and black forelock. Shamgar snorted.

He belonged here. Bailey hadn't truly fit in Austin. And apparently, he'd been nothing but a diversion for Jaz. A wrenching feeling behind his breastbone made him gasp. He closed his eyes and rested his forehead against the gelding's.

Her silky face beneath his hands. Those berry lips eager against his. The smile that lit up the world so much more than the sunshine ever had. Green eyes that delved into his aching soul. Moments together played on the back of his eyelids, as fictional as the latest film.

"Fool." He growled the word.

Shamgar shied back a step. Barking from the house pulled Bailey's attention in that direction. The screen door slammed, and his bubbly blonde sister stood on the porch. "I didn't expect you for hours."

Bailey ground his teeth together. He didn't want to face Tess any more than he wanted to relive his months with Jaz. As usual, his preferences didn't matter much to God.

He slid between the rails and jogged toward the house. The siding glowed a pale taupe, a dark blue porch and trim with barn red shutters beside the windows accenting it nicely. Above the front door a sign read "Homestead of Fritz and MaryAnn Travers." Emotion stung his eyes.

Tess had done it. She'd brought her dream to life and honored their parents by naming the ranch for them.

He wrapped her in a hug, noticing how her shoulder blades dug into his forearms. Had she lost weight?

When he stepped back, his gaze swept her from head to toe. She looked the same. Maybe those purple smudges hadn't been beneath her eyes, but the smile crinkled the edges as it always had.

"Guess I can throw another potato in the pot." Tess pinched his cheek and turned toward the door.

Her braid swung out and he tugged the end of it, stopping her in her tracks.

"A man needs meat with his potatoes."

"Ha."

As soon as she opened the screen door, Poppet bounded out. Bailey crouched down and let the lolling tongue bathe his face. He caressed her floppy brown and white ears. She yipped and groaned, her fluffy tail shaking her backside left and right.

He'd been missed. All the animals greeted him like he'd been gone for years instead of weeks. And Tess's arms around his waist grounded him.

When he entered the house, his phone rumbled against his hip. He pulled it out. Jaz's text sat on the lock screen. *Ca! me.*

Since they'd begun dating, Bailey had always responded immediately to her messages. Within ten minutes. There was never a meeting at work that would keep him longer than that. And he would happily pull over if he was driving.

Hearing her voice had meant more to him than anything.

A vacuum sucked the heart from his chest. Today, the thought of hearing her voice made him nauseous. He didn't want to hear how the guy she really loved had shown up to reclaim his spot in her life.

Whenever he tried to convince him he had nothing to offer her, she'd argued that she was the one without a purpose. But he'd been right in the end. He shrugged the thoughts away and hung his hat on the peg inside the door.

When his phone rang twenty minutes later, he still wasn't ready to face Jaz. He almost ignored the call, but Tess looked at him with raised eyebrows.

He sauntered onto the porch before answering.

"Hey." *Beautiful.* But the usual greeting stuck in his throat.

"Hey, cowboy. Sorry I couldn't wait for you to call. Did I interrupt anything?"

He evicted the frog from his windpipe. "Nope. What's up?" His heart pounded so loudly, he nearly missed her next words.

"I got a letter from Drew today."

*Huh?* Her brother had been buried for seven years. How could she get a letter from him?

Bailey leaned over the porch railing. "What? How?"

"It freaked me out, too. He was carrying it in his pocket on that final mission." Her voice faded away.

His chest tightened at the thought of her choked with tears.

*Buck up.* A replay of the embrace she'd shared with that stranger accompanied the reminder.

He straightened and gritted his teeth.

"It wasn't like a goodbye letter. More like the letter he'd been writing to me before the mission. He asked Billy to deliver it."

Billy? Was that whose arms she'd fallen into?

"Seven years to deliver it?" He grunted. That was hard to believe.

"Billy was injured, and then he was fighting PTSD. But he came through." She choked to a stop again.

He supposed a good boyfriend would ask about the letter. But he'd seen her in another man's arms, and this might be his only chance to end it, walk away with his head held high.

"I saw you."

After a short pause, she asked, "What are you talking about, Bailey?"

Did she sound guilty? Had there been a different pitch in her tone? If he could look her in the eye, she wouldn't be able to hide anything. But then, she would be able to read the devastation on his face, too.

No. It was better this way.

"I'm at the ranch. I left Austin at lunch."

He heard her breathing on the other end of the line. "Why didn't you come by here?" As

if she would have been there.

"I drove by the high school." He gritted his teeth again. "I saw you."

She gasped. "That was Billy. The guy from Drew's squad."

"You were in his arms." The ice in his voice coated his throat and his chest. Good. Maybe it would numb the emptiness aching there.

"To thank him for delivering Drew's letter."

"He's the guy you broke up with a few months ago. And now you're back together."

"What?"

Her outrage almost convinced him he'd been wrong. A small voice whispered to let her explain, but Bailey squelched it. He'd heard it all before. He was too much trouble. He wasn't worth loving.

"I'm out."

"Bailey — no —"

He pulled the phone from his ear, ended the call, and then powered off the phone.

God help him, he wouldn't survive hearing her voice for another second.

# Twenty-one

Jaz stared between the phone and the letter. Nausea and vertigo spun the room on its side. Her knees crumbled, and she sagged onto the bed.

He's *the guy you broke up with. Now you're back together.* What was Bailey talking about?

Jaz wanted to share the contents of the letter with someone who would listen to her heart. If Mom wasn't in her own world of pain, she would gladly share this with her. But for several months, the only person she revealed—even wanted to reveal—her deepest thoughts and feelings to was Bailey.

*I saw you. You were in his arms.*

Tears flooded her eyes. If he thought he could just hang up on her, he should know better. The man had moved to Austin to win her heart and trust. His words, not hers. And he'd done it.

But he didn't trust her? And he wouldn't even let her explain about Billy or the letter?

Jaz lay back on the pillows. After her eyes stopped burning, she unfolded the paper that had initiated all this drama. And her lips twitched. Because she could hear her brother, as if he stood beside the bed and spoke the words swimming in ink.

*Hey Slugger,*

*I'm not surprised to hear your batting average. You're a natural, oh, and I know the guy who taught you that amazing le"-handed cut.*

*Things are hot and du$ here. Most of the time we're prepping for missions, but there's not much actual action. Until there is, and then it's fu$-on adrenaline for a few hours and back to boredom. I'$ try to sign up for COM time and ca$ you and the folks. I guess you'$ be back home end of May?*

*We're breaking in a new guy. Doc says he looks about 18, but he can put a spiral on a football. And no, I'm not having second thoughts about college. Thanks for asking, Dad.*

*This job is more important than touchdowns and college de-grees. Around here, someone has to stand up and protect the ones who need it.*

*I'm proud of you. I close my eyes and imagine I can hear the crack of the bat against the bat when you bring another runner home. Can you hear me cheering? Mine is the loud, obnoxious voice chanting, "Slug it."*

*Always follow your dreams. I've found that's the secret to being fulfilled and feeling centered in God's will (bet you never thought you'd hear me use preacher terms like that, huh?) Sending a hug and a noogie.*

*Your Bro,*

*Drew*

Her eyelids fluttered, and tears dribbled down the side of her face.

He loved her. He was proud of her. And he made it sound like Dad nagged him about college, too. Jaz couldn't imagine that. Drew was the golden child, and even if the Army wasn't Dad's choice for Drew, he still supported him. She knew be-cause the man's chest swelled with pride as her parents watched her brother parade across the field, graduating from boot camp, then Special Forces training, and finally his demo-litions training.

But only her mother showed up for Jaz's military gradu-ations

The hum of the garage door startled her. Jaz sprung up from the bed, splashed cold water on her face, and stared at her reflection—eyes a little puffy, but not an obvious "I've been bawling" look.

She sauntered into the kitchen where her mother was try-ing to pull herself up against the counter.

"Mom!"

Geraldine jerked and crumpled. Her backside grazed the wheelchair and spun it to one side.

Jaz dove forward in a second-base-slide under her mother, taking the brunt of Mom's weight against her chest. Air whooshed from her lungs.

Jaz grappled for purchase against her mother's yoga pants and Lycra tank top. Their grunts mingled. Jaz twisted onto her knees. She slid her arm across her mother's slender chest and beneath her armpits. Thank the Lord years of batting practice made for a strong upper body. Her legs chased the wheelchair against the bar.

With a surge of effort, she used her other hand to lift Mom's hips and settle her rear onto the seat. With a groan, Jaz sagged her head into her mother's lap. Sweat itched against her scalp, and her chest heaved like she'd stolen home plate.

*Thank you, Lord, for keeping her from falling.*

"Does anything hurt?" Jaz glanced up.

Mom's honey-colored skin was ashy, and her lips pinched in the way that meant she fought tears. Jaz massaged the knee that wasn't attached to the leg in a brace. The jarring had to have sent pain searing through the broken femur, and maybe even the cracked fibula. The boot protecting the lower leg cut into Jaz's thigh.

Jaz grasped the arms of the chair, and Mom scooted until her butt was fused against the seat back. Jaz sagged against the cabinets behind her, still kneeling at her mother's feet.

"Do you want some painkillers? You haven't taken any today."

Mom shook her head. Her lips trembled. "I thought I could balance against the counter."

Jaz squeezed her mother's hand and stood. "Maybe if you locked both wheels, the chair wouldn't have fought you. Next time wait until I'm beside you."

Mom's chin quivered as she ducked it. "Thank you, Jazlyn."

Jaz patted Mom's trembling shoulder and opened her mouth to reassure her.

Her father breezed through the doorway, changed from his work clothes to long athletic shorts and a t-shirt emblazoned with the hospital's logo.

Jaz stepped away from her mother and toward the pot on the counter where a pork roast had simmered all day. She jerked the refrigerator open and snagged the bottle of her grandfather's special barbecue sauce.

"What's going on?" Suspicion clouded her father's tone.

Jaz kept her back to him and removed the lid from the slow cooker. Then she drained some of the juice and shredded the tender meat with two forks.

"Jazlyn?"

"Want to eat on the porch?" She was proud that her voice sounded firm, not at all shaky after the close call.

"Gerry? You're practically crying. Did you have words with your daughter?" The last question rang with accusation.

Jaz straightened her spine and twisted open the bottle of sauce before pouring a generous portion over the meat. Savory-smelling steam rose from the crock, and her clenched stomach groaned.

"Let's eat in here." Her mother sounded collected, but Jaz resisted the urge to look at her.

She wanted to offer the pain pills again, but that would be waving a red flag. The past few days, her mother took a dose with breakfast and one thirty minutes before bed. There was time for an additional dose today, but it would mean she'd need to stay up an hour later.

Jaz returned the crockery to its electric base and covered the saucy meat. She grabbed dishes and silverware and set the table in the nook overlooking the front of the house. The pacing between refrigerator and table calmed her nerves further. Soon, the coleslaw, bean salad, and buns sat in the center of the table.

Her father rolled her mother into place, his hands colliding with Geraldine's as they both reached to set the brakes. Jaz lowered her chin. Good. Her mother wouldn't be forgetting about setting those any time soon.

After carrying the pot of pork to the table, Jaz poured three glasses of iced tea. Her mother's slightly sweet tea recipe was nothing like the instant stuff served in the chow hall. Although she had loved the structure and routine of military life, there were plenty of things she didn't miss. The food topped the list.

Jaz settled next to her mother and across from her father. He bowed his head, and the women followed suit.

"Gracious and loving Father, thank You for providing this bounty. Thank You for Your many good gifts, and especially for speeding my wife's recovery. Amen."

They passed the food, and Ron asked his wife about her day. "Is the pain worse? You seem quiet."

"I might be trying to do too much."

Her father gave Jaz the side-eye. "That's why your daughter is here, so you won't do too much."

"I'm tired of sitting around."

He squeezed her hand. "You need to heal, darling. Let us take care of you for a change."

The sounds of scraping forks and clinking silver on glass filled the room. Jaz relaxed, savoring the spice of the pork and the crunch of the slaw. Her mind drifted to the letter, and she wondered if she should mention it. Maybe she'd tell her mother tomorrow.

Mom picked at her food. When she shifted, she gasped in pain.

Ron bolted to her side, massaging her shoulders. "What is it? What hurts?"

Jaz's fork dropped to her plate. The sumptuous meal

hardened to marble in her gut.

"I tried to stand at the counter. I fell."

"You fell?" His voice roared over the hum of the refrigerator and gentle *whoosh* of the ceiling fan in the family room. "Where were **you**?" His glare pinned Jaz in place.

*Reading Drew's letter. Crying about Bailey.* But none of that would matter to her father. Her mother's gaze held a million apologies.

"I was just coming through the door. I caught her before she hit the floor."

"You shouldn't have left her alone."

He was right. When Billy dropped Jaz off, Mom had been visiting with Tabitha. Jaz had slipped into her room to read Drew's letter. She'd heard Tabitha leave, but by then she was on the phone with Bailey. His coldness made her forget all about her mother.

Her father stomped his way over to the bottles of pills beside the sink. His fingers fumbled with them, and he grunted while depressing the childproof cap. He was back in a minute, holding the caplets out toward his wife.

"You volunteered for this, daughter. Is it too much to expect you to stay with your mother?"

Geraldine coughed. She'd chased the pills with tea, and her eyes widened as her hand went to her throat. Ron slid closer, leaning her forward, and reaching toward her abdomen. She shook her head, finally catching her breath.

"Okay?" His tone dropped from the railing to a near whisper.

Her mother nodded and squeezed his hand, her mouth opening and closing. A boa constrictor slithered up Jaz's spine and wrapped around her lungs until every breath took a concerted effort.

"How often has this happened? You're so busy with your work, you can't look after your mother." He sat stiffly in his chair, throwing daggers at Jaz with his narrowed eyes. "Why say you'll take care of her if you don't?"

Jaz gritted her teeth. "I've been taking care of her for weeks. She's fine, better every day. I thought..." But she hadn't been thinking about her mother at all. The rat of guilt gnawed at her stomach.

"You didn't think." His fork stilled beside a half-eaten lump of beans.

"Something happened today." Her heart dropped. She hadn't meant to share anything with him.

"Yeah, you let your mother fall." His square jaw was a brick.

Why was she even trying to explain? He never listened to her.

"It was my fault." Her mother's soft words cut across the tension. "I thought I had set the brakes. If Jaz hadn't come into the kitchen when she did, I would have spilled to the floor."

Her father reached for her mother's arm, and his gaze softened. "It's not your fault. She should have been with you."

"I—I'm sorry."

"*She* should apologize." Her father quirked a bushy eyebrow at Jaz, daring her to argue.

It was too much. The stress of being a caregiver and the argument with Bailey collided inside her. Never mind the shock of hearing from her dead brother.

Jaz leaned back in the chair and crossed her arms. "The list of what I should apologize for is so long, where should I start?"

A scowl twisted her father's pale lips, dousing the ember of irritation inside Jaz with fuel. Fury flared to life, hot and unstoppable.

"I'm sorry I'm not ladylike, Daddy." The supposed endearment dripped with venom. "I'm sorry I would rather play softball than the piano. I apologize for being everything you didn't want in a daughter."

"Jaz—" The word was a plea from her mother.

Jaz mowed over it. "I'm sorry my scholarship was for something useless like playing ball. I'm sorry for dropping out before I became something respectable."

"Are you really sorry?" His jaw flinched, and his eyes bored into her.

"Actually, no. I'm not sorry for any of that. But I am sorry that Mom nearly got hurt today. And I'm sorry that I couldn't live up to Drew's example." Her throat closed, and tears stung her eyes.

*No.* She would not cry in front of him. She didn't care enough about what he thought to reveal her vulnerability.

Her father crossed his arms over his chest, matching Jaz's pose. "Tears won't work on me."

Jaz threw up her hands. "This is why I avoided coming here for years. You act like everything I do is to manipulate or irritate you. But guess what, Daddy: it's not about you." She sprang up and her thigh slammed the table, jangling the silverware and sloshing the tea. "After Drew died, there was nothing here for me. Sorry, Mom." She glanced at her mother, and the tears bubbled up again. "I love you, but you've got someone who worships you like a goddess, and I have never been able to measure up to that."

She twirled toward the doorway. Spots danced around the room.

"Run away, Jazlyn. That's what you know how to do."

His words froze her. Molten emotions long suppressed bubbled up from her soul. She whirled to face him, slamming her hands on her hips.

"Shows what you don't know. I tried for years to win a drop of approval from you. If it weren't for Drew, I would have given up long ago." Her shoulders shuddered. "I've spent the past seven years trying to live up to what Drew would want, because he's the only one who ever loved me. I wasn't running away; I was striving toward the standard he set." She clenched her teeth. "Of course, I didn't measure up to that either. Just like you always thought, I'm not good enough."

Her feet slapped against the wooden floor. She rushed into her room, snatched up her phone and handbag, and slammed out the front door.

She was to the turn onto Armstrong Road before she realized Bailey was angry with her.

*Really, Lord? What else can go wrong?*

"Forget I asked." She whipped a U-turn in the next driveway and drove toward Mill Creek Park. Her fingers sought out the crumpled paper in her pocket.

Jaz needed her brother's words more than ever, but she doubted they could fix her shattered heart.

# Twenty-two

The hammer's pounding reverberated through his bones until his elbow tingled. Sweat trickled down his cheek and glued his shirt to his back. Bailey missed this honest exertion. His designing job challenged his mind and awakened his creativity and logic, but the strain of his muscles during the simplest of ranch chores fueled something else.

Or maybe it burned the emotions he couldn't seem to exorcise any other way.

*Have you prayed?* MaryAnn chided in his head.

She'd asked him the same question every time he'd ever groused about his problems. By the time he was in high school, he'd stopped saying anything that sounded like a complaint in her presence. Back then, he was praying.

Did it help?

He drove another nail into the partition between the two stalls. Sweet straw scented the air, overpowering the other barn odors. Mucking stalls had always been a favorite chore. Once finished, no matter how much his shoulders and lower back burned, or his boots stunk, Bailey's accomplishment stared him in the face.

With the claw end of the hammer, he rattled the boards, working his way clockwise around the stall. Gray and white hairs clung to the post at the corner. Shamgar did like a good scratch. Once everything was tidy and secure, Bailey strode out the back door and into the paddock.

Earlier he'd shoveled manure and spread a thin layer of

wood chips in the soggy spots. He glanced toward the sky. The sun hadn't climbed much beyond its zenith.

Poppet rolled to her feet, ducking beneath the fence to trot in his direction. She'd been glued to his side since he'd walked in the door on Friday. If he owned his place in the city, he'd take her with him. He shook his head. She probably wouldn't be any happier there than he was.

Or maybe she would. Anywhere was bearable when you were with someone you loved.

The gaping wound in his chest ached. Without Jaz, he doubted he'd be able to endure the separation from everything familiar. She'd been right to tell him the ranch was in his blood.

Shamgar side-stepped as Bailey came within arm's reach. He muttered and ran his palm across the gelding's speckled rump. The horse continued ripping grass from the base of the post on the pasture side of the corral. Likely he remembered Bailey's empty pockets from his last couple attempts to nuzzle his way to a treat.

Bailey fingered the snarls from his horse's mane. Rhythmic chomping played a lullaby. He patted the sleek neck until Shamgar raised his head and stared at him with an unblinking brown eye. Bailey's fingers worked under the black halter, scratching at the base of the gelding's ears.

Maybe it was the connection with the animals he missed. Shamgar snorted at him and bobbed his head before returning his attention to grazing.

Bailey rested his arms across the horse's back, recalling a time when the backbone jutted up and he could count the ribs. The gelding wouldn't endure any human touch in those days, but Bailey's patience earned the horse's trust.

He stared across the fields. Wasn't that what he'd promised Jaz? That he would go slowly and earn her trust.

The scene from the school flashed into his mind. She'd said the guy was from her brother's platoon, not the ex she'd been emotionally battered by when she'd stopped in Sweet Grove a few months ago. It was an innocent hug. A thank you for delivering an overdue goodbye from Drew.

*Am I overreacting?*

Poppet snuffled around his boots. Shamgar's teeth ground together on the grass. Aromas of horse sweat and cedar mingled into his nostrils.

*God, if You could offer a little guidance, that'd be great.*

But the echoing hollowness between Bailey's heart and soul couldn't muster an ounce of faith. God had made it clear years ago that Bailey was on probation. If he worked hard and stayed out of trouble, things would go fine.

Bailey's immediate assumption that Jaz had reunited with an old flame answered the real question. Did he deserve her love? Nope. If he couldn't trust her, he couldn't love her.

His stomach clenched. Okay, he loved her. Too much. Like he'd loved MaryAnn and Fritz too much after his blood relatives couldn't be bothered with his care.

Hadn't he stood on the other side of this paddock and told her to go to Austin and have a happy life? But then he'd let Tess convince him to chase her. And once he caught her, he treated her with the same understanding and persistence as he had all the wounded animals he'd helped.

Maybe now that she was healed from her mistrust, it was time to let her go.

Dust pooled and spun as a car turned in at the gate. Shamgar's head swung up, and he stopped munching for a moment as he eyed the dust. His ears flicked toward the rumbling motor.

Bailey patted the horse and eased his hat lower. The red brown flurry dissipated, and a red car stopped behind his old truck.

A dance of anticipation stirred in his chest. Somewhere in the abyss where he'd tried to bury it, his heart pounded, a horse galloping to food.

Poppet growled, and Shamgar stomped one foot. Jaz

stepped from the car. The dog's brown and white tail slapped Bailey's boots before she loped toward the visitor.

A vision in jeans, Jaz strode toward the paddock, arriving at the fence at the same moment as Poppet. The woman bent down to ruffle his dog's fur. Poppet yipped, her joy clanging into the pit of his chest.

It was no use trying to avoid her. Jaz wouldn't leave until she'd had her say. But then, maybe she would go, and he could try to find his life without her. He'd lived it for thirty years, so it seemed feasible he could do it for longer.

Shamgar nudged his shoulder. Bailey patted the horse's lean neck and shrugged his shoulders back.

As he swaggered across the corral, his boots sent up puffs of dust. Her eyes locked on him, and he dropped his gaze so she wouldn't snare him with the turbulence he knew he'd find in the sage depths.

"Can we talk?" She lifted her chin, turning the question rhetorical.

Bailey ducked his head, focusing on the fence in front of her. He curled his hands around the white rails and dug his short nails in. *Don't look at her face. Don't touch her.*

She jabbed a ragged looking envelope under his nose. "This is what was delivered to me yesterday."

"Okay." He gripped the rail tighter.

"Read it. I want you to know what sort of emotional state I was in when you were grunting at me and accusing me of... of...whatever." Her voice rose in pitch, and Poppet whined.

He shook his head. "I shouldn't have doubted you."

Her sigh could have been a blustery east wind. She stepped closer and reached for his hand. Bailey sidled backward.

Her mouth dropped open and then shut with an audible snap. "What's really going on, Bailey?"

"I realized I shouldn't have chased you to Austin. That I belong here. That you...should..." But he didn't believe it. He wanted her to love him and stay with him.

She tossed her hands in the air and shoved the letter into

her back pocket. He tried not to think of her backside or holding her hands or wiping away the tension on her face with a kiss. He shoved his hands into his hip pockets and gritted his teeth.

"Since you saw me with another guy, it made you realize that I should be with someone—" She gasped. "Black. Is this because Billy is black?"

Bailey jerked back like she'd slapped him. The sight of the dark-skinned arms so near the deep brown neck had appeared right to him. He'd immediately assumed she would be better with that guy. But because of *that?*

Jaz pressed against the fence and reached for him with an open palm. He shuffled backward again.

"I can't deal with this." She huffed out a sigh. "My dad came unglued on me last night." She choked to a stop.

Bailey peeked under the brim of his hat. Tears turned her eyes into a stormy sea. She pressed her hand to them. She hated crying.

His fingers twitched toward her. He wanted to comfort her. A groan caught in his throat as he stared at the ground.

"It was great to read Drew's letter and hear his voice again." She swallowed. "And it helps to know how he died." She'd learned the truth of the so-called training accident? Bailey shuffled his feet but then stiffened his knees. He would let her talk. Then she would leave, and he could find something else to pound nails into.

She slammed her fist into the fence. Poppet shied away, and Bailey's heart thudded in surprise.

"We're past all this. No more one-sided conversations."

Before he could react, she stepped onto the middle rail and climbed over the fence, dropping a foot away from him. He balked, but her hands locked onto his wrists. She glared at him as she shoved the hat higher on his head, and his hiding place disappeared.

"What. Is. Going. On?"

His skin tingled at the contact, and his shuttered heart banged into his breastbone. He couldn't look away from her penetrating stare. He didn't want to. He'd rather close his eyes and kiss her until the sting of betrayal was forgotten.

He pressed his lips together. "I didn't think it was…his skin. But maybe that's part of it." He swallowed hard. "I was sure it was the guy who broke your heart. It looked like a reunion."

"It was a sister thanking a stranger for delivering her brother's last request. If Captain Clayton—" She ground her teeth. "Showed up, I'd slap him across the face like I should have done when he gave me that line about ruining his career and not fitting the Virginia mold." She tugged on his arms and tried to place his hands on her waist.

Bailey curled his fingers into fists. He wanted to touch her and hold her, but if he did, his resistance would fail. Even now her hands burned his skin, sending a trail of fire straight to his empty chest.

"I'm done with lies." She pursed her lips, and he couldn't stop staring at them. "My family is driving me crazy, and I probably burned the last bridge to my father. I need you."

It dawned on him then—he didn't have any strength to offer her. The moments he saw her in another man's arms, he was ten years old and shivering in a courtroom. He was the skinny kid with a bloody nose who everyone picked on. She deserved someone who was truly strong, not someone who'd been faking strength his entire life.

Bailey shook his head. Words jumbled in his mind, but he couldn't make his mouth form them. She wouldn't understand. As much as she fought with her dad, she didn't know what it meant to be worthless. It was one thing for your family not to appreciate your accomplishments, but when they kicked you out because it was too much trouble to keep you, that told a different story.

"I don't have what you need." *I am nothing.*

Her hands slid up his arms. A host of sensation chased them. He ground his teeth until his jaw ached.

"You are what I need." Her eyes proclaimed it. "Right now. Exactly as you are."

He closed his eyes. His heart strained toward her, wanting to believe, wanting it to be true.

"My grandmother called it when I was a kid. I'm too much trouble. I've never had the backbone to fight for anyone or anything."

"You fought for the ranch."

Bailey shrugged away her touch. He gripped her shoulders, shaking her a little. He had to make her understand.

"You fought for the ranch, Jaz. *You* did that. And I let you rescue me because I'm too weak to rescue myself." The truth crushed his chest until he panted, out of breath at the admission.

She stared at him with wide eyes.

"I'm not what you need. I can't be your hero. I'm nothing like Drew."

She blinked. Moisture clung to her black lashes. Her pale eyes were luminous and wounded.

Bailey stepped back. "I'm sorry." He turned and strode toward Shamgar.

"That's not how I see you." She took a shaky breath. "I see the strength you show in standing up for Tess. The strength to chase me to Austin."

He wanted to believe her, but the broken shards of his soul stabbed him. He was good at pretending to be whatever people wanted him to be, needed him to be. But in the end, he wasn't anyone's hero.

"Don't walk away from me, Bailey. I mean it."

He slipped his fingers in the halter ring beneath Shamgar's chin. "C'mon boy." The horse flicked his ears in Jaz's direction but followed Bailey toward the barn.

"Stop, Bailey. You proved yourself to me, and I love you." The final words garbled with the emotion in her throat. "Why are you doing this?"

At the back door of the barn, Bailey halted and glanced

over his shoulder. He couldn't look at her. He was too weak to resist the pull of the lasso that connected his heart to hers.

"Go home, Jaz. Make things right with your folks. You don't need me for that."

He tugged the gelding forward. The barn shaded them, and whatever else Jaz said was lost beneath plodding hooves.

Bailey dropped into the corner of the sweet-smelling stall, huddled into himself, and let the horror show of his childhood replay.

Where was God in all that?

# Twenty-three

**J**az pedaled the bike in circles on the back roads outside of town. A breeze tossed dust into her eyes. Nothing could make them redder.

When she got back from the forced exertion on Saturday night, the motion-sensitive lights snapped on, blinding her as she wheeled her bike into the garage. Her legs wobbled, drained of energy. She guzzled water in the kitchen, glad her parents had already gone to bed.

In her room, she picked up her phone. There were several texts from Tess. Jaz read them, but they didn't compute. Words didn't matter. She'd committed her heart to Bailey, and he'd thrown it back at her like a hot coal.

*We're done. Let him tell you why.* After her fingers tapped out the message, she tossed the phone onto her bed and trudged into the bathroom to wash the sweat from her face and neck.

Another message blinked on her screen. *Come for breakfast tomorrow. We'll double-team him.*

Jaz blinked, recalling another breakfast. Her heart cramped worse than her rubbery legs. She'd been jealous of their sibling teasing that day, but it hadn't stopped her from laying a lip lock on the handsome cowboy.

She shook her head and covered her face with her hands. She was tired of chasing after dreams that didn't want to be caught.

*Always follow your dreams*, Drew's letter said. But some dreams cost too much. His had cut his life short, and hers had carved out her heart.

*You love him. He loves you,* Tess's next message read.

No, if Bailey loved her, he would at least give a reasonable explanation for why he was pushing her away. Because his family had dumped him when he was a kid wasn't a legitimate reason.

*And your dad's disapproval is reason enough not to have a relationship with him?* her thoughts countered.

Jaz choked at the sudden thickness in her throat and stilled. Her father battered her with a lifetime of scorn. That wasn't the same as one day in court.

But what about the years that led up to that day in court? Hadn't Bailey's mother and father been choosing drugs over him? He really believed he wasn't worth fighting for, worth loving.

*But I fought for him.* She tried to rationalize away the chiding voice in her head.

And now? Why wasn't she fighting now?

*Because I can't. I can't be rejected again and again by a man that I love.*

There. She'd admitted it. He'd pushed her away, and that made him just like her father, just like Captain Clayton.

*What about me?* Drew's voice sounded as clear as it had when she'd read his letter.

*What about me?* The second voice was barely a whisper, but it twisted a knife into her bruised soul.

Another line from Drew's letter echoed across her heart and mind. *I've found that's the secret to being fulfilled and feeling centered in God's will.*

The phone vibrated. Tess had given up on the texts.

Jaz pushed the answer icon. "I can't do it, Tess. He doesn't want me."

"He does want you. He does."

"Sending me away like that? I don't think so." Agony slammed through her chest like it had as she stood in the paddock.

"He's afraid." Tess's voice quavered.

"So am I." Jaz sighed. "I know you're trying to help, but leave it alone, Tess. Let us lick our wounds in peace."

"If you'd just talk to each other, you wouldn't be alone."

Jaz grunted. It seemed like the words had run out. She'd given him her heart, and he'd shoved it aside like a pile of manure.

"Please. Don't give up on him." Tess sounded near tears.

"I don't know what more I can do." He'd sent her away. He didn't want her, no matter how much her heart wanted him.

A sniffle from Tess's end. "He always puts others first. He thinks this is best for you."

Jaz snorted. "Yeah, I don't need him telling me what's best for me. My father's been doing it forever, and I'm done with that."

"If he chased you again—"

"He only did it because of you, right?"

Silence. "You have to push him out of his safe zone."

"Apparently we did. And now he's heading back."

A loud sigh. "He's in the barn. Wouldn't even stay in the house."

"You're a good sister, a good friend." Jaz meant it.

"He thinks loving you puts you at risk, don't you see?"

Did she? Not really. She'd stopped playing it safe when she dated him. She still didn't understand why he'd drawn back again.

"He needs to figure out what he wants, Tess. Let him." Jaz hung up.

The man who had promised to prove his love had decided she wasn't worth loving. Like every man in her life.

❧❧❧

JAZ ALMOST TALKED HERSELF OUT OF GOING TO CHURCH the next morning. But the vacancy in her soul ached, and she didn't want to be trapped in her parents' house all day.

Still, she should have timed it better. The instant she

stepped into the vestibule, Elise Nelson looked up from chatting with three teenagers.

Jaz's eyes hadn't adjusted to the interior lighting when the greeter shook her hand.

"Welcome." He extended a folded bulletin.

Before Jaz glanced at the brightly colored paper, Elise swooped down and pulled her toward the women's restroom.

"I was going to ask how you are." Elise backed against the bathroom door. "Puffy eyes say you're still tired. But that might be from staying out late with a certain cowboy."

Elise stopped for breath, and Jaz held up her hand. Tightness in her chest at the mention of Bailey lengthened the pause.

Elise's eyes widened. "I heard he was in town. I expected him to come to church, but Tess was alone."

"It's over." A tidal wave of weariness made Jaz wobble.

Elise grabbed her arms and furrowed her brows. "What's over?"

"Bailey broke up with me."

Her mouth dropped open. "He broke up with you because you're staying with your parents?"

Jaz shook her head. "I can't talk about it, Elise. Please." Jaz poured her grief and fatigue into the look she leveled at her friend. "I really need church today."

Elise patted her shoulder, apparently stunned into silence. Jaz figured it would be a short reprieve, so she bolted from the restroom while Elise gaped after her.

An usher opened the door to the auditorium, and Jaz crept to a seat on the far side, practically in a corner.

She melted into the cushioned chair. Arpeggios floated from the piano. The worship leader stepped to the microphone and called out a number.

Jaz pulled the hymnal from the basket beneath her seat. Her hand rested on the cool cover. The words and melody circled in her mind. Slowly, tension bled out her pores.

Peace seeped into empty spaces. Calm infused her, chasing away the fatigue.

When Pastor Bernie took his place behind the lectern, Jaz's equilibrium had returned. It unnerved her to discover she'd begun to depend on a relationship with some guy to get her through life's struggles. Did she really want to be that person?

*Lord, I'm sorry for depending on everyone but You. Show me how to have faith in Your plan.*

Jaz stroked the pages of the hymnal she'd opened for the responsive reading and hadn't closed. She imagined ribbons of peace spiraling up from the printed words and wrapping around her heart and mind.

*I know You'l take care of Mom. Thanks for helping her heal.*

She blinked as her eyes burned with emotion.

*Be with Bailey. Show Him how much You love him. Take away his pain.*

The room blurred. Jaz widened her eyes and stared at the cross on the front of the pulpit. She imagined directing her prayers to Jesus, the one who died, was buried, and then rose from the grave.

*Help me let go of these feelings I have for him.*

Where she'd been filled with an overwhelming sense of God's presence, something twisted in her chest. It would take more than one prayer to release her love for Bailey.

*I didn't want to love him, God. I'm tired of being hurt by men.*

The peace ebbed further from her. Jaz stared at the pastor, not really comprehending anything he said. Somehow, her prayers were pushing God away. How could someone get further from God while praying?

The preacher's voice penetrated the bubble surrounding her.

"Forgive, and it shall be forgiven you. Jesus is clear that if we want His grace, we must extend grace. People hurt us. That will never change." Bernie scanned the rows and his gaze seemed to rest on Jaz for an instant. "But if we don't forgive them, that's what really hurts us." *Forgive.*

Jaz swallowed the sour taste that welled from her gut. Her father didn't think he'd done anything wrong. How could she forgive someone who wasn't sorry?

The thoughts wrestled in her heart and mind. The congregation stood for the closing song. Jaz slipped out of her seat and jogged to her car.

She'd gotten the message she came for. But what was she supposed to do with it?

⁂

BACK IN AUSTIN, DAYS RAN TOGETHER. BAILEY GOT UP IN the morning and headed to work. After work, he played ball at the gym with some guys from the office. Then he returned to the tiny studio to eat and try not to think.

Once he went to sleep, which sounded easier than it was, his mind replayed the final conversations with Jaz. Sometimes he dreamed of their dates and at the end she'd be standing in the dusty paddock, crying. They ended the same as real life: he told her to leave. She always left.

He'd wake up with a thousand-pound dumbbell smashing his chest, unable to draw a breath until he sat up. Most days, he gasped out a plea—"God, help me." But God had gone silent again.

That didn't shock Bailey. He wasn't following the rules and toeing the line. He hadn't been to church since he'd attended with Jaz. It was easy to imagine God glaring at him, arms crossed over His chest, a stance his biological father used right before inflicting pain.

Bailey crushed thoughts of that man and those nightmarish years. He got up, showered, and went to work.

At the office, everyone stayed at arm's length.

On Thursday, Bailey sat in a client meeting with his boss. Bailey was designing a million-dollar home for the couple—a businessman and his realtor wife—so he listened as his boss talked them through their options and wants. With the design software open on his laptop, he made notes about everything.

At the end of the meeting, his boss said, "Bailey. A word."

Bailey nodded and returned to the seat at the conference table. He kept his laptop closed and stared at the man who had hired him. Now in his mid-50's, Dick Clarkson had started out when architects used drafting tables, not computers. His graying hair receded from his forehead, and gray eyes stared from beneath slender brows.

"Your probationary period ended a couple weeks ago."

Bailey stiffened.

"We've been swamped, but I wanted to take the opportunity to discuss how you've been doing. Ask what you expect for the future."

Bailey swallowed. Now that Jaz was gone, he didn't care to look into that crystal ball. The family he'd always dreamed of would never be his.

"I've got your file on my desk." His boss waved to him. "I'll be back in a minute."

Dick strode out, and the room felt vacant.

Bailey leaned his elbows on the table. The future? He could barely manage each day. The gnawing in his stomach told him he was a little concerned about losing the job. But why? Hadn't he decided he belonged on the ranch?

*Tess needs the income.* A niggling at the back of his mind rose to the forefront. *Stop using your sister as a cover for your decisions.*

He wasn't ready to go back to Sweet Grove. But he didn't want to stay in Austin either.

Without Jaz.

He closed his eyes, and her lovely face swam across his eyelids. So beautiful. So out of his league.

"All right then." His boss shut the door and sat across from Bailey. "First, everyone thinks you're a great addition to the team. You picked up the new software in no time, and you follow directions without question."

*You're a sheep.* He hardly recognized the growling voice he'd heard condemning him for the first nine years of his life. His stomach bucked, and ice tingled in his fingertips.

He straightened and banished the thought of his biological father. Why was he intruding now?

Dick opened the folder and glanced at the papers inside. "I'd like to set you up with your own client list."

Bailey blinked. "You want me to handle meetings like the one today?"

His boss nodded. "We'll start with smaller projects, of course. Designers with their own portfolios earn bonuses for on-time and below-budget projects."

"I don't think that's for me." Bailey gulped. "I mean, the money would be great, sure, but I prefer being in the background."

His boss squinted. "You're limiting yourself, Bailey. There's only so far you can go in the background." But

he'd be safe there.

"I enjoy designing, but I don't like trying to figure out what a client wants."

Dick nodded. "It takes finesse and practice, but you could learn to do it."

Bailey shook his head. "I'd rather design."

His grandmother's voice rang as clear as it had been in the courtroom two decades before. *The boy's too much trouble.* He rubbed the heel of his hands against his ears. The past hadn't intruded on him for months. What had changed?

After a gulp to clear his throat, he said, "You said everyone's happy with my designs." He was making himself useful, like always.

His boss tapped the folder. "Sure, but designing's entry level. I hardly touch the designs these days, except to review them before presenting to clients."

"Designing is what I want to do, sir." That much was true. "I wouldn't want to do anything else."

Dick studied Bailey, who forced his gaze to remain steady

even though the back of his neck itched like he'd stepped on an ant hill.

"You don't have to decide today. I'm happy to have you drawing plans for my clients." He shut the folder. "But if you want to go anywhere in this business, you're going to have to learn to work with customers and ferret out their vision."

Bailey reached toward his skull, realizing his hat wasn't there for him to tilt. He scratched his ear. "My sister's been struggling with her startup. I've been spending extra time there."

"Sweet Grove, right?" Bai-

ley ducked his chin.

Dick cupped the lower part of his face, running his index finger beneath his nose. His eyes stared past Bailey. "I've worked with a couple businesses in Rosewood and Harrison. If you need to be there and were willing to see clients, I could probably find some work for you."

Bailey's heart stalled, and his breath froze in his lungs. He could be with Tess and do the designing he loved? *If you're willing to see clients.*

His heart sped again. The twisting below the pulsating beast told him that the idea reeked of a setup for failure. But he wanted to move back to the ranch, didn't he? And he needed the money.

"Think about it."

Bailey nodded. He wasn't interested in meeting with clients, but if it meant he could move home?

*Home.* Pale green eyes in a square face flashed into his thoughts. He stiffened and slammed the door on the vision.

The men stood, shook hands, and Bailey returned to his desk.

After work, he drove to the gym. Jaz's face haunted him. Would she still want him? The ache in his chest hadn't lessened during their time apart. If anything, he thought of her more often and reached for his phone to text her at odd moments, choosing instead to stare at the photos he had of her.

But he'd driven her away. She wasn't chasing after him.

*Go home, Jaz.* She'd done exactly as he said.

At the gym, a group of guys—half of them from Dick Clarkson Architecture—invited him to join in a pickup game of basketball. He'd enjoyed playing years ago at college in Colorado and with guys from his first job in Houston. Surprisingly, his muscles recalled the moves with remarkable ease.

Most of his shots bricked off the rim, but he moved in on defense to make several steals and block a few shots. After an hour, the other men called it quits. Sweat glued his clothes to his frame, but Bailey pumped weights for another thirty minutes.

Why go to his apartment? No one waited for him.

Again, he wished he'd brought Poppet to the city. At least then the loneliness could be assuaged with some pets, and the silence could be broken with a conversation of meaningless questions and barked replies.

After eight, he reached his apartment. His phone told him he'd missed a call from his sister an hour previously. She would listen to his recounting of the day.

An ache deepened in his chest. He hadn't given Jaz much of a choice. Besides, she deserved someone who wouldn't doubt her at every turn.

Bailey drained two glasses of water and threw open every window in the small apartment. As he circled, he punched up his sister's number.

And after the first post-breakup conversation, Tess stopped talking about Jaz, too. Still, his sister called him most nights with questions about the ranch or stories about the animals. Like she knew he was barely hanging on.

Tonight, she answered on the second ring and listened to his rehashing of the meeting with his boss.

"You should do it." Her tone was teasing. "Not that I need you at the ranch."

The clenching around his heart relaxed a tad. She did need him at the ranch, but she'd never say it.

"I could finally design an addition for the barn." He snapped his fingers. "Or a large dining area for guests on the main level of the house."

The vision of the larger barn and expanded dining room swam in his creativity center. His fingers itched for a pencil or even a mouse linked to the company's design software.

"Someday." She sighed. "Travers Guest Ranch will be a dude ranch rather than a bed and breakfast. Then I'll be getting the family discount on those plans."

"Family discount? Who said anything about that?" He wanted to make her smile.

She chuckled. "I did. And you just repeated it."

*Have you seen Jaz?* But he swallowed that question. "Such a tricky little girl you are." He snorted, almost feeling the mirth. "I want to winterize everything this weekend."

"Should I plan to make you supper tomorrow?"

His stomach dropped. He told himself that it was because he anticipated home cooking, but a voice in his head called him a liar. For a moment, he wanted Tess to mention Jaz, and he hated his weakness.

He shrugged and sucked in a deep breath. "Maybe just pie."

She laughed. The musical tone thawed the ice in his chest. He needed to see Tess, so her joy could rub off on him.

"Pecan?"

"Why not peach?" He slumped against the headboard of his twin bed.

"So much work to blanch the fruit." She let out an exaggerated sigh. "But since you're my favorite brother—"

"Only. I'm your only brother."

She giggled. It took him back to the days when they had a real family. "You lucked out." After a pause she said, "Peach it is. But you have to bring your own ice cream."

"Done." The word released more tension from his gut.

*We're going to make it, sis.*

But wasn't there more to life than making it?

# Twenty-four

Another Thursday appointment at St. Joseph's in Rosewood, and today they were meeting her father for lunch. Jaz wrinkled her nose as she rolled her mother's chair toward the cafeteria, and the stench of deep-fried okra overwhelmed her.

Jaz pushed the wheelchair along the various counters, snagging a banana, yogurt parfait, and extra granola for herself. Her stomach flip-flopped. She told herself it was the disgusting combination of frying food and antiseptic.

Her spirit chided the dishonesty.

After paying for their lunch, Jaz wheeled her mother to a window overlooking the courtyard. With autumn underway, cooler air made the patio inviting, but not when angry clouds glowered at the windswept bushes.

"I don't see your father." Her mother plucked the salad off the tray.

Jaz scanned the sparse crowd, a sign it was early for lunch, and didn't see the tall man with side-slicked hair either. She pulled out her phone and opened a message. *We're in the cafeteria.*

She scooted around the table to sit across from her mother.

"You know he doesn't text." Geraldine pulled three napkins from the metal dispenser and dealt them to each place at the table.

Jaz stifled the urge to huff and groan. At what point would Ronald Rolle enter this century? She scrolled to her contact list, selected his name, and pushed the call button. After four rings, his voice mail picked up.

"He doesn't answer his cell phone at work, honey." Her mother drizzled orange dressing on her salad. Her glossy lips pursed, and her eyes screamed an apology. Like her husband's quirks were her fault.

Jaz sipped her water, wishing for a caffeine infusion from tea, but she knew better than to trust sweet tea from a mess hall.

She fidgeted with her yogurt cup and watched the people trickle through the lines. No pale-complexioned man with a white shirt and monochromatic necktie. She drummed her short nails against the denim of her capris. Why couldn't he show up on time? He'd be the first to glare disapproval if she was even a minute tardy.

"He probably got caught in the middle of something." Her mother's fork dangled an inch above her salad.

"I'm going to check his office."

Her mother arched a shapely eyebrow. Today, they'd gotten great news from the doctor, and Jaz wanted to see the worry and tension drain out of her father when Mom relayed it. Maybe he'd lighten up. Maybe she'd be able to return to Austin.

Her heart wrenched. Other than her job, it didn't seem like there was any big hurry to get back. Bailey wouldn't let her explain about Billy Jefferson, and she'd been handling all the research assignments remotely, which had become as stale as two-month-old Wonder Bread.

She shoved her chair back and stormed toward the exit. Blood pumped through her and swept the anxiety away.

Patients, employees in scrubs, and one white-coated physician populated the elevator. Jaz stepped off on the second floor and headed toward the administrative offices, trying to recall the last time she'd been there. But she couldn't. Most of her life she'd resented her dad's job because he used it to excuse himself from every event she held dear.

The desk in the reception area was empty, but the three

doors behind it were clearly marked. She chose the "Department Administrators" door and pushed into another short hallway. Black signage on the second door read: *Ronald Rolle, Imaging Administrator.* On his rise from an x-ray technician, he'd attended many weekend trainings and conferences and worked countless sixty-hour weeks at the hospital. Home had been a comfortable place when it was her, Mom, and Drew.

She knocked and turned the handle. It spun beneath her grip, and she walked in, only hesitating a moment on the threshold before letting the door shut behind her. A panel of fluorescent lights burned overhead, but no one sat behind the desk.

Piles of folders cluttered the desk and a table behind the wide, gray office chair. One tall bookshelf was the only other furniture behind the desk, and two stiff-backed chairs with teal cushions sat in front of the polished black surface.

Her eyes swept the office, freezing on the photo frames on the right-hand wall. The requisite framed diplomas sat nearest the desk, and a large portrait of her mother took center stage. Two collages hung beside her mother. In one, the photo from Drew's Advanced Individual Training graduation ceremony caught her attention, his dark face and shapely jaw stern beneath the Special Forces beret.

Jaz stumbled closer and grappled with the back of the chair to steady herself. Seeing the favored son was no surprise. Her heart seized.

Beside the frame containing Drew's photos and clippings of his military accomplishments hung a shocking sight. A colorful photo caught her eye, the red jersey and Longhorn emblem doubly familiar since she'd been wearing them only a few months ago.

It couldn't be the posed portrait taken during her final year of college softball. In the photo, she gripped the bat and stared into the lens with the same intensity she focused on every pitcher she'd faced.

She sidled closer to the wall. Her fingers brushed against

the gold edged frame. Beside the picture were several newspaper clippings. "Local Girl Gets Full Ride at UT" and "Rolle's Hitting Scores Shorthorn Championship" leapt out and clawed across her soul.

He'd never even congratulated her for those accomplishments. When she'd been fresh from the scholarship signing, he'd said, "At least that bat will get you an education. Still planning on being a lawyer, I hope."

Her stomach clenched at the memory. Every atom of joy that floated her through that day exploded and evaporated into a mist of insignificance. Nothing she did earned his praise.

During that golden moment, Drew had been in the military, so he couldn't give her a double-thumbs up or sweep her into his arms, swing her around, and praise her until the sting of their father's rejection faded. Instead, her mother had hugged her, kissed her cheek, and said, "I'm so proud." In the next breath, Mom asked if she had homework or could help with dinner.

Years of practicing, sweating, and training had rewarded her with top honors, but it didn't even merit a celebratory dinner or positive word from Mr. Hard-to-Please.

And yet, he'd clipped the article the Rosewood paper had run. Its prominent position on the wall beside Drew's accolades and his beauty queen wife's portrait surprised her the most. Did it mean he was proud of her?

Jaz stared at the headlines. Her eyes scanned through the once-familiar articles. In the bottom corner of the collage she saw a small clipping. It was the general announcement many hometown papers ran about military achievements under an "In the Service" headline on the community page. It read "PFC Jazlyn Rolle graduates with top honors from the JAG Paralegal Program," followed by the date and the name of the fort.

*"Your father couldn't get away."* Her mother had embraced her then held her at arm's length.

*Light had spilled from the sparkling hazel eyes. Jaz never longed for her mother's pride or adoration. It was always freely given.*

That day, Jaz's stony heart had hardened. She recalled the bustling plans to drive across three states to attend Drew's graduation from his training program. Pride beamed brightly enough from their father's eyes that it could have scorched Drew.

Her father never congratulated her, but this framed collection on his wall meant something.

Maybe her mother had documented these important moments and hung the proof there so everyone could see the Rolle family successes.

The door clicked behind her. Jaz swung toward it and knocked the frame askew.

Ron Rolle stalled in the doorway, his tie slightly crooked and reading glasses mussing his slicked brown hair. He glanced toward the wall behind her and strode in.

"I'm late." It wasn't an apology.

He circled his desk and dropped the folders he carried in a neat pile. He removed his glasses and folded them into the empty case beside his widescreen monitor.

"Mom's waiting in the cafeteria. We already bought our lunch." Jaz's voice sounded high.

He smoothed his palm over his hair and continued around the desk ending up a foot from Jaz. He pinched the corner of the crooked frame, straightening it. "Alison put this together for me."

Jaz wasn't sure who Alison was, but it debunked her theory that her mother was responsible.

"It surprised me." A hollow ached beneath her stomach. She wished Bailey was there to hold her hand, prove she was lovable.

Except he'd been a typical man and sent her away.

Her father twisted his head toward her and then returned his gaze to the framed pictures and articles. "I don't know why. One for Drew and one for you."

Jaz curled her lips and narrowed her eyes. "We all know you

were proud of Drew." She clenched her fingers into fists, surprised by how cold they felt. "Me, not so much."

He stared at the clippings, and Jaz willed him to say the words, admit that she hadn't been a complete disappointment.

He sighed and turned toward her. "I wanted you to be like your mother."

Her stomach flopped to the floor. "I'm no beauty queen."

He tilted his head and furrowed his brows. "Unfortunately, you got my facial structure. And your grandmother's stubbornness."

He fingered his stubbly chin, then brushed past her to hold open the door. "Let's not keep your mother waiting."

Jaz tried to swallow, but her mouth was arid and her throat tight. *Just ask.*

Her father gestured for her to go ahead, a gentlemanly act he always performed for her mother. With leaden steps, Jaz shuffled toward him. A shock ricocheted up her spine when his fingers settled on the small of her back, another small act of care he spent on her mother.

She froze and turned, barely needed to tilt her chin to stare into his face. Yes, she saw the square jaw and too-wide nose in the mirror every day. For once his lips weren't pressed into a thin line.

"Does that mean you were proud of us?" She flipped her hand toward the wall they'd been studying, and her fingers grazed his upper arm. "Me?" It was little more than a squeak.

"What else would it mean?" His tone was tempered, softer than he usually used with her.

"It would have been nice to hear it from your lips. That's all." Jaz shook her head and stepped through the door, sudden energy lengthening her stride.

"That's not my way, Jazlyn."

Her stomach bucked into her chest. While her mind flipped through every childhood encounter starring Drew as the center of parental approval, they walked through the halls and to the stairway. As their footsteps echoed in the stairwell, Jaz replayed those moments. Her heart vaulted into her throat.

Her father's eyes may have shone, and he might have said "Good job" to Drew's accomplishments, but the words "I'm proud of you, son" were noticeably absent. How had she not realized that? Why had she yearned for something from him he'd never bestowed on the son everyone bragged about?

*I waited for something he's never given, might be incapable of giving.* For too many years, she let the absence of "I'm proud of you" slash her confidence to ribbons. Worse, she'd fostered anger and resentment, believing if her father wasn't proud, he must be ashamed. But she'd never once doubted his approval of Drew.

*Lord, I'm an idiot. I distorted his angry words about not being like Mom. He didn't understand me, but that didn't mean he wasn't proud.*

Unmet expectations weren't disapproval. While her father might have been disappointed she wasn't more like her mother, he didn't despise her success in softball or her service in the Army.

As he held the cafeteria door for her, Jaz shed the burden that oppressed her for two decades. Let him have unmet expectations of her, but she wouldn't hold it against him. Instead, she hugged this small concession from him close to her heart and spread its blanket over the hollow where his approval had been absent.

Her lips trembled into a smile. "Thanks."

His eyes widened, and his mouth softened from their stiff line. "Ladies first."

Since she knew her Heavenly Father showered her with approval, this small acknowledgment from Dad was enough.

# *Twenty-five*

**O**n Saturday afternoon, Bailey sat at the stop sign and stared down Orchard Way in the direction of the Rolle house. He missed her. He'd been wrong to doubt her. His heart played gopher in search of a home into his hollowed-out stomach.

Had it only been a week since he'd given her the cold shoulder? His barren heart screamed as if it had been ages.

But he didn't want it to be forever. He'd been wrong, stupid even. What could he say to make it up to her?

His chest ached. The war raging there wouldn't ease up. One part of him fought to make things right with Jaz and return to the happy state of coupledom. The darker side thumped the cartons of back issues. Bailey's broken past had crippled his present. People Bailey cared about left him.

*But that doesn't have to be the future.*

Words from six months after he and Tess moved in with the Traverses came to mind. Mary Ann's voice echoed through his memory, *I love you, Bailey. Fritz and God love you, too. But you're the only one who can decide to be loved by us.* She'd repeated the statements many times in those first few years.

By the time he turned twelve, he had accepted their love. And they loved him well until they died.

*You're the only one who can decide to be loved by us?* And loved by Jaz.

He pictured Jaz weeping in the paddock. Warmth surged through him. He gasped for air and flipped on his turn signal.

He cranked the wheel away from Jaz's parents' house, unable to face her right now.

His cool treatment accused her of betrayals he knew she'd suffered at the hands of other guys and would never commit against him.

He drove past the browning fields. The apple groves greened the roadside, and his truck slowed. Almost automatically, he steered onto the narrow dirt track to the special place. Drew had made it important to him, but he hadn't been back since Fritz's funeral.

His heart thrummed as he recalled Jaz pulling up behind him that day. And the shared joy they felt when she'd helped him remember to check Fritz's Bible where he found the will.

The kisses they'd shared. His heart leapt like a horse escaping over a fence.

After everything she'd done for him, he'd stomped her trust into the dust. She wanted a man to love and accept her, but he'd doubted his worth so thoroughly it had altered his perception of her.

Branches encroached from one side of the rutted path. He slowed for the final dip in the road and had to swerve to avoid rear-ending a red car. He slammed the brakes. The motor coughed and died.

She was here.

He twisted the key off. His fingers tightened and started to crank it the other way. That's when he noticed her shapely legs dangling from the willow branches.

When Drew brought him here, they'd climbed that tree. They tossed rocks out into the pond, Drew coaching him on how to get more distance. Thunder had rumbled, and the sky opened, drenching them in seconds. They'd whooped and laughed, and Bailey felt free from his curse of doing whatever it took to prove his value.

What happened to that freedom? At what point had he picked up the manacles again?

His hand slipped away from the keys. He slouched into the

seat and wrapped his fingers around the steering wheel.

*Lord, I screwed up. I don't know how to make it right.*

A gentle prodding tugged inside him. It was the first stirring he'd experienced in any conversation with God since he'd sent Jaz away.

After a few deep breaths, he yanked the door handle. The door squealed, announcing his arrival. As if she hadn't heard the engine when he came up the road.

He shoved his fingers into his pockets and slithered between the two automobiles. Her muscular calves had stilled. As he crept closer, he glanced up, tilting his head to see between the yellowing leaves. "I was headed to your house." Well, he should have been.

"I'm not there." She sounded tired.

His stomach twisted. She'd been taking care of her mother who had been bound to a bed and wheelchair for six weeks.

He opened his mouth. Closed it. What was he going to say? *I'm a jerk.*

True enough but admitting it didn't solve anything.

The branch above him dipped. He looked up to see Jaz shifting toward the trunk.

"Wait." He held his hand toward her.

The rustling stopped. "We need to look each other in the eye for this conversation."

He gulped. "I need to apologize."

"Got that right."

The branch wobbled again. Bailey rose to his tip toes and grasped it. The bark scratched against the thinning callouses on his palms.

"It'd be easier if I didn't have to face you."

The branch bowed, nearly knocking his hat off. He let go of the tree and squatted down.

"I'm not making it easier for you."

He deserved the heat in her tone. And he certainly didn't merit any concessions.

*Lord, give me words.*

The limb shifted. Leaves shivered, and a handful floated around him. Then the gorgeous woman who owned him stood a foot away.

His heart lurched toward her, but his fingers scrabbled for pebbles. His mind whirled, repeating his four-word petition for help, while his arm tossed the first stone into the pond. Divots set the water in motion.

After straightening, he threw another one, harder this time. His stomach clenched.

*Plop.* No apology would earn her forgiveness. Why should she forgive him? He'd been wrong and cruel.

After he'd emptied his hands, his palms slid down the back of his britches before pocketing his fingers. With a huge sigh, he made a quarter turn and studied Jaz.

Crossed arms molded a gauzy blouse to her shapely form. Her toned, bronze biceps bulged where the short sleeves cut into them.

*Cowboy up, Bailey. Time to admit the truth.*

"I'm sorry for saying you betrayed me." *You would never do that.* He gulped. "That was my own insecurity talking."

"Why wouldn't you let me explain?" The betrayal he saw in her eyes gouged him. "You wouldn't listen. It was too much like my dad."

The comparison stung. "Ouch." But he deserved it. "I betrayed you like you would never betray me. I'm a jerk."

She sighed, dropped her arms, and shifted closer to him. A breeze whispered through the trees and carried her citrus scent to him. He curled his fingers against the bottom of his pockets.

"You're going through a lot of family stuff." He ground his teeth together. "I'm sorry I didn't listen. That I wasn't there for you."

Her fingers brushed down his arm, stopping on his forearm. Hairs stood at attention, and he stiffened his knees, so he wouldn't give in to the compulsion to lean against her.

"I forgive you."

Her husky whisper sent awareness slithering through him. He turned his face toward her, and she gazed up at him. Her kissable berry lips twitched.

"How's your mom?" His voice sounded too husky for such a serious question. "And everything else? It's like we haven't talked for months.

Something flashed in her pale eyes before they narrowed. She gazed at his chest.

"Great. Her pelvis is healed." Her dusty black sneaker slid next to his boot. "She's using crutches even though her right leg is in a cast for at least one more week."

"That's great." His fingers twitched again, and he dropped his hands to his sides. *Are we okay?* But he couldn't bear it if she gave him the answer he deserved.

"I'll be heading back to Austin soon."

Bailey's stomach leapt at the announcement. She'd be back where he could see her every day.

Her lips parted and then pursed. Why didn't she sound more excited?

A bird chirped nearby. A plop from the water announced a fish jumping. Silence stretched between them, reminding him of when he pushed her away.

He lifted one hand to her shoulder. Her heat zinged through him.

She tipped her head back. Those green eyes snared him.

"I missed you." The words struggled through his tightening throat.

She arched an eyebrow. "Really?" She licked her lips and his gaze dropped to her mouth.

She scuttled backwards. "I mean it, Bailey. I need you to be sure. I can't take another break up."

His other hand reached for her waist. Bailey gazed deep in her eyes, opening his heart so everything he felt flooded his eyes. She blinked, and her eyes widened. Were those tears in her eyes?

"I messed up. I never want to hurt you again." He choked back the wave of panic that welled at the thought. "I'm not alive without you."

"What can I do so you believe that I'm yours?"

*Marry me.* But it wasn't the right time. He had to prove she could trust him again.

"Knock me upside the hard head?" His lips slid upward.

She sucked in her breath and tilted her chin up, inviting him closer. He angled his face and tasted her lips. Sweet and salty, and so much Jazlyn. He breathed her in, and when her tongue tapped his bottom lip, he opened to her, losing himself in the rush of sensations.

Surely, she could taste the loneliness and regret he'd suffered during the past week.

She gasped and dropped her forehead to his chest. He rested his cheek against her hair. The curly strands rasped against his whiskers. Shudders of longing coursed through him.

"I need you to know I would never betray you."

"I know." He'd let the sight of her in another man's arms remind him of everything he'd already lost. He'd chosen doubt over faith, but she hadn't done anything but stand by him.

She sidled back and stared into his face. "You made me trust you. Love you." Her frame trembled, and his fingers tightened on her waist. "I've never loved anyone this way."

He endured her scrutiny, pouring the emotions she made him feel into his eyes.

"I love you. But I don't deserve you." He would never deserve love, but if his mom was right, that's not how love worked.

She blinked. "Maybe I'm the one who doesn't deserve you."

His heart and stomach twisted together. She doubted a man could love her because of her own childhood traumas. Were they doomed to let the past bar them from having a future?

Something his father had told him years ago flashed into

his mind. He let that wisdom flow from his lips. "Since God loves us, I'm sure He wants us to love each other."

Her lips quirked. "I think you're right."

He skimmed his hands down her sides. She shivered and threaded her fingers through his, leaning against his arm.

"My dad practically said he was proud of me." A tremor shook her words.

Bailey stepped closer and touched her cheek. "'Bout time."

"He admitted he can't verbalize his feelings." She choked to a stop. "I realized he never told Drew he was proud of him, either."

Bailey's heart pounded, and he pulled her against his chest. He drew circles on her lower back with the hand that she wasn't squeezing in a vise.

"But the way he looked a Drew." She turned her face upward, and their gazes locked. "I saw the pride in his eyes."

The eyes. Love flared in her pale green orbs, and fire heated Bailey's chest.

Jaz swallowed. "I may not be the daughter he expected, but I think he's proud of me."

Her breath warmed his collarbone. Hairs prickled along his back, and his lips made a case for kissing away the hurt in her tone.

She sagged against him. Bailey drew back enough so he could meet her gaze. An uneasy expectation swirled in her soulful eyes.

"You're an amazing woman. I'm proud to be with you."

Her lips trembled into a smile, and she dropped her chin in a small nod. "And I'm proud to be with you. Don't ever doubt it again."

His chest ached from the thrumming of his heart. "I'm an idiot."

Her hand slithered out of his and up to his chin, where it rasped over his whiskery cheek. "I think I need to do a better job showing you how I feel."

Her gaze dropped to his mouth an instant before she pushed up and kissed him. His pulse skittered as his tongue tasted her. Her fingers tangled in his hair and tugged him closer, and a whimper rose from her throat.

Bailey pulled back, his forehead on hers. "I love you, Jazlyn. I promise no more breakups." He smoothed his thumb over her lower lip.

She tapped the brim of his hat, pushing it further back on his head. One corner of her lush lips curled upward. "Those lips are pretty convincing."

The ache eased from his chest. He kissed her again, slow and sweet until her passion deepened the embrace. Giddiness exploded through him.

Hope flamed in his chest, burning away the mocking defeat. Jaz pressed into him, warm and real.

Another gust showered willow leaves around them. He imagined the wind carrying away his past, and his arms tightened around the waist of his future.

Before the seasons changed again, he would ask Jaz to marry him and seal their hopes and dreams together once and for all.

# Book Three

# Twenty-six

**B**ailey Travers tossed his hat on the rack beside his desk and thumbed through the stack of mail his landlord had handed him on his way out of the apartment. The scrawl of blue ink on an obviously government-issued envelope drew his gaze.

*Is this you?* Was written in barely legible printing. Two forwarding stickers covered the original address, but the name on it scalded through him and he nearly dropped the envelope.

*Bailey Dyer.* Bailey Dyer was a scared ten-year-old boy whose mother was dead and whose father was in prison. A boy whose maternal grandmother claimed, "He's too much trouble."

A venomous snake coiled in Bailey's stomach. There was only one person this letter could be about.

Memories sliced through him of pain searing his bare back, of baby Tessa screaming in the other room, the cat urine smell of his mother's rare hugs, and the scorn dripping from his father's voice. Ugliness tugged him toward the past, but Bailey blinked his way back to the present.

He dug his fingernails beneath the flap of the envelope, tearing with enough force to make it a pile of scraps. With shaking fingers he opened the single sheet, and his gaze scanned the lines of text.

Daddy Dyer had made parole. This letter was to inform him that the man who'd scarred more than his flesh was walking the streets of Texas once more.

*Don't let him find me.*

A knot tightened in his shoulders. Bailey ground his teeth together and tossed the letter into the trash. That was where memories of his old life belonged. He had a new life now. Today he had an important meeting with his boss, Dick Clarkson, and no time to consider ancient history.

Ever since mentioning a branch office closer to Sweet Grove, his mentor had been pushing Bailey out of his comfort zone. Bailey sat at his drafting table and slammed the door on his past as he opened up the drawings he'd made to convert a strip mall in Rosewood, Texas.

Hours later, Dick stared at the monitor on the conference room wall. Bailey gulped. His plan for creating an indoor marketplace was displayed on the huge screen. Bailey had reworked the sketches after every meeting with potential occupants, with a total of four revisions during the past week alone.

Everyone had their own idea about what would work the best, and Bailey thought he might go bald trying to please them all. This was the reason he'd argued against taking on design clients. Still, he hoped to present the final plan at the investor meeting the following evening. But only if Dick believed it checked all the boxes for the string of entrepreneurs who were going out on a limb to create something unique to Rosewood.

Rosewood, Texas, where the love of his life's father worked. The small city was only thirty minutes from where he grew up, a place his younger sister was converting into a guest ranch.

At the thought of the two women in his life, Bailey fought the urge to check his phone. It had vibrated a few minutes earlier, and he suspected it was Jaz with the most recent update on her mother.

Geraldine Rolle had been involved in a serious accident nearly eight weeks previously, and Jaz had moved to Sweet Grove to be the primary daytime caregiver. Since Bailey had shared the caregiving role with his younger sister Tess during the final weeks of their foster father's life, he understood the emotional toll it could take on a person.

Today, Jaz was hoping the orthopedic surgeon declared her mother beyond the risk of reinjury.

His boss swiveled his steely gaze with the force of a horse's kick. "Looks great, Bailey." Dick extended his hand. Bailey's calluses rubbed over the man's smoother palm. "I knew you could do this."

"That makes one of us." Bailey released a sigh, but the tension in his shoulders remained.

Dick laughed and slapped his mentee's back. "The good ones are always hardest on themselves. I guess you should draw up a plan for that office space in Rosewood we found, huh?"

"I can start on that." Bailey ducked his chin in a nod. "If you're sure that's the office you want."

Dick nodded. A strange warmth puddled beneath the terror clawing at Bailey's gut.

The branch office close to his hometown would be much smaller and, initially, a one-man show. Once he built a solid list of clients, he could hire an administrative assistant and — hard to fathom — another designer to help him carry the load.

For someone who hadn't wanted to work directly with customers a few weeks ago, this was a huge step.

*You can do anything you set your mind to.* Jaz's husky voice had whispered those very words in his ear as he was ushering her into her car four days ago for her return to Sweet Grove.

He yearned to be back in the same city as she was, but for how long? If he moved to Sweet Grove and she came back to her job in Austin, they would be separated again.

He jerked his mind out of the quicksand pulling his sense of accomplishment into a funk. They would work it out. They'd been through too much together to let something like a hundred miles conquer their love.

"I'll be at the meeting tomorrow, but you'll do fine." Dick stood and stretched. Bailey jumped to his feet, ignoring the niggle of doubt that came from too many years of trying to earn his place but falling short.

"I appreciate your vote of confidence, sir." Bailey reached for the brim of his hat to tap it with his customary salute of respect. But since he was inside, the hat was on its peg near his drafting table.

Dick's eyebrow twitched upward, and the corners of his thin lips trembled. "You haven't let me down yet, son."

*Son.* The word echoed through Bailey as his boss strode out of the conference room. He'd already lost two fathers. Not that he'd considered the abusive man who spent most of his life in prison a father. No, he'd buried his father six months ago because Fritz Travers had reared him, supported him, believed in him, and left him everything but a legal adoption to claim they were father and son. Dick Clarkson would be a poor substitute for the second man but a vast improvement over the first.

Bailey had another Father, too, one he'd been trying to renew a relationship with ever since realizing his humanity could cost him the woman he loved more than anything.

*God, I'm struggling here. I feel like this move is from You, so help me ace this presentation.*

As he methodically moved through disconnecting his laptop from the meeting room's system, Bailey let the thought of God and Fritz smiling down on him shove aside the lingering doubts about the presentation.

On his way back to his desk, he passed his coworker Mark.

"Coming to the gym?" Mark asked.

The ache in Bailey's shoulders reminded him that he hadn't worked out that morning. Nor had he been to the gym the night before. He'd rather be heading out for a horseback ride, but maybe that could be on the agenda for the weekend.

"Let me finish up a couple things."

Mark shook his head. "Don't let a couple things turn into an hour." He punched Bailey lightly on the shoulder. "You work too much."

Easy for Mark to say, since he'd been with the firm since graduation from his design program four years ago. And the twenty-five-year-old seemed young to him, younger even than Tess who was the same age. Tess would be thrilled to hear he was moving home.

As he saved all the pertinent files and cleared his desk, he let himself imagine that conversation.

He snorted. Okay, thrilled might be an overstatement. She'd accuse him of trying to interfere in her fledgling business plans. Like he knew anything about running a guest ranch. Although he did know how to keep the stock happy and calm the mounts for any greenhorns who might think they wanted to take a trail ride. Now that autumn had cooled the temperatures and brought occasional rains, the pasture would spring to life until the cold winds of winter required regular feedings of hay.

The thought of hay made him itch for the barn. This past

weekend he'd harvested the late crop from the Wells' field with help from Adonis and Herman. If it wasn't for them, he wasn't sure how Tess would be managing the ranching side of her business. She didn't need him? Ha. She'd always need him.

After sweating through his t-shirt in a couple games of basketball at the gym, Bailey headed into the weight room. He let visions of running with Jaz push him through his push-ups, pull-ups, and sit-ups. When he got home, he'd call her to update her about his move and find out how her mom's doctor appointment went.

Back at his studio apartment, Bailey rushed through a shower. He dumped a can of chili into a bowl and tossed it in the microwave. While it heated, he pulled up Jaz's name at the top of his contact list.

"Hey, cowboy." She sounded tired, but her sultry tones revved his heartbeat.

"Hey, beautiful. What did your mom hear from the doc today?" He scooped the steaming chili into a bowl. His stomach groaned as he pulled crackers from a cupboard, a poor substitute for homemade cornbread.

"The doctor released her from home health. Looks like I'll be heading back to Austin." She didn't sound as excited at the prospect as he'd expected.

"That doesn't make you happy?"

"I'm ready for Mom to be well, but..."

Bailey took his bowl to the card table and sat in the camp chair beside it. He listened to her talk about her father and missing the kids at the office.

Now that he was moving back to Sweet Grove, the idea that she would be two hours away in Austin made the move home less exciting.

Before he could share his big news, his phone buzzed. He stared at the screen. It was his sister.

"Tess is calling," he said when Jaz paused. "Can I call you back?"

"Sure."

Before he said anything else, the call ended. That was Jaz. She wasn't much for drawn-out goodbyes.

"Hey, sis." Bailey shoveled a bite of chili into his mouth.

"Our father is here!" Tess said, and the spicy meat and beans nearly choked him.

Bailey coughed. "What?"

"Lonie Dyer," his sister hissed. "He looks like a really *ancient* you."

Bailey had just gotten that notification. How could his father already have made it to Sweet Grove? And how did he know where to find them?

He gripped his damp hair. Yanking it out wouldn't prove anything. The stupid letter from the corrections department had been forwarded from Houston to Sweet Grove and finally found him in Austin. It could have been a month old.

He dropped his fists onto the table, rattling his bowl of chili.

Tess squealed. "Did you just punch something?"

"Tell me you made him go away."

"How would I do that? It's not like I wasn't standing on the porch of a huge farmhouse."

"You don't know him."

"You're right. I don't." A squawk sounded from her end of the phone. Her voice raised. "But he is our father."

"He was a sperm donor. Fritz and MaryAnn were always our real parents. Especially to you."

Tess sighed. "I have a guest, a man doing surveys for Liam James. I put them at opposite ends upstairs."

Their ranch was much closer to James' place than the bed and breakfast, but it was unusual that singles stayed at the ranch. Bailey despised the idea of Tess being alone with strange men.

A shiver convulsed through Bailey's gut. Lonie Dyer was not to be trifled with. He was a conman and a petty thief. Although he couldn't be bothered to sign away his parental rights and kept making parole at just the wrong times during Bailey's youth, the man hadn't been any sort of father.

And Tess should never be alone with him. Not for any reason.

"I'm in the barn, but I don't know what to do. He showed up asking for you. Then he was all, 'Are you Tessa? You're even more gorgeous than your mama.' And he meant it."

So, the snake hadn't lost the charm he'd used to con his way into marrying their mother. Not that he'd ever used it on Bailey.

"Go stay with Elise."

Tessa huffed. "I'm not leaving my guest. I haven't finished breakfast for tomorrow. And Pastor Bernie preached about loving our enemies on Wednesday—"

"Pastor Bernie doesn't know Lonie Dyer. I do."

"Well, I don't. You've never said a thing." He heard the pout in her voice. She probably had her arms crossed and her chin aimed at the ceiling.

Bailey pounded the unsuspecting card table, and the chili nearly spilled. "You. Don't. Need. To. Know." He shoved away from the table and paced to the windows

.Energy zipped through him, screaming for an outlet. *I'd like to pound my fist into Lonie Dyer's face.*

But violence had never solved a single problem for Bailey. Instead, it made things worse.

*Blessed are the peacemakers.* The words from the Bible he'd been listening to on his walk between work, the gym, and his apartment came back with haunting clarity.

*He isn't seeking peace. I guarantee he's looking for money or something else.*

And Tess was an innocent. She had no clue how to defend herself against a vile predator like Lonie Dyer.

"I'm coming tonight."

He had planned to drive up in the morning for the meeting with the investors and to meet with the owner of the prospective office space.

"I'm fine."

"You don't know that." Bailey shoved back the livestream of horrors he'd lived until Lonie was convicted and sent to prison. Eight years as the man's victim taught him all he needed to know. There would be no changing the man. If anything, prison had hardened him further. "I'll feel better if I'm there."

"Whatever. I just wanted to talk to someone who would understand how freaked out I am."

Bailey had an excellent thought and straightened. "Why don't you call Jaz? Have her come out and stay with you until I get there."

"Any excuse to see your sweetheart." But the relief in her tone was evident.

Jaz wouldn't fall for Lonie's crap. And she could handle him if he got any ideas about laying a finger on Tess. Bailey's shoulders slumped a little.

"If anyone will understand daddy issues, it's Jaz."

She'd been working through hers, but until a few weeks ago there was more tension than friendliness between her and Ronald Rolle.

"I don't have daddy issues." There was a snort in the background. "Did you hear what your horse had to say about it?"

Bailey's mouth twitched. He was sure Shamgar was complaining about Tess talking so loudly near his stall. Man, it would be good to get home and spoil that big guy again.

"Whatever you say, Sissy."

"Don't call me that." Her growl was playful and a sign she'd calmed down.

"You're getting bossy in your old age."

"Ha! You haven't even seen me being bossy."

"I'm scared." He tossed shirts into a duffel bag.

He should probably give his landlord notice. He glanced around the single room. Nothing here felt like home.

"Bye."

"See you in a couple hours."

But she'd hung up before he finished. Once he got on the road, he'd call Jaz and verify that Tess followed through on his request.

Because he wasn't leaving his sister at the mercy of the man who'd made his life Hell for years.

# Twenty-seven

**L**onie Dyer was a piece of work. Jazlyn Rolle had met sweet talkers like him during her six months with Boldt & Associates. It wasn't the false charm that grated against her as much as the expectation to get something for nothing.

By the time he'd spoken two sentences, Jaz had known that the striking physical resemblance between Bailey and Lonie was all there was. Even without the sharp planes on his face and hardness in his eyes, Lonie wasn't at all appealing.

"And who might you be?" That was the first sentence he'd spoken.

"This is Jaz." Tess stepped around her as the two of them entered the parlor.

Lonie's hand settled possessively beside a photo book of Central Texas on the edge of an antique table.

"A Sweet Grove native like my little girl?" His tone dripped honey, and Jaz figured he could con a starving man out of his last meal.

Probably how he'd convinced the parole board a man with one armed robbery after another shouldn't serve out a full sentence. Jaz had entered the man's name into the county database as soon as Bailey had mentioned he was out of prison. Not that she expected him to show up in Sweet Grove. He'd burned whatever bridge he might have had to his children years ago.

"I thought you'd be in your room." Tess gazed at him with expectation.

That's when Jaz saw herself in her friend's posture. Tess wanted his approval. Since she'd always yearned for Daddy love, Jaz knew the feeling exactly.

But Lonie's narrowed eyes told Jaz that Tess was heading for heartache.

Jaz stepped closer. Lonie's gaze flashed to her and roamed lasciviously down her body. The very same thing had happened so many times during her six years in the Army that Jaz was surprised when she glanced down at herself. The uniform she expected to see was only loose boyfriend denim and a form-fitting sweatshirt. Judging from the lust-filled gaze on Lonie's face, it should have been something much more revealing.

"I'm Bailey's girlfriend, and he's on his way here."

Lonie's lips thinned into a reptilian smile. "Boy couldn't wait to see me." His dry chuckle sent a hoard of shivers down Jaz's spine.

"Tess and I are going to hang out until he gets here." Jaz turned Tess toward the doorway. "Let's get some sweet tea. What's on the menu for breakfast?"

She forced her backbone to steel as she marched her friend into the kitchen. Tess responded about breakfast, but Jaz didn't pay attention. Now that she'd met the man and seen the open desire in Tess's eyes, she realized Bailey hadn't been overreacting to send her to the ranch.

Jaz blocked the doorway into the kitchen by leaning on the side of the bar. Lonie pulled up a stool like he belonged there.

"Sweet tea?" Tess paused to glance over her shoulder at Lonie while pulling glasses from the cupboard.

"I never did sweeten to it."

Once Tess turned away, Lonie shifted a leer to Jaz. She glared, unblinking. Maybe it would be smarter to pretend to fall for his slimy charm, but she couldn't do it. Men like Lonie Dyer had too much power over women, and Jaz refused to be another conquest for him, even if only in his mind.

Tess handed her a glass of tea and sipped hers.

"What are your plans?" She set her glass down. "Did you want something else to drink?"

This wasn't part of her normal B&B hostess routine, and Jaz wanted to snap at Lonie to leave the kitchen since it wasn't generally open to guests. But Tess's hopeful expression killed the protest before it reached her lips.

"A shot of Jim Beam would be nice." Lonie chuckled again, this time the sound more authentic, although it still grated on

Jaz.

"How about a Coke? I have Sprite or cola."

Lonie shrugged. "Don't go to any trouble for me, darlin'."

As if she hadn't already by loaning him a rent-free room. The front door opened and closed, and footsteps plodded toward the dining room. Jaz's heart leapt, but Bailey would use the kitchen entrance, so it must be Tess's other guest.

"That's Mr. Gary." Tess brushed past Jaz and into the hallway.

Lonie arched a scraggly eyebrow at her and smirked. "How long you been goin' down on my boy?"

Jaz clenched her fist. "He's not your boy any more than Tess is your darlin'." She mimicked his syrupy drawl of the endearment.

"Feisty, too. I see my boy didn't fall too far from his father's good taste."

Her short fingernails jammed into her palms.

*Lord, I want to deck his smarmy face. Help me here.*

"Cat got that tongue o' yours? I could show you a few things to do with such a tricky tongue." He leaned closer, reaching toward her.

Tess flew back into the room. "He has everything he needs. Checking out in the morning. And he's convinced me to make apple tarts."

Lonie retreated into his own space. Jaz tried to relax her combative posture, but it wasn't easy.

Tess pulled out a mixing bowl. Lonie's voice returned to syrup as he talked about his plans to "find a good job close to his family." Jaz doubted hot wiring cars and waving a gun while wearing a mask qualified him for decent employment, and Bailey would be sending him packing in short order.

Tess moved through the kitchen with practiced ease, getting out ingredients and then sifting them together. "Would you grab a gallon of apple slices from the freezer on the porch?"

Jaz shook herself from her dark meditations to amble into the adjacent room. She stared through the glass into the darkening night. No headlights coming up Armstrong Road. It would be at least another hour until Bailey arrived.

She wished him home as soon as possible—before her self-control broke and she hurt Tess's feelings by hurting Lonie

Dyer's face.

❧❧❧❧

BAILEY STOMPED UP THE STAIRS FRIDAY NIGHT. The back door flew open and Jaz flung herself on him.

"Thank the Lord! I'm about to kill him."

The instant of relief from holding his girl perished in the fire of increased tension in his shoulders.

"What did he do?"

"The man's a slime ball. And Tess can't see it."

The scars between his shoulders itched. Only he knew the exact caliber of Lonie's sliminess. He hugged Jaz close, breathing in the scent of coffee and sugar. Their lips met and the sweet tea he tasted made him want to deepen the embrace, but the need to rescue Tess from the nightmare of Lonie Dyer curtailed the enjoyment of the reunion.

"Thanks for coming." His voice sounded harsher than normal.

Jaz nuzzled her nose against his chin. "I love Tess almost as much as you do."

His hands squeezed her waist and trailed to latch onto her fingers. She glanced toward the door but turned to the driveway.

"How about coming to dinner tomorrow night?"

The longing in her voice tore at him.

"I'm not leaving Tess alone with him."

She cocked her head. "What about when you head to your meeting?" He'd filled her in on the eminent move back to town when he'd called her during her drive to the ranch.

"I'll make sure to drop Lonie off somewhere in Rosewood."

Jaz blinked. Something in her pale eyes told him she didn't think it would be so easy to get rid of the man.

A wave of dizziness plowed through him. He was exhausted and didn't want to confront Lonie Dyer.

"I'll text an invite to Tess in the morning."

She brushed her lips over his, then she strode off the porch. He watched her disappear beyond the sphere of light from the porch and steeled himself.

He twisted the doorknob and clambered into the screened back porch. As he shoved through to the kitchen, Poppet yipped, her entire body wagging. He shrugged off his Carhartt jacket and hung it on the tree beneath his hat. Scents of cinnamon and sugar swirled around him. His stomach roared like an angry grizzly.

Tess looked up from behind a curtain of steam as she rinsed dishes in the sink.

"Where is he?"

She slapped her hands on her apron-covered hips. "Welcome home, Lee. Coffee?"

His stomach balked worse than an inexperienced pitcher, and he shook his head. A floorboard creaked and Bailey twirled.

A man an inch shorter than him and a few pounds lighter entered from the hallway. The dark blue eyes mirrored the color of Bailey's, but something hard lay beneath them. Light brown hair barely covered the top of the man's head and was threaded with gray at the temples. His thin face looked wolfish, and the lipless smile baring browning teeth didn't dispel the image.

"There's my son." The smooth tones slid like oil over glass, but the hairs at the base of Bailey's neck stiffened.

Poppet whined and shied behind his boots.

"You turned out all right." He raked narrowing eyes down Bailey's frame. "I think I'll turn in."

"How about you get in my truck and I take you to a motel?"

Lonie's thick eyebrows lowered. "Not very hospitable, are you? Haven't seen your pa in years—"

"Save it. I buried my dad six months ago."

Tess slid an arm around Bailey's waist, startling him. "Lonie has a room here."

"He should move along." Bailey stood to his full height and glowered at the man.

Lonie laughed, and the menace in the sound sent a pack of rats scurrying down Bailey's back. The man didn't intend to walk out of their lives so easily. "I could use an extra pillow." His beady eyes flicked toward Tess. "Can you get me one, girl?"

Tess nodded, shooting Bailey a warning glance as she squeezed his waist. "He is our father." Her lips wobbled as she smiled toward the strangely familiar man on the other side of the counter.

That hopeful look undid the belt cinching around his heart.

She didn't know anything about the past, and Bailey didn't want to tell her now.

"They're upstairs. I'll put one in your room."

"That's a good girl."

Bailey's hands clenched as Tess hurried into the hall.

Lonie narrowed his eyes. "Looks like Old Dona did you a favor by signing you over to the state. This is a nice spread." Lasciviousness glinted in the man's gaze.

Here it was. Now the demands would begin.

Bailey crossed his arms over his chest. "The ranch hasn't been profitable for years." He had done his best, but the marketplace didn't reward small, family operated beef ranches.

"Land is money. How many acres?"

"It doesn't concern you." Bailey leaned toward the intruder, glaring down at him although he didn't have much of a height advantage.

"Not happy to see me, boy?" Thin lips sneered. "Then you better find a way to pay me off, so I'll get out of your hair."

Something hardened in Bailey's chest. He would not be bullied by this man now that he was grown.

"You think you scare me?" He curled his fingers into the front pockets of his jeans so he wouldn't reach across the counter and wipe the leer from the pinched face.

The stairs creaked.

"What about her?" Lonie glanced toward the sound. "You'd best consider your little sister, boy."

Then he strutted from the room like he owned it.

Bailey gulped the acid that welled from his stomach back down. Lord help him, he would destroy that man if he laid a finger on Tess.

# *Twenty-eight*

Jaz shrugged the ache out of her shoulders and rested the paddle across her lap. Water slapped against the hull of the borrowed kayak as she floated toward the far shore of Mill Pond.

After what happened at Tess's the previous night, she needed the physical exertion. In fact, it was Tess who suggested she ask Jack Bryant at the Cider Mill about borrowing a kayak. He'd been experimenting with renting some equipment in the park during the summer, and Jaz had had to dig one out of a locked shed beside the small pier where Mill Creek dumped into the pond.

A gray band of clouds scuttled overhead. She dipped the paddle into the murky water and stroked closer to the willow marking the special place that Drew had brought her to get away from her tensions. He'd also shared it with Bailey, and now it had become something of a sanctuary for them. They'd discovered the will that saved the ranch from the clutches of Honey Campbell there, and two weekends back Bailey had apologized beneath the old willow for accusing her of betraying him.

As the front of the boat stirred up the silty bottom matter, Jaz caught movement near the old fence. Behind the trunk of the willow, a mass of reeds and bushes stretched five feet to the stained cedar planks that marked the edge of the county park. Ruts from vehicle traffic cleared a central area of foliage, and the opposite side of the clearing had a leaning wooden fence that bordered the ramshackle homestead that had been vacant for as long as Jaz remembered.

Bushes jerked by the old fence. The end board wavered as if struck by a boulder.

Jaz ran the kayak ashore. Her booted feet sunk up to the ankle as she stepped out of the rocking boat, steadied by the buried paddle on the water side. Mud slurped as she tugged her foot free, and her lips curled in disgust.

From the opposite side of the rundown fence, a clatter sounded. A limb from a pecan tree raked along the top of the planks. An animal could be causing the commotion, but she'd been certain she'd seen a flash of denim dodge around the willow tree. If someone was there, why would they hide? And choosing to trespass on the old homestead could prove a dangerously poor choice.

When she was eight, Jaz had tried to explore it, and Drew jerked her away from the fence that had been more upright in those days.

"It's a nest for rattlesnakes," he'd hissed. And as much as she loved the outdoors and could "man up" as well as any boy her age, snakes freaked her out.

But what if some other kid was in there?

After dragging the kayak completely out of the water, dropping her life jacket and leaning the paddle against the willow, Jaz strode toward the dilapidated cedar planks. Browning scrub snagged her yoga pants. She ignored the tugs and found two missing boards beside a third plank that raised up when lifted.

She crouched through the opening, duck-walking through the underbrush on the opposite side of the fence. Twigs snapped beneath her hikers and leaves snagged her ponytail. After several feet, she emerged into a dusty patch between the overgrown vegetation and a leaning structure. It was too small to be anything except an old pump house or other outbuilding. Smudged footprints in the reddish dirt marked a path around the side of it.

Jaz opened her mouth to call out but shut it an instant later. Any kid who was playing around in here would know it was trespassing and wouldn't want to be found. She stepped lightly over the tracks and sidled along the building. A door hung off one hinge, closing the weathered building off except for an angular gap at the top corner where something had taken a chunk out of the wood.

She paused outside the doorway, holding her breath. A whisper of sound from inside gave away her quarry. Jaz pulled out her phone and selected the flashlight application. May as well stun the kid—or the possum, whichever she was about to unearth.

A rusty latch remained as the only handle for the door. Jaz grabbed the metal and at the same moment it croaked in contempt, she flung the door ajar and shined the beam from her phone into the narrow building.

Behind a slab of cardboard, a pair of pale eyes stared out at her. A slender hand, covered in grime, blocked her view. "Turn it off," squawked the cornered trespasser.

"Come out." Jaz lowered the beam so it pointed at the sagging box hiding the boy. "It's dangerous to play here."

"Not playing." He snapped the words like a trapped animal.

"Neither am I." Jaz straightened and gestured with her free hand.

After a scuffle, the child dodged around her and slumped against the sliver-infested exterior with enough force to rattle its walls. His red hair was ratty, and his freckle-smattered face bore deep smudges of dirt. Bony shoulders reached to Jaz's elbow, but the oversized sweatshirt didn't hide the emaciated state of his body.

"How old are you?"

"What's it to you?" He raised his chin, emphasizing the filth covering every inch of his skin.

Jaz arched an eyebrow and crossed her arms. "Where do you live?"

"Here."

A stab ached inside her gut. Where were his parents?

"I ain't going nowhere without Fl— my sister."

"And where is she?" Her heart leapt. Was the girl hiding somewhere else? Hurt from a fall or even a snake bite?

Thin shoulders shrugged, and a fraction of defiance drained away. "Some house in Sweet Grove. That's why I took off from that lady's house in Harrison."

His pale lips pressed together.

He'd run away because he wanted to be with his sister.

"How old are you?" she repeated.

After a pause, during which he studied Jaz and she felt the strength of his perusal, he dropped his chin.

"Nine. She's only five. She needs me to take care of her."

It could have been Bailey standing in front of her, neglected and worried about protecting Tess. Not that Bailey had ever run away from the system, but he surely would have fled his biological parents if there was a way to ensure Tess could escape safely, too.

Hopelessness bled into the boy's amber-flecked, whiskey-colored eyes. They'd seen too much, and now they'd be forced to see another place where he was unwanted. Why had he been separated from his younger sister? Had he come from a drug-using home like Bailey? A place where he or his sister had been abused? Was living in this rundown homestead more dangerous than whatever he'd faced before?

Warmth exploded in her stomach. He needed help, and she was the one God had put in his path. The thrill of determination spiraled through her chest. Decision and purpose steeled her spine.

"Come with me. I'll help you find your sister." She knew it wouldn't be easy, but the boy deserved to see his sister, even if only for a minute before being whisked to wherever kids who ran away from foster homes went.

His eyes narrowed, and he slouched away from her. "Why?"

"Because my boyfriend was a foster kid when he was your age, and he would have done anything to keep his little sister safe." *Then and now.*

After a quick scan of her face, he slipped back into the leaning pump house. Jaz ignored the fidgety feeling in her stomach. She had no idea how she'd help him find his sister, but when had that ever stopped her?

A moment later he emerged with a ratty camouflage backpack slung over one shoulder, and he tried to shrug his other arm in the strap.

Jaz lifted the pack so his arm slid in place. It felt heavier than she expected. "What's in this thing? Rocks?"

"I can't eat rocks." He scowled.

As they walked toward the fence, shimmying through brush, Jaz debated how to get him back to town. Her car was across the pond in the park's lot, but two people couldn't fit in the kayak. Making a quick decision, she pulled out her cell phone and scrolled to the sheriff's number, which he'd encouraged her to keep on hand during her dealings with Honey Campbell.

He answered with a blunt, "Grant."

"Jaz here."

Her companion stopped beside the kayak, kneeling to touch its smooth surface.

"I'm by the old homestead off Orchard Way. Need a ride, if you could come in quiet."

He sighed. "I'm not a taxi service."

"I have a one-person kayak and a passenger. One you've likely been looking for."

After a pause, Grant asked, "Red-haired boy?"

Jaz grunted, hanging back from the kayak.

After a grumpy mutter, the sheriff said, "Be there in fifteen," and ended the call.

Jaz slid her phone into her pocket and approached the boy with her hand out. "I'm Jaz."

"Kenton." His grubby hands were thin and surprisingly warm.

"How long have you been hiding out here?"

Kenton squatted beside the boat. "Are we going in this?"

She shook her head. "It's for a single person."

The glint snuffed from his pale eyes. Jaz wanted to zip him into the life vest and paddle him around the pond—anything to bring the glow of life back to his expression. It reminded her of working with the children in the law office while their parents had consultations about malpractice lawsuits. It was the only part of her job she'd missed while taking care of her mother the previous six weeks.

"You're pretty brave to hide in that dump."

Skinny shoulders shrugged. His gaze traveled around the lake, and he fumbled with some pebbles on the bank. He tossed one into the water. The motion, not smooth or manly like Bailey's, still reminded her of him. Each time they'd been there, he'd expended part of his nervous energy by tossing stones in the pond.

She needed to help this boy and his sister. Bailey would claim she had a hero complex, and if she did, she'd gotten it from her older brother, Drew, who'd sacrificed his life to save his squad from a surprise attack in Afghanistan.

"Did you see any snakes?"

"Snakes are cool." The boy gawked at her over his shoulder. Watching for her reaction to that startling viewpoint?

Jaz stopped the shiver that wanted to disagree about scaly

creatures. "So, you did see some? Rattlers are poisonous, you know."

"No rattlers. Only a few black snakes, and they didn't want to share the shack with me." His skinny body shook with the raise of his shoulders.

"When did you last eat?" Jaz slid beside the kayak and pulled out her day pack.

When her zipper opening broke the silence, his gaze homed in on her movements with feverish intensity. She handed him her water bottle and the granola bar she'd tucked in the week before when she'd gone on a six-mile run.

By the time he gulped down the water and gnawed through the food, a dark truck bumped down the road. At least the sheriff arrived in his hunting rig instead of the patrol car he normally drove.

Kenton's eyes widened. He flinched when the uniformed man stepped from the vehicle. "You called the cops?" The accusation burned through her hotter than his venomous glare.

"I'll stay with you. Promise. Sheriff Grant's a good guy. He helped my friend a few months ago."

Kenton's head whipped from side to side, but there was nowhere he could run. He shriveled into himself, and Jaz draped her arm over his shoulders.

"I promise to take care of you."

His wide eyes begged for more than a few moments of time. Her heart melted.

"Who do we have here?" The sheriff's gruff voice eased at Kenton's fearful expression.

"This is my bud, Kenton. And this is Sheriff Grant. He's going to give us a ride to my car and return the kayak to Mr. Bryant." Jaz projected an appeal through her eye contact with the lawman.

"So I am." He held his hand toward the boy.

Kenton looked skeptical for a few long moments, then shook it quickly.

"Want to grab the other end of this thing?" The sheriff nodded to the stern of the kayak, a hand resting on the bow. His taser rattled against his boots as he squatted down to grip the plastic.

Kenton scrambled to pick up the other end of the boat. His backpack bobbed with each step and something in his face relaxed. Jaz followed behind with the paddle.

*Lord, show me how to help this boy and his sister. I promised.*

And she always kept her promises. Drew had taught her that.

# Twenty-nine

**B**ailey hurried back from his two meetings in Rosewood only to discover Lonie with his filthy feet on the desk in the office while Tess worked on her computer. The man's eyes scanned the room, resting on the large painting of the ranch in better days that concealed Fritz's in-wall safe.

"I can run you into Rosewood now." He nudged the booted feet from the desk.

Lonie lurched upright as his feet swung to the floor. "Thanks, son." The sound of the word from his lips made Bailey's skin crawl. "Tessa's gonna run me in to pick up a few things from Walmart."

Tess glanced up, distracted. "I need some cleaning supplies. And the groceries are cheaper there, too."

"You're not buying him anything." Bailey glared between the two of them.

"I've got a little pocket cash." The glint in Lonie's eyes reminded Bailey of his demand for money.

Tess waved her hands at them. "I'm trying to work here. I'll be ready to go in thirty minutes."

Bailey jerked his thumb toward the door. Lonie's lips curved in a lazy smile and he stood with the speed of a sloth. Bailey glared, but the expression made Lonie's smile grow.

In the hall, Bailey hauled the man toward the front door.

"Don't touch me, boy." A dangerous glint shone from Lonie's dark eyes.

Bailey swung wide the door and gestured for Lonie to precede him. Lonie plucked a strand of long grass from beside the porch and chewed on it.

"I'll pay for your motel room in Rosewood."

"I said I ain't leaving here until you make it worth my while." He settled his back against one of the posts. "Besides, your sister wants to get to know me."

"I know you well enough for both of us."

"Do you?" He quirked an eyebrow. "'Pears you didn't tell her anything about me." The man's low chuckle reminded Bailey of a rattlesnake.

"Look, we don't have any money."

"I am looking." He gazed around the porch and to the paddock and barn. "I see plenty of dollar signs."

Bailey ground his teeth together. He needed to get rid of this man, and he'd prefer to do it without unearthing the abuse he'd endured at his hands. Somehow, he needed to convince Tess that he was dangerous.

*Show her.*

He ignored the voice. He'd been the one wearing a tank top at the swimming hole, the one who never took his shirt off in the locker room. And he didn't intend for his sister to see his scarred back. Ever.

"I'm going to get ready for my afternoon with a pretty girl." Lonie tossed the grass away and stepped toward the door.

Bailey blocked his path. "Leave Tess alone."

Lonie blinked slowly. "You know how to make me."

His breath smelled like tobacco and beer, making Bailey wonder where he'd gotten either.

Lonie shoved his shoulder against Bailey's arm and swaggered inside.

Bailey needed to get away. The dogs yipped as he headed toward the barn, and the horses in the corral raised their heads. Shamgar whinnied, but Bailey ignored the pull to spend a few minutes with the horse.

Instead, he jumped into his truck and twisted the key. The back end rattled and swung wide as he roared out of the driveway onto Armstrong Road. Gravel sprayed the brown weeds in the ditch. Bailey steered into the slide and lifted his boot from the pedal.

He didn't want to give Lonie Dyer the satisfaction of knowing how much their faceoff upset him.

"I'm not that kid anymore." He growled the words to no one and reached for the knob on his ancient radio.

He cranked the volume only to hear some country song crooning about no one understanding the heart of a cowboy. A cowboy. That's what he'd always be, even if he could draw and run his own office, he felt most comfortable on Shamgar's back.

He slowed as he entered Sweet Grove city limits. His jaw ached, and he tried to relax his gritted teeth. Tess thought she wanted to know why Bailey hated and distrusted Lonie, but he didn't want to see the look of pity in her eyes. He bore scars in his flesh, and she didn't need to see them.

*Jesus bears scars in his flesh.*

He'd been twelve when a fight had landed him on his back. The scraped skin burned, and MaryAnn walked in while Bailey tried to clean himself up.

Reflected in the mirror, her eyes widened above the marks he bore. As she took the cloth from him, he'd turned, hating the way his lip trembled and tears blurred his eyes.

*You're in good company, son.* She'd talked about the scars on Jesus' back and in his hands and feet—scars he'd shown his disciples, but Bailey wanted to cover his up. The shame of them diminished that day, but it had never disappeared.

*Were you thinking you'd hide them !om Jaz once you're married?*
He shook away those thoughts.

Without his by-your-leave, the truck bounced into the parking lot of First Street Church. At that moment, Pastor Bernie emerged from the door at the back of the building.

Bailey swung the truck into a parking spot and slammed it into park.

Bernie raised his hand in greeting and sauntered over to the driver's window. "Afternoon, Bailey."

He rolled the window down. "Afternoon."

"How about some coffee?" The pastor nodded toward Mabel's. According to Jeffrey, the pastor took two coffee—and pie—breaks there every Monday through Friday.

Bailey shook his head. "I need to talk to someone about our visitor." The man's wife helped Tess with meal prep or cleaning at least one day each week, so he would know about the uninvited guest.

"Your biological father." Both men nodded.

"Unexpected, I hear."

"Unwelcome."

Bernie furrowed his brow. "Not to Tessa." He gestured toward the church. "Want to sit inside a spell?"

Bailey heaved a sigh. "I want him gone."

"You had a rough go before Fritz and MaryAnn adopted you."

*They didn't adopt me.* Bailey bit back the denial. That was old news. The Traverses loved him and Tess, no matter what legal documents were never filed.

"I know you'd be stopping to see the sheriff if you had a legal question." Bernie leaned his forearm on the rusty mirror. "So, I'm guessing this is about forgiveness."

Bailey blinked and sat back. The springs beneath him groaned at the sudden movement. He drummed his fingers on the steering wheel. He didn't want to talk about forgiveness.

"I want to marry Jaz." That would get an eyebrow raise.

Bernie's eyebrow twitched. "I hear she's heading back to Austin, and you're back in Sweet Grove."

Bailey shrugged. "We've done the distance thing before."

"But it doesn't work for a marriage."

"If she married me, she could stay here. With me."

"Did you ask her, son?" The word sounded so natural coming from the preacher, and Bailey's heart leapt at the sound of it. Unlike when Lonie uttered it like a curse, this made warmth pool inside him.

He shook his head. "I've got nothing to offer her."

"What about love? And family?" Bernie smiled. "You might be surprised to realize there's more to keep her here than you think."

Bailey's phone vibrated in his pocket.

"You've grown into a man who made your parents proud." Bernie cocked his head. "Now MaryAnn would want to see you in church more regularly..."

Bernie grinned, and Bailey's stiff lips responded. A light of truth pushed back the dark thoughts plaguing him. A little more church would probably give him a sharper perspective about everything. Why did he let Lonie's lies make him doubt? Tess loved and respected him, but she didn't understand.

"Let's pray." When Bailey nodded, the pastor squeezed his shoulder. "Lord, give Bailey wisdom in dealing with his family issues, and strength to walk in the path You have for him.

Amen."

Warmth oozed straight to his churning stomach and aching chest. The prayer had power, like so many Fritz had prayed over him in the years before MaryAnn had passed away. Wistfulness for the peace Bailey had once known with God overwhelmed the doubts.

"God's got this. You think you can trust Him?" Bernie held his gaze.

Bailey ducked his chin. "Thanks, pastor. That prayer reminded me of Dad—" Emotion choked the words.

Bernie patted his shoulder again. "Fritz was a good man. A godly man, and he'd be thrilled to see you helping Tess with the ranch and finding a woman like Jaz to marry."

Surety coalesced in his gut, chasing away the last remnants of anger.

"Now, there's a slice of pie calling my name at Mabel's." A smile bloomed on the serious face. "Sure you don't want to join me?"

Bailey shook his head and pulled out his phone. *Meet me at the sheriff's office,* the text from Jaz read.

His heart leapt. He hadn't heard from her all day, and now this. Was everything all right?

"Who's that?" The pastor asked. "You look worried."

"Jaz. She's at the police station."

Bernie's concerned expression melted into a smile. "Oh, she rescued a boy out by Mill Pond this morning. A runaway."

Bailey's hand dropped to the gear shift. "I guess I don't need to bail her out, then."

Bernie laughed and raised his hand as Bailey backed out of the parking spot. The sun glinted off his windshield, and for an instant, light ringed the pastor's auburn hair like a halo.

*Thanks for sending your angel, Lord.*

The rattling truck carried Bailey the few blocks to the woman who owned his heart.

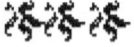

JAZ PACED ALONG THE FRONT OF THE STATION, craning her neck toward the conference room where the county attorney, a social worker, the sheriff, and another woman sat with Kenton. She hadn't intended to spend her day at the station, but her heart cried out for the plight of the scrawny, homeless boy.

When she paced toward the outside, a leggy cowboy crossed the parking lot. Jaz pushed through the glass doors of the station and jogged down the three steps to meet him.

"Hey, cowboy." She grinned up at him.

He caught her hand in his and pulled her against his side. "I guess I don't need to post bail?"

She elbowed him. His chuckle seemed forced.

"What were those meetings you had today? We were so busy debating how to run Lonie out of town, you never said."

They strolled toward the parked cars. She picked out his rusted truck closer to the library's section of the lot.

"He's still here."

The growling tone made Jaz swing her gaze to him. His jaw bulged as he gritted his teeth. She squeezed his hand, wishing she knew how to solve his problem.

"What about the meetings in Rosewood?"

When they reached his truck, Bailey leaned against the tailgate, reminding her of the first time he'd given her a ride in the old Ford. She stopped a step away from him and tilted her chin up, glad she could see all the lines of his handsome face from this angle.

"A project for work. And it looks like I'll be opening a branch in Bryant County."

Jaz blinked, her mind spinning on the words. "You're moving back to Sweet Grove?"

The first month of their relationship had been across the distance, and the past six weeks reminded her how much she despised it. She wanted to spend every evening with him rehashing the day or streaming sitcoms. It wasn't a good night for her without his lips brushing along hers and flashing his killer half-smile.

He nodded. "Just in time."

Her heart dropped into her shoes. He meant in time to protect his sister. She knew that, but she heard something else: "Just in time for you to go back to Austin."

Her face must have showed her misgivings because he ran a finger gently along her jaw. "We can do the long-distance thing for a while longer."

But what if she didn't want to?

His mouth quirked into the grin she adored.

"Now, why are you at the sheriff's office?"

She explained about finding the boy. As she talked, something twisted in her chest. She'd promised to help Kenton find his sister, but all she'd done was get him back in the system that separated them.

"He wants to be placed with his little sister." She tossed her hands in the air. "As soon as I saw him, he reminded me of you."

Something dark flashed in Bailey's blue eyes before he ducked his chin so the brim of his hat shaded them from view.

"He wants to protect her, like Drew protected me and you protect Tess."

"It's what brothers do." Bailey's drawling words were quiet.

Jaz furrowed her brow and reached to push his hat up. In the pocket of her bedraggled sweatshirt, her phone vibrated against her abdomen and when she looked down, her kinking hair fell from her loosening ponytail.

"It's my boss." She glanced away from the phone. "I called to ask for advice about Kenton."

"Better take the call." He pecked her cheek, but the action made her shiver instead of filling her with warmth. "I should check on Tess."

"Dinner at six?"

Bailey rounded to the driver's door and nodded once. "We'll be there."

Jaz slid her finger to answer the phone and strode back toward the police station. "Mr. Boldt, thanks for returning my call."

"Sounded important." He cleared his throat. "Call me Evan."

She shook her head. "I need some legal advice. About foster care group homes."

Because as she'd listened to Kenton's story of a mother who abandoned him to her sister and the aunt who foisted them on friends at every turn, she couldn't stand the thought of the boy being separated from his sister for another day.

They needed a home, and apparently, since Kenton had fled from every placement, no one wanted him.

Bailey's truck rattled past and Jaz waved at him. He raised his hand in return, but he wasn't smiling. Already thinking about confronting Lonie again? Or did she say something that hurt his feelings? Evan's voice drew her attention back to the phone.

"It's not my specialty, but I possess some general knowledge."

The standard legal disclaimer. It made her lips quirk into something like a smile. How very lawyerly of him.

"There's a nine-year-old boy who wants to be placed with his younger sister. She's five. They've been in and out of the foster system for six months, but now their legal guardian has been deemed unfit."

Jaz clenched her fist, gripping her yoga pants in a way that wasn't healthy for the spandex.

"Their parents are out of the picture, then?"

"Dad isn't named on the birth certificates. Mom left two years ago and hasn't been back."

"FPS will search for her."

Jaz nodded. She had no delusions that the mother who'd abandoned her three-year-old daughter to a woman who sold herself for drugs would be considered any more fit than the aunt. Yes, there'd be a process, but there wasn't any reason to expect the kids wouldn't be in the system.

"Grandparents deceased. No other known relatives. But the sister has been accepted into a family that doesn't have room for the boy. Kenton." Naming him made it more real.

"Sad but not unusual."

Spoken like a man whose family was intact. A man who had never had to protect his sister from anything worse than unwanted attention from the guys at school.

Jaz gritted her teeth. *Lord, help me handle this the right way.*

Which wasn't spewing disdain for the man she prayed would assist her. Even if her home life hadn't been ideal, she didn't fully understand Kenton's situation either. But she knew the results. She witnessed them daily in the life of the man she loved. Parents who left didn't do it without causing internal wounds.

"According to the sheriff, this isn't an isolated event. And now that Kenton has run away, he's considered a higher risk and no local fosters will take him in."

Evan made a noncommittal sound, so Jaz pressed on. "We need a residential facility for older kids and siblings. A safe place where they can be together."

"That'll require two monitors, one of each gender."

Of course. Nothing she wanted could be easy.

*I don't need easy.* Determination revved her heart rate.

"Seems like at least a half-dozen kids have been bounced around, some clear out into the sticks. There are ten families in Rosewood, but half are for emergency placements and the other half have been filled up all year."

"What did you need?"

"A place for them to stay right here in the community."

She took a deep breath. Once she said it aloud, there'd be no going back. "I'm going to start a group home."

She straightened. The fire in her middle that had burned brightly when she'd first joined the Army flared to life. Passion for a mission. It had been the missing ingredient these past weeks while she'd been chained to a computer doing research and taking care of her mother.

On her boss's end of the phone, she heard a door open and close. He sighed. "I know an attorney who specializes in family law and deals frequently with FPS. I'll have him call you."

"These kids need someone to advocate for them."

"You'd make a fine attorney, Jaz. With a heart for the underdog, you'd be a favorite with families." After a pause, "You are a favorite with our clients. The kids have missed you."

"I've missed them." She pictured the diversity of faces among the clientele.

"It might be next week before he contacts you." Evan sounded resigned.

"That's fine. After help from Google, I have a starting place. I'm hoping the FPS social worker will discuss it with me once she finishes with Kenton and the legal team."

His sigh was louder this time. "You'll be in the office Monday?"

Her galloping heart sank into her stomach. She needed to return to Austin and get back to her job. Even the returning hope of finding a new mission didn't negate the drudgery of details.

"I'll be there."

By the time she returned to the station, the door to the conference room opened. Sheriff Grant strode out and caught her eye. She followed him back.

The door barely closed before Kenton jumped up and stepped toward her. She let him hold her hand. Both the social worker and Jedediah Gowan, the county attorney, took note of the physical contact. Funny how the standoffish boy had warmed up to her during the hours they played checkers at this very table.

"Jaz Rolle is the one who found our boy out by Mill Pond." The sheriff gestured toward the attorney. "You know Mr. Gowan. Donna is a court reporter asked to transcribe the conversation today. And this—" His hand extended toward a mousy looking woman whose brown eyes squinted at them over large, round glasses, "is the representative from FPS, KaroLynn Vance."

Jaz shook hands all around before squeezing into a chair beside Kenton. The boy fidgeted, kicking her in the ankle on accident. Jaz gripped his hand tighter until he stilled.

"Could you relate the story for us, on the record?" Jed Gowan folded his hands and gazed at her.

She could see how those light brown eyes could be both comforting and menacing, depending on if he was for or against you in court. Jaz relayed the morning events.

She ended the tale with her own question. "So, is it possible for Kenton to see his sister?"

Jed turned to the social worker. KaroLynn's mouth worked like a fish in search of food. She cleared her throat and pulled off her glasses. "We feel for the boy's situation but reuniting the children could disturb a happy placement."

"What do you think will happen?" Jaz raised her eyebrows. "Is Kenton going to scoop his sister up and run?"

The social worker glared. Jaz didn't want to make an enemy of the woman. She needed help to move forward with her plan, but there was red tape and then there was ridiculousness. A boy wanted to make sure his little sister was safe, and anything that kept him from doing that was ridiculous.

Jaz turned to Kenton. "You just want to see her, right?"

He nodded. His Adam's apple bulged as he swallowed. "I wish I could stay with her, but I know no one wants me."

Jaz's heart plunged into her feet. She wanted to pull the boy into her arms and reassure him that he was wanted. But since she couldn't take him home with her because of the state fostering hullabaloo, she wouldn't offer false hope or additional promises.

She ground her teeth. "What can we do to make this meeting happen?"

KaroLynn huffed. Jed and the sheriff exchanged glances.

"Look, ma'am, I plan to hunt up enough support from investors to open a residential home for foster kids who are difficult to place and especially for siblings. I think it's in the best interest of the children if families can stay together."

"And a group home is better than living with a family?"

Jaz shook her head. "No, but it's better than being separated from the only family you have." She sighed. "Ms. Vance, we might have gotten off on the wrong foot here. I don't care so much about regulations as I do about this little boy."

The women's gazes clashed and held. Understanding dawned in the social worker's eyes. However long she'd been working for FPS, it had been long enough to drain the soul from her, but Jaz saw the woman's buried ideals awakening.

KaroLynn shifted in her seat and cleared her throat. "I can certainly call the foster home and see if a visit with Flossie May can be arranged."

"Thank you." She squeezed Kenton's hand. The boy wilted against her arm. "And any information you could give me that would expedite my own project would be greatly appreciated."

The woman nodded. "Let me make that call before we take the boy to his emergency placement."

She shuffled out of the room clutching a folder in one hand and a cell phone in the other.

"Thanks for your help, sheriff." Jaz smiled at the man.

"Thanks for staying with Kenton here." The sheriff squatted to the boy's level. "Although, I bet he's hungry. I've got a sandwich and chips in the break room."

After a nod from Jaz, Kenton followed the sheriff out. Once the door shut, the court reporter began collecting her gear.

"Jed, you got any insight on opening a halfway house for these kids?" Jaz asked the county attorney.

"It's a big undertaking. Judging by how things have been going this year, I think it'd take some pressure off the foster parents in the area."

As nice as his approval of the idea was, that wasn't the sort of information she needed. "I have the procedure from the Internet, but I have a feeling the state isn't going to see an unmarried woman my age as a suitable sponsor for such an undertaking."

He raised a dark eyebrow. "If you had a social work degree, they'd look on you more favorably. Still, residential foster care homes for youth are in demand. Most sponsors specialize the tenants, like children of drug or sexual abuse."

"Something for siblings and runaways isn't specific enough?"

The corners of his lips lifted. "Oh, it's specific. And pretty high risk. They'll want lock-ins and a certified counselor, most likely. As well as—"

"A live-in chaperone of each gender."

His smile appeared, transforming him into a good-old-boy. "You have done some homework."

"Evan Boldt told me that."

"Evan Boldt? That's right. You work for the Boldt brothers in Austin."

"I hope they understand." She stood up. "This project is about to become my full-time focus."

Jed hurried to open the door for the reporter. He thanked her for her help and waited for Jaz to follow her out.

Jaz locked her gaze on his. "This halfway house is happening."

"I'll support you anyway I can."

She nodded. "You can start by steering me toward potential investors."

Jed coughed. "You don't ask for much, do you?"

For these kids, she'd ask for the sun and moon and wouldn't stop asking until she got them.

# Thirty

The old farmhouse felt empty as Bailey worked on preliminary drawings for the new office space. Dick had signed the lease earlier in the day after all four investors for the conversion project had signed on the dotted line. Next week he'd meet with contractors and shuffle through bids to get his first solo project underway.

The sun lingered low on the horizon, and he checked his cell for the umpteenth time. It had barely been thirty minutes since Tess said she was heading home. He wondered if he should shower before taking his sister to the Rolle house.

*As soon as I saw him, he reminded me of you.* Jaz's words cut into him. Did she really see a scrawny foster kid when she looked at him?

She felt sorry for him. And here he was planning to ask her to marry him.

He shook away the thoughts. That hadn't been what she meant. Hadn't his past attempts to break up with her taught him anything? Jaz loved him. As much as any woman ever would.

*More than you deserve.*

Bailey surged to his feet and closed the laptop. He didn't need to listen to Lonie's lies inside his head. Soon enough, the man would be back and tossing out threats in person. He might as well use this time to sneak into the barn and give Shamgar a treat.

After he stowed his laptop in its bag, he pulled some baby carrots out of the small refrigerator in the manager's room. A quick glance in the mirror told him he should at least comb his hair. After all, he'd have his hat off.

The smell of hay, dust, and animals embraced him as he strode down the path toward the paddock gate. At his whistle, four heads came up and four horsey faces turned.

"Hey buddy. I've got carrots."

Shamgar tossed his silvery mane and wheeled toward the barn. When another horse made a move in the same direction, his gelding cut in front and trotted a few steps. The bay snorted and stomped, staring toward the barn, tail flicking side to side.

Soon enough, Shamgar followed Bailey into his stall, nose nuzzling along the hip pocket of Bailey's jeans. Bailey offered him one carrot on a flat palm to entice the horse into the wooden enclosure.

Shamgar nudged his chest.

"Demanding, aren't you?" Bailey scratched the black star on the horse's forehead. He could still see ghostly creases, scars remaining from the rope marks that had crisscrossed the speckled coat when he'd first rescued the animal.

After Shamgar snuffed up the final carrot, Bailey ducked across the aisle to grab a brush and curry comb.

"Never pictured you with animals."

Bailey flinched at the jarring words in the solace of the barn. Lonie Dyer didn't belong in this world.

One of his hands closed on the curry comb as he swiveled toward the doorway.

The man slouched against the door frame, with work-booted feet crossed at the ankle and jeans a size too large sagging to his hips beneath an oversized sweatshirt. He looked like he'd been dressed from a dumpster, and that was probably close to the truth. Wasn't he getting some clothes today?

Bailey didn't care enough to ask. He sidled toward the shelf of brushes.

"Your sister is sweeter than candy." Lonie shook his head. "Got too much religion along the way." His lips puckered in disgust.

"The Traverses were great parents."

Lonie raised an eyebrow. "Anyone who needs the crutch of religion is weak."

Bailey blinked. Fritz and MaryAnn were far from weak. He recalled the strength of the peace and assurance he'd felt after his short conversation with Pastor Bernie. Lonie was the weak one.

"Time to talk business, boy." Lonie straightened as he growled the words.

"I don't care to do business with you." Bailey scorched the man with a glare.

"You should." A scratchy chuckle that sounded like metal grinding into glass set Bailey back a step. "I know you care about your sister."

"You only care about yourself." The metal edge of the comb cut into his palm.

"I've been reformed." The man's thin hand clutched at his chest like Bailey's words wounded him, but the crooked tilt of his lips told the true tale. "Colorado and Texas penitentiaries have been contributing to my education, healthy eating, and fitness for two decades. I am a poster boy of the system."

"Hardly a positive endorsement," Bailey muttered and edged back until his shoulders nudged a peg holding a bridle.

"My parole officer would argue that."

"Got him snowed already, huh?"

"Son, it don't snow in Texas. I'm a charming man." He smirked. "That's how I convinced your mama to marry me."

An urge to pummel the sneering face welled in Bailey's gut. It burned through him, but he gripped the comb and an empty peg to anchor himself away from the despicable man.

*Lord, don't let me sink to his level.* The prayer came suddenly, unbidden. Tension eased from his shoulders.

"Pay me off, and I'm gone."

"For how long?"

A thick eyebrow rose toward the receded hairline. "Pay me enough and you'll never see me again."

*I couldn't be so lucky.*

"The guest ranch took all our capital." *All of Wynn's capital.* They'd never had any money in the bank. "There's no money."

"I've seen some antiques around the place."

He'd been casing the farmhouse and barn. Bailey shouldn't have expected any less. He fisted his hands again. Pain as the curry comb gouged him shook away the cyclone of fury.

"There's nothing for you here. You should move along."

"You gonna make me?" Lonie straightened into a semblance of a fighting stance.

Bailey gritted his teeth and snarled, "I can take you."

Lonie laughed. The sound crawled over Bailey's skin like a horde of locusts. A buried memory rose from the back of his mind.

⁂

PAIN *SEARED THROUGH HIS BACK.*

*"I told you to take the trash out, boy. Are you too stupid* for *that?"*

Bailey's *six-year-old #ame shook #om the agony of the* lit *joint pressed to his bare back. He'd been in the bathroom* washing *baby Tessa when his father slammed into the room* and jerked *him toward the kitchen. He couldn't leave the* baby *in the water. She would drown!*

*He'd been back in the kitchen in less than a minute, but by then his father's rage burned as hot as the smoking weed.*

*Bailey scrambled toward the paper bag. It seeped liquid on the scarred linoleum, wet #om something his parents had discarded. His fingers fumbled to scoop up the bottom.*

*The rancid scent of burnt sauce made him gag. That had been from his mother's attempt to heat up a can of ravioli, but she'd been puffing on her pipe and ruined what had been one of his favorite foods. It hadn't tasted much better than it smelled, but Bailey knew better than to complain. And if he hadn't eaten it, he would have been hungry.*

*A smack knocked his face into the soggy coffee grounds on the top of the bag. Bailey stumbled into the side of the door and struggled to keep his grip on the bag with one hand. He hadn't thought of how he would open the door with his hands full.*

*"Corine! Open the door for your stupid son!"*

*Bailey flinched, waiting for another fist to find its way into his flesh.*

*"He's your son, too," his mother hollered back, her voice coming closer.*

*"Something so dumb couldn't come from me." His father puffed out his chest.*

*"Look at him," his mother demanded, coming out of the main living area. "His eyes and the color of his hair."*

*The scent of cat urine surrounded her. They didn't have a cat, but that's what his mother always smelled like.*

*She jerked open the #ont door. A gust of air shoved the rotten garbage smell up Bailey's nose. "He looks just like you."*

*"Well, he acts like you. Stupid."*

*Bailey slithered through the door, scraping his arm on the metal workings. He hardly felt the pain, what with the scorch mark throbbing on his back and the chi! wind biting his shirtless torso.*

*"I must be stupid to stay with a loser like you," his mother snarled.*

*Thankfully, the door slammed and spared Bailey from hearing the exchange of insults.*

⁂

BAILEY BLINKED BACK INTO THE PRESENT, SHAKING his head. Lord help, he would not stoop to this man's level. He slid one booted foot toward the doorway.

"I'm sure you think you can take me, boy." Lonie reached toward his boot and pulled out a hunting knife easily as long as his forearm. "I'll be here to console Tessie when they find your bloody body."

Bailey stopped. The ice in the dark eyes meant business. He knew that merciless expression. Years in prison had probably given Lonie plenty of experience in self-defense.

"I've got places to be."

"Your sister was cleaning up." Lonie grinned, rotating the knife so light glinted off the blade.

Bailey sucked in a breath. Saddle oil and a hint of horse filled his nostrils.

"She said she'd be ready in a few minutes."

"I need to clean up, too."

"Don't let me keep you." But he made no move to clear out of the doorway.

Bailey clutched the curry comb, considering it as a projectile. He could bean the vile face, but the knife would still be there.

"Do we understand each other?"

Bailey nodded. "You're going to play Papa with Tess until I give you incentive to head out."

"I've charmed smarter women." He snorted. "Not that your

mama was one of them."

The metal brush gouged deeper until Bailey relaxed his grip.

*Lord, I really want to lay him out. Make him move out of my way before I lose control.*

"Aren't you supposed to get a job?"

"I've got several lined up. And I'll be doing some junk hauling tomorrow." Lonie held his gaze again, then slid the knife back into the cover hidden beneath the denim.

"I better let you go get some of that chocolate pie." His leer raised Bailey's blood pressure, but then the slime ball oozed away as quickly as he'd appeared.

Bailey stared at the ceiling, listening until the creak of the sliding doors told him the man was truly gone. His breath hissed out in rushed exhales. He paced to the shelf and placed the comb where it belonged. A moment staring at the grooves in his palm from the death grip on the tool helped him steady his breathing.

"Thank you, Lord." His whisper seemed to echo through the saddles, blankets, and bridles.

Fritz taught him to fight as a final measure and that some principles had to be proven with violence. MaryAnn showed him that prayer almost always delivered a person from the fight. God could cool your temper or move your opponent out of range. He'd done the second today.

"If you could erase the flashbacks, that'd be even better."

But Bailey knew it would be an unanswered plea. Sure, the nightmares hadn't lasted after the first year on the ranch, but there were always things that would trigger those shadowy childhood years.

*They're part of you. They made you the man you are as surely as working this ranch has.* Fritz's reassurances didn't make the shame disappear. Just like he bore the scars of Lonie's abuse on his flesh, his soul bore them even deeper.

A nicker woke Bailey from his stupor. He trudged back to the stall and scratched behind the ears tilted toward him. "I'll have to brush you later, boy. I've got a date."

The soft nose dipped toward Bailey's pockets.

"I'll bring you more carrots then."

Shamgar snorted and stomped a foot almost like he understood. If anyone could, it would be an animal that had been just as mistreated before coming to the ranch.

And maybe big-hearted Jaz, who shared her brother's passion for helping the underdogs.

*And me,* whispered the One who had answered his plea only moments before.

For once, Bailey wasn't facing the bully alone.

THE SCENT OF CHILI POWDER AND SWEETNESS embraced Jaz as she darted into her parents' house. She hadn't meant to leave her mother alone all day.

"Mom?"

"Kitchen." The sing-song quality that had been missing for weeks rang in the lilting call coming from Jaz's left.

She dropped her bag on the counter. A quick glance showed her that no matter what her nose said about the state of dinner, the table still wasn't set.

Her mother stood at the sink, wrists buried in soapy water.

"Sorry to desert you."

Mom's smile lit up the room. "Tabitha stopped by." She pointed her elbow to a square dish sitting on the stovetop.

Jaz pecked her mother's cheek and leaned over the stove. Cinnamon battled with the other delicious scents. "Peach cobbler?"

"It is Bailey's favorite."

The man had a sweet tooth that wouldn't quit, and her mother catered to it whenever he shared a meal at their house.

"You and Tess spoil him."

"You've already got his heart, so I'll settle for his stomach." Mom chuckled at her own joke.

Jaz slid beside her mother and scrubbed her hands. "He's moving back, you know."

"Oh? Right when you're heading back to Austin."

Her mother's perfect lips curved down.

"Let me finish this and set the table. Dad should be home soon." Jaz didn't want to think about returning to a long-distance relationship with Bailey.

Mom pulled a hand towel free from the stove's handle and kissed Jaz's cheek. "You're a wonderful blessing."

Jaz didn't feel like a blessing. More like a spilled box of spaghetti. What had changed?

Although the past six weeks had been a misery in many ways, she'd managed to come to terms with her relationship with her father. As much as she enjoyed the group of younger Christians in Austin, she'd found spiritual peace at First Street Church. Her friendships with Elise, Kristina, and Tess added a hometown feeling, too.

The buzz of the garage door opening pulled her back to the tasks at hand. She dried her hands before pulling five deep bowls out of the cupboard.

"Something smells delicious." Her father's voice carried down the hallway from the laundry room.

"Chili and cornbread," her mother replied.

The words cut off abruptly, and Jaz shook her head. It used to hurt to see the love and adoration her father had for her mother because he had none to offer Jaz. Having Bailey look at her with love helped, but Jaz knew her father was proud of her in his own way.

Jaz hurried to the oven and cracked open the door. Sweetly scented hot air washed over her. Yellow batter rose evenly in the rectangle baking dish.

The doorbell chimed, and a knock sounded an instant before Tess called, "We're here!"

Jaz let the oven door fall shut as she skipped to the entryway. Tess met her at the kitchen entrance, but Bailey stood on the stoop, a frown marring his good looks. "The point of ringing the bell—"

"She was expecting us." Tess hugged her quickly and shot a rolled-eye grimace toward her brother.

"We're practically family. Family doesn't ring the bell."

Jaz waggled her finger in a "come here" motion. Bailey swept his hat off. Something in his eyes told her his frown was about more than his sister's breach of etiquette.

She rose on her tiptoes to peck his cheek. "Hey, cowboy. How about a smile for your best girl?"

His lips tightened, tilting in a poor excuse for a grin.

She arched an eyebrow at him. "I'll take your hat and coat."

Tess reappeared, holding her jacket. "On your bed?"

Jaz nodded and Tess whisked the items a few steps down the hall. At the end of the hallway, the master bedroom door opened, and her mother strolled out, fingers laced with her father's. He walked a step behind her, clad in jeans and a sweatshirt.

"Welcome, Bailey." She stopped to hug Tess, who emerged with empty hands from Jaz's room. "Tessa."

Jaz reached for Bailey's hand, but he'd turned to shut the door, taking an unusually long time to secure it. What was wrong? Something must have happened with Lonie.

Tess bubbled about the guest ranch being booked solid from Thanksgiving through the first weekend of January. Jaz finished setting the table, with bread plates beside each bowl and butter, jam, and honey for the cornbread.

Her mother stirred the chili in the slow cooker. Jaz's stomach growled but with less force than before. What had upset Bailey?

Her father pulled out a chair for Mom and leaned in to kiss her cheek. Tess jabbed Bailey with an elbow, and he quickly pulled out the chair to the right of Mom while Tess rounded the table to sit beside Ronald Rolle.

"How close is the hospital to Bailey's new office?" Tess asked as she scooted her chair in.

Jaz caught the faint scent of horse as she brushed past Bailey to her seat. "Thanks, cowboy."

Bailey nodded and sat at the foot of the table opposite Mom. The Rolles had fallen into this seating pattern while her mother was in a wheelchair for three weeks.

Her father caught her eye. "I didn't know Bailey's office was moving to Rosewood." He placed his hand palm up on the table and her mother slipped hers in it. "Let's pray."

It was a brief prayer, and Jaz stood to serve the chili from the pot in the center of the table while her mother placed generous slabs of cornbread on each plate. Conversation fell into an easy pattern—compliments on the food to Geraldine.

"Oh, it's my grandmother's recipe," about both dishes. And, "Jaz started the chili this morning."

"Tell me about this office in Rosewood." Her father turned his hazel gaze on Bailey, who had his head down and was methodically spooning chili in his mouth.

After a moment, Bailey looked up. "Clarkson is opening a branch. We have a big contract to repurpose the strip mall on Eastside into an open concept marketplace."

"Interesting. Where's the office located?" Her father fingered his cornbread, preparing to take a bite while Bailey answered.

"It's a small building located on Branch and Southwest 73rd." Bailey slathered his cornbread in butter.

Her father mentioned a friend who lived out near the 80th block of Branch Street, including her mother in the conversation. Jaz listened, spending her glances on Tess who savored each crumb of cornbread and Bailey whose wide shoulders seemed unnaturally tense.

"So you'll be back in Sweet Grove?" Her father reached for another slice of cornbread.

"Yep. Staying at the ranch for the moment."

"Sounds like you'll have to bunk elsewhere in a few weeks." Mom smiled. "I'm so pleased to hear the resort is doing well."

"It's picking up. Mostly thanks to my investor."

Tess's cheeks pinked, and she stirred her chili.

"And you're heading back to Austin on Sunday?" Her father glanced at her.

Jaz nodded. "I'm working on something, though, and I might want to pick your brain."

His bushy eyebrows shot toward his slicked-back brown hair. He wasn't used to her seeking out his advice.

"I'll miss you." Her mother squeezed her elbow.

"She'll be back." Tess elbowed Bailey. "To see me."

Bailey shook his head. "Me, you mean."

"I don't think so." Tess cocked an eyebrow. "And if you argue with me, I'll eat all the peach cobbler."

Bailey straightened, a twinkle lighting his eye. "There's peach cobbler?"

"Tabitha helped me make it." Her mother shook her head. "I fear she's going to expect me to visit First Street Church."

"She's not like that." Tess smiled. "She has a servant's heart. She says she loves helping me strip and make beds, but that's crazy, right?"

The women laughed, but Jaz's gaze drifted to Bailey. He reached for the honey, and she slid it closer to him, hoping to catch his eye. He dipped his chin in thanks but didn't meet her gaze.

Finally, dessert was served, and Tess was claiming dish duty. "You two pair of lovebirds go on now. Take a walk or something."

Jaz steered Bailey toward her room. She shrugged into a sweatshirt and coat and snagged his coat and hat. "You heard the boss," she said as she handed him the items.

"She's not the boss of me," he hollered into the kitchen.

"I am if you want biscuits and gravy on Sunday," Tess called back.

Jaz grinned when Bailey's mouth twitched. She loved the way they interacted.

Outside, they strolled toward the road, hand-in-hand. Jaz inhaled the crisp night air, smelling the sage and tasting the dust—so different from the city smells of Austin.

"So, what happened with Lonie?"

A few steps later, Bailey answered. "He threatened me. He wants money."

Jaz snorted. "Don't we all." She could build the perfect haven for foster siblings if she had money. Instead, she'd be returning to an uninspiring job in Austin.

"I told him we didn't have any. He mentioned the antiques MaryAnn collected."

"Are they really so valuable?"

Bailey shrugged. "No idea. But she does have some jewelry and crystal heirlooms. Not that he's getting anything."

"Of course not."

Gravel crunched beneath their feet as they circled beyond the end of the subdivision. Silence stretched in the absence of droning insects.

After several minutes, Jaz pulled Bailey to a stop near a cluster of fruit trees. She wove the fingers of her free hand over his other hand and looked up into his face. Light from the street they'd left cast him in shadow so she could barely make out his profile. "What else is bothering you?"

Bailey stared down at her, and she wished she could read his eyes.

"I'm not a scrawny orphan anymore."

Jaz flinched at his words, squinting to see if he was joking. "Who says you are?"

He answered with the barest whisper, "You."

A dog barked from somewhere nearby, and another answered from further away. Jaz pressed her lips together to keep from blurting out a denial, cataloging everything she'd said to Bailey that day. "Does this have something to do with Kenton? That orphan I found?"

"You saw me when you looked at him. I haven't been that skinny eight-year-old for decades. But you and Lonie can't see that."

"He's nine," she said, and the words died on her lips. She and Lonie? He was comparing her with a creepy convict?

Jaz pulled her hands free. "Now I'm like Lonie, huh? Well, good thing I'm heading back to Austin. You can get rid of me without any sort of payoff."

The chili bubbled and burned at her throat. She would not throw up although she'd barf long before she gave in to her burning nose and eyes.

Bailey stepped forward and grabbed her hand. "That's not what I mean."

"That's what you said."

He growled, "I said you can't seem to look past my past. I'm not a scrawny orphan, Jaz."

"I never said you were."

"Then why do you look at one and think of me?"

"Because you were one!" Jaz tried to snatch her hand from his, but he tightened his grip. "And if I could have helped you then, I would have."

"Is that all I am? Someone you can save?"

Jaz stomped on his foot, but he barely flinched. Stupid cowboy boots! "I love you. I'm dreading going back to Austin because I don't want to be away from you. And you think—"

He stepped into her and pulled her against his chest. The brim of his hat collided with her skull a nanosecond before his mouth covered hers. It was a fierce kiss, hot and possessive.

Jaz bristled for an instant before melting into his masculine embrace. Her arms found his neck, and warm hands settled against her lower back. Bailey's insistence cooled to an apologetic plea. The night sounds became the thudding of her heart and his indrawn breath.

When he inched back, he rested his forehead on hers. "I'm an idiot. You already knew that."

Her palms trailed across his broad shoulders and down his back. He sucked in a breath and stiffened. Ticklish?

She rested her hands on the waist of his jeans. "I know Lonie is upsetting you. I wish I could kick him off the ranch."

Bailey shook his head. "Not this time, beautiful. This time I'll rescue myself."

She smirked at him. "But I'm the big, strong, soldierly type."

He nodded. "And I'm the man who adores you."

He nibbled at her lower lip. After another breathless kiss, she stepped back.

"Are we really going to do this long-distance thing again?" The misery sucked away the joy she found in his arms.

"Unless you're staying here. Or I'm refusing this promotion to Rosewood."

She shook her head. "You're not refusing that job, Bailey." *But I would stay here if I could.*

And that shocked her.

"Yes, ma'am." Bailey threaded his fingers through hers.

A shiver of longing shot through the connection. With matched steps, they walked back to her parents' house. In the quiet evening, Jaz prayed, *Please, Lord, work this out.*

# Thirty-one

Saturday devolved into a nightmare worse than those that had plagued Bailey the first few months after Lonie had gone to prison. The man clung to him like a leech, trailing him to the barn and insisting on a ride around the property.

After the guest checked out, Tess arrived in the barn in jeans and boots, happy to take a ride with Lonie. Bailey had been putting the man off by grooming each horse from head to hoof. Now he'd have to give in to the man's request.

Lonie charmed Tess with stories of his childhood and unbelievable plans for working in Rosewood or Harrison so he'd finally get to know his "two great kids." His sister lapped it up like the barn cats did the occasional pan of milk.

Back at the house, Tess made lunch for the three of them, but Bailey couldn't stand the hooded looks from his father whenever his sister's back was turned.

He paced into the parlor, gripping the second sandwich Tess had made, to try and get away from the falseness ringing in the man's tone. As he scanned the room, his gaze landed on one of the antique side tables. A brass urn used to sit there, he was sure. It was from Germany and came with Mary-Ann's great-grandparents when they'd emigrated years before. It had the designer's name engraved on the bottom, and Bailey wasn't sure if it was worth much cash, but he knew it had been there the last time he'd been home. Why would Tess move it?

The bread he'd swallowed seemed to expand. He pounded his chest to move it along, forcing himself not to breathe or choke.

Had Lonie lifted it? The man would steal his sister blind while she bought into every falsehood he weaved in that fake Southern accent.

Bailey strode through the rest of the house, eyeing each table. The crystal decanter and goblets sat askew on the silver tray in the study. Those items might have more monetary value than the urn, but to Bailey their intrinsic value was immeasurable. He could still see Fritz pouring out the Texas whiskey and cuddling on the love seat with Mary-Ann. That had been their nightly routine for his entire life.

They'd handled those glasses forever, and even though the silver tray was a newer addition, it had an engraving on the bottom. Without thinking, Bailey moved the crystal onto the wooden surface of the console table and flipped the tray over.

Silver. It was real silver that his mother had polished every few months and Tess had polished in the wake of Fritz's death.

*To my beloved MaryAnn who is a saint to put up with me for twenty-five years. My heart is yours, Fritz.*

He gulped again. No matter if they were parted by a hundred miles or a thousand, he felt love like this for Jaz. Reading the inscription firmed his resolve to keep Lonie away from Tess and get him out of the house before he could rob them blind.

But he couldn't do it alone. Not while opening the new office. That had been the plan all along—work to keep his loneliness for Jaz at bay because she'd be returning to Austin. Would they ever live in the same town again?

He shook away those thoughts. His mind went through the catalog of people who he'd trust to look after Tess. It wasn't a long list, and Bailey hated the idea of telling anyone in town about Lonie Dyer. Especially since he hadn't even explained everything to his sister.

He jerked his shoulder forward, imagining the movement

would scratch his back. The scars were painless now, but the burns had itched horribly as they'd healed. Those were old wounds, and Lonie couldn't push him around anymore. But Tess was another story.

His gaze fell on the closed laptop. A corner of a business card peeked out. It felt soft and cool between his fingers. *Javier Wynn, Domestic Property Manager, Wynn Investment Properties International.*

The man had spent most of the summer at the ranch helping renovate the rooms and setting up the manager's quarters in the barn. He'd even moved in there.

And he could again.

After ducking away from Tess and Lonie, Bailey headed to the barn. He dialed the number from the business card. After several rings, the man answered.

Or did rich men answer their own phones? He asked, "Mr. Javier Wynn?"

The answer seemed hesitant. "This is Javier."

"Bailey Travers." He paced in front of the barn, watching to see if Lonie would follow him again.

The man on the other end sucked in a breath and something desperate entered his cultured voice. "Is Tessa okay?"

Bailey grunted. "For now. But I need your help to keep it that way." Admitting he needed help to protect his sister made him grit his teeth.

"What do you mean?"

How did he explain to this stranger? He was a business associate of Tess, so he probably didn't know anything about their family. "Can you come to the ranch for a few weeks?"

After a pause, a stilted question: "What's going on?"

Bailey sighed and shut himself into the manager's quarters. "Our biological father showed up, and Tess gave him a guest room. He's a convicted felon and he's trying to blackmail me." He paced the small space, clenching and unclenching his fist.

"Will he hurt her?"

"Yes. Probably." Bailey pushed the phone away and

growled, "He hurt me often enough." But Javier surely didn't need to know about that.

Bailey shook his head to chase away the ghosts. So many memories wanted to haunt him. "Look, he's an abusive jerk and he won't leave us alone until I pay him off."

But the Traverses had no money. That's the only reason Tess had contacted Javier in the spring. The only reason he'd been able to finagle a not-quite silent partnership with her. She needed his money to get the guest ranch up and running.

"Do you want me to pay him off?"

"Heck no." What kind of person did he think he was talking to? Bailey pushed down the indignation as Lonie's voice whispered, *Apple don't fa" far #om the tree, boy.*

"What do you want from me, then?"

Bailey was nothing like his father, and maybe rich people always thought payoffs were the solution. Bailey wouldn't know because he'd never had excess cash.

He swallowed the welling frustration and steadied his voice. "Look, Wynn, it's obvious you care about my sister." That's why he'd called the man. Not because he had money.

"She's my business partner." Bailey snorted. "I'm not blind or stupid. You care about Tess and..." *Are you really doing this? Once you bring him here, there's no going back.* "I want you to be her bodyguard."

He'd rather protect her himself, but with his new job, that wasn't a possibility.

"Bodyguard?"

Bailey pictured the lean man. He wasn't buff or intimidating, but surely he could protect Tess from Lonie.

"Yeah. Someone to stick like glue to Tess's side so she's never alone with Lonie."

Javier's voice lowered, as if he'd pulled back from the phone. "Did he threaten her?"

"He is a threat. The man's a bully. Always has been."

The scars on his back itched. The memories pressed hard against him. *Please, Lord. Not now.*

Javier's voice pulled him from the edge of the nightmare. "I've got to redirect my team to another project. It will be a few days before I can get there."

Bailey locked the door to the room and slumped beside the barn door. Javier would come. There would be someone else to depend on so he could keep Tess safe.

"Get here as soon as you can. I'm back in Sweet Grove, but my job takes me away from the ranch every day." Bailey pushed the door open. "But Lonie's always here with Tess."

"I'll try to be there mid-week."

Bailey closed the barn door and jogged toward his truck. "Thanks. I'll owe you."

"Bailey."

Something in the man's tone prickled Bailey's skin. He froze beside his truck and steeled himself for a bombshell.

"You can count on me."

*I told you I wouldn't leave you alone.* Peace whispered through his chest as a breeze whipped the pecan branches against the roof of the porch. He should have trimmed those trees back.

Bailey slammed his truck door and gulped. "I hope so."

After he ended the call, he tossed the phone on the seat and prayed all the way to Rosewood.

## Thirty-two

On Sunday after morning services, Jaz snagged a donut from the table in the fellowship hall and headed to Harrison City Park. KaroLynn hadn't let her down, and she was heading to keep her promise to a little boy who probably expected it to be broken.

*Not on my watch.*

The saying had passed her brother Drew's lips often, even before he'd decided to become a soldier.

She had time to park, polish off the donut, and guzzle her ever-present bottle of water before the social worker pulled up in a late model Toyota Camry.

Kenton's face bloomed at the sight of her. He raced toward her but stopped short of a hug. Jaz glanced at the social worker watching them with raised eyebrows, arms crossed over her chest.

"Thanks." Jaz raised her hand to the woman before turning her attention to Kenton.

"Is she really going to come?"

A minivan rattled around the corner and pulled into a space near the restrooms. Kenton stared at it, eyes wide. When a girl with a mop of red curls bounced out of the back seat, he sprinted toward the vehicle.

They embraced like long-parted lovers—if such a reunion involved girlish giggles. Kenton twirled the girl around, and her short hair rustled in the wind. The girl's head barely reached her brother's chest, and her legs and arms were nearly as spindly as his. His freckles were darker, and her eyes were browner, but the resemblance between them was clear.

The wiry middle-aged woman beside the van peered at the kids and then joined KaroLynn. The women perched on a bench.

"How is it?" Kenton's voice filtered to Jaz as he and his sister strolled hand-in-hand toward her.

"The bwuthers ignoe me." The girl's lisp was more pronounced because she was missing two of her front teeth, but Jaz noticed her tongue was a little tied.

"Good. I'll punch them if they hurt you." Kenton fisted the hand that wasn't holding his sister's.

His sister's brown eyes scanned him, and he puffed out his chest. "They twice your size."

Jaz bit her lip.

"So? I'll protect you from giants."

Her heart soared. The granite set of his jaw reminded her so much of Drew's determination. And even more recently, she'd seen that stubborn set on Bailey's face when Tess argued with him about allowing Lonie Dyer to stay there.

Kenton introduced Jaz to the girl—Flo—and they shook hands. Clear, brown eyes squinted at her. "Jaz is the one who found you for me."

Warmth rushed through Jaz's chest. She wanted so much more for them, but this reunion was a good start.

"I'll push you on the swing." Kenton clenched his sister's hand.

Jaz followed them to the swing set. Hair on the back of her neck bristled, and she turned to see the two women glaring at her. They didn't understand why she wanted to be at the visit. One smile from Kenton melted Jaz's heart and made missing an hour with Bailey worth every minute.

After Kenton settled Flo and launched her higher than Jaz's head she asked, "You want me to push you?"

"I can do it—" but he bit off the retort. "Sure."

"Betcha can't catch me!" Flo chortled, throwing her upper body back as she pumped her legs.

"Betcha I can."

Jaz smiled, alternately pushing each of them, thrilling at Flo's squeal every time she went a smidgen higher than her brother. His weight helped him soar, and Jaz spent most of her energy on Flo.

"Jump!" Flo begged.

"Don't." Jaz knew the watchers would disapprove.

"They think you'll get hurt." She jerked her head toward the bench.

"I've done it a million times."

Sure. A million times in his nine short years. Jaz's lips twitched. "I know you can do it, but let's keep the ladies happy so you can see Flo again real soon."

Once the kids had been loaded up, Jaz reminded KaroLynn that she was still waiting for information and statistics about children who would benefit from the halfway house.

The woman's sober eyes studied Jaz for a long time. "Why are you really doing this? Planning to run for office?"

Jaz almost choked. Politics? Not in a thousand lifetimes. "You know Tess and Bailey's background, right? I hate for siblings to get separated during a time when they need each other so much."

"This is outside your experience. How can it possibly succeed?"

"Because I care about it." Jaz swallowed. As for the other question? "God placed the passion in my heart the moment I saw Kenton."

The social worker's dark hair scuffed across the wool coat collar as she shook her head. "You have no idea how difficult this will be."

Jaz straightened. "I like a challenge."

"And when you can't scrape the funds together? What then? You've given that little boy so much hope."

Jaz blinked. She'd thought about this, too. "I've already

signed up for the foster parenting courses. I'll take them in myself."

KaroLynn gasped. "The state doesn't want single foster parents."

Lead pinged in Jaz's stomach. She knew it was true. "I have an excellent job in Austin and great character references."

The women stared at each other for a few moments until the social worker shrugged. If Jaz couldn't win KaroLynn over, how could she find support for the halfway house?

"Thanks for letting me hang out with those two." Jaz stepped toward her parked car. "Same time next week?"

The frown creased her chin and forehead, but KaroLynn nodded tersely before gathering up her satchel. Jaz backed out before the woman reached her car.

Her smart phone showed enough time for the rest of her Sunday plans—plans that included a long kiss from a certain cowboy after he took her on a horseback ride.

Her heart raced as she steered back to her parents' house to change, pack her car, and start the first of many goodbyes.

⁂

MONDAY STARTED EARLY. AN AUTUMN HAZE HUNG over the city while Jaz completed her three-mile run through the UT campus. Traffic buzzed in her ears and the sulfuric scent of exhaust choked her.

She entered Boldt & Associates before the receptionist and hurried to her desk. The setup of her monitor looked foreign, and the scent of disinfectant spray stung her nose as she pulled open the bottom drawer of her desk.

Everything was the same, so why did her heart race with first-day nerves?

By Tuesday evening, her eyes sagged. Staying up late with her eyes glued to a computer screen was taking a toll. Maybe she'd sleep in the next morning, but no. If she didn't get her physical exercise, her energy would deplete all the faster.

Emails from Jed Gowan and Anna Ring encouraged her.

Both of them were sold on her idea and using all their contacts to help her. Fortunately, Anna had worked with nonprofit startups in Dallas before her marriage fell apart and she'd needed a fresh start.

Sweet Grove was a perfect place for fresh starts, she said. Although Jaz only knew her in passing, Tabitha Olsen had mentioned Jaz's project — the Bryant County Pit Stop, she'd decided to call it— to her working women's Bible study group, and that was all it took for Anna to throw her weight behind it. Unfortunately, the woman expected Jaz to spend Saturday with her making follow-up calls to the businesses in Sweet Grove and Harrison that Anna had emailed about the group home.

Her phone buzzed with a Facetime request. Jaz rubbed her eyes and answered the call. Bailey's face filled her phone's screen. Thick stubble lined his square jaw and the indentation in his light brown hair testified that he'd probably worn his hat most of the day.

"Hey, cowboy." A yawn cut off her greeting.

"You look tired, beautiful."

"Is it Friday yet?" Not that the weekend would offer much respite.

Bailey chuckled, and the sexy grin she loved quirked his mouth. "Tess has a surprise for you. Do you think you can answer your phone to a strange number around 5 p.m. tomorrow?"

"If Tess is calling, it won't be a strange number."

"It will be a strange number." He glanced away from the screen and frowned. "That was the barn door. Probably Lonie."

"No change there?"

"Oh, he's rude to Javier and sweet to Tess, but I'm sure he wants to threaten me again." Anger flooded his dark eyes.

"If you can catch him stealing, that will violate his parole."

Bailey shook his head and a knock sounded from his end. "I'll figure something out. Get some sleep."

He tapped his invisible hat. Jaz pressed a kiss to her fingers then held those to the camera. She ended the call.

*I'! figure something out.* What happened to them working as a team?

Although her brain was so frazzled, she could hardly concentrate on the state's tedious video curriculum. And if she started the university degree program in December? Would she have any time for Bailey?

"Lord, I need some restful sleep." She paused the video and plugged in her phone on her way to bed.

Maybe things would look brighter in the morning.

⁂

WHEN THE PROMISED CALL CAME, JAZ WAS PUTTING the finishing touches on a research assignment at work. As if she didn't have enough eye strain. It seemed six of her eight hours at the office had been glued to the computer monitor.

She shoved the negative thoughts away and lifted her cell phone. The area code was for Texas, but she recognized nothing else.

"This is Jazlyn Rolle."

"Miz Rolle. Liam James."

Liam James, the multi-millionaire web designer who lived in Sweet Grove? Her mouth went dry. This was Tess's surprise?

"Uh, Mr. James. How can I help you?"

"My wife thinks you have a startup I should hear about." He sounded grouchy about the idea.

Something gnawed at Jaz's stomach. His wife, Jennifer, was good friends with Elise and Kristina, but Jaz didn't know her except in passing. How had she heard about the halfway house?

"You've got five minutes to pitch it to me."

Good Lord. Jaz took a calming breath. A single investor like James could be the answer to all her prayers for this project.

*Prayers?* The still small voice reminded her she hadn't been praying as much as she should. Nope, she'd gone into determined, hard worker mode instead.

*I know I'm not relying on You, Jesus. If You can work this conversation in my favor, I'! do better.*

She took a deep breath and poured her passion out. By the looks of the office around her, she spoke for more than five minutes. Whenever she paused to take a breath, Liam James asked her a question about accommodations or certifications or something.

"All right, Miz Rolle, you've convinced me that Sweet Grove needs this foster care home. What do you need from me?"

*Money. Contacts.* But then something else came out of her mouth, "A partnership."

During the silence that stretched after she said it, Jaz fought with herself to take the request back.

"Indeed. I'll get my attorney on an agreement. Could you email me so I'll have your address to forward to him?"

Jaz blinked. "Um, you want to be my partner?"

"Not exactly." He sighed. "But I don't think the Lord is giving me a choice. I think I'll be more of a silent partner."

The Lord wasn't giving him a choice?

He rattled off his email and Jaz scribbled it on her desk calendar, repeating it back to him.

"You should hear from him by week's end."

With that, he was gone.

But Bryant County Pit Stop suddenly seemed like a sure thing rather than a pipe dream.

# Thirty-three

After a week of running and remodeling, Bailey wanted his new office space finished. On Friday, he folded up the laptop and glanced around Rosewood's library. It wasn't a horrible place to work as long as he didn't need to draft anything, but he did.

His phone vibrated in his pocket as he stood to stretch. Crackles eased the stiffness from between his shoulders. These chairs weren't the right distance from the desk for him, either. He needed that stool he'd molded to himself during his months with Clarkson in Austin.

He glanced at the screen of his phone. *Still on for dinner?*

More tension bled away. Jaz had been back in Austin, back at her job this week, and they'd hardly talked more than five minutes each night. His evenings stretched long without her. At least they had the weekend. But how long would weekends be enough?

After dumping the laptop and cord on the seat of his truck, Bailey typed, *On my way to Mabel's now.*

It would be good to eat some of Jeffrey's cooking. And maybe even plan a little guy time.

But first he needed to dig the burr—one Lonie Dyer—out from beneath his saddle blanket. No matter how business was going, it did little to take his mind off the big issue: how to eject his thieving father from their world once and for all.

But he had an inkling of a plan, and with Jaz's legal background and super intelligence, they would figure something out. It rankled that she'd be rescuing him again, but if he'd learned anything, it was that two could handle a problem better together. Wasn't there a Bible verse that said so?

He considered it as he sped toward Sweet Grove. Whatever they decided, they needed to do it soon. Wynn had run some promotion and the guest rooms were booked starting the weekend following Thanksgiving, which was only two weeks away. And the room in the barn wasn't big enough for Lonie Dyer's ego.

Bailey parked along the curb on Maple Street keeping his truck heading toward the ranch. Wind gusted, trying to close the truck door on his legs. Bailey zipped his jacket, turning the collar up and pushing his hat down. He tossed a blanket over his laptop and slammed the door, turning the key in the lock. That wasn't his computer to lose, but it still felt strange to lock anything in Sweet Grove.

A warm gush of cinnamon-scented air greeted him as his pulled open the door to Mabel's. His stomach groaned, and he salivated like a starving dog. As much as he appreciated the lunches his sister made, a cold sandwich couldn't satisfy a man's needs.

"Hey, stranger." Kristina waved from the direction of Jeffrey's office. "Expected to see you more often."

Bailey tipped his hat and then pulled it off. "Getting the office in shape while overseeing another project steals my hours."

"We're glad to have you back."

"Especially me." Jeffrey swung through the kitchen doors. "You're just in time. I'm about to take my gorgeous fiancée away from here and test out my night chef."

The men bumped chests and slapped each other's backs.

"And here I was primed for Berkely's special prime rib. It *is* Friday night."

"We've got two orders left. One pretty rare and then the end." Jeffrey turned back toward the kitchen. "Grab a booth and let the waitress take your order."

"I'm meeting Jaz."

"Of course." Kristina's grin lit up her dark face. "Table for two it is. Jeffrey will hold that rare beef for you. Don't worry."

Bailey wove through the mostly full tables, raising a hand to several old-timers at the counter. He hoped the night chef could cook like Jeffrey, because everyone had expectations that Mabel had laid in stone years before—old-fashioned home-cooking at reasonable prices with pie to top it off.

Before the waitress brought his water, the door opened, and Jaz strolled in. Her dark hair was smoothed into a clip at the nape of her neck and the slacks covering her muscular frame swished with each step. She called a greeting to Kristina over her shoulder before leaning down and giving him a peck on the lips.

Something besides his starving gut growled for more. She slid into the booth across from him and squeezed his hands with her cool ones before shrugging out of her coat.

The waitress slid water onto the table. "I'll give you a few minutes."

"Oh, I'll take the chicken fried steak with country gravy dinner." Jaz glanced at the waitress. "And sweet tea."

The woman whipped out her tablet.

"Jeffrey's holding a prime rib—rare—for me," Bailey said. "I'll take it with a loaded baked potato and a glass of milk."

Jaz shook her head at that last. She'd told him he was a little old for milk with dinner when he'd requested it at her house. His reply, "Boys never grow up. Haven't you heard?" made her grin while her father chuckled.

The waitress turned away. Jaz wilted against the booth, and he noticed the shadows beneath her green eyes.

"Rough week." He reached his palm toward her, hoping she'd hold it. She dug through her handbag and placed a folded sheaf of papers in his hand.

"This is what they require for the halfway house. Do you think you could figure out how much it would cost to convert a regular house?"

He frowned at the papers and then met her beseeching gaze. "I want to hold your hand."

She glanced at his hand, immobile with the papers on it. "Sorry. It's not very comfortable to do it this way. Want to sit beside me?"

*Yes.* But he wouldn't because he couldn't afford to be distracted from the serious conversations they needed to have, either. It looked like she wanted to vent about the injustices of the child protective services requirements first.

"Yes, I'll get the pricing. Once you find property, I'm sure we can incorporate everything the state wants."

"For a price." She leaned back again. "It's like they don't want anyone to be able to help these kids."

"They're trying to give them some sort of stability and protection."

Jaz closed her eyes. When she opened them, raw pain radiated from those sage pools. "How did you manage it? I see Kenton and Flo and it's like I'm forced to watch you and Tess suffer."

Bailey stuffed the paper into his coat pocket and shrugged out of the jacket. He leaned forward and hung his hand off the edge of the table. Jaz lowered her palm to his, and he squeezed. A sizzle like raw meat on a grill shivered against his flesh.

"We weren't in the foster system that long. MaryAnn said God planned for us to be with them, and a few weeks after our grandmother relinquished us to the state, we were out of Austin and at the ranch."

"But they're keeping Kenton and Flo apart. Can you imagine?"

He shook his head. He recalled stepping between a scary policeman in full gear and Tessa when they busted his mother for manufacturing meth. His fist had been raised, but the man had talked him down and let him carry his sister from the house.

"I see you've partnered with Liam James. And you're planning a fundraiser next Saturday."

Everyone in town was talking about it, and Tess had handed him a stack of fliers yesterday that he'd been dropping at every business near his office in Rosewood.

"Everyone's been supportive." Her eyes glinted. "And you know that big house in Harrison that used to be an antique shop?"

Harrison was closer to Sweet Grove than Rosewood, but Bailey hadn't spent much time in the little burg. Before Mary-Ann died, Fritz had sold a few of his wood projects to the antique store.

He nodded.

"It's been closed for a couple years, but the heirs are pretty well-off." Jaz clapped her hands together, and Bailey missed the warmth of her touch. "Anna thinks she can convince them to donate it as a write-off."

He whistled. "That would be a boon."

"I can't believe Tess convinced Liam James to sponsor a table at the fundraiser, giving away a few hours of consulting time. His wife has been handing out those fliers everywhere, too."

She pointed toward the window behind their booth. One of the fliers was posted there, and as he glanced around, he saw several more tucked next to napkin holders and by the take-out menus.

"What did your bosses decide?" His stomach knotted at the thought of her working long hours and going to school for even more hours.

The waitress sashayed up to their table and shuffled their plates with a flourish. From the small plate between them, the yeasty fragrance of fresh rolls stabbed into his ravenous hunger. He reached for the bread, sighing when it warmed his fingertips.

A pang of longing for MaryAnn's fresh-baked bread reared its head. Tess still hadn't perfected those old recipes.

Conversation lulled while they dug into their food. The

prime rib, juicy and flavorful, melted in his mouth. Jaz offered him a corner of bread smothered in the creamy gravy, and it tasted so much like his mom used to make that he wanted to shout. Or devour all of it.

"Need a side of gravy?" Somehow Jeffrey had snuck up on their table, his fingers laced with Kristina's.

"How 'bout sending your recipe to Tess? She's missing something in hers and this is perfect."

"He could tell you the secret ingredient, but then he'd have to shoot you." Kristina winked.

Jaz shook her head. "It's all delicious. Where are you off to?"

"Dinner with my folks, and then a movie in Harrison."

Jeffery tugged Kristina closer. "Plenty of discussion of wedding dates during the conversational lulls."

A pang resounded in Bailey's chest. His gaze slid to Jaz, who smiled and nodded. When things settled down in their lives, would she say yes to him?

*You've got to ask her first.*

"See you Saturday night. Dad and I are pushing it with the local chamber. We didn't realize there was such an influx of runaways in our area."

"It's sad." Jaz shook her head. "I'm touched by how everyone has rallied around this cause."

"We just needed someone to bring the need to everyone's attention." Kristina squeezed Jaz's arm, and they shared an understanding smile.

After the couple left, Jaz pushed her plates away, and Bailey finished off her remaining mashed potatoes, rolling his eyes in pleasure at the taste of the gravy.

The waitress refilled the water and sweet tea. "Pie? There's peanut butter chocolate cheesecake tonight."

Jaz patted her flat stomach and stared at him. "I'll have a couple of bites of whatever you want."

Bailey knew the glint in his eye at the mention of dessert couldn't be hidden. His sweet tooth had been conditioned over years of special occasions with Mary Ann's famous cream pies and cakes.

"Did I see cherry?"

The waitress nodded. "Warm? With ice cream?"

"Perfect." Bailey leaned back with a sigh. "Maybe a cup of coffee to go with it."

The waitress bussed their dishes.

Once she left, Jaz met his gaze. "What's new with Lonie? Anything missing?"

"No, but I've seen him casing the antiques Tess set aside in the study."

"The ones she wants refinished?"

He ducked his chin. "I think I can set a trap for him."

She shook her head. "It will still be your word against his."

"You think people won't believe me?" A wave of shock jarred the contentment in his stomach.

"That's not it. A court needs irrefutable evidence, not hearsay."

She threw around legal jargon like a second language. And it was for her. Which reminded him.

"What did your bosses think about you going for the child psychology and social work degree?" A boulder dropped inside him at the thought of her in college for several years. Somehow, they'd get through it.

"They're talking it out." The look on her face seemed sober. She must have thought they wouldn't go for it.

The waitress set a plate of pie between them, offered up two clean forks and napkins, and poured coffee for him. A puddle of ice cream formed around the flaky golden crust swimming with ruby globes of deliciousness.

Jaz nibbled at the crust and Bailey polished off the pie.

"Let's see if Sheriff Grant will help with your trap," she said.

"Isn't there a law against that?" Bailey thought he'd heard something against entrapment somewhere.

She shook her head. "But he'll be able to figure out some way to get the proof we need."

Bailey hoped so. He didn't care if Lonie Dyer went back to

prison, but he needed to get out of their lives.

# *Thirty-four*

**S**aturday dragged as Jaz and Anna called every business in the county but sped up when Anna got the news that the property owners of the antique store in Harrison were more than happy to donate the building to a nonprofit for a huge tax write-off.

Jaz and Anna danced around the woman's apartment and quickly made plans to see the building. It was mid-afternoon before the realtor could meet them at the property. Jaz begged Bailey to join them so he could take measurements and make sketches. Anna ordered a banner so she could photograph it on the house for the open house fundraiser the next weekend.

During their long day of calls, Anna managed to get three dozen items donated for the silent auction and pledges for one-fourth of the estimated startup cost. Jaz had wrangled support from three-fourths of the Sweet Grove businesses, but it hadn't come out to the same amount of cash.

Hopefully it wouldn't matter. If they could raise the rest with the auction, Liam James would match the funds and they'd have enough to begin renovations on the house.

Jaz stared up at the two-story building. It looked like a storefront, but they could change that.

A warm hand settled on her lower back. "Daydreaming?"

The husky voice sent shivers of delight through Jaz.

"Maybe." She turned into the broad chest she'd learned to lean on. Strong arms circled her. His face dipped toward hers until the brim of his hat nearly touched her forehead.

"How's my girl?" His whisper tingled through her entire body.

"Amazed how everything is coming together." She tilted her head up.

Their gazes met. His blue eyes tried to drown her, but she blinked away their hypnotic effect.

"You've been working your tail off."

Jaz let her attention linger on his full lips as he spoke. When they crept into the sexy grin she loved, she smacked his shoulder playfully. "Stop distracting me, cowboy."

His chuckle made heat curl inside her like a cat in front of a fireplace. The man didn't know his own appeal, and that made him all the more appealing.

"You've been distracting me for months and years, beautiful."

She shook her head and held her hand out to him. His calloused fingers felt right laced with hers.

As they approached, the real estate guy arched an eyebrow at something Anna said.

"Jazlyn Rolle?" The man held his hand out. They shook, and Jaz was surprised to feel the ripple of callouses along his palm. More than a sales guy, then.

"Bailey Travers." Bailey shook the extended hand.

"Bruce Anderson, assistant broker at ReMax Bryant County. Nice to meet you. Let's get this open."

Light filtered through windows in need of cleaning. The solid oak door clicked closed behind them. Dusty relics from past centuries crowded against the walls.

"All the furnishings are marked to be transported to storage until the heirs can sort what's valuable from the lesser pieces." Bruce spoke without the usual Texas twang, reminding Jazlyn of her time in the military.

Jaz walked up creaking stairs to the left of the entry. Polished wooden railing revealed itself when she rubbed her hand over the banister. The men's voices droned below her.

A narrow hall divided the second story and three doorways opened on one side, with four on the other. An old-style split door closet stood at the end of the hall. Each room was roughly square shaped with a small closet. Somehow, they'd need to open up a storage space for two occupants in each room. Perhaps built-in drawers and shelves could work for the boys' rooms. Only one bathroom upstairs, which would be a problem. They'd need separate spaces for boys and girls, if her sibling plan was going to come to fruition.

Bailey found her staring at the ancient claw footed bathtub in the bathroom. It was a decent sized room with a full-wall storage closet, a screened area beside the tub for the toilet, and a single vanity. They'd want multiple toilets and showers, wouldn't they?

"Lots of potential here." Bailey rested his arm across her shoulders. "What do you think?"

"It's going to cost thousands to get this ready for occupancy."

"Good thing it's being donated, then."

She turned to him. Her stomach roiled. "What if I haven't budgeted enough money?"

"Then you go back to the investors or look for grants." His face was placid.

"But I wanted to open it by summer or sooner."

He traced the line of her chin. "What was that you were telling me about God working everything out?"

Jaz blinked. Things had been falling together for this project, and the only way to explain it was that God was working His plan. Why start worrying now?

"Thanks for reminding me." Her smile was rueful.

"You can remind me later when I have doubts about my stuff." He lowered his head toward her. His pupils dilated before his eyelids closed.

Her lashes fluttered as she sighed into his lips. Too soon, he withdrew, sliding his fingers down her neck and taking her hand.

"Want to check out the basement with me?" He waggled

his eyebrows.

Heat washed through her, and she laughed.

With his strong hand in hers, the worries faded to a tinny echo.

# *Thirty-five*

**B**y Sunday afternoon, Bailey's plan had come together with approval from the sheriff. Now, he needed to get Tess on board, which was why he invited her and Javier into the impromptu meeting in his room in the barn. Anywhere Lonie Dyer wasn't had been hard to find around the ranch lately.

Just as he opened his mouth to begin the explanations, the barn door squealed. With his sister, his girlfriend, and his sister's business partner seated around him in the future manager's office, it could only be one person. Bailey sucked in the aroma of horse, hay, and old boards—scents that screamed home to him— steeling himself for the upcoming confrontation.

"Where's my baby girl?"

At the sound of Lonie's voice, Tess bolted to her feet. Javier flinched toward her, but she was leaning out the door and calling, "In here," before he could stop her.

A look of understanding passed between Bailey and the other man who stood a couple inches shorter than Bailey.

Tess shuffled back into the room, leaving the door open. Lonie Dyer sauntered in, making the office feel hot and overcrowded.

"There's my girl." His eyes narrowed as he took in their stiff postures. "Why are y'all crammed in here? There's a nice office up at the house."

Yeah, where he could eavesdrop. Bailey knew all about the thin walls and old floor vents in the farmhouse.

"We just finished up with the horses." *Not that it's your business.* Bailey glowered at the interloper.

Lonie didn't bother to meet his gaze. Instead, he shifted closer to Tess. "You said you'd run me to Rosewood for that appointment." Lonie's tone dripped charm.

Bailey squeezed his hands on the arms of the office chair and leaned forward. A squawk from the old inner workings made Lonie jump. Good.

Javier stood. "I'll take you, sir." His bronze skin and dark eyes gave him a foreign appearance, and the slight accent in his speech sounded exotic. "Tess and Bailey need to work out some details about the ranch."

Lonie's blue eyes slitted. "Are you even legal to drive in this country?"

Bailey huffed in exasperation and opened his mouth to reply.

In an even tone, Javier said, "Yessir. I'm a legal citizen with a current New Mexico automobile operator's license."

Lonie snorted. "New Mexico. Shoulda guessed."

Like that was the same thing as Mexico? Besides, Javier came from Brazil and could probably buy everyone in the room five times over again.

Lonie reached for Tess's chin and Bailey bristled.

"I was lookin' forward to spendin' time with my girl."

The man could lay it on thick. Bailey had learned the truth about him when he was too young to fall for the charm, so he saw through the veneer.

Tess softened toward him, squeezing his hand. "I'll be here when you get back."

Lonie scanned the room again, leering at Jaz and smirking at Bailey.

"After you, Mr. Dyer." Javier's politeness grated against Bailey. Lonie Dyer hadn't earned the man's respect. His sneer in Javier's direction certainly didn't repay the etiquette.

Once the barn door squealed again, Tess shifted from foot to foot. "We should go inside. I'll make a fresh pot of coffee. And there's muffins."

Bailey's stomach rumbled. After he nodded, Jaz stood. His eyes watched her smooth movements. She hooked her elbow through Tess's. "We've got to double date."

Tess shook her head. "It's not like that."

Bailey checked the lock on his door and dragged his feet. He'd done his best to keep his secrets for decades, but today might require peeling back more than just his shirt.

*Lord, help.*

The girls had already reached the porch by the time he emerged from the barn. Jaz had her head thrown back, laughing at something. Tess was grinning and shaking her blonde tresses like a horse tossing its mane. His chest clenched, making it hurt to draw his next breath. They meant the world to him, but would they see him differently once they knew the truth?

The steps squeaked as he bounded up to the porch. He whisked his hat off at the same moment he opened the door and nearly plowed into Jaz. The summery scent of her wrapped its fingers around his heart and wrenched.

"There you are, cowboy." She flashed white teeth at him and whirled toward the kitchen door.

It took his heart a moment to restart, but he let the link between them draw him after her. He would follow her anywhere, as he'd already proved by going to Austin. Was it possible her new project would be bringing them back to the same town again?

His stomach knotted at the thought of her working with foster kids. After today, she'd probably never stop seeing him as a pitiful representative of an abusive childhood. But he'd do whatever it took to convince Tess not to fall for Lonie Dyer's lies. They needed to be free of the man.

Bailey hung his hat on its peg atop the coat rack and veered toward the scent of baked goods.

Tess flipped the coffee pot on and flicked a towel at him. "I'm still mad at you, Lee."

"As long as you make me muffins." He snaked an arm toward the plate holding several muffins.

She hip-bumped his arm away. "I didn't make them for you."

"She made them for her boy*friend*." Jaz drawled out the first half of the last word.

Tess's cheeks flushed. Bailey stalled in his next move toward the muffins and caught an elbow to the gut.

"Oof." He backed away. "I'll let you girls bring me one."

"If you say please."

Bailey nuzzled next to Jaz's ear. Her breath caught in her throat, making his heart rev into stampeding herd mode. "Thanks for bringing me a muffin."

His voice sounded husky. Would she continue to affect him this way forever?

She nipped the end of his nose and swatted his arm. "There might be a bite missing."

"You can bite my muffin anytime."

Poppet raced around them yipping, but not loud enough to keep the words between them.

"Gross. Stop already." Tess punctuated her demand by beaning him in the neck with the towel.

Bailey snapped it out of the air and tossed it back to his sister. "You started it."

"Ha. Jaz started it."

"And now I'm finishing it."

Their laughter followed him through the doorway and to the end of the hall. A glance showed him Tess had at least closed her door. He resisted the urge to test the knob and see if she'd locked it. She was too trusting, and Lonie Dyer was not to be trusted. Not even a little bit.

Bailey paced behind the desk and stared out the window toward Armstrong Road. Even with the laptop computer on the desk and the light-filtering drapes on the window, he still felt his father's presence here. So many nights the man had sat on that sofa with MaryAnn and then after she'd passed, he'd sat in the chair poring over pages in his Bible. But the light had gone out in his eyes. Would that happen with Jaz when she found out how truly scarred he was?

Chatter preceded the girls into the room. He turned, watching Jaz slide a muffin with a bite out of the top across the desk. With a shake of his head, he reached for it and she arched an eyebrow.

"Coffee." Tess set a cup beside the muffin and then dropped into one of the chairs in front of the desk. Her shoulders slumped.

"Missing Mr. Tall, Dark, Brooding and SO HOT already, huh?" Jaz kneed Tess's leg before perching on the other chair.

Tess rolled her eyes. "I'm tired of having the same argument with my brother."

Bailey broke off the bottom half of the muffin. Purple marks pocked it where the blueberries had been. His stomach groaned for the food but thinking about the upcoming revelation made it twist. He chased the oversized bite with a swallow of hot, black coffee. The scalding down his throat braced him.

"No more arguments." Jaz sounded comfortable. "It was nice of Javier to get Lonie out of the way."

Tess grunted.

Bailey finished off the muffin, still staring out the window. Not that he would have noticed if the yard caught fire. He was too busy trying to formulate an easy admission.

He turned and set the cup on the desk. "Lonie is a controlling sociopath. I know what I'm talking about."

"It's been years, Lee. Don't you think he could have changed?"

Bailey gritted his teeth. "No. He's already threatened to hurt you if I don't pay him off."

She gasped. Jaz squeezed Tess's hand. This wasn't news to her, but it was about to be.

"What can he really do to us?" Tess straightened. "I know that's why you brought Javier back and why Jaz has been hanging around all the time."

"Oh no. I need your connections to help me with the foster home." Jaz had come once at Bailey's request, but the girls were friends.

"Right." Tess rolled her eyes. "I'm giving him a chance." She crossed her arms over her chest. "There's nothing you can say to change my mind."

Bailey blinked. *Really, Lord? It has to come to this?*

"Fine. I'll just show you what Lonie's capable of then."

His fingers struggled with the buttons on his shirt. Were they trembling? He untucked the tail from his waistband and curled his fingers under the hem of his white undershirt. He paused. Once they knew, they would never be able to unsee the evidence of his horrible past.

But if it convinced Tess to believe him about Lonie, it would be worth it. Wouldn't it?

*Lord, help.*

He took a fortifying breath, trying not to notice how much like jelly his knees felt. With a jerk, Bailey shrugged both shirts up to his shoulders and turned the evidence written across his back toward the women he loved.

Their gasps sent a rush of cool air over his exposed skin, raising goosebumps. Tension coiled like a rope in his shoulder as he stood bare before them, letting them see the assortment of burns across his shoulder blades. He hadn't paid attention to them in years, but he knew the rippling white scars looked puckered and gruesome. The reactions from the school locker room had taught him to wear an undershirt that he only changed in the privacy of his bedroom.

Cool fingers touched his back. He shivered.

"He burned you?" Jaz's voice simmered with a fury he'd heard in her brother's so many years before.

"With his cigarettes, joints, pipes, and matches. Multiple times through the years."

Her fingers moved across another scar and then fell away. No longer able to delay the inevitable, he straightened his shirt.

As he turned, Tess threw herself against his chest. "I didn't know," she choked out.

Was it selfish that he wished she still didn't? His hand trailed into her silky hair. He dropped his chin onto her head and patted her back.

A few steps away, Jaz stared at them, but it wasn't pity on her face. Her green eyes burned with righteous indignation. She clenched her denim-clad knees and the stiffness of her jaw announced her teeth were grinding together. As their gazes clashed, his stomach reared into his heart.

"He should be in prison for that." Her voice shook.

"Why would anyone hurt a child that way?" Tess voiced the question that used to haunt Bailey. "Why did our father hurt you?"

*Because I was worthless.* The old accusation slithered in quick answer.

*That's a lie.* This time, it was Fritz's voice rising to Bailey's defense.

"Now you know what happens to kids whose parents don't really care about them."

"I already knew." Jaz fidgeted and paced toward the door. "All the more reason for me to get funding for the foster home."

Relief spun through him. Maybe she wasn't motivated by pity, but she still wanted to save those kids. And him? Did he still need saving?

He hugged his sister and set her away from him.

"I've got some ideas about how to catch Lonie and convince him to leave us alone."

Tess swiped her hand across her cheeks. "I hope it lands him back in jail."

A thousand pounds lifted from Bailey's shoulders—relief, he realized. He had no secrets left to hide.

# Thirty-six

The next Saturday, Bailey worked in his finished office drawing plans, losing track of time. By the time he realized he needed to get to Jaz's open house, he didn't have time to change from his work ensemble. He tugged the bolo tie, glad his boots were freshly polished.

Cars overflowed from the parking lots, making Bailey continue past the courthouse and pull into the high school lot. A stiff breeze blustered, sending a few errant leaves rattling against the pavement. He adjusted the brim of his hat and told himself he could rub elbows with half the people in town for a good cause.

And anything Jaz loved was a good cause. Her latest passion for helping foster kids happened to dredge up old ghosts. Still, he realized running from the memories wouldn't alter his past or the future for kids like Kenton and Flossie May.

Kenton reminded him of a scrawny ginger cat Tess had snuck home from school under her coat. The thing hadn't looked like it could survive a day but had kept the barn free of pests for a decade before disappearing.

Today Bailey would wrestle his past into oblivion. As he stepped inside the courthouse, he shucked off his coat and jacket. The alcove where tables of volunteering information usually sat had been converted to a stuffed closet.

A teenage boy slipped his phone into his hip pocket and offered to take Bailey's coat. "We don't have check tickets," he said, "but someone will be here at all times to keep things secure."

"I'm still worried about my hat."

The boy gaped at the battered brown Stetson that was three different shades inside from all the sweat it had soaked up over the years.

"Joshin' you, kid." Bailey flashed the grin he knew Jaz loved and strode toward the stairs.

Voices floated down from the hallway and out of open courtrooms. Several tables lined the circular passageway where he'd waited to sign in for jury duty, but he bypassed everything for the circuit court room.

Jaz had outdone herself setting up several display boards featuring the dozen foster children in the county that sought permanent placement. Beside it, another board showed the old antique store and some rough sketches he'd drawn up to show how the house could be modified to fit state standards for residential foster care.

Before he took three steps up the aisle, Jaz hugged his arm. Her skin glowed like a smoky quartz, and the joy gleaming from her pale eyes twisted something inside him. His girl was gorgeous when she smiled.

"The house will be donated. They're signing it over on Monday." Her husky whisper filled his ear.

Warm breath trailed anticipation across his chest and down his arm. She pressed her lips to his gaping mouth for a quick second and then drew back far enough to admit another person between them.

Not that anyone approached, but when he blinked away his shock at her greeting, he noticed Liam James standing across the room with a knowing smirk on his mouth.

Bailey ducked his chin in acknowledgment. The man raised his hand, and the little girl beside him turned her gaze on them. She was a beauty, with curly hair and plump cheeks.

"Great news." Bailey returned his attention to Jaz, enfolding her fingers in his.

"Do you want a snack? The donations Tabitha managed to wrestle up are amazing, very professional."

Bailey never turned down food. His stomach churned a bit at the thought of what lay ahead once he left this shindig, but not enough to keep him from sampling the deli meat and a particularly decadent cupcake with bacon sprinkles on it.

"Buttermilk cupcakes with maple frosting. The bacon is perfect on them."

Who'd ever imagined such a combination? Bailey wouldn't have thought it would work, but the cake melted together with the frosting, and the bacon reminded him of MaryAnn's special recipe pancakes and syrup.

When Anna Ring pulled Jaz toward a clump of people in suits, Tess sidled beside him and took his arm.

"I'm scared, Bailey. Aren't you?"

It wasn't the place to talk about this. Church folk and even their neighbors milled through the various courtrooms.

"No. The plan is sound."

"But he hurt you before."

"I was a child." Bailey tugged her close for a one-armed hug and kissed her blonde hair. "I'll be fine."

"The sheriff is going to follow you, right?"

"I'll be with him," a voice interjected. The ranch's not-so-silent investor stopped behind Tess with a multitude of female eyes following his movements.

"That doesn't make me feel better." Tess frowned at the man.

"What do you mean?" Javier's face blanched. "I can handle myself."

"He had a knife. And he's a criminal." Her nails dug through Bailey's sleeves.

"We'll be fine," Bailey said. "And the sheriff will be right behind us, waiting for my text."

"I'm sorry for doubting you." Her blue eyes sparkled, but

she blinked the moisture away. "I didn't mean to hurt you, either."

He conked a loose fist beneath her chin and when their gazes locked, he held hers. "I'd do anything to protect you."

"I'm glad you told me the truth. But it makes me sad for you."

Bailey bristled. "Don't feel sorry for me, Tess. Like Dad always said, I'm the man I am today because of everything I've lived through."

Her lips quirked. "You are a pretty awesome man. And even a good kisser if Jaz is to be believed."

Heat inched along the back of his neck. He had no intention of discussing kissing with his little sister.

"I'll take care of things. Don't worry."

"*We'll* take care of it." Javier's dark eyes smoldered, a hidden message zinging toward Tess when their glances met. "About time I acted like your partner in this ranch."

"Silent investor," Tess muttered but her smile didn't dim, and the admiration glowing in her eyes brightened them like a sunny sky greeting the dawn.

Bailey might be a late bloomer in the romance department, but he figured the attraction between these two was mutual. Not that he'd encourage the guy, even if he did like him.

During the hour Bailey stayed at the event, waiting for night to fall, he passed by the silent auction tables, surprised to see a weekend at the Travers Guest Ranch up for bid.

He shook his head at seeing Wynn's name and a bid for $500, at least double the value of the voucher. What was the man going to do with a weekend to a place he stayed for free?

Bailey shook his head. As darkness lapped at the barred windows of the courtroom, he jostled through the crowd and pulled Jaz aside. In an alcove outside the judge's room, they found a little peace.

"We're heading out."

"Lord help."

Bailey raised an eyebrow. "I hope that's a prayer and not a grunt of disbelief."

Cool fingers stroked his whiskery cheek. "I believe in you, cowboy. But divine intervention is always welcome."

Something reared inside him, wanting to protest. Her eyes glowed with pride and desire and things he'd need a code book to decipher.

He brushed his lips over hers. A flock of birds burst to life in his chest, and his mouth tingled. As she pulled back an inch, her breath tickled along his jaw, sending heat flooding through his legs.

"Truth will prevail, cowboy. It always does." If only his life experience agreed with her optimism.

After another quick kiss, he led her back to the thinning crowd.

"Only thirty minutes left to get your bids in." Anna Ring's voice rose above the general banter. "Better check to make sure you're getting that auction item you want."

Jaz squeezed his fingers and sidled to Tess's side.

Javier rubbed his sister's elbow and they shared another look, then the man followed him downstairs. After they reclaimed their coats and Bailey's hat, the men pushed against a cool gust of wind toward their vehicles.

"I'll wait until you're inside," Javier told him, "then slip across the pasture."

Bailey nodded. "Not sure I'll catch him in the act, but I'll be checking the rooms."

As his truck roared to life, Bailey gritted his teeth.

*Let this be the end of Lonie Dyer.* He wasn't sure if it was a wish or a prayer, but something inside him steeled.

⁂

JAZ IMPRESSED THE FEELING OF BAILEY'S BROAD calloused fingertips on her heart and let him go.

*Keep him safe.*

"Only thirty minutes left to get your bids in." Anna Ring's voice swelled above the hum of the crowd. "Better check to make sure you're getting that auction item you want."

Something dark shadowed Tess's pale eyes, and Jaz slid to her side and tucked the slender woman's arm under hers.

"God's got this." Jaz leaned close, catching the scent of cinnamon and cedar from Tess.

Bailey's sister stared until Javier's dark head disappeared down the stairwell. With that sort of look, she announced her interest in the man to the entire world. Jaz fought a grin. Tess blinked at Jaz, and the shadow withdrew.

"It's going to bring back the worst of Lee's memories." She swallowed hard. "Facing down our da —Lonie."

Jaz squeezed her arm. "He's got Javier and the sheriff for backup." She nudged Tess's ribs with an elbow. "You know, that hot Brazilian guy who follows you everywhere like a puppy?"

Tess frowned. "I don't need another puppy. And he's only here because Lee told him I was in danger."

"Right. He doesn't want you to be in danger because he *likes* you."

Tess jabbed her elbow into Jaz's side. "He cares about his investment in the ranch."

Jaz laughed. "Keep telling yourself that. But, how does he kiss?" She dodged as Tess gasped and wound up another pot shot.

Liam James held court at the display near the silent auction tables encircled by a crowd. Jaz made eye contact with her own "silent" business partner.

Before she reached him, someone gripped her elbow. Jaz glanced to see KaroLynn wearing a wool dress covered by a fluffy pink sweater. For once, the woman's makeup looked touched up, although the lipstick had worn away, leaving a smudge of liner on her bottom lip.

"Thanks for coming, KaroLynn." Warmth puddled in Jaz's middle. Maybe she was finally winning the social worker over.

"Well, yes." The woman cleared her throat and stared over Jaz's shoulder.

Not a good sign. Maybe she was embarrassed by the gratitude.

"Liam James is really behind this project." Pastor Bernie's voice came from the direction KaroLynn stared. "It's given our youth group something local to focus fundraising efforts on."

Jaz turned to thank her pastor for his support, but Karo-Lynn's hand tightened like a vise.

"Can we talk privately?"

"Uh," Jaz looked around the crowded room. "I suppose, but I was going to talk once the auction closes." It was a way to pass time while Anna collected the bidding forms so she could announce the winners.

"I'll only take a moment of your time." KaroLynn practically dragged Jaz through the crowd surging toward Liam.

It would have been easier for a fish to fly, and Jaz did her best not to knock into any of the people she'd basically begged to invest in her idea. She lost track of how many times she apologized, and she wasn't feeling especially charitable by the time the social worker pulled her into a briefing room.

"That might be the rudest thing I've ever done."

And she'd been in the military for six years. Jaz jerked free from the woman's hold and crossed her arms over her chest.

KaroLynn picked at her skirt. "I'm sorry, but I need to go."

"Fine. What was so urgent that you made me shove my way through a crowd I invited here?"

"It's the kids."

Jaz's intestines curdled. There were only two kids the woman could mean. "What about Kenton? Is he okay?"

If he ran away again, they might send him back to Austin where there was a lock-up for frequent flyers. She'd never be able to arrange visits with his sister then. And what about seeing him? She had to get this house up and running.

"He's fine. They're both fine." KaroLynn paused until Jaz met her troubled gaze. "For now."

"What do you mean?" Jaz shifted, suddenly feeling her boot pinch her little toe.

The woman rubbed her palms down the outside of her skirt a few times until she finally clenched them over the gray fabric. "Their mother petitioned the San Antonio office. She's back in the area."

Their mother? The one who abandoned them for who knows what reason, entrusting their care to a drug addict? Jaz gritted her teeth. There should be a law about having children.

"Of course, she isn't financially able to care for them, so she's been referred to other departments."

"Financially? She abandoned them. She's completely unfit!"

KaroLynn touched Jaz, her fingers gentle on her forearm this time. "She's their mother."

A surge of frustration pushed Jaz's stomach into her lungs, and her breath caught. Heat burned her eyes and heaviness stopped her nose. Tears wouldn't help Kenton and Flo.

"There must be something I can do." Her voice sounded mouse-like in the empty room.

"Build the Pit Stop. You'll help plenty of kids with that place." KaroLynn's mouth pushed into a tight smile. "The first rule of foster care is don't care too much."

*Don't care too much.* The problem with the system shone through that statement. But Jaz couldn't take her heart back. She'd already given it to the redheaded boy who only wanted to protect his sister. Only wanted to be the big brother Flo needed. Like Drew. Like Bailey.

Jaz clutched her hands over the pang in her chest.

"I wanted to let you know. Maybe as early as next week, Kenton and Flossie May will be together again." KaroLynn tried to sound hopeful.

Jaz nodded, and the woman left her alone. How was she supposed to speak with passion and hope now that the motivation behind this whole thing was torn away?

*I gave you this dream.*

The echoing whisper pounded the inside of Jaz's skull. Even an hour ago, she'd been extolling the way God had answered prayers and moved mountains to make the Pit Stop a reality. But now? Because of one piece of bad news, she was ready to show her belly to the opposition?

Jaz threw her shoulders back. She would go out there and thank everyone for believing in her vision. Work on the halfway house would continue.

And Jaz would keep the hopeful expression of a certain little boy fixed in her mind. Because somehow, she would give him the family he deserved.

# Thirty-seven

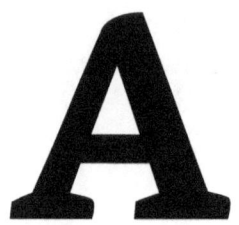wild animal lunged for release from his stomach. Armstrong Road seemed longer and bumpier than it had a few hours earlier. Dust swirled behind his tires, blocking out the sight of Javier's SUV. A glance toward the Wells' drive showed the sheriff's vehicle, dark but not vacant. He'd be two minutes away.

Bailey's clenched teeth chattered as he bumped down the drive. Maybe he could borrow the Bryant's tractor and smooth away the ruts before the guests Wynn had booked arrived next weekend.

The truck groaned to a stop outside the barn. Bailey switched off the engine and headlights. A shadow swept across the covered window of the parlor.

*Lord, let this plan work.* Bailey needed Lonie Dyer out of his life so Tess would be safe.

The familiar squawk announced the opening of the truck door. His stomach clenched.

Two dogs whined, shimmying beneath the paddock fence and trotting over to him. After he'd petted the barn dogs, Poppet arrived, sitting on the toes of his boots, slapping white fur onto his slacks with her exuberant tail.

"You need to stay out, girl." He had no idea what might go down with Lonie.

She whimpered, but when he commanded her to stay, she curled up beneath his truck. He could feel her eyes drilling deeper than an oil rig as he strode up the steps and into the house.

Stale coffee, nutmeg. and something flowery rushed to greet his nostrils. The bulb on the hood over the stove cast shadows through the kitchen. Faint tendrils of light brightened from the downstairs hallway and flared on the upstairs landing.

His boots thudded on the hardwood floors. Tess's bedroom door was open a crack and he knew she'd shut it. He resisted the urge to check on the bait and headed toward the beacon flooding from the half-open door to his father's — no, Tess's — office.

He steeled his spine and pushed into the room.

Lonie Dyer's filthy boots rested on the desk and he reclined in the office chair, a half-full glass held in one hand. The crystal decanter that held Garrison Brothers bourbon — "straight from Hye, Texas" he could hear Dad say — sat empty a few inches from the toe of the intruder's foot.

A sly sneer creased the weaselly face. "Son. I've been waiting for you."

"To say goodbye?"

"If the price is right." He sipped dark liquid from the heavy glass, his gaze glued to Bailey.

Bailey wanted to snatch the glass away from the man. That crystal had been his father's gift to Mary Ann—his mother—on their fifteenth wedding anniversary. That was the third year he lived with them, and the look on her face remained in his mind.

Lonie hefted the glass as if toasting Bailey. "This crystal might be a nice going-away present."

His teeth ached from clenching them. "That's not up for grabs." *Although you've already had your grubby hands on it.*

Bailey flicked his finger over the button on his phone. He'd set it up to record. He walked closer, arms crossed over his chest.

"I've noticed a few things missing. What have you lifted?"

Lonie chuckled. "I told you to pay up, son. You should

know I mean what I say."

Darkness entered the man's eyes. A shudder rumbled beneath Bailey's arms.

Lonie scanned the room. "Is there a safe in here? Anything valuable in it?"

"A pistol and some documents. Nothing of value to you."

"Want to grab the gun and run me off?" The glint in the narrowed eyes screamed danger.

Bailey shook his head. "Those are your methods. But you need to leave. You've pilfered enough."

"I'll say when it's enough."

Bailey paced toward the window, wondering if Wynn was close. It didn't matter. Lonie would be leaving tonight if Bailey had to hogtie him and dump him by the interstate.

"The rooms are booked starting next weekend, so you need to find somewhere else to stay."

"Your sister's immigrant boyfriend already mentioned that. About the same time he took over the room across the hall." Lonie sipped more bourbon. "She can do better than some wetback."

"He's more than you think." Why did the man insist on using ignorant racism whenever he talked about someone with skin darker than his own? "Do you need help packing your bags? A ride out of town?"

"I've got a few days."

Bailey shook his head slowly. "You're leaving before Tess gets back. Tonight."

Lonie drained the glass and stood. "Why don't we have a look in the safe?"

Bailey turned toward the door. He'd check on the ring and send the sheriff a text from Tess's room.

"Don't turn your back on me." The growling voice sounded animal-like.

Footfalls scuffed across the floor. A shove slammed Bailey into the wall. The tip of the knife rested on the door frame, its sharp blade blocking passage. Bailey stared at his father, whose lips curled into a snarl as fierce as anything a coyote could muster.

His legs shook and gymnastics rumbled through his intestines, threatening to send him into a ball. But Bailey raised his chin. *Lord, help.* "No more threats."

"I haven't even begun to threaten you. Or your pretty little sister." Lonie licked his lips. "Or your hot little girlfriend."

Bailey chopped his hand against Lonie's wrist. The man grunted, and the knife gouged a chunk from the wood as it fell away from the doorway.

"Collect your things." Bailey hardly recognized the steely voice. "I'll drive you to the bus station in Rosewood."

Bailey strode into the hallway, but he'd hardly taken two steps when a sharp jab wrenched his lower back. The scars between his shoulder blades tingled, and memories avalanched him.

Pain. Humiliation. Screams.

Bailey twirled toward the attack, arms raised. The knife slashed his forearm. Agony flared through him.

Bailey grunted and stomped Lonie's instep. The man howled, and Bailey jammed his elbow into the bony throat, turning the sound into a moan.

The leering face from his nightmares sneered at him before Lonie doubled over, choking. Something unknotted in Bailey's soul.

"You're leaving tonight."

The front door burst open. A moment later, Javier twisted Lonie's arms behind his back. The knife clattered to the floor. Javier's grunts mingled with Lonie's wheezing breaths.

"Send your text." Javier shoved Lonie face-first into the wall. "You're bleeding."

Bailey stared numbly at his arm. Red seeped around the cuff and dripped down his hand. He staggered into the kitchen and wrapped a towel around his arm, pressing it into the counter while he alerted the sheriff by text.

Air swam around him, and he seemed to move underwater

as he followed Javier, pushing Lonie in front of him, onto the porch.

The sheriff arrived. Javier explained things while Lonie looked surly.

"Assault with a deadly weapon." Bailey raised his arm then jerked his head toward the house. "Knife's inside."

"You realize you're in violation of your parole?" Sheriff Grant asked while directing Lonie to spread his hands on the hood of the patrol car.

Lonie's snarling answer was lost to Bailey. He slumped onto the porch. Another patrol car bounced down the drive, and the sheriff nudged his shoulder.

"Recognize this?" Grant held a rose-gold ring toward him. MaryAnn's wedding ring.

Bailey nodded. "I have plans for that."

"I have to bag and tag it for now, but we'll get it back to you as soon as we can."

Bailey reached to tip the brim of his hat and sucked air at the stab of pain.

"You need to get that looked at." The sheriff reached for the radio on his belt.

"I'll take him to the hospital," Javier said, materializing from the deepening night outside the halo of porch light.

As they walked to the man's rental, Bailey saw a deputy helping Lonie into the back of the patrol car.

A strange lightness filled his chest, and he staggered into Javier. The man's hand steadied his shoulder.

"Thanks." Bailey's voice sounded gruff.

Javier nodded as he waited for Bailey to get into the SUV.

*Thanks, Lord.* The hollow soul he'd tried to ignore for so long flooded with soothing peace. *This must be my father's faith.*

As the door shut out the sounds of the arrest, Bailey closed his eyes. With the past finally corralled, he had a future to plan.

AFTER GETTING TEN STITCHES AND A TETANUS shot, Bailey seemed no worse for wear. In fact, his concern was all for Tess and her disappointment that Lonie hadn't cared about her at all. Again, their situation brought Kenton to mind, and Jaz could only pray to keep the gnawing doubts away.

By Wednesday, Jaz completed the official foster home Family Protective Service's application packet, so there was no more delaying her decision. Her stomach churned. She tried to replay the positive conversation with Liam James about sufficient funding and community investment, but the echo of KaroLynn's voice drowned it.

Jaz fingered the envelope that contained the letter she'd printed from her mother's computer on Sunday.

She picked up her desk phone and dialed Evan's assistant. When she hung up, she glanced at the time on the computer screen. He could see her in thirty minutes, and she needed to get to the DFPS office by three to drop off the application. Was she really doing this? Moving home to focus on getting a college degree?

Did she want to stay two hours away from Bailey for the next two years? Of course not. And as things progressed with the renovations and the application, she wanted to be on-site at Bryant County Pit Stop. Liam was making that possible with his generosity.

Jaz half-concentrated on the document she was preparing for one of the associate attorneys, and when her reminder dinged, she snatched the envelope out of her drawer and climbed the stairs. She paced beside the assistant's desk, and the woman looked relieved to finally admit her to Evan's office.

"I wasn't expecting to meet with you today." Evan stood as Jaz approached.

She handed him the envelope, glad to see her hand wasn't shaking although her legs could double as wilted lettuce. She and her boss sat at the same time, and Evan peered at her, tapping the corner of the envelope on his desk.

"I don't think I want to read this."

Jaz blinked, but what could she say?

The paper crinkled as he withdrew the sheet from the envelope. It took a minute for him to read the short missive. She'd wanted to resign and walk, but her parents talked her out of it. Unless she wanted to burn her bridges with these prominent attorneys, giving proper notice made more sense.

"I'd prefer not to accept your resignation." He settled the letter on the file he'd been working. "But you've been burning the candle at both ends these past couple weeks."

Jaz nodded. "Things have come together in a way that makes me sure the Pit Stop is God's plan for my future."

"So, you've decided to get the child psychology degree?"

"With a minor in social work. Jed says that will pacify FPS." Jaz rubbed her hands on her thighs. "I know two weeks isn't enough time for you to find a replacement, not if you want me to train them."

Evan shook his head. "HR will handle it. Don't worry." He cleared his throat. "I have something for you as well, but I was hoping to take you to lunch on Friday."

And she was hoping to have lunch with Anna on Friday and iron out her next actionable steps. What could he have for her? A pay raise she wouldn't be getting now?

"I can get that on my calendar, sir."

Evan's lips twitched and he arched one dark brow at her. "We use first names, and that's not changing because you're heading home to Sweet Grove."

*Home to Sweet Grove.* She hadn't thought of it that way, but as he said the words, her heart repeated them.

*Home to Sweet Grove.* The small town where she'd grown up was filled with friendly faces and a certain ranch where the man she loved tossed his hat on a peg.

"Are you going to stay for two weeks? Or will I lose you when you head up there on Friday night to see Bailey?" Evan leaned back in his chair and his hands dropped to his lap.

"I've given my word. I'll be here until a week from Friday."

Not exactly two weeks, but it had taken two days to talk herself into such a drastic change.

"Let's not keep you in suspense." Evan leaned forward and used his mouse. The printer in the corner hummed to life. He rolled his chair back and retrieved the printed sheets.

He signed the top sheet and curled a corner up so he could sign the second sheet, then he folded the paper into thirds, deftly creasing the pages with his well-manicured thumb. After he pulled an envelope from a drawer, he slid the pages inside but didn't seal it.

He held the envelope toward her. Jaz reached for it. "Should I read this later? You went to so much trouble to make it look official."

Evan's mouth curled into a half-smile. "I didn't want Lisa's work to be wasted." He nodded at the letter in her hand. "Open it."

Her fingers trembled, and she lowered them onto her lap, hoping he couldn't see. If it was anything to do with her job, he wouldn't have bothered to give it to her, would he? Unless he hoped to dangle a carrot in front of her nose.

She closed her eyes. *Lord, I know you want me to start the foster home, so help me deal with this news in the right way.*

Her hands steadied as she unfolded the sheets to reveal a letter on Boldt & Associates letterhead.

*Dear Miss Role:*

*It's with pleasure that we inform you of our intention to support Bryant County Pit Stop.*

*Attached to this letter is an initial donation of $5,000 to assist you in furnishing the foster home. In the future, we plan to sponsor each resident's back-to-school shopping trip. The request for reimbursement forms can be located at this link on our website.*

*Best of luck as you spend your big heart on the needy foster chil-*

*dren of your home county.*

It had signature lines for both Evan and Daniel but Daniel's was blank.

"Wow. This is very generous."

Evan steepled his long fingers. "There's a $500 maximum per child on the annual grant, but I know other local businesses offer similar programs. I'll make sure you get a list."

Her throat tightened. "Thank you, Evan. Since I'm jumping ship here, I didn't expect your donation to be so substantial."

He cocked his head. "You've been happiest working with the kids, so I'm not that surprised you want a career where they're your focus."

Jaz hadn't realized her passion for the clients' children had been so noteworthy. Was she the last one to realize she wasn't suited for a legal career?

"Not interested in the second page?"

Jaz straightened. "I just assumed..."

His brows shot up to his hairline. She flipped the back page forward. It was a legal document. The subject header "Tuition Reimbursement" held her attention. She read through it, and suddenly things blurred. It was an extension of the standard reimbursement policy of the company to coursework in Child Psychology. This paper alone was worth thousands of dollars.

But she was quitting.

She handed it back to him, happy to see her hand was steady, although her heart did a gymnastics routine worthy of a silver medal.

He made no move to take it. "I knew you'd leave eventually, Jaz. That offer stands for three years from your separation date with our firm."

Her arm sunk to her lap. "How did you convince your brother?"

Evan waved off her question. "His teeth look sharper than they are. Maximum of eighty percent reimbursement."

"If I maintain a perfect GPA. I'm familiar with the company's policy."

He chuckled. "You'll be missed around here."

"This is so much more than I expected."

"You don't expect much, and we can afford to be generous with veterans who continue to serve others." Evan shrugged to his feet. "I've got another appointment."

Jaz bolted from the chair. "Of course. I'm heading to the DFPS to turn in the foster application. I cleared the early hours with HR."

"Good luck, Jaz."

They shook hands, and even though he towered above her, Jaz felt like his equal.

After such incredible revelations, meeting with the state felt anti-climactic. Again, things seemed to be rolling along smoothly, and that made the acid burn into her throat. If she was supposed to help Kenton and Flo, then why were they going back to an untenable situation?

*Lord, I don't understand.*

*Just because you can't see God working doesn't mean He isn't.* Those were Elise's words on Sunday after she'd repeated Karo-Lynn's bad news.

Clouds had rolled in while she was inside, but they didn't dampen her excitement about the coming adventure.

Jaz headed into a semi-empty coffee shop. Apparently the late-afternoon caffeine rush hadn't begun. She ordered a sweet tea and parked at the round table furthest from the door.

The stack of papers from her meeting mocked her. She highlighted her liaison's contact information and dog-eared the page that outlined the process for successful liaison inter-actions.

Between sips of tea, she texted Tess and Bailey to let them know things were moving along. Then she dialed her business partner.

Was chairing a nonprofit a business? She wasn't sure when it would start paying her a salary, but since she had a roof over her head, clothes to wear, and a way to pay her tuition, she fig-ured it wasn't as urgent for her as it was for the kids she wanted to help.

"James."

Jaz straightened. "Hey, the application is dropped off. The manager I met with said to go ahead with the construction."

"Great. I'll get the contractors on top of it."

Jaz sighed. "Not sure how long an approval will take."

"Let's leave that in God's hands. What else did you learn?"

"They assigned us a residential contract manager from the San Antonio office. I guess we're in a region with a bunch of other large counties with smaller populations."

"Did you get all the contact information for this guy?"

"Gal. And yes." Jaz swirled the straw in her tea. "Mr. Ives even sent her an email while KaroLynn and I were in his office."

Liam whistled. "Wow. Sounds like things will be moving along. KaroLynn knew what she was talking about."

Jaz's stomach lurched. "About that. I want to thank her somehow."

"Getting foster kids off the street will ease her load, believe me."

"True, but I appreciate her help, and I know she still thinks I'm a little sketchy."

Liam's laugh made her push the phone away from her ear. She glanced around, glad the only other patron was far away, certainly not disturbed by the booming laughter.

"I'll come up with something," she said.

"I don't doubt it." She sensed his grin. "You're the most determined woman I've worked with in a long time."

Determined—well, there were worse things she could be.

"Thanks for going above and beyond." Her chest cramped, and she sipped her tea to ease it.

"A year from now you'll have this in hand, and I'll slip into the role of silent partner."

Jaz snorted. "We'll see about that."

But as she drove back to her apartment, energy hummed through her veins almost as if the caffeine from the sweet tea had carried electrical charges. She'd come to Texas in March feeling like a beaten dog, never imagining she could pulse with so much purpose. Had she ever felt this way before?

Maybe when she was standing in the batter's box, but not since leaving college to follow Drew's dream.

*Always follow your dreams,* Drew told her in his last letter. Finally, she was.

Only one thing would make life even better, and she would see that man's blue eyes later this evening during their nightly call.

Come Friday she'd fall into his strong arms, and then she'd be home.

# Thirty-Eight

The Saturday when Jaz returned to Sweet Grove for good couldn't come fast enough. When it finally did, Bailey prayed his way through feeding the stock in the reddish predawn light, and the chilly breeze seemed to say, "Today is the day."

An hour later, rocks scraped the bottom of the canoe as he and Jaz neared the flailing willow branches of Drew's special place. Bailey dug the paddle deep, sinking it into the gooey mud at the bottom of Mill Pond. The bow carved its way into the beach and halted inches from the tree trunk.

A smile tugged the corners of Jaz's full lips. With athletic grace she leaned into the beach, swaying the canoe in the direction Bailey wanted. His stomach clawed into his ribcage, but Bailey swallowed away the swelling nausea.

He could do this. If he could stand up to Lonie Dyer and the shadows of his childhood, he could face anything. His pulse pounded in his ears louder than the scrape of beaching the canoe.

Bailey stabilized the boat with his paddle. Jaz stepped onto the rocky shore, and his gaze followed her toward the loose fencing behind swaying cattails.

*Was this the right place?*

Shaking off the wave of indecision, Bailey climbed onto the soft dirt littered with thin willow twigs and curled leaves.

He stopped beside Jaz. His fingers caressed the coarse hair

peeking out of her sweatshirt collar. "You found him just in time."

Jaz turned. Her pale green eyes swam with emotion. "I wish I could keep him."

Bailey stroked her smooth cheek. "He'll be fine. You'll see to that."

"I hope I'm not doing this for all the wrong reasons."

Bailey waited for panic to unlock his abysmal memories. Nothing. Was he truly free?

"Once your place it set up, you can petition the state about Kenton." Bailey tilted his head. He hadn't come here to talk about the foster home.

She pushed the brim of his hat higher. His heart plowed against his breastbone, anticipating what often came after that simple movement.

"You're amazing. So supportive of me." Her finger traced a path from his ear to his chin.

A shudder coursed through him, but he told himself to wait. Let her finish.

"I hate that I couldn't stop the bad things from happening to you." She blinked, her gaze locking onto his.

He dove into the depths of her green eyes. How had he ever managed to earn her love?

*You don't earn love.* MaryAnn's motherly voice assured him. *It's freely given.*

She proved it. Fritz proved it, and even God had proved it once again.

"Bad things happen." For once, the scars on his back didn't itch to remind him of the horror.

Her white teeth flashed in her beautiful dark face. "I'm going to make sure these kids have a better future."

He squeezed her hips. "I'm proud of you. Those kids might never know how awesome you are, but I do."

She shook her head and glanced around. "Is that why you brought me here? To Drew's place?"

Bailey's stomach twisted. Another wave of dizziness

slammed into him. He ground his teeth. This clearing would always remind them of Drew, but that wasn't a bad thing. Instead, Bailey planned to build on those positive memories because that's the tone he wanted to set for their future.

*Their future.* Pressure bubbled beneath his ribcage.

"He'd be proud of you, too." Jaz's words had him stepping back.

Bailey reached for the brim of his hat. "Why?"

"Because you're a great big brother."

Bailey snorted. "Tess would argue that."

Jaz squeezed his hand. "You protected her. And got hurt." She narrowed her eyes.

The healing cut on his arm tingled. Yes, he'd put himself in harm's way for Tess, and he'd do it again.

Bailey cupped Jaz's strong chin. "Some things are worth getting hurt for." He sucked in a breath. "He'd be proud that you've found your dream and are following your own path, rescuing kids from the system."

"Foster Child Advocate right here."

He grinned, and her breath shuddered, drawing his gaze toward the emblem of a Texas Longhorn on her red pullover. His throat tightened.

"Still speaking legalese." He curled her hair behind her ear, leaving his fingertips on her earlobe. "My girl's smart and sexy."

She opened her mouth, but he didn't let her argue. He covered her parted lips with his own, drinking in the taste of her strength. He'd need it for what came next.

Jaz leaned into him. His hands tightened on her curvaceous hips, holding her a breath away from him. Her fingers burrowed into the hair at the nape of his neck. Shocks and tingles spiraled down his back.

He levered away from her until her hands slid onto his arms. Her eyelids flickered open. The dazed look there mirrored his feelings every time they kissed.

"Yum." Her smile lit a fire in his gut.

*Don't get distracted.*

He grazed his lips over hers again.

She groaned, and he pulled away. "Bailey." Her breath hissed along his neck.

"I want to say something, so stop distracting me."

She slapped his bicep. "*You* kissed me."

He grinned and tapped the brim of his hat. She had him there.

He threaded his fingers through hers and tucked his other hand into the front pocket of his jeans, trying to reclaim his cowboy pose. "Looks like we're both living in Sweet Grove."

She nodded. "I hate staying with my folks, but rentals near the halfway house are non-existent."

"Javier's staying in the manager's quarters for now, so I'll be looking for a rental, too."

"Are you going to move to Rosewood? There'd be more options."

He shook his head. "Two of my clients are in Sweet Grove."

"You're welcome." Jaz squeezed his hand.

They stared at ripples on the smooth water. A breeze dislodged the curl from behind her ear.

He wasn't doing this right. But then, everything about their relationship had been a little backward, starting with her pursuing him. But he could cowboy-up now.

"Are you sure about the online courses? I'll stay in Austin if you want to go to classes at UT."

Jaz faced him. "Jed says I can fill the advocate position as long as I'm working toward the degree. The kids need me here."

"They aren't the only ones."

She tilted her head. The stretch of neck she exposed taunted him. "Are you trying to say you need me?"

He ducked his chin, keeping his gaze locked with hers. "Need you. Adore you. Don't want to live without you."

She raised an eyebrow. "A month ago, you were sending me off to Austin with your blessing to find someone more deserving."

His grunt came from the bottom of his lungs. "I never said I was smart. But I'm certain."

A glint lightened her pale eyes. "What are you certain of?"

"You."

She pushed onto her tiptoes, but he shuffled backward. Her quirking eyebrow twitched.

Bailey dropped her right hand and reached for her left. The warmth of her fingers slithered up his arm, prickling his hair to attention.

"Do you love me?" The question came out breathy. He sucked in air.

Jaz nodded. "You're the man for me."

A thrill electrified his heart into a frenzy of bucking. Those words meant more to him than any standard love proclamation because men hadn't been kind to Jaz.

He fumbled in his pocket. The slender band slid to his pinky's knuckle. "I don't want any more misunderstandings between us." He gulped. "If you'll have me, I want to marry you."

She blinked at him. A bubble of unease built inside his chest.

"Are you asking?" She sidled her sneakered foot between his dusty cowboy boots.

Sweat itched where the hat seemed to tighten around his head. His fingers twitched to move the brim, but his hands were full of Jazlyn and a ring.

He pulled the band out, and the diamonds glinted.

"Be my wife?" The words were husky, straining to get through his scratchy throat.

Jaz glanced toward the ring hovering above her left hand.

"The ring is beautiful." Awe filled her tone.

"It was MaryAnn's. She wore it until her silver anniversary when Fritz bought her a new one."

She gazed up at him through thick black lashes. "A ring that belongs to a strong marriage."

Did that mean she didn't think they would have one? His heart pulsed forlornly in his stomach. If she said no...

*I'll ask her again later.*

Pale eyes studied him for another endless moment.

*Lord, I was so sure.*

But he wouldn't give in to the failure snapping at his feet. They belonged together. He was positive.

"If I say yes, you'll be stuck with me forever."

It was his turn to blink at her. "Sounds like Heaven."

A dazzling smile broke the stern lines of her face. "That was the right answer, cowboy."

What answer? She hadn't said anything.

Jaz laughed. A bird fled the branches above them, squawking as it fluttered away.

"That was a yes, cowboy." She held his hand still and slid her finger through the ring.

Bailey's heart didn't start beating until she pressed her lips to his. Then he came alive, wrapping his arms around her and hugging her to his chest. Their mouths celebrated the beginning of forever, sliding together with heated enthusiasm.

She said yes.

Bailey buried his nose in the skin of her neck. The brim of his hat jarred against her, going askew. He grabbed it and settled it on her head.

Her lips parted, and his chest tightened.

That old battered hat looked at home on her dark hair.

As her lips caressed his again, Bailey relaxed into the truth of Jaz. She loved all of him, even his scars and weaknesses, and she shared his ideal of family.

Together, their faith soared. Wrapped in the arms of his future, Bailey understood the meaning of home.

# Acknowledgements

This book has been through so many hands because it began as a single novella that morphed into a trilogy that became a miniseries before the rights came back to me.

A hearty virtual hug to Savannah Jezowski for her insightful alpha reading that transformed a blah storyline from caterpillar to butterfly.

A huge shout out to Susan May Warren and the Deep Thinkers Retreat group who helped shape Jaz and Bailey into the dynamic and realistic characters on these pages.

A bouquet of rose-shaped gratitude to editor extraordinaire Megan Harris of Megan Writes Media, whose excitement for this story nearly equaled mine.

A flirtatious wink to my own personal hero and husband who supports me emotionally and financially and encourages me to keep writing on the days I'd rather give up.

A shout of gratitude to the Lord, my Heavenly Father, who calls me to the craziness that is fiction writing and gifts me to pursue it even when doors close.

A meaningful smile to you, the reader. Read on, my friend.

# About the Author

Nurtured through her troubled teens in Narnia, Sharon Hughson appreciates the power of the written word. For years, she devoured books by Dee Henderson, Lori Wick and Karen Kingsbury. All the while, unwritten stories beckoned. In 2014, she finished her English literature degree and started writing fiction.

She writes full-time from her home in Oregon, where she resides with her husband and three helpful cats. This novella is her first with Sweet Promise Press, although her published works number in the double digits.

When she's not writing, Sharon works as a substitute teacher at local middle and high schools and stays active walking, hiking, and biking. When the rain settles in, she enjoys scrapbooking and crocheting.

See all her titles at sharonhughson.com. Visit the Newsletter page to get a FREE story and the latest updates about new releases, events and giveaways. To connect with Sharon, join her **Facebook Group** and follow her on Amazon to be notified about new books.

# More from Sharon

**Contemporary Fiction**
**Mimi and the Banker**

**Biblical Fiction**
*Reflections: A Pondering Heart*
*Reflections: A Laboring Hand*
*Reflections: An Adoring Spirit*

Or maybe you're still not sure you'll LOVE Sharon's story. You can read a sweet romance novella for FREE by clicking here.

# More Sweet Grove

*An Unexpected Homecoming* was originally published as *Love's Texas Homecoming*. It was part of the First Street Church Romances series based on writing by Melissa Storm. This tie-in story is being published with the permission of Melissa Storm.

**Interested in checking it out?**

**Start with Love's Prayer.**
Ben Davis has lived in the shadow of his family's mistakes for years. Forced to give up all his dreams, he wonders if death by his own hand might be the only way out. A desperate plea sent to the God he isn't even sure he believes in is soon answered by a series of miracles that bring Summer and Ben crashing into each other.

Summer loves the busy life of the city, but agrees to spend the season in Sweet Grove, running her aunt's flower shop while figuring out what to do with her life after. On thing's for sure, she's a terrible florist. Luckily, her latest mishap leads her to a man with pleading, soulful eyes she's all too happy to get lost in.

Ben tells Summer she's his miracle, but Summer's not so sure she sees it that way. Can he convince her to share the rest of her life with him before the seasons change? And might the tiny town have a place for Summer to finally, truly call home?

If you love tales of faith, hope and finding home, then don't miss your chance to fall in love with Ben, Summer, and the entire town of Sweet Grove, Texas, in this heartwarming romance.

**Grab your copy of Love's Prayer and start reading today!**

www.ingramcontent.com/pod-product-compliance
Lightning Source LLC
Chambersburg PA
CBHW031552240626
47153CB00002B/477